MORE PRAISE FOR *SIRENS*

"*Sirens* is a hard-boiled garden of disturbing delights. Joseph Knox's prose is wonderful, both surprising and lyrical, and his protagonist, Aidan Waits, pulls the reader through his wicked world at a relentless pace. I truly loved this debut, and look forward to seeing what Joseph Knox does next."

> —NICK PETRIE, author of *The Drifter* and *Light It Up*

"Knox presents the city as pungently and uncompromisingly as Ian Rankin does Edinburgh."

> —*The Guardian*

"Great read. A powerful piece of Manchester noir, brutal, poignant, and dark as tar."

> —CATH STAINCLIFFE,
> bestselling author of *The Silence Between Breaths*

"A firecracker of a crime tale. His writing is taut, atmospheric and studded with eye-catching descriptions. An arresting new talent."

> —*Metro*

"Fresh and darkly stylish, *Sirens* is a striking debut that marks the arrival of a major new crime-writing talent."

> —CHRIS EWAN, author of *Safe House* and *Dark Tides*

"A fierce, assured, and utterly compelling debut."

> —STAV SHEREZ, author of *The Intrusions*

"Thrilling, breathless stuff."

> —*The Observer*

SIRENS

SIRENS

A Novel

JOSEPH KNOX

CROWN
NEW YORK

Copyright © 2017 by Joseph Knox

All rights reserved.
Published in the United States by Crown, an imprint of the Crown Publishing Group, a division of Penguin Random House LLC, New York.
crownpublishing.com

CROWN is a registered trademark and the Crown colophon is a trademark of Penguin Random House LLC.

Originally published in hardcover in Great Britain by Doubleday, an imprint of Transworld Publishers, a division of Penguin Random House Ltd., London, in 2017.

"Heart and Soul," words and music by Ian Curtis, Peter Hook, Bernard Sumner, and Stephen Morris Copyright © 1980 Universal Music Publishing Limited. All Rights Reserved. International Copyright Secured. Used by permission of Music Sales Limited.

Library of Congress Cataloging-in-Publication Data is available upon request.

ISBN 9781524762872
Ebook ISBN 9781524762896

Printed in the United States of America

Jacket design: Gregg Kulick
Jacket images: (woman) khoa vu/Moment/Getty Images
(background) Christelle Vaillant/EyeEm/Getty Images

10 9 8 7 6 5 4 3 2 1

First American Edition

For Johanna

"The past is now part of my future, the present is well out of hand."

—*Joy Division, "Heart and Soul"*

SIRENS

Afterward I went back onto the night shift. They'd never trust me in the daylight again. I spent my time responding to 4 a.m. emergency calls, walking up and down dead escalators and trying not to think. I'd been good at that once. I could hardly believe it, a few months later, when I saw my breath in the air again. Saw November coming back around.

"Shittin' it down," said Sutty, refusing to get out of the car. Sometimes it was hailstones and sometimes it was slush. Tonight it was sheet rain, catching the light and cleaning down the streets. They needed it. My partner handed me his newspaper and I got out of the car, holding it over my head as an umbrella.

We were responding to a call from the manager of a charity shop. I watched his mouth moving. He wanted me to shift along some homeless people sheltering in the building's doorway. It didn't make a lot of sense but, then again, I wasn't paying close attention. His nasal hairs were jet black and matted together, like the start of Hitler's mustache. I looked at the sleeping man and woman in the doorway, told him he was wasting police time and walked back through the rain to the car.

I climbed inside and handed Sutty the wet newspaper, his punishment for not coming with me. He gave me a look and then turned to a dripping, folded-down page.

"See this?" he said, holding out the paper and gauging my reaction. "No way to die, that, is it?"

The picture was blurred with rain, the text too, but I recognized the girl. She'd been one of a group, one of three I'd known briefly, the previous year. The subheading said she'd been twenty-three years old when she died. Twenty-two when I knew her. I looked out the window, at November, coming back around. She was the last of them. Sutty leaned in, cleared his throat with a graveyard cough.

"Come on," he said. "What happened there, really?"

I looked at him steadily. "You're asking the wrong person."

All I knew was where it had started, a year before. The three strikes against me and all the reasons I couldn't say no. I couldn't have explained the girls, the women, who had briefly entered my life. Briefly changed it. He wouldn't have understood their laughs, their indignations, their secrets. For the rest of the night my eyes drifted to the people on the street, the girls, the women, and I felt like I was seeing the lives they wouldn't live.

I got home in the early hours of the morning, made myself a drink and sat down. I flicked around the radio stations until I couldn't put it off any longer. I reread the newspaper and let myself think about it properly for the first time in months.

"You're killing me," she'd said.

What had happened there, really?

UNKNOWN
PLEASURES

1

The young couple crossed over to avoid me, and I heard the jingle of loose change in someone's pocket.

A street you see every day can look unfamiliar, lying facedown on the ground, and it took me a minute to work out where I was. The pavement was frozen. Low-hanging fog blurred the air, and nothing could pass through it without being altered somehow. It threw the whole city out of focus, taking the shine out of another Friday night.

My left arm had gone numb and I rolled off it to check the time. The face of my watch was shattered. Assuming it had stopped when I hit the floor, assuming that had only been a few minutes ago, I still had over an hour. I could get into some dry clothes and be at the bar in plenty of time to see the handover. I felt my way up a wall and got to my feet. My face hurt and my brain felt like it had come loose, rattling around inside my skull, erasing pin numbers and names of childhood friends.

I watched the young couple disappear into the fog. In spite of social media, CCTV and the state, we still live in a world where you can disappear if you want to. Or even if you don't. It had been about a month since the story leaked.

A month since I'd gone missing.

I felt the back of my head where someone had just hit it, hard. My wallet was still in my pocket, so I hadn't been mugged. I'd been warned. There was no one else around but I could feel eyes all over me.

The street swayed and I held on to a lamppost to steady it. When I started to walk I went for long stretches with my eyes closed, not even thinking about bumping into things.

Turning a corner, I found myself on Back Piccadilly, immediately recognizing its exhausted red bricks by their external fire escapes. These buildings wall in a narrow alley on both sides, making a claustrophobic throughway. The evening rain had caught the moonlight, and I started walking out of nostalgia as much as anything. There was an all-night coffee shop at the other end, and I'd spent some time there in another life. It had been years since I stopped going, and the city had changed so much that I knew I wouldn't see any of the old faces.

I was a few steps into the alleyway when I heard a car start behind me. An engine growled into life, flexing its muscles before falling into a smooth rumble. Light flooded the narrow path and a crooked silhouette grew out from my feet.

Thinner than I remembered it.

I looked over my shoulder, into blinding high beams. The car was idling at the alleyway's entrance. *Nothing to see here.* I turned and kept walking. I was halfway along when the beams shook. When they started following me.

The engine revved and the car moved closer. It sounded just two or three feet behind, and I knew then that I'd never really disappeared. I could feel the headlights, burning into my back. I didn't want to turn and look through them at the driver anymore. I was afraid of who it might be.

I pressed myself into an alcove so the car could pass. It stayed where it was for a few seconds. Squinting into the light I saw a BMW, all gleaming black paint and chrome. I could feel the night in my lungs. The blood, singing through my veins. A window came down but I couldn't see inside.

"Detective Constable Waits?" said a man.

"Who's asking?"

I heard a woman's laughter from the passenger side.

"We're not asking, handsome. Get in."

2

The rain tapping against the windscreen was making faces at me. My veins felt threadbare and weak, and I sat in the back of the car trying to make a fist for my own amusement. I thought of the speed in my coat pocket.

"True what they say, then?" said the driver, reading my mind. He looked to be in his late forties. He had broad shoulders and weaved them like a middleweight each time he turned the wheel. He wore a fitted suit jacket, charcoal gray in color, which nearly matched the hair on his head. When he used the rearview mirror it was casually, looking through me like I wasn't there. The woman was a dishwater blonde with an efficient ponytail.

I didn't say anything.

In the back seat I felt the chill of my sodden clothes and clenched my jaw to keep from shivering. The only thing in the car that hadn't come straight from the showroom was a police scanner. It was turned right down. I could smell a designer vanilla perfume but didn't recognize the brand. It didn't match either of the people in the front seats, though. It smelled like money, like youth.

We were driving emphatically away from where I'd been. Out of the nightlife, the glare. Past the empty shops and the going-going-gone local businesses. The huge, vacant buildings. The dying high street.

"What's he want?" I said.

The man made eye contact in the mirror. "Didn't ask."

We pulled onto Deansgate.

Over a mile in length, Deansgate stretches from one side of the city to the other. In that space it does it all, from invite-only restaurants to down-and-out soup kitchens, with everything you can think of in between.

"Well, where is he?"

"Beetham Tower."

I must have sworn.

"Been there before have you?" said the woman.

The tallest building outside the capital, Beetham Tower had been one of several skyscrapers planned for the city. The idea was to expand farther and farther upward, each structure a few meters taller than the last, like some great, dull-metal graph, charting endless growth. Developers had decided they could make millions by mortgaging small, overpriced rooms to single men and women, our only commodity. But their heads had been in the clouds. When the economy came crashing down around them, the owners, investors and builders lost everything. The male suicide rate rose slightly and everyone else carried on.

Now, most of these derelict building sites are cannibalized for scrap. The others are left to rot, collecting rainwater in exposed foundations. Rusting like open sores in the ground. There were times during its three-year construction when it seemed that even Beetham Tower wouldn't be finished. It went up, though, in spite of everything, extended like a middle finger to the entire city.

We turned off Deansgate and pulled up to the tower's carport. A beaming valet dressed like Sinatra leaned into the window. He recognized our driver at first sight, stopped smiling and waved us on, down to the subterranean car park.

3

Beetham Tower is shared by a Hilton hotel, residential apartments and, right at the top, bespoke penthouse suites.

Although the structure itself is streamlined, the four-story annex at its base is much broader. It has to be, containing as it does a ballroom, swimming pool and the smiling sons and daughters of the top 2 percent. The walls of the lobby and lobby bar are made almost entirely from windowed glass. The design is such that, should someone accidentally look outside, all they'd see is their own reflection.

I had been here before.

The previous year, after a young woman crashed through a nineteenth-floor window and fell to her death. Dasa Ruzicka was an underage sex-worker from the Czech Republic. She had been trafficked through Europe when she was fourteen, having been sold by her father to a local trader. It was easy to take girls from these places because they went missing so often. Each one was camouflaged against a backdrop of habitual disappearance. But there was another, more elemental, reason she was taken.

Dasa had been beautiful, and not the emaciated version of it they throw around these days. She gave meaning back to the word. Her clear complexion had naturally lent itself to sex work because, in spite of all the sadness life could parade past it, she went on looking pure somehow. A recurring frustration of my job was that girls, women, were things to fuck and throw punches at. To throw through windows. I wondered what it said about us now, that graceful was the worst thing you could be.

I was sure Dasa couldn't have propelled herself through the window with such force. The hotel room she fell from had been empty, though. I kept guests and staff there for hours, questioning anyone whose key card might have allowed them access to the floor. When enough money had complained, a Detective Inspector was sent to relieve me. I took him into an empty room on the nineteenth floor, tried to explain the situation.

When he still wouldn't listen I backed off toward the door, my eyes on the window. The city below. He realized what I was about to do and shouted at me to stop. I ran at the glass to see the look on his face as much as anything, but he managed to get in the way before I could hit it.

It was the second of three strikes against me that would eventually lead to front-page news. To my total disgrace. To my taking the only job left open to me.

Dasa's death went down as a suicide and stayed that way.

I hadn't been back to Beetham Tower since.

4

Detective Sergeant Conway," said the female officer, holding out her hand for me to shake.

Her colleague was talking to the receptionist while we waited in the lobby. By my estimation of a Special Branch officer, I would have called him overfamiliar. There was a roar of laughter from a group of men in tuxedos, entering through an enormous, ornate revolving door. They danced beneath a chandelier the size of a family car. I was wishing it down on them when I looked at DS Conway.

"What's his problem with you?" she said, nodding at her partner. The man turned from the desk, walking back toward us, and she fixed her posture like she hadn't given me a second thought.

The lift went endlessly up toward the penthouses, a part of the tower I had never been in before. The man used a key card that granted us access to these upper echelons. A Muzak version of "My Heart Will Go On" ended, faded out and then faded back in again at the start. Like everything else in the building, the lift was decked with mirrors and reflective steel.

I looked at my shoes.

We stopped on the forty-fifth floor and the doors opened with an affected whoosh. Before the mechanized schoolmistress voice of the lift could finish speaking, the man had taken me firmly by the arm.

We moved down a long, tastefully minimal hallway, leaving Detective Sergeant Conway behind. We passed two other apartments, the only others on this level, before coming to a stark black door. The man used his card to open it and directed me into the lounge area of a large, anonymous residence.

There had been a lot of talk in the press about these penthouses. Only the ultrarich need apply. The suite itself wasn't quite worth it, but you weren't paying for that. You were paying to be five hundred feet in the air. A once-in-a-lifetime opportunity to look down on millions of people or, if your head was big enough, have them look up at you.

The room was dark, lit ambiently by the neon city below. Three walls of the lounge area were made of huge panes of glass, offering a near-panoramic view.

"Take a seat," said the charcoal man. I stayed standing. "Fine. He'll be with you in a minute." With that, he turned on his heel and walked toward the door. He opened it just enough for a person to pass through and made sure that it closed quietly behind him.

Discretion.

As soon as it shut I went after him, my eye to the peephole. The hallway was completely deserted and I wondered if he could have moved that fast. For a second I thought he might have squatted down out of view, but the idea was too ridiculous.

"We're alone, Waits, if that's what you're wondering."

I turned to the voice. I could see the dark outline of a man against the glow of the city from outside.

"How'd you get the shiner?" he said, that unmistakable Oxbridge accent.

I touched my eye. "Right place at the right time."

"I thought Detective Kernick must have taken a dislike to you . . ."

"He did seem disappointed that someone beat him to it."

"That was the impression he gave me as well." The man stepped into the dim light and smiled. "I should introduce myself. David Rossiter, MP."

I crossed the room. He was a tall commanding presence. In his mid-forties, wearing a tailored suit and projecting the warmth of a good politician. He gave the firm handshake of a man who meets people for a living, using both hands to cup mine. His skin was warm but his wedding ring was cold to the touch.

"Do take a seat," he said. I sat down and after a slight pause, so did he. "Interesting."

"What's that, Mr. Rossiter?"

"I motioned to the seat on my left, you chose the one on my right—and call me David." I smiled, feeling a dull ache across both my eyes. "You're probably wondering why I asked you here, Aidan."

"Waits," I said. "I assume it's not a social call."

"Very well then, Waits. Do you follow politics?"

"Only when I can't help it."

He smiled again. When he smiled, he looked directly at me, assuring me each time that I had amused him in some special way. I'd seen him on the covers of newspapers, giving war criminals the same look.

"I wouldn't want to presume you know who I am."

"You're David Rossiter, MP."

"And what do you know of my career?" he said, cradling the last word.

"Only what the papers say."

"You should know better than most not to believe what the papers say. *Disgraced* Detective Aidan Waits . . ."

I ignored him. "Your father was an MP and did all right out of it. You were more idealistic, though; when your brother went into frontline politics, you were still grifting it as a barrister. You married young and it worked. But I suppose a man would make it work with a vodka heiress."

The smile again.

"You got into politics at a funny time. The Tories had spent four years out of power, and another four after you joined. In spite of that you brought credibility to the old boys. Didn't toe the party line, spoke in favor of gay marriage, women's rights. Even immigration. Just the right kind of reckless to be a cabinet MP. It was no surprise when you were made Secretary of State for Justice, particularly with the law background. And I suppose it helps that you're a well-turned-out family man with two good-looking girls."

"You should write my biography," he said, the last word tailing off as he noticed that my hands were shaking. Without missing a beat, he stood and poured two large cognacs from a bar in the corner of the room.

"Thanks," I said, as he handed one of them to me.

"And where do you land, politically?" he asked, sitting back down.

"I'm still up in the air."

"An undecided?"

"Policy just seems too vague to solve the problems I come up against."

He took a drink, swilled the liquid round in his mouth for a second and then swallowed. "Save the world one person at a time?" I nodded. "There's probably some truth in that." He shifted in his seat. "So what if I were to tell you about one person? One person who desperately needs saving?"

"I'd tell you there are better people to do it than me."

"And I've already told you I don't believe what the papers say."

I took a drink. "I'd do what I could, but it's nothing that old charcoal down the hall couldn't manage. It's probably less."

He seemed to like that.

"In fact, Waits, you're the only person who can help me. What does the name Zain Carver mean to you?"

I didn't say anything.

"This morning," he went on, "I spoke to your superior. Terrific chap by the name of Parrs."

"Why am I only just hearing about it?"

"You've been living off the beaten track. It took Detective Kernick a few hours to find you."

"Well, I'm glad he was so discreet about it. That beamer blended right in."

"My apologies. Special Branch get too comfortable blending into affluent areas."

"And here's me blending into the bad ones."

"That's why you're here . . ."

"I can't talk to you about Carver until I've spoken to Superintendent Parrs."

Rossiter considered me for a moment then took a phone from his jacket pocket, holding it out for me to take.

"I'd rather you dialed," I said.

He smiled, scrolled through his address book and waited for an answer. As usual, Parrs picked up immediately.

"Have your man Waits here," said Rossiter into the mouthpiece. "Looks the part. Very authentic. Even accepted a drink on duty. Won't speak to me until he's spoken to you, though." He held the phone out again and I took it.

"Sir."

"*Waits*," said Superintendent Parrs. His Scottish accent was a low growl. "You'll extend the Minister every courtesy. We'll speak tomorrow." The line went dead and I handed the phone back to Rossiter.

"Zain Carver," he said.

"Drug dealer."

"And what's he to you?"

"A weak link, if I'm lucky."

"It's your job to get close to him?"

"I have a feeling my job's about to change." He didn't say anything. "If Carver succeeds it's because he's a one-off. A businessman among thugs. It's my job to see if that's exploitable."

"Exploitable how?"

"Three ways, really. With the right pressure applied, he might inform against other dealers. He isn't the biggest or the brightest, but might topple someone who is. Alternatively, he might tell us which police officers are on his payroll. Most interestingly, he could just be a frontman."

"A frontman for what?"

"There might be a dozen people above him who we've never heard of."

"I'm curious, what do you get out of all this? I mean, your name's mud now . . ."

"My name wasn't much to begin with. Why am I here, Mr. Rossiter?"

He took another drink. I heard his teeth collide with the glass.

"What do you know about my daughter? My youngest, Isabelle."

"Pretty girl and pretty young. Eighteen, nineteen?"

"She's seventeen," he said. "And mixed up with this Carver character."

"She's a minor, then. Send a squad car round and bring her home."

"That was what Superintendent Parrs suggested. I'm afraid it may take a little more finesse." I could see thick spots of rain hitting the panes of glass surrounding us. For a few seconds I could distinguish every one of them, then they became heavier, faster, until the room was wrapped in a blur. I waited. "A well-read lad like you might remember when Isabelle was last in the news."

"She collapsed," I said. "Exhaustion."

He didn't move.

15

"Suicide attempt?"

He nodded. "Isabelle suffers from depression. Part of the inheritance from her mother's side. There've been other attempts, but none so forceful as the last. There was too much blood, too much disturbance to keep the papers out. So we gave them exhaustion." He was staring somewhere off to my right, reliving it all. "I went to the editors myself and begged them."

"I see," I said.

"Do you?" he returned, before moderating it into a different question. "Do you know the only thing worse than your daughter stabbing herself in the neck?" I shook my head. "Her waking up, coming home and hating you for saving her life." He finished his drink. "She spoke to me, Waits. Said she understood her condition, understood there'd be black days. And said very calmly that this wasn't one of them. She was thinking clearly and couldn't forgive me for calling the ambulance."

"Takes a long fall for an MP's daughter to end up with a Zain Carver."

"Well a long fall's what she had," he said. "She got involved with them through a friend, I think. Far as I know, she's been living there at Fairview for a month."

"A month?" He didn't say anything. Fairview was the name of Zain Carver's home. A large Victorian property, south of the city in a young student-dense area. It was infamous for its house parties, attracting everyone from university heartthrobs to local celebrities. "I don't know what Parrs told you, but my orders have been to stay on their periphery. I've seen cash handovers, drunk with low-level dealers—"

"And some job you're doing of that," he said. "As of today, your orders have changed. You're to cross the threshold. Get your hands dirty. Make contact with the main players."

"And your daughter?"

"I can't risk having her brought home by the police."

"With respect, sir, the papers listened once, they'll listen again. Anyway, what's a scandal next to getting her home?"

"Scandal?" he said. "I'd give up this job in a heartbeat if it brought her back." I believed him, but that should have been my warning. He talked about Isabelle like she was dead already. He composed himself. "I can't be the one that makes her hurt herself again. Understand?"

Perhaps if I could have seen his face clearly I would have, but we were shrouded in darkness.

I shrugged.

"You're a young man. Just wait. You'd do anything for your kids."

"What do you want me to do for yours?"

He stopped, as if he hadn't properly considered that yet. "Can you get close? Can you see that she's OK?"

"I could even ask her how she is."

"I'd really rather you didn't make direct contact."

"You're not exactly making this easy, Mr. Rossiter."

"I won't have my daughter brought home against her will. And certainly not by the police."

"She wouldn't know," I said. "Even Special Branch down the hall's having a hard time working it out." He didn't say anything. "Look, these are bad people."

"What kind of trouble do you think she's in with them? Sex?" The word cost him a lot.

"I don't know, I wouldn't think so. Carver considers himself a gent. A businessman."

"A good thing, surely?"

"Depends on your experience of businessmen. I'd say it's a dangerous thing. There are other ways a girl can be exploited, especially a girl with a name. There are other pushers in the city who'd have treated her badly. She'd have been back home and in counseling by now, however much she might hate you."

With effort, he ignored the slight. "But Zain Carver?"

"He's different. More likely to know who she really is. More likely to charm her. He sells Eight and—"

"Eight?"

"Heroin," I said. "H is the eighth letter of the alphabet. It's a decent brand name, but mainly it sounds more innocent on a street corner or in a club."

"Out of the question. Isabelle's had her problems, but she wouldn't use—"

"None of them would until they do. Anyway, it's a university town. The last few years, Carver's done all right with party drugs. Does he know she's your daughter?"

"It's possible." He swallowed. "Although she's generally ashamed of the fact."

"Even if he did, he'd be playing a dangerous game, not knowing you won't just have her dragged home."

"Hm," he said, playing idly with his wedding ring.

"Has she run away before?"

"Only to five-star hotels on my Amex."

"And do you have a picture of her to hand?"

Rossiter reached into his breast pocket. He produced a photograph and handed it over, cupping it with his free hand like a naked flame. Isabelle was a pale, pretty girl with dull blond hair and intelligent blue eyes. In the picture, she was staring above where the camera would have been. At the person holding it, I thought.

"Look." He leaned forward. "I'm sorry about the crack I made, about you drinking with the dealers. You must be under a great deal of stress."

We sat in silence for a moment.

"Is there anything else you need from me?" he said.

"The name of the friend who introduced her to Carver?"

"I'm afraid I never met her."

"Her?"

"Him, them; whoever."

"Perhaps your wife—"

"Alexa's an unwell woman. She's not to be bothered."

"I see. And why are you so interested now?" He raised an eyebrow. "If Isabelle's been gone for a month?"

"Well spotted," he said, flexing his jaw. "You might as well know. I'm fighting a war on two fronts, Waits. Alexa also suffers from depression. We've been . . . strained now for some time. I'm afraid Isabelle got lost somewhere in the middle."

"How should I get in touch with you?"

He handed me an embossed business card. I ran my fingers over the raised letters.

"You'll get me on this number anytime, day or night."

"Well, thanks for the drink. I'll be in touch."

I left him slouched on the sofa, looking worn out and bereft.

5

Rubik's was one of those cavernous bars that evolves into a night-club as an evening wears on. In more honest days it had given the Hacienda a run for its money, hosting a who's who of post-punk bands. That was long behind it now. It was just off the Locks, looking out onto a canal that ran the length of the entire city. The beer hall itself had a backlit red glow, with no direct light during trading hours. It was one of the biggest rooms in the country, holding a few thousand people before anyone touched elbows.

There were four bars over three floors.

I had watched the central bar manager there for the last three weeks. He was a big man who wore his stubble as a fashion statement, cultivating a permanent five o'clock shadow. He had a calculating, ob-servant air about him. Never more so than on Friday nights, when he would hand over large sums of drug money to one of Zain Carver's employees. I had established that the drugs were delivered here, and then franchised out to other clubs in the area by this bar manager.

It was a slick system.

The best place to hide a few high people is among a few thousand drunk ones. For Zain Carver it meant that the bar manager took all the risk. He had a mixed portfolio, boasting party drugs in every line. Each was branded with a corresponding number. Coke was Three, Ecstasy was Five, Ket was Eleven. Customers could hold up the right number of fingers and get served without ever mentioning a drug.

The real secret to Carver's success was that he had more in com-mon with a white-collar criminal than some street-level thug. He simply had a product dropped off one day and the money collected another. It made this human connection of Isabelle Rossiter an inter-esting anomaly.

This was payday.

Because of my meeting with David Rossiter I'd arrived too late to see the handover itself, but things had changed. It was time for the direct approach.

It wasn't difficult to spot the girl on collection duty. She stood out at the bar, ordering her usual tall, neat vodka. She wore black tights and short black boots, flashing a high-watt grin through hot pink lipstick. She had long chestnut hair and wore a vintage suede jacket, probably older than she was. She was something else, somewhere in her early twenties, the textbook definition of hiding in plain sight.

When I knocked over her drink, she took it well. For a moment her thick, monkey-puzzle eyelashes widened in outrage. Just as quickly, though, she got the bar manager's attention and ordered another, resuming the cool indifference which I assumed was in her job description.

"Sorry about that."

"No problem," she said.

"It's Cath, isn't it?" She paused a second before turning her head to look at me. "I think we met at one of Zain's parties . . ."

"Really." There was no question mark.

"Well, just for a minute."

In fact, I had seen her speaking to Carver once or twice but never met either of them. The sad, plain girls standing at the backs of the rooms had given me her name. They talked about her like she was famous. *Cath*, they said, *she's one of his favorites*. She had started life like them, at the backs of the rooms, not knowing anyone, and then worked her way forward, from party girl to partner. They assumed that her tenacity was the difference-maker, that they might work the rooms harder and will themselves into her shoes. The sharper ones might realize before it was too late that it would never be the right time for them.

The bar manager brought her a fresh drink, glaring at me as he did so. A memory sparked. I thought I recognized him from somewhere and wondered if he recognized me. Catherine seemed calmer as soon as she had her drink in hand, turning to me with a pretty, nice smile. It was a world away from the bright, play-acting grin she'd worn earlier. She had that mark of a great actor, putting just enough truth into each role to keep it convincing. Even when she switched persona mid-sentence, one didn't make a lie out of the other.

"Well," she said. "I'll definitely remember you now . . ."

"Let me pay for that."

"Next time you knock over a girl's cocktail so you can buy her another, make sure she's not drinking on the house."

She made to leave.

"You wouldn't have talked to me otherwise," I said to her back.

She turned. "I might have, you know? That black eye suits you. Your face'd be lost without it."

"Whenever it starts fading I go out looking for another."

"Right. Tell me something, erm . . ."

"Aidan."

"Aidan." She stopped smiling. "Are you really looking for trouble?" I didn't say anything. "So you don't intentionally put yourself in harm's way?" Her eyes moved to the bar manager and then back over to me. I looked. He was standing, watching us, arms folded across his barrel chest.

"No," I said. "Course not."

"Then let me give you some advice." She stepped closer. "Go home. Save yourself another black eye."

"Like you say, my face'd be lost without it."

Her eyes went back to the bar manager. "Getting lost might not be a bad idea, babe."

"Sorry to bother you."

Satisfied, the barman moved farther away, started serving a group of girls. Catherine took up her glass, had a good pull and then set it down again. She slid a card discreetly beneath it as she did.

"I'd say you can buy me a drink sometime . . ." Her smile was wide and garish again, but for a moment I thought I'd seen the real thing.

"I'd probably just knock it over. Goodnight."

She crossed the room with wide, lovely strides and left.

I palmed the card she left under the glass and waited a minute. Then I walked out the door, down the road, to the rented room where I was staying. I threw my broken watch away, took some speed and changed my clothes.

6

The third strike against me was no one's fault but my own. After it, I was lucky to even get a job following Franchise collectors from bar to bar.

I'd been graveyarding, on and off, for a few weeks. Begging, stealing, borrowing my day shifts, swapping them for all-nighters. I loved watching the city, the town I knew, transforming into something else between the hours of nine o'clock at night and five in the morning. The smiley faces, smeared by kids on windows, pierced with neon light.

I liked the people.

They were young, drunk and in love. The girls were lightning bolts and the boys were all talk. The transsexuals, goths and gays took back the night, diversifying the high street, screaming words en masse I didn't even know the meaning of. And it was working. Keeping me vaguely sober. Vaguely out of trouble.

The only problem was my boss. Detective Inspector Peter Sutcliffe. His real name. Perhaps he was doomed as soon as they printed it on his birth certificate. Perhaps he was taunted when he was young, associated from the word go with a national hate figure. Either way, it's a bastard's name, and he filled every inch of it. They called him Sutty. The nickname helped avoid confusion but also made fun of his photosensitivity.

Sutty was corpse pale, allergic to daylight.

I learned a lot from him, not all of it good. I started graveyarding with a romantic view of the nightlife which quickly got realistic. I didn't know about vamps, the dealers who only came out at night, and I couldn't have told you anything about the gangs, who sold what, and how you could tell them apart. The only ones I could spot on sight were the smilers. So-called because of an inch of scar tissue at each corner of their mouths, where dealers had bladed them, branded them for late payment or too much lip.

Sutty knew which ones were Rushboys and which ones were Whalleys, just by the way they'd whistle for attention. Sutty could spot a Burnsider who'd wandered too far south. He could point out Franchise collector girls, the sirens, gliding from club to club. And he had an almost supernatural eye for trouble. It was a Sunday morning but only just, 2 or 3 a.m., and we were working Oxford Road. Connecting student digs with the university, then the university to the city center, the road saw the best and the worst of things. Working girls and curb crawlers, dealers and users.

It also leads onto one of the city's most lauded landmarks. The curry mile. Hundreds of Pakistani, Bangladeshi, Kashmiri restaurants, door to door, as far as the eye can see. A thriving, vibrant and diverse Muslim community. That was interesting because of a technique we'd started to see.

"*The shawl thing*," as Sutty called it. Young women wearing burkas, a common sight on the road at all hours, to camouflage their movements. Some dealers had been known to operate out of them, and some of the more nervous tweakers had started to wear them, too. This incensed Sutty. Possibly dark skinned. Possibly a user. His enemy squared.

We were standing by an all-night street vendor, drinking coffee while he smoked a cigarette. He jabbed me in the ribs, nodded straight ahead.

"There's our girl."

"What? Where?"

He pointed at a small woman in a black burka, on the other side of the road.

"Looks like someone on their way home to me."

"Come on," he said, crossing through the cars. He gave them an all-purpose hand gesture and I followed. He jogged up beside the woman, got in front of her and blocked her way. She tried to move around him but he held up his hand.

"Allahu akbar," he said, still getting his breath back.

The woman didn't say anything.

"Come on," said Sutty. "Off with your head."

The woman looked left to right. She looked trapped. Finally, she took off her black headpiece. She had thinning hair, the color and consistency of straw. She was white, plainly a user, almost the same pallor as Sutty. As I came alongside them I saw that she had been branded. That inch of scar tissue at either side of her mouth.

"Wipe that smile off your face," said Sutty, laughing at his own joke. The woman's expression didn't change. "Do you wanna show me what you've got in your hand, sweetheart?" The woman's right hand was clenched in a fist by her side. Reluctantly, she held it out, opened it. She had two sweaty, crumpled ten-pound notes. Sutty took them from her, said, "Thank you very much," and turned to leave.

She stared down at her empty hand. Then around, confused, to me.

"Sir," I called after him. It sounded weak. "Sir . . ." I said again. When he didn't turn I shouted: "SUTCLIFFE."

He stopped then, looked at me. His expression was blank.

"You can't do that," I said. He didn't move for a moment; standing still against the people streaming past us on the pavement. Finally, he nodded. Walked over to the girl, fumbled in his pockets and handed back the notes. Then he took her by the arm and dragged her toward me.

"Search her," he said. I looked at him. "Search her, that's a fuckin' order."

I turned, reluctantly, to the woman. People were walking around us, trying to give Sutty a wide berth. She held out her hands again, opened the one with the money. Except now, pressed between the notes, was a bag of blow that hadn't been there before. Sutty stepped forward, frowned like he was surprised.

He tutted, twisted her arm backward and handcuffed her. As he dragged her across the road to a waiting squad car, he flashed me a nasty smile.

"Good job I gave her that cash back, eh?"

She cried in the car. We booked her in and handed the drugs over into evidence. I didn't wrestle with my conscience for long. The next day I walked into police headquarters on Central Park, signed in and took the lift up to the fifth floor. I input my security code and passed into the secure area where seized drugs were held in evidence lockers. I took the cocaine and swapped it for talcum powder. That would have been that. I just happened to do it on a day when Superintendent Parrs was having the lockers examined. I remember walking down the corridor, the blood roaring in my ears.

Then a thin, reedy voice. "Excuse me, Detective Constable . . ."

I knew immediately. I was sitting outside Superintendent Parrs's office, scared to death, for two hours. When he opened the door to call me in, it was the first time we'd ever spoken. He told me to take a seat and took what I'd come to think of as a quintessentially Parrsian course of action.

He said nothing.

We sat there in silence until I couldn't take it anymore. I told him my story, acknowledging that I was ending my career before it had started. He didn't argue with that but as I finished speaking, as he sat back to take it in, I thought I saw a flicker of interest.

That Scottish accent. "Think the rules don't apply to you, Waits?"

"Sutcliffe—"

"I'll deal with Sutcliffe. I've been having a squint at your record. It's actually all right, if a little prone to lonerism. You might be what I'm looking for."

"Sir?"

"I'll be clear, son. I'm gonna give you two choices. Honestly, I advise you to take the first." I waited. "I can dismiss you on the spot. Raise criminal charges. Pursue a conviction and show you the inside of a cell. I'd also take it to the press, tell them you're dirty. Render you unemployable for the rest of your life."

"What's my second choice?"

"You can do a wee job for me. By now, the rumor of what you did is all over the station. By lunchtime, it'll be all over town. That might be useful."

"Useful how?"

He leaned forward. "I need someone who looks dirty."

He outlined the plan.

It was an open secret, he said, that Zain Carver kept police officers on his payroll. There had been years of missing evidence, of failed, fruitless raids on his holdings. It would be my job to find out who was in his pocket. My job to look even dirtier than them. My job to leak bad intelligence and set the trap.

"Either way," he said, "you'll be suspended with immediate effect while awaiting trial. Free from casework. Free to move about. Free to mix with the bad elements." He gave me his shark's smile. "If you want to be my man, if you get it right, those charges we talked about can just disappear . . ."

"And you advise me to take the first option?"

"The first option will ruin your career. The second could ruin your life."

"When do you want my decision?"

"Tell you what, I'm gonna start writing up the charges." He picked up a ballpoint pen and clicked it. "If you don't want to go to prison, you won't let me get to the end of this sheet."

The first option was bad, but it was the mention of a cell that scared me. I'd grown up in a group home. Had my fill of cots, cafeterias, curfews. I looked at Parrs. He was writing fast, and when I saw the words on the paper—conspiracy, corruption—I saw that my choice was actually no choice at all.

"I'll do it," I said.

I thought I had nothing to lose. At first I even liked the idea of vanishing into the Franchise. Superintendent Parrs had a fear of me being found out that bordered on paranoia, and only three people knew I'd gone under.

I gave up my flat and put my things into storage. I was moving into the city center. The thick of it, where I'd go from bar to bar, following the Franchise. I thought hard about what I might say to the people from my old life, but when I told the girl I'd been sleeping with that I was going away for a while, she laughed.

"*Going away?*" she said, throwing her things into a bag. "You were never really here in the first place."

I stopped going to work. I went missing. They briefed a story to the press and everyone believed what they read about me in the papers.

Disgraced Detective Aidan Waits.

My mind coursed, making connections. I toyed with the card that Catherine had left in the bar. It was an invitation to an after-party at Fairview. The home of Zain Carver. I could go there that night and track Isabelle Rossiter.

I found a bottle of wine and got my jacket on. The speed lifted me immediately. I stood by the window for a minute, breathing deeply, looking out at the endless blocks of buildings.

Fifty stories of unblinking lit windows.

7

I banged on the door and waited.

Bass-driven music beat through the building like a pulse. Shaking windows and walls gave the impression that the house was edging toward me, inch by inch. The sound system attracted strangers in from the street who hadn't dared knock and they clotted together at the end of the path, watching me like I was their leader.

Fairview was on the border between West Didsbury and Withington, two of the city's wealthiest suburbs. It looked like the ancestor of some fine family of buildings, raised on the best of everything. I took my bottle of red by the neck and banged its base into the door a few times.

It opened to a girl in a black evening dress. She had a hospital-white complexion and real red hair. She said something to me but it got carried away with the music escaping from indoors. Her eyes were framed by mascara and they, along with that timeless dress and those lost words, made her look iconic, like a silent film star from the twenties. I stood there with a helpless look on my face. She must have been used to this reaction by now because she took Catherine's card from my hand and beckoned me in.

I walked inside, into what felt like solid air. It was a madhouse of laughter and limbs, and there were people dancing, sweating, kissing, everywhere I looked. Turning to thank the redhead who'd opened the door, I saw she had already bolted it behind me and picked up a conversation, mid-sentence, with another man. As expected, I stood out in the room, closer to thirty than twenty.

I couldn't see Catherine anywhere but another girl caught my eye. She was standing off to the right, looking hopelessly out of place. Punkish, electric-blond hair had replaced her natural color, but it still sat atop that pretty face. She had the fine, slim figure of a seventeen-year-old girl but had tried to dress older. She gazed vacantly about, chewing a strand of hair, absorbing knowing looks from swaggering, slightly older boys.

Isabelle Rossiter.

She wore a light frayed scarf, which she toyed with constantly, checking it was still there. Her father said that she had stabbed herself in the neck and I assumed that it covered a scar.

I moved out of the doorway, muttered some kind of thanks for being let in and threw the redhead a dying look. She took it with that necessary indifference of the beautiful, who kill by the hundreds every day. I gave Isabelle Rossiter a friendly nod and moved on.

The hallway was constipated with people and I shoved through them, parting a shit-faced sea of twenty-somethings, drinking straight from the bottle. Some people were glassy-eyed from shooting or smoking Eight, but the main force tonight was Ecstasy. *Five*, as they called it. I felt too foreign an object to join the ones dancing in the next room, too tired to fight this back-and-forth shit-tide in the hallway and going up a floor was impossible. The stairs were made invisible by couples, all queuing toward toilets, showers, bedrooms and sex.

"Can I have a swig?" a girl said into my ear.

I saw a flash of porcelain skin, white teeth and manic blond hair. I thought of the picture her father had given me. Isabelle Rossiter was thinner than that now, but it didn't mark her out in this room. The other girls were between five and ten years older than her, but all had similar frames. Like they'd refined themselves to within an inch of their lives, paring back anything extraneous.

"Course," I said, handing over the bottle. In the time it took her to have a drink and wipe her mouth, she lost interest in me. She looked around the room, like she hoped someone else was watching us. When movement in the hallway forced us closer together, she considered me, up and down. Her eyes met mine again, looking disappointed.

"What brings you here?" she said, over the music. It was a bright question. My age, my disposition, my dark clothes made me stand out against a backdrop of youth, energy and color.

"Thought you might need a drink."

She showed me her perfect white teeth. "How do you know Sarah Jane?"

"Sarah Jane?"

"The redhead whose feet you just fell at."

"I was meeting her for the first time."

"She only ever lets in people she knows . . ."

"I've got one of those faces."

"One of those faces?" She contemplated me properly for the first time. "Is that how you got the black eye?"

"Case of mistaken identity."

"Yeah yeah," she said, taking another swig from my bottle. People passing pushed us closer together. "I bet it's makeup to make you look dangerous."

"Why bother with makeup? I just go to parties and throw insults at the biggest man I can see."

She raised an eyebrow. "Have you met Zain?"

We were so close together our lips almost touched. I leaned into her neck so she could hear me better over the music.

"He here tonight?"

"Haven't seen him."

"You know him, though?"

"Yeah," she said, face vacant.

"Only, from what I hear, I'd get more than a black eye."

"How did you say you knew Sarah Jane again?"

"I said I didn't."

She moved away from me. "Then what are you doing here?"

"Meeting nice girls . . ."

"Zain doesn't do nice girls."

"What about you?"

She wrinkled her nose up at the schmaltz. "I wasn't very nice when I got here and I'm even worse now."

"Worse how?"

She started to turn and I took the bottle back.

"I wanted that," she said.

"Yeah, well."

"Come on . . . a drink's the least you can do."

I nodded and took a swig.

She tilted her head to one side, tried to look bored. "I'll blow you for it." People pushing through the corridor forced us closer together again and I thought I saw her blush. I handed back the bottle and gave her some space.

"Free of charge."

She looked at it in her hand for a few seconds. "Sorry," she said. She half-smiled, embarrassed. "Don't know what's wrong with me tonight." She stepped backward and was absorbed into the hungry, swelling crowd.

I drifted from room to room with the movements of the party. There was just one locked door, and I wondered what was behind it. I didn't see Sarah Jane, the redhead, or Isabelle Rossiter again that night. As far as I could tell, Carver and Catherine never even showed up. It gave me the odd feeling that they were all together, somewhere else entirely. That all this had been for my benefit. I wondered what Parrs had got me into.

8

I woke early on the Saturday. The last day of October. I found David Rossiter's card and dialed ten out of the eleven numbers before hanging up. Instead I dialed a different number altogether. Superintendent Parrs answered on the first ring.

"*Waits*," he said. Parrs always picked up the phone in the same way. Like he'd glared at it a moment before you called, expecting your name to appear any second. His voice was a low growl with a light Scottish accent.

"Superintendent."

"How was Rossiter?" he asked.

"The elder or the younger?"

"Elder first."

"We had a drink. I was surprised. And surprised you weren't there."

"Hm," he said. "That was decided at a higher level. The Minister, in conjunction with our beloved Chief Superintendent."

"What's her take on it?"

"She decided if I were there, things might take on an official tone. She's keen, for appearances as well as the legitimacy of our case, that the two prongs of your work stay separate."

"Good of her," I said.

"Hm," he replied. Whenever Parrs talked about Chief Superintendent Chase, it was accompanied by an inflection of doubt that I was grateful to hear. He was unreadable in every other way. It made sense to me that Chase had forced the Rossiter affair on Parrs, and he resented it. That went double because the order had come from a woman.

He cut into my thoughts. "Make no mistake about who you're working for and where your priorities lie. You were due to make contact with the Franchise in a couple of weeks anyway. That's the only reason I agreed to this."

"Understood."

"You went to the house last night."

Without seeing him, I couldn't tell if he was asking the question or telling me what he already knew.

"Sir."

"And?"

"And no Carver."

"Drugs?"

"Around, but student stuff."

"So what about Isabelle Rossiter?"

"She was there. Mr. Rossiter asked me to keep my distance but she seemed OK." I thought of her taking the bottle from me, felt grateful not to be lying to Parrs's face.

"She's staying there at the house?"

"Far as I could tell. I thought I'd give the Minister a call but wanted to run it by you first."

"You'll keep him fully apprised, but only after checking what I want him kept fully apprised of. He can have the vague outline of it. Seen a paper this morning?"

"No, not yet."

"Course not. I'd be surprised if you've seen your shower and razor. I'd planned to run the Greenlaw appeal later in the year, once you'd made contact with the Franchise. Given that we're ahead of schedule, I managed to get it in today's *Evening News*. There'll be a repeat early next week." Despite its name, the *Evening News* ran a morning edition. I'd be lucky to catch it.

"What's the angle of the appeal?"

"Ten years since she disappeared, give or take."

I heard him breathing down the phone. In spite of his stated interest in the drug trade, I had the feeling that the Superintendent's main fascination was in the disappearance of Joanna Greenlaw. A notorious cold case with links to the Franchise.

"Are her family involved?"

"Didn't have any. There was a kid when she was fifteen but given up for adoption. I want to know how Zain Carver reacts to the appeal. If he doesn't react, prompt him."

"I'll try."

"I want him rattled on the subject," he reiterated. It didn't matter to Parrs that this would put me in danger. It probably made it better. He had nothing to lose in our deal either. "Aside from that, proceed as planned."

"Sir."

"Is there anything else?"

I thought of Isabelle, blushing with the wine in her hand. I didn't feel like turning her life over to a blackmailer as well.

"I think that's everything," I said.

9

The Greenlaw appeal was the Superintendent's passion project. It hadn't been part of our original deal, that I'd study the Franchise like a delicate ecosystem. It dropped a rock in the pond. Turned my covert operation into a suicide mission.

Joanna Greenlaw was one rung above an urban myth.

She had been a cash collector for Zain Carver back in the early noughties. His first. She passed into police legend when she agreed to give evidence against him. The old guard still used her name as shorthand for a long shot.

You'll never get anything on him, son. You'd need Joanna fucking Greenlaw.

I got up, got dressed and found a copy of the *Evening News*. The appeal was prominent, sure to catch the eye.

POLICE APPEAL FOR INFORMATION ON GREENLAW DISAPPEARANCE

Ten years.

It said that Greenlaw had been a popular twenty-six-year-old woman with connections to the criminal underworld. She had severed these connections and started a new life when she went missing. The truth was slightly more complicated.

Carver's bar franchise had been her idea. Before that, he'd been small-time. Selling recreational quantities of soft drugs while he worked out what to do with his life. The Franchise changed that. He had qualities that the city's chaotic drug market hadn't seen before. Professionalism and a strategy. Unfortunately, that came with ambition. When he insisted on market growth, the scene started getting bloody. Joanna went to the police when another collector, a friend of hers, was killed.

She'd been placed under Special Measures, a budget version of Witness Protection, and installed in an abandoned house on Thursfield. A ghost street in Salford, Thursfield was an entire row of derelicts. Empty and isolated, not even worth knocking down or renovating. Ideal for hiding somebody.

Due to the low scale of the operation, there was no budget for a man on the door, but when an officer stopped in at the end of his shift he became concerned. He knocked repeatedly to no answer and then kicked it in. He wiped his boots once he gained entry. There had been black and white paint daubed all over her doorstep.

I studied the picture alongside the appeal. Joanna had dark, naturally curly hair, and wore a long, thick jumper over black leggings. She looked more like an art student than a drug dealer. The expression on her face was half-formed, the prelude to either a smile or a frown. She was standing in a lounge, by a fireplace, backed so far into the wall's alcove she looked like she was trying to disappear into it.

Ten years ago.

The officer searched the house for her but she was gone, along with her suitcase and clothes.

As far as we knew, Joanna Greenlaw was never seen again. Personally, I didn't want to know what Zain Carver had to do with it.

10

spent the following week returning to the mundane surveillance of the previous month. I haunted local bars, establishing in my mind how far the Franchise reached. I usually enjoyed this time alone, but Friday's party had left an impression on me. I wanted to walk into the lives of the people I'd met, and the ones I hadn't. There was a certain thrill in maintaining a double identity, but it was more than that. I felt like it was a second chance to absorb some of the life I'd missed out on.

I put a call in to David Rossiter on the Monday, to update him on his daughter. He insisted that I meet him for coffee at his penthouse, to share my impressions.

"I can be there within the hour," I said.

"I'll send a car."

It didn't occur to me until after we hung up that I'd never told him where I was staying. Ten minutes later the black BMW arrived. Detective Kernick, alone this time. He drove us, wordlessly, back to Beetham Tower. I was escorted up in the lift. The background Muzak went impassively on. There was a thrill, an electric charge, to being on the forty-fifth floor again. Detective Kernick led me along the corridor to the same penthouse suite. He opened the door and closed it behind me, remaining outside.

Thin winter light gave the room a sepia tone. This time, David Rossiter was already seated, waiting for me in the lounge. Even sitting down, he cut an impressive figure. He didn't speak until Kernick had closed the door.

"Waits," he said, standing to shake my hand.

"Mr. Rossiter."

"Please, take a seat."

We sat down.

"There really isn't much to say."

"I'll decide that, if it's all the same to you."

"Well, after our meeting on Friday I went to a bar on the Locks. For the last month or so I've been watching a man there who I believe to be involved in the Franchise."

"The bar's name?"

"I'm afraid not."

He raised an eyebrow.

"It's my understanding that my work for you amounts to a personal favor. This is an ongoing investigation. There's only so much I can share . . ."

He frowned. "Go on."

"Fridays are of interest to me because it's also when Carver has his money collected."

"Collected how?"

"He employs a network of young women, feigning to be on nights out. They chat and flirt with the bar staff, then collect the money and get cabs home to Carver."

"Is that safe?"

"It is if you own the cab company in question. After our conversation I made contact with one of these girls and got myself invited back to the Carver house. There's a party there most Friday nights. Drugs, DJs, dancing, et cetera."

"Drugs?"

"Ecstasy, mainly."

"And Isabelle?"

"She seemed OK."

"OK?"

"Like a young woman enjoying herself." It was right at the edge of the truth but, from what I'd seen, she had done nothing that warranted my spying on her. And nothing that her father needed to immediately know about. There was a pause as Rossiter took this in.

"Your assumptions?" he said.

"I don't make assumptions, I only know what I see."

"I rather think that's true." He looked me firmly in the eye. "This won't do, Waits. How are you to know what's relevant to Isabelle? Relevant to me? You'll tell me everything, and I'll decide. I'm sure you think you know what you're doing, but you're a young man. You won't notice every detail and you won't always see its importance when you do."

"With respect, sir—"

"I have quite enough respect. What I want are the facts."

Neither of us spoke for a moment.

"Why do you take off your wedding ring, Mr. Rossiter?"

His gaze flickered.

"I beg your pardon?"

"Your wedding ring. Why do you take it off?"

He fingered his temple. "I'm not sure what you're—"

"It was cold to the touch the first time we shook hands. Your skin was warm, though. Same thing today. In future, you should put the ring in a trouser pocket if you have to take it off. Somewhere it'll keep the approximate warmth of your body. Dropping it into a loose coat pocket, especially if you're out in this weather, will only make it colder than your hand. Raise unwanted questions."

"What is this?"

"A detail I noticed."

We sat in silence for a minute, Rossiter staring into the middle distance over my shoulder. It made me think there was someone else in the room, standing behind me. I didn't move. Finally, his eyes drifted back onto mine. He smiled coldly.

"That'll be all."

11

rationed the more interesting parts of the job for regular intervals in the week. As Friday drew closer, time moved slower and I became restless for the next party. Only Rubik's, the bar on the Locks, carried the same thrill.

I watched the staff. Their movements.

It was the central hub of Zain Carver's business. The bar manager was an integral part of that. I took a paperback one day and watched him over a couple of beers. Everything he did, from making a cocktail to taking a tip, was done hatefully. There was more to it than that, though.

I recognized him from somewhere.

Once I was certain, I walked up the road to St. Peter's Square. The central library had recently reopened its doors after a four-year renovation. An enormous circular building, it had taken inspiration from classical Roman architecture and stood out against the gray office blocks surrounding it. It was the first time I'd been back since the refit, and I had to ask for directions to the newspaper archive.

I flicked through endless *Evening News* articles until I found what I was looking for. A photograph of the bar manager, beardless and smiling on the court steps. Sweating through a cheap three-piece suit. He looked like he'd won a regional darts tournament.

SMITHSON ACQUITTED.

Glen Smithson, the bar manager, had been arrested for the date rape of Eleanor Carroll, an eighteen-year-old fresher, away from Ireland for the first time in her life. Despite a CV including theft, domestic violence and the sale of Rohypnol, the case against him had fallen apart. The judge had blasted detectives for "contaminated, tampered with, and missing evidence." Reading between the lines, I wondered if the girl had been intimidated, too. She had dropped the charges, dropped out of university and gone back home.

The Franchise in full effect.

I contemplated his picture for a long time.

Everyone else I'd met so far had personality. I could believe they were people in a shady world doing a job. But the bar manager hated. It was interesting.

12

November. Fairview. Friday night. The same thick pulse of music, beating out through the walls. Same gaggle of people standing at the end of the path, wanting to go in but not quite daring. Having got in and out once, I was nervous about going back. I took a pill before I set out, then another when I arrived. I didn't knock this time. As I was about to, the door swung open. Sarah Jane, red hair in corkscrews, white skin in another black dress, inclined her head. The look said: *I remember you*, but not much more.

The truth is that she was a cruel kind of beautiful. Someone you might remember on your deathbed, wondering where your courage had been on the day you met, wondering why your courage only ever surfaced at the wrong time and for people who weren't worth it.

I stepped inside and she closed the door behind me. If anything, the party was busier this week. Life was exploding in every corner of the house and the walls looked like they were sweating. Turning to thank Sarah Jane, I saw the reason why.

Zain Carver.

He was standing beside her, radiating charm and cold, clean malice. The oldest man in the room, some thirty-six years of age, Carver was rich enough in money and drugs to overcome any stigma. He dressed casually in designer clothes, like a hip-hop entrepreneur. He was mixed race, with a brilliant, bright smile. The house belonged to him, although his height meant that he had to slouch in the hallway. It gave the impression that he was holding up the ceiling and I think he liked that. Fairview had been left to him by his parents, along with a small property portfolio and an annual income. There was no real need for him to inhabit such a violent world, but I suppose that's how you can tell a man who comes from old money. There's no one so keen to get hold of the new kind.

Sarah Jane was half-turned toward me and about to speak.

Carver interrupted her.

"Right, though, aren't I?" he said, with the kind of Southern accent people only get from not living there.

She turned to him, speaking quickly, quietly. He half-listened while scrolling through messages on his phone. My arrival had brought an atmosphere in with it and I thought about leaving. Instead, I moved warily out of the doorway with a nod in their direction.

I'd been drinking in the hallway for a few minutes when I saw Sarah Jane again. Next to the other girls, their jaundiced, liver-failure fake tans, she was pale and smooth. She ghosted her way through the human wall with an ambivalent, removed ease.

I called her name over the music but she didn't look back. I started to follow but was forcefully shoved from behind. I fell into a group of people and, finding my feet again, saw our celebrity host, Zain Carver, strong-arming his way through the crowd after her.

I reached out for his shoulder but someone pulled me back. He was a small mountain, all piss and uproar that I'd spilt his drink. I recognized him as Carver's enforcer, Danny Gripe.

Grip to his friends.

He pushed me. "The fuck's your problem?"

Close up, there was something off about him. His eyes seemed to be swelling out of his skull, his left arm looked smaller than his right and his hair was thinning in patches. He kept looking from his fallen glass to me in mock-awe at the power of gravity.

"I said, what the fuck's your problem?"

I didn't reply. I didn't know. He pushed me again and I laughed at him. His mouth shrank down to a small puckered circle of outrage. There was no chance of fighting in such a cramped space, but when he clenched his good fist some people held him back.

I could leave now or go deeper inside, after Sarah Jane and Carver. Reluctantly, I turned and pushed through the crowd in their direction. Whether it was earned or not, Carver had a reputation for making women disappear.

I arrived in the kitchen to see ten or so people standing around closed patio doors leading out into a garden. The music was much quieter, and I could hear them all speaking in the same hushed tones. The unhappy couple had already passed through. I went to the doors and saw them in silhouette, standing at the end of the garden path.

They were having a heated argument. I could see their breath in the cold but couldn't hear them. Carver's frame loomed over Sarah Jane's. I expected the worst and shouted over my shoulder to the room.

"Hey, everyone out. Zain needs some privacy."

His name scared most of the gawpers back into the hallway. One man dragged his knuckles across the room, tried to look past me.

"What's he doing out there?" he said, all admiration.

"Proposing," I said. "What the fuck do you think he's doing?" He huffed out like I'd hurt his feelings.

Because the light was on indoors, I could see Carver and Sarah Jane framed in a reflection of my own face. They looked like a two-headed monster, but began to struggle and pull apart. I pressed up against the glass and made to open the door, when one of the shapes hit the other bluntly about the head.

They separated into two and stood, motionless, in the gloaming. I saw their breath in the lantern-lit November night, puffing out excitedly, bridging the gap from one to the other. In a matter of seconds they seemed to grow calmer, their breath less dense in the air, until there was nothing left between them.

I refocused and caught my own reflection in the window. There wasn't an expression of concern or shock on my face. I just looked interested.

I turned away and was surprised to see Isabelle Rossiter, watching me from the corner of the room. She was backed up against the wall with a bottle of wine, and I could tell she'd seen my fascination reflected in the glass. Her blond hair was neon under the lights.

"Hello again."

"Oh, hey," she said, like she'd only just noticed me. She drifted over, looking at nothing in particular. She nodded out at Carver and Sarah Jane. "They can be really good for each other, sometimes."

"What's good about them?"

She shrugged. "I've seen him get a smile out of her."

"Is that so rare?"

"Have you got one yet?"

"I'm still working on you."

"I could use one," she said. "What are you doing right now?"

"That depends."

"On what?"

"When you were born." She raised an eyebrow. It reminded me of her dad. "I'm just big on astrology," I said.

"I'm sure we'd be compatible . . ."

"Really? Do you have a name?"

"You're old-fashioned. It's boring." She smirked. "All you need's my number." She was half-joking by this point, and I liked her more for it. When I started to leave, she took my hand. Dropped the femme fatale act.

"It's Isabelle. My name's Isabelle."

"Three syllables? I'll never remember that."

She smiled, finally. "My friends call me Izzy."

"Friends?" I said. I looked out into the garden. Carver and Sarah Jane were walking back toward the house, both of them expressionless. My reflection in the glass of the patio door still stared back at me, but it wasn't even interested now. It was cruel. "Is that what they are?"

She tugged my hand. "How do you know Sarah Jane?"

"I told you, I don't."

"And I told you, she doesn't let people in unless she knows who they are." She passed me her bottle of wine. "Thought I owed you one, for last time." I gave her a weak smile and walked out of the kitchen, back into the sea of bed-wetter twenty-somethings.

She doesn't let people in unless she knows who they are.

I wondered if that had been a warning. The people moved slowly, but I had almost reached the front door when a large, hot hand squeezed my shoulder. I turned to see a bloody-nosed Zain Carver staring straight at me. He jerked his head back toward the kitchen, then leaned into my ear and said, "A word, brother."

13

The house party crowd parted easily for Carver, owing more to reputation than size. They glanced at me with fading smiles, even concern. They'd seen the bloody nose that Sarah Jane had given him. Music still blared from the next room but I barely heard it. He walked ahead into the kitchen. I took a breath and followed.

Isabelle was gone but there were three of us. Zain Carver, myself and Grip, the man I'd argued with earlier. He looked like a reanimated corpse. In the direct light of the kitchen I could see that his left arm *was* smaller than his right, but there was more to it than that. The entire left side of his body was warped and diminished. His eyes were inflamed and painfully wide.

"That's him," he said.

"Close the door," said Carver, to no one in particular. I reached out to do it, felt the sweat on my palm when I touched the handle. I was blocking off one of my possible exits and some chemical survival instinct said *Don't*. I tried to ignore it. With the door shut the music was almost entirely blocked out.

"*That's him*," Grip persisted. "Fucking took a swing at me."

Carver smiled off into the silence. There were several lights on in the kitchen, each facing a different direction. Because of where he was standing, he cast two stark shadows.

"You took a swing at Grip?" he said.

"No, I didn't."

Grip spat in the sink as though I'd put a bad taste in his mouth. His left arm didn't move naturally with his body, but trailed behind it like an afterthought.

"He's a liar, then?" said Carver.

"Confused. I'm sure he gets that a lot."

Grip took a step forward, then thought better of it. Instead, he took a wine bottle by the neck and smashed it into the wall. He held the sharp end up at me and said, "Keep talkin' shit." Glass and red wine pooled together on the floor.

Carver looked at him. "Was an accident, I'm sure. This guy—"

"Aidan," I said.

He paused at the interruption. "Aidan had the presence of mind to clear the room while I was . . ." he smirked, searching for the word, "*talking* to Sarah."

Grip stood, flushed in silence. He seemed to be mentally scrolling through every word he knew, searching for the right one. He still held the smashed bottle by the neck.

"Where's Sarah Jane now?" I said.

Carver nodded at Grip. He paced across the room, shoulder-barged me and walked out. For the moment that the door was open again, the music, the world, boomed back into the room. A rapper was shouting about starting out from the bottom, over a brooding, moody beat.

Then the door swung shut.

Carver took out his phone, leaned against a work surface and started scrolling through messages. Occasionally he stopped, tapped out quick replies and then went on. A couple of minutes passed before he said anything. He didn't look up.

"Why you asking about Sarah Jane?"

I started to answer but he cut me off.

"Why you hanging round Rubik's? Why you telling Cath you've been here before?"

"I have been here before."

"Come onnnn." He smirked. "You hadn't last Friday when you told her you had . . ."

I didn't say anything.

"You've been noticed, Aid." He was still scrolling through messages. "And not just by Cath, not just at Rubik's. Staff in the Hex have seen you seven times in two weeks. Likewise The Basement, and we've got you on CCTV at The Whistlestop." They were smaller, satellite clubs that the Franchise operated out of. Spotted around, from the Locks, into the city center and even into the northern quarter. Carver glanced at me then went back to his phone. "Mystery white boy. You're turning into my best customer."

"Seemed like a way in."

"Fake it till you make it? Not here, brother. I told Cath to slip you an invite if you were angling for one."

"Why?"

"You keep showing up. You're persistent." He shrugged. "Thought you must have something to say for yourself. Double-time, though, I've got a hundred unread messages competing for my attention."

"I'm no one, really—"

"Filth are one rung lower than no one in my book. Detective Waits, innit?" He looked up, over my shoulder. When I turned I saw that Grip was standing outside the patio doors, smoking a cigarette, still holding the smashed bottle by his side. He winked at me. It looked painful. I felt the sweat pooling on my lower back. That animal survival instinct, now saying, *run*. Carver laughed and went back to his phone. "Don't look so worried, brother. I read the papers. No one gets in unless I know 'em."

"You don't know me."

"Stealing drugs from evidence? Taking bribes? I know enough. You sound like my kind of copper. With one difference. They binned you off. *Suspended, pending further investigation*." He was reading from a news story about me on his phone. He scrolled down and winced. "Bad picture of you, there, Aid." He squinted. "No black eye, though."

"They haven't binned me yet."

"Near enough, and I'm drowning in friends as it is. Some of whom have actually managed to hold on to their jobs. So if that's all—"

"Got any friends on the ghost squad that's investigating you?" He looked up from his phone for the longest time since we'd started speaking. "Any friends who even know what a ghost squad is?"

"Go on, then."

"A completely off-the-books operation designed to sting corrupt police officers."

"Off the books, how?"

"Granted special powers for a particular focus on officers who neutralize evidence and betray law enforcement operations." He didn't say anything. "Sounds like that might describe some of your friends."

"Why wouldn't my friends know about this?"

"All confidential. All staffed by older heads."

He smirked. "Why would some old heads after some bent cops be interested in me?"

"Cuz it's your lucky day, Zain. It's always your lucky day. It's been your lucky day every day for the last ten years."

He nodded at Grip through the glass. I saw him turn and walk farther down the path into the garden. Carver took a drink, pushed himself off the work surface and walked over to the doors.

There was something physically unnerving about him, aside from his size. He moved like an actor in the round, always aware of his surroundings and the effect they had. Low ceilings, light configurations and phones became props when he was in a room, and he used them at will to amplify or diminish himself. Even his accent altered slightly depending on who he was talking to. It went further than that, though. He projected parts of people back at themselves in a disconcerting way. The laconic passivity of Sarah Jane, or the controlled aggression of Grip. With me he became opaque and difficult to read. It was like talking into a funhouse mirror reflection of myself.

"Maybe I'm just lucky, brother. What can I tell ya?"

"That's probably what they're wondering, too. What can Zain Carver tell us if he stops being lucky . . ."

"What makes you the messenger?"

We both spoke quietly now. "I'm not coming at you like a man on the turn, because I'm not. But you said it yourself." I nodded at his phone. "There's a bad picture of me there. My job ended in a pretty public way and I'm wondering if I've got anything valuable. This is big, and it touches people with money. Where else would I be?"

"If this ghost squad's so confidential, how come you know about it?"

"Got me where I am today."

"You were on it?" I didn't say anything and he guessed again. "No." He started to laugh. "They busted you?"

"That's just it. They had the chance to, but they didn't. Whatever I was or wasn't taking from evidence should have been untraceable by existing standards. It was untraceable. Until one day my clearance to the fifth floor was restricted."

"So someone got wise."

"No. Someone had set a trap. I was pulled into an interview room and questioned. The cop in charge was an out-of-towner, reading from a script. First alarm bell, they didn't want to give away who was running the thing locally.

"The questions focused on money troubles, third parties, blackmail. Second alarm bell, they already had a profile in mind.

"Now, this was more than a sackable offense. It was heavy jail time. Instead, when they realized I wasn't their man, I was transferred out of headquarters without a word. Third alarm bell, they didn't want any noise.

"And all the time I'm wondering who's got the clout to spot me, restrict my clearance and hush it up. Then I start to wonder why they'd take the trouble." Carver pocketed his phone, full attention now. "The only thing that made sense was that I'd walked into a sting, and that they had their hearts set on something, someone, bigger than me. Dirtier than me. An arrest at headquarters might send the real target underground. So, I'm transferred away from the operation and a few weeks later some flimsy charges arrive. The ones you read about in the paper."

"And you pluck a ghost squad out of thin air?"

"Better than that: I found them. I knew it had come from a higher-up, and I knew it had come from inside Central Park. So I spent a few days watching who came and went. I crossed a lot of names off my list, made a note of some others. Then I saw Derek Wright."

"Should I know him?"

"Chief Inspector. Apparently retired in March, but still showing up to work in October. Then I spotted Redgrave, another supposedly retired old head, then Tillman. Retired cops sneaking in and out the back door. That's why your friends won't know about it."

"And how would these old heads be filling their days?"

"Working through historic case files, finding patterns, taking appropriate action. I'm betting when it comes to cases where Zain Carver got lucky, the same detectives' names keep cropping up." I let that hang in the air for a second before I went on. "Then it's just a case of applying the right kind of pressure to those detectives, telling them whose boyfriend they'll be in prison. They get your so-called friends to feed you the wrong information and your luck starts to run out."

49

Carver massaged his jaw with a knuckle. It was a bad habit of mine and I tried to remember if I'd done it in front of him.

"Why should I believe any of this?" he said. "You've been fired, you're after one last payday—"

"Take it or leave it. But if you've got a friend on the force, they can confirm the gist easy enough."

He eyed me. "Go on, then. How?"

"Between five and six p.m., if they're watching, they'll see Wright, Redgrave and Tillman leaving police headquarters on the east side."

"Any day?"

"Tuesday to Friday, from what I've seen so far. Wright and Tillman usually clock in between eight and nine. Redgrave's variable."

He let me see that he was thinking on it. "And what do you get?"

"What happened to Sarah Jane tonight?" I wanted to sound conflicted. To steer the conversation toward the personal. He frowned like *Who the fuck do you think you are?* I looked back. Neither of us moved for a second and he started to laugh.

"Y'mean, is she buried in cement at the bottom of the garden?"

"I read the papers as well."

His smile curdled and he took a step closer. "You're gonna come in here talking about Joanna?" I didn't say anything and he pushed me. "Eh?" I didn't think he'd actually lost his temper. He was just showing me it was a possibility.

"I told you, I can't come here like a man on the turn, because I'm not one. I can work for a businessman without thinking twice. I don't know about a killer, though."

"Sarah Jane went out to cool off, but she'll be back." He paused. "Some days I think Joanna will be, too. I haven't read this appeal, but I'm glad it's happening. They shouldn't have forgotten her for so long. I never did."

"What happened to her?"

He frowned again. His phone started vibrating and he patted down his pockets for it. "Wright, Redgrave and Tillman?" I nodded. "Come back next week. If there's something in it, I'll do right by you." He answered the phone and I started to leave. Before I got to the kitchen door he raised his voice. "It's true what I said, y'know." He sounded sincere but I didn't know if he was talking to the phone or to me.

14

I didn't see Carver again that night and when the music stopped shortly afterward, people seemed to fall down dead wherever they'd been standing. The floor was littered with passed-out bodies. Relieved, I took a long drink from Isabelle's wine. I decided to climb the stairs now that they were clearer, and felt calmer with every step. The incessant beat of the music had been replaced by a ringing in my ears that felt vital and alive.

I reached the landing and turned right into a large, perfumed bathroom. There was the outline of a girl sitting on the toilet. The seat was down and she was fully dressed with her head in her hands, looking every inch the pregnancy scare. I turned on the light and saw an abject Isabelle Rossiter. She was blacked out but breathing.

I picked her up and gently sat her down on the floor. She was so light she almost wasn't there. I cleaned two abandoned glasses, filled them with water and sat with her quietly as she drifted in and out of consciousness and drank. My own vision had started to blur before I sat down but now everything fell out of focus, started to move in slow motion. I felt my perspective altering, falling out from under me.

The wine.

Thought I owed you one, for last time.

It felt like a strong sedative. Rohypnol or GHB. I hoped I hadn't drunk enough to knock me out but it would blur the edges. When I floated up to my feet I think I was laughing.

Isabelle's head was back in her hands. Her tousled, punk-rock hair and bare legs. She was barefoot, too, and the colorful varnish on her toenails made her look like a child. I'd bent to nudge her awake but saw that her scarf had fallen open.

I tilted her head backward.

The scar on her neck was bigger than I expected. And darker, considering it had healed over a year ago. It was shaped almost like a Z. Two deep, definitive lines, joined by a lighter one in the middle. When she attempted suicide, she had stabbed herself in the neck, drawn the knife back on itself and made a second, deeper cut.

I drew together the frayed ends of her scarf and tied them lightly back around her neck, making sure to cover the scar. I covered her legs with a thick, dry towel, turned the light off and left her there.

Dizzily, I opened the first door I came to, letting my eyes adjust to the darkness. It was a large room with a king-size at one end and some sleeping couples on the carpet. I tripped over them to the bed, where I heard a man snoring. I pushed him onto the floor and lowered myself down, shattered and shaking. The bassline of my pulse moved my whole body, and the room was spinning.

Time moved fast, back and forth, and it might have been an hour or a few minutes. The door opened hard. I saw people on the floor roll away from the light. I pretended to be asleep when the door closed.

It was dark again.

I heard the soft, searching footsteps of a girl, padding across the room toward the bed. She lay down beside me and drew herself closer. She smelled of cigarettes and fresh air, but I could feel the sweat through her skirt.

"Hello again," said Catherine, into my ear.

The room carouseled and her voice felt like a beacon. Our fingers linked together in the darkness, she took my hand and guided it slowly up her thighs. She was warm between the legs, and I realized she had no underwear on. "Still looking for trouble?" She laughed, a wonderful sound, and her shallow breaths got me hard. She unbuttoned my trousers and I felt her hand moving on me. Even at the time it felt more like a memory. Or the memory of something someone else had told me. I came after a few minutes and she peppered my face and neck with light, breathy kisses.

I thought I heard her say *Zain*.

Lying back, exhausted, I became conscious of heavy breathing. I tried to exhale open-mouthed to make it quieter but it had no effect. The breathing was coming from someone in the darkness at the far side of the room. I passed out into a solid, dreamless sleep.

I opened my eyes, sat up suddenly and saw strained daylight coming through the curtains. The room spun. Experience told me I'd be OK as long as it went clockwise. When I rolled over I saw the bed was empty. Catherine had gone. I could still smell her on the pillow. I got up unsteadily and left the room. There were sounds of life in the house but no one on the landing or stairs. I descended and, pausing in the deserted hallway, heard muffled voices behind a closed door.

"*Sheldon White?*" It was one of the girls talking. I didn't recognize the name but heard something familiar in the tone of voice.

It was fear.

I could have opened that door and joined the owners of those muffled voices, but at the time I didn't think a one-night stand mattered. At the time, I didn't think. I opened the front door, glad to have seen no one, and walked back out into November.

Squinting into the light, I saw what looked like a large smear of bird shit on Carver's doorstep. Black on white. It was still wet when I stepped over it.

15

T he state of you," said Parrs, motioning me to a chair. It was Monday morning. His Scottish accent still stood out, but everything else about him blended into the background. He was a gray man in almost every respect. His hair and clothes had faded prematurely when he was promoted to Superintendent. They suited him, hinted at the thoughtful, internal life he seemed to lead. We were sitting in a miserable greasy spoon off Oxford Road. It wouldn't do for me to be seen in headquarters.

I pushed a newspaper across the table.

Parrs opened it in the middle and read.

Minutes went by as he sat, frowning into my report.

The edited highlights.

I had left out my own drug use and one-night stand, and I'd tried to downplay Isabelle's fall, too. If anyone had known, if anyone had asked, I would have said it was to protect her. In truth, I wasn't sure why I kept it to myself. Perhaps I didn't trust Superintendent Parrs. Didn't trust David Rossiter, MP.

Even with a weekend between me and the last party, I still felt wired. The buzzing light bulbs and humming oven fan sounded like synths. Parrs stopped reading and looked at me over the newspaper. I realized I'd been tapping my foot against the chair leg ever since I sat down, and stopped. His index finger was pressing hard into the page, saving his place. He reread a line.

"What'd you make of Carver?" he said, like it was the third time of asking.

"Big character. Definitely has friends on the force. He was all ears when I told him about the ghost squad."

"He'll follow up?"

"If his man sees Wright, Redgrave and Tillman leave headquarters a few times, I think we'll be good."

"Who's living at Fairview?"

I glanced over my shoulder at the door. We were the only cus-tomers.

"Carver and Grip, definitely," I said. "The girls, Catherine, Sarah Jane and Isabelle, I think. Not the barman."

"And Friday night?"

"Same story as before. There's nothing too evil happening there, but a lot of bad vibes. An atmosphere."

"All those stories in the press about their boss's ex-girlfriend going missing." Parrs smiled, gleeful at the thought. "You pushed Carver on the subject of Joanna Greenlaw?"

"I think it hit a nerve. He pushed back."

"Oh?"

"Didn't go the way you'd think, though. He said he hadn't read it but was glad to see something happening. Said Joanna Greenlaw shouldn't have been forgotten about for so long."

"What do you think?"

"He said it like he meant it, but a bit of performance goes along with everything he does."

"Any indication he knew more?"

"No," I said, wondering if the Superintendent had told me every-thing. "He said that some days he still expects her to walk through the door at Fairview. As far as he's concerned, she went missing ten years ago. The appeal hit a nerve but . . ." I tailed off.

"You think there's something else?"

"Maybe Carver's always so well informed, but I got the feeling I'd been noticed because of heightened security."

"Hm," said Parrs.

"I heard mention of a Sheldon White, and—"

His eyes darted up at me. "Who said that name?"

"One of the girls at Fairview."

He looked at me. Closed the newspaper with my report in it. When he spoke again, his voice was lower than usual.

"Sheldon White's the ghost of Christmas past, son. A mover and shaker for the Burnsiders back in the day. He just got home from a seven-year stretch."

"Right."

His eyes sparkled. "He was also investigated in connection with the disappearance of Joanna Greenlaw." He snorted to himself. "If they're talking about Sheldon White, they must be rattled."

"Why am I only hearing about this now?"

He'd almost forgotten I was there. "I want you focused on Carver."

"You can't keep sending me over there with half the story."

He glared at me. "I can do anything I want with you, son. If you feel like backing out, I'll send you down with them." He reopened the newspaper, referred to my notes. "Isabelle Rossiter. Tell me about her."

I realized I was tapping my foot again and stopped.

"Mixed-up kid, but no more than most seventeen-year-olds."

"Seventeen," said Parrs, rubbing his face. "No clue what she's doing there?"

"Carver keeps a lot of young girls around. I assume she'll join the others and start collecting cash from bars. She looks the part."

"Looks can be deceiving, son. She seem stable?"

"More than I was at her age."

"That doesn't fill me with confidence."

"I saw the scar on her neck. Whatever happened there, it was no cry for help."

"Hm," said Parrs, not really interested. "When are you going back?" He was hungry for more. He'd have driven me over to Fairview there and then.

"Carver invited me to the next party."

"Ah." Parrs smiled. "The shit Friday agreement."

When Parrs smiled, the lines around his eyes deepened, like gills on a shark.

"I'll hear then what his man makes of our ghost squad."

He nodded, then considered me for a moment. "Don't get too carried away with this Isabelle Rossiter shite. Her ladyship, Chief Superintendent Chase, can stick her tits in all she likes, but I'll not have some slut jeopardizing my investigation. Your focus remains absolutely on the Franchise."

This Isabelle Rossiter shite. "Sir," I said.

"And tell me something. Honestly now."

I held eye contact and nodded.

"Are you using, son?"

I stopped tapping my foot again.

"No," I said.

I got up and left before they even took our order.

16

I made sure the cubicle was locked and laid a line on the back of my hand. It was Wednesday night. I had made the same pub-crawl tour of Franchise places as the previous week, making a note of who I saw and where. I'd been drinking in The Basement, a small subterranean bar with sticky floors and no natural light.

When I left the Gents', the back of my throat was burning and everything smelled of speed. Things seemed to move faster but that might have been the shock of seeing Sarah Jane. Stark red hair, the devastating cut of her dress. She was working tonight. I had never seen her in Rubik's, but she seemed to collect from these smaller, satellite bars.

"Hi," I said, as she turned from the barman. She gave me something less than a look and strode out of the room toward the stairs and street level. She would probably have blanked me either way, but I wondered if Carver had shared the story I'd told him.

The ghost squad.

Wright, Redgrave and Tillman had been entering and exiting police headquarters on cue. Tipped off, a corrupt officer would have no choice but to wait, watch and corroborate what I had said so far. I wouldn't know for sure until Friday. The next party. If I had gained their trust, or something close, that would be my chance to lay groundwork for the sting.

It was an exciting time and, although I didn't have the Superintendent's zeal for the Franchise, I was starting to see the appeal of the operation. Joanna Greenlaw's disappearance ten years ago. Zain Carver's pseudo-empire. His bars and his girls. His sirens. Isabelle Rossiter, seduced by it all. And now the added layer of this Sheldon White, this grudge, another blast from the past.

If it had worked, the mark would have been in custody a week later and I would have gone back to my old life, muddied name and all.

Zain Carver would have been arrested, his bars shut and his girls dispersed. Who knows what Isabelle might have done.

I keep going back to that moment. The last before I lost control. If it had worked, I might have saved myself a lot of trouble, a lot of pain. I might even have saved some lives while I was at it.

I drank a beer for my throat. The speed made me feel omnipresent and untouchable. I was everywhere, setting a hundred different moving parts in motion. The people were just things seen from a distance. The unblinking, lit windows on a tower block.

17

I spent the next couple of days apart from the Franchise. Bereft of it. It had begun to feel like a force, pulling me toward Fairview. When Friday came and I went back up the path to the Carver house, it was quickly. I walked straight past the try-hards and onlookers attracted to the throb of bass. I didn't know what I was walking into. It could have gone either way.

Sarah Jane opened the door and stood aside without looking directly at me. The hallway over her bare shoulder was heat and people and *life*. Strobe lights flashed and vanished in time with bass drops in the music. I stepped inside and she closed the door on a couple of people coming up behind me.

"Hi again," I said, over the roar.

She cut me off. "He wants to see you."

I picked out Catherine in the crowd behind her. Long chestnut hair, spilling out against the wall. I thought of our night together, I couldn't believe it was real. She was pressed against the left side of the corridor, talking to a man who had his back to me. The lights made her ultravisible one second and gone again the next. When she saw me her eyes widened.

"Hey," said Sarah Jane, snapping her fingers in my face.

"Lead the way."

It was difficult to follow her through the crowd. Too many people in too little space. They parted ways for Sarah Jane like she was royalty, surging back together in her wake. The strobe slowed everything down, making the walk seem like a series of snapshots. I glanced over my shoulder for Catherine. The man was still talking to her, but she was looking at me. Communicating something.

"Watch where yer goin'," said Grip, connecting hard with my shoulder. I looked at him. He flicked my forehead and smiled. His bottom lip split open when he did, and a drop of blood ran down onto his chin. He flicked my forehead again. I couldn't see Sarah Jane and pushed past him toward the kitchen. I got there in time to see her open the door and walk through it without checking if I was still behind her. I was sweating from the heat of the crowd, she was completely untouched by it.

Isabelle Rossiter was standing by the door on her own. She wore the same frayed scarf, same punkish style as before, and looked down at her faded, stamped-on Doc Martens. When she saw me following Sarah Jane, she called out over the music:

"You said you didn't know her."

I went past her into the kitchen and closed the door. The light was dim, steady, and the music was muffled. Zain Carver was where I'd left him a week before. Leaning against a work surface, scrolling through the messages on his phone. He had a bottle of expensive-looking liquor and two glasses at his side. He finished reading a message and then looked up at Sarah Jane.

"Give us a minute, sweetheart."

He went back to his phone. She gave him a go-fuck-yourself smile and turned on her heel, closing the door behind her.

"See," he said. "Alive and kicking."

"Does she know?"

"Not from me. Why?"

"I thought I got a frosty response."

"You're doing all right then. That's a few degrees higher than her usual temperature." I waited while he typed out a message.

"Hennessy?" he said finally, nodding at the liquor.

"Sure."

He set down his phone, broke the seal on the bottle, poured two large measures and handed me one. The glass was bespoke, sitting comfortably in the palm of my hand.

He held his up in a toast. "To new friends." We both smiled and touched glasses. Cognac. I had never knowingly drunk the brand before and it was beautiful. I felt that familiar effect of a good drink, relighting a fire inside me that I didn't know had gone out.

Carver looked at me. "Wright, Redgrave and Tillman. All seen going in and out of police HQ this week."

"What's your man make of it?"

"Enough to get you back in this room, Aid. He made some *discreet inquiries.*" He twisted the words in an impression of the person who'd said them. It wasn't familiar. "He's friendly with a girl in admin on the sixth floor there. Yer men've got a room blocked out, permanently—6.21A. The girl couldn't see who'd authorized it, but it was for something called the Parks Road Monument Committee."

"Three serious crime detectives, picking out a war memorial . . ."

"I know." Carver smiled. "Take at least five of the fuckers. I didn't give my man the full story, but he saw it himself. Put it together and came back talking ghost squad, too."

"He worried?"

Carver picked up his phone, which had been vibrating with regular messages as we spoke, and started scrolling again. The message to me was that my role in this was over.

"Said I'd do right by ya, so name a price. The Hennessy's yours, by the way."

"In that case . . ." I picked up the bottle, examined it and poured us both robust refills. "Ten?"

"Nowhere near, pal. Try again."

I took a drink. *Glowed.* "Seven."

"Five it is." Carver smiled. "Speak to Grip."

"I get the feeling he doesn't like me."

"Doesn't like anyone. That important to you?"

"If he makes life difficult."

"He won't," said Carver, scrolling through his phone. "He knows all about it." I waited a minute while he typed out another message.

"So what's next?"

He frowned. "You don't wanna know." I was sure that this dismissive attitude was designed to prompt me further. To try and double my money with more information.

The pitch. "I might have more to say."

"Such as."

"Some of the quirks of a ghost squad. Worth more than five."

"On blast, then."

"Why would they do something like this on-site at headquarters?" Carver shrugged. "Ready access to physical files," I said.

"Nothing's physical, these days."

"Something's keeping them in that building. Specifically, that room. To the point that no one else is allowed in there. They can't be using police HQ data networks or shared drives. Too obvious, too visible, too easily accessed."

"So?"

"In all likelihood, anything and everything they've got on you, me and your man is in that room. Probably on one segregated hard drive." Carver had put his phone down again now, full attention. "Wipe it and they've got nothing."

"How?"

"I watched the place for two weeks before I came to you. Wright, Redgrave and Tillman never went in on a Monday. Your man was watching last week. He see them go in then?"

He thought. "Not Monday."

"Your man just needs to get into that room."

"Simple as that?"

"They're hiding in plain sight. We know where it is and when it's empty. They can't install security measures beyond a locked door because that would draw attention to it. And anyway, no one in their right mind would be interested in the—what? Parks Road Monument Committee, and on the sixth floor, no less." I could see that he was interested. "Your man could get to the room this Monday."

"Hm."

"Maybe he goes straight in. Maybe he leaves it for the following week."

Carver looked at me. "Maybe that is worth more than five."

We spoke a little more and finished our drinks. Carver was noncommittal but lit up. When he sent me back out into the party, he insisted I take the Hennessy with me, and I found that I was suddenly popular. Grip shunted over. He was drenched with sweat and moved uncomfortably. He held a carrier bag and handed it over with a grunt. When I nodded, he lumbered back into the crowd. There was money in the bag. Five evenly sized wads of fifty-pound notes. With effort, I managed to get them inside my jacket pocket.

I searched for Isabelle. I wondered if there was something between her and Sarah Jane. I had heard the disappointment in her voice when she saw us together. The Superintendent's lack of interest in her scared me. *This Isabelle Rossiter shite.* Her own father hadn't even noticed she was gone for a month. Don't let her disappear, I thought.

"Celebrating?" said Catherine, nodding at the bottle.

"Every day." I handed it to her and she gave me a smile. The first real one I'd seen in some time. It went all the way to her eyes, and had no place in that building. No place between the two of us, really. She took a drink, winced and handed it back.

"Bit rich for me."

I thought of the cash in my pocket. "If you like 'em poor, I might be the man for you."

She smiled again. "Might you?"

"Well, I could at least waste some of your time."

"Or accidentally knock my drink over . . ."

"I'm still sorry about that."

"Don't be. It got me away from Neil."

"Neil?"

"Bar manager at Rubik's—thinks he owns me. He shower-curtains round all the girls . . ."

"Shower-curtains?"

"Clings."

"The guy with the designer stubble?"

"That's him, looks like he's been up all night, trying to solve a murder or something." I laughed. *Neil.* So Glen Smithson, acquitted date rapist, was using another name. Good to know. "Most men don't dare talk to us," she said.

"Glad to hear it."

"Are you? What really made you knock my drink over, Aidan?"

"I wanted to meet you."

"Not meet Zain?"

"You first," I said. I realized that I meant it.

She put her hand on my chest and looked me in the eyes. "Waste some of my time, then . . ." She said it like a dare.

"I'll make you wonder where your life went." We drank a little more. Moved backward and forward with the crowd, until, without even noticing it, we were upstairs again. When I kissed her I felt like everything might change. My personality, my body. My life. When we stepped apart I was still myself. It was bearable, though, for the moment. She was there with me. She laughed and hit me in the chest when she saw the way I was looking at her. Then we kissed again.

I left about an hour later. I closed the front door behind me and felt something wet on my fingers. I looked. Black on white, like the smear of bird shit I'd seen on the doorstep a week before. There were no birds around and I put my fingers to my nose. It smelled like paint. I walked down the path, wiping my hand on a leaf as I went.

When I got back to the northern quarter, gone midnight, everything was pleasantly blurred. I drank some water, took two painkillers and sat down to sleep. I saw I had a new text message. It was from a number I didn't recognize and simply said:

Zain knows.

18

The next morning I got up early. Showering, I saw the smear of black and white paint, dried onto my fingers. I thought about the bird shit I'd stepped over on Carver's doorstep, a week before. Then I thought about Joanna Greenlaw's disappearance.

There had been black and white paint daubed all over her doorstep.

I picked up the phone. I needed to speak to an expert and there was only one I knew of. I took a deep breath and dialed Sutty's number. I hadn't seen him since we arrested the woman in the burka. As far as he knew, I'd stolen drugs from evidence the next day and been suspended. If he was still working the night shift, I'd probably find him in bed, sleeping it off.

He answered with a gurgle. "Yurgh."

"Sutty."

"Yurgh."

"It's Waits."

"Waits?" That woke him up. "The fuck do you want?"

"I need some help . . ."

"More than I can give ya, son. You've got some bloody cheek calling me, after what you pulled."

"I know."

"We shouldn't even be talking. If yer charges make it to court, I'll be testifyin' against ya. And gladly."

"I know. I wouldn't call you if it wasn't urgent—"

"Ah've got no fuckin' money and ah've got no fuckin' time, so—"

"It's not about money. It's about gang tags." He didn't say anything but I knew that would intrigue him. "You're the only person who knows this stuff inside out."

"What's it for?"

"Private work. Security."

"Paid?"

"Hundred quid for an hour's work." He snorted. "Two hundred— that's as high as I can go."

I heard him rolling his tongue around his mouth, mulling it over. "Where?"

"Town? I could meet you at The Temple?" A converted subterranean public toilet, The Temple was owned by the frontman of a famous local band. He kept it suitably dingy and the prices reasonable. It was Sutty's favorite bar.

"Bring the money," he said, and hung up.

19

I descended into The Temple, felt my eyes adjusting to the darkness. There was never much space but it had the best jukebox in town. Today it was playing *Exile on Main Street*. Sutty was sitting by the bar with a pint of Guinness. He necked it when he saw me and slammed down the glass.

"Two more," he said to the barmaid. "He's payin'." I sat down, paid for the drinks and took a sip.

"How's it going?"

"Cash," he said, scratching himself all over. I handed it to him. I had taken it from the five grand that Carver had given me. Four fifty-pound notes.

Sutty counted it twice. "Right, come on then . . ."

"Joanna Greenlaw," I said.

"What kinda private security's that?"

"It's background. When they went to the house, there was something on the doorstep."

"Black and white paint." He sniffed. "Old Burnsider tag."

"So—"

"So fuck-all, anyone could've put it there. At the time they looked into it but a bit o' paint's not much to go on."

"What do you know about them?"

"Everythin'." He shrugged. "Burnside Estate was an industrial complex. Couple of miles north, outta town, along the Irwell." He took a drink and I saw him warming to his subject. "Whole place backed onto the river so factories could dispatch an' receive goods by boat. All shut down when the industry went abroad in the eighties. Became the shithole we know today."

"I've never been."

"I'll save yer the journey. Abandoned warehouses. Junkies, slags, homeless people."

"What about the Burnsiders?"

"Not much left of 'em. They eke out a livin' on tar."

"Tar?"

"Yurgh. Made from cookin' fentanyl. Hundred times stronger than morphine. Cheap to make, cheap to get." He smiled. "Bone-shakin' highs, but a strong risk of infection. Amputation. Et cetera."

"And the paint—"

"They don't even use it anymore. It was just a turf thing, it marked their property. These days, they haven't really got any."

"And why's that?"

He eyed me. "What's this about?"

"The person I'm working for's been finding black and white paint on his doorstep. It rang a bell." I paused. "And I thought I could get him to cough up some cash for you. As an apology . . ."

He sniffed. "Black and white paint on his doorstep's more likely to be a zebra crossin' than the Burnsiders. They're finished. In their box and not coming back out."

"What put them there?"

"Zain Carver. Started playin' with the big boys about ten years ago. It never got too bloody, but even the junkies could see. Eight's purer than tar, and reasonably priced. Plus you won't get bladed for late payment. He gentrified the trade, so to speak. They're obsolete. So's that tag."

I took a swig of Guinness. Thought about it. The fact that the tag was obsolete didn't count out its relevance. Especially if someone was using it to hark back to the glory days when it had been more widely used. Its use now didn't feel gang-related, though. There had been no corresponding threats or violence that I knew of. It felt personal. Rooted in the disappearance of Joanna Greenlaw.

"While we're sharin'," said Sutty, pulling an envelope from his pocket. "This arrived at the station for ya. 'Fraid I had to open it . . ." I accepted the envelope. Pulled a sheet of paper from it. The paper had lost its crispness. Been unfolded, read and passed around a few times. I looked at the signature. Tried to swallow my surprise. Then I refolded the letter and put the envelope in my pocket.

"Funny that." Sutty sniffed. Smiled. "You told me you grew up in care."

I changed the subject. "Does the name Sheldon White mean anything to you?"

He looked at me again. "Course, but, I mean, he's inside . . ."

"He got out recently."

"You don't say?" He thought about it. "Forget what I just said, then. That might change things for the Burnsiders."

20

I went home. Hung up my jacket. The letter was still in the pocket but I didn't open it again.

The first strike against me was my history. Who I was and where I was born. I enjoyed getting older because every second was like distance traveled away from my childhood. Or so I thought. Later, when Parrs got his hooks into me, I saw how inescapable it really was. The setup to some fucking joke that pays off in the third act.

Our mother didn't want us.

I never told anyone when it might have changed things, and over the years I forgot it myself. I don't remember much about being young now. Some people can talk in forensic detail about their childhood, or at least reel off the odd anecdote. For me, it feels like a lifetime ago, and some days I wish it were further. But when you forget certain things, you're letting other people down as well as yourself. That fading smile on an old friend's face when they see you've forgotten some shared story.

I've started forgetting about my little sister.

I have a clear picture of her in my head, but I don't know how accurate it is. In it, she's a chubby, scruffy toddler. The scuffs on her dress, her one-up, one-down knee socks speak to her character. Adventurous and knockabout. Wide-eyed and brave. Quiet for her age, though. A thinker. An unusually hot forehead. She wouldn't even look up when I warmed my hands on it, just carried on with whatever she was pulling apart or putting back together. I remember her curls, her small, concentrating frown.

And I remember the way she'd flinch when grown-ups at the home moved too quickly around her. I'll remember that and then walk into doors. Stop dead in the middle of roads. I'll be standing in the shower, not thinking of anything, and suddenly be sitting down with my face in my hands. I couldn't look at the letter. It was the first strike against me. My history. Who I was and where I was born.

21

put in a call to Superintendent Parrs.

"We're on."

"Monday?"

"Room 6.21A. His man'll most likely check it out this week, with a view to breaking in Monday next, if it's clear."

"I'll make sure it is. Good work, son. Anything else to report?"

I thought of Sarah Jane's icy disdain. Isabelle's disapproval. Her disappearance from the party. Grip's bloody smile and Catherine's real one. *I felt like everything might change.* I thought of my conversation with Sutty. The paint. I thought of the money. Five grand in cash. More than I'd ever had to my name. I had taken it to the lock-up where the few things from my old life were in storage. Just until the job was done. I thought of the message I'd received from an anonymous number.

Zain knows.

"There's nothing else," I said.

II

SUBSTANCE

1

Saturday. The cubicle was bathed in ultraviolet light. City-center bars go in for that because it means users can't see the veins in their arms to shoot up with. Rubik's was no exception. Sometimes the tweakers would find a vein out in the street, mark the spot with a biro, then go into ultraviolet-lit toilets and stick a needle straight in it. When they drifted out, marble-eyed, the cross hairs on their arms looked like small bloody kisses on a birthday card.

I made sure the door was locked and stood on the toilet seat. Using a screwdriver I'd brought with me, I carefully pulled out the screws surrounding the light fitting and took it down from the ceiling. I had been watching Smithson, the barman, for weeks. Despite there being a dedicated cleaning team, he spent a lot of time in these toilets. I reached my arm into a small hole and felt around.

Bags.

The first one I pulled down was coke. There were three different varieties of pills and then a zippy containing tiny, shoot-ready packs of Eight. I replaced almost all of the drugs, and the fixture, and got down off the toilet.

I laid a line of coke onto the back of my hand. The whole arm trembled. I closed my eyes and breathed deeply, tensing everything, trying to get my body back under control. When I looked down again I found myself focusing on some graffiti written above the cistern.

Forget the night ahead, it said.

I stared at that graffiti a full minute then carefully poured the coke back into the clear plastic bag it had come from.

I flushed the toilet, unlocked the door and left.

The bar was waking up. Out of its last tragic hour and into a happy one. The day-timers' ranks were swelling with people getting off work, meeting friends. I saw Catherine at the bar ordering her usual tall, neat vodka. Her chestnut hair was loose over her shoulders. Casually raising the heart rate of every man in the room.

Isabelle Rossiter was with her.

It was the first time I'd seen them together. I wondered if Catherine was the friend who brought her into the Franchise. I hoped that wasn't the case. It suddenly struck me that I was working against Catherine, and probably to put her in prison. I caught my reflection in my beer and pushed it away. Isabelle fingered her neckline and flirted shyly with the barrel-chested bar manager. I thought of the article I'd read about him.

SMITHSON ACQUITTED.

The bar manager said something that caused Catherine to look up. An argument broke out between them. At one point Catherine even stood in front of Isabelle.

I heard her say: "*No more.*"

In the end, Isabelle calmed her down, seeming to come to some kind of arrangement with the man. Catherine left them to it, walked off to a corner table. The bar manager said something to the girl working with him, walked round the bar and out the front door. Isabelle waited a minute, then followed. There were men at tables staring so hard that she almost dragged their eyes out with her. I watched Catherine, waiting to see if she'd follow, but she didn't.

The barmaid was serving three people at once when I went over. She was a cheerful blond Australian. A student, I thought.

"Quadruple vodka, please."

"Try something legal."

"She got one," I said, pointing to Catherine in the corner. The barmaid glanced over, then smiled at me.

"She's special, hun. You're not."

"Jameson's and soda, then." I tipped her for the zinger, took a sip and turned from the bar. Walking through Catherine's sight line, I sat at the next table with my back to her. I was wondering what to do next when I heard a chair scrape behind me, then heels on the hardwood floor. My left hand started trembling again and I wished I'd just taken something.

"Aidan," said Catherine. I looked up. Past black suede heels, a leather pencil skirt and a low-cut top. Past the chestnut hair, loose over her shoulders. This girl I'd only known a few weeks. It was a miracle when my eyes met hers.

"Cath."

She smiled. "Still looking for that black eye, I see."

"Getting closer every day, though, aren't I? Join me?"

She got her drink from the other table.

"So who's in the running?" she said, sitting down opposite.

"There was a moment where I thought Carver might hit me, but it passed."

"I'm sure it'll come back around." I could tell she was still annoyed by whatever had happened between Isabelle and the barman, and our conversation felt terse for it. "What do you think of him, anyway?"

"Zain? Throws a good party."

"Is that all?"

"I haven't spent much time with the man."

"He spoke to you. It's more than most people get, believe me . . ."

"What do you think of him?"

She didn't answer. Didn't let me change the subject. "Why are you always hanging round, Aid?" We'd slept together twice and she was realizing she knew nothing about me.

"I'm looking for a job. It's what I was talking to Zain about on Friday."

"You want to be one of his girls?"

"Is that how you think of yourself?"

"I don't think of myself that much." She paused. "But I don't belong to anyone, if you're asking."

"Not even people who pay you?"

"Not even people who fuck me."

Off to my right, the barmaid dropped a tray of glasses. They smashed and half the tables started cheering.

"I hate it when people do that," I said.

"Drop glasses?"

"Draw attention to a mistake."

"A mistake?"

"I wasn't talking about—"

"No." She silenced me with a squeeze of the hand. "I gave you the chance to and you talked about something else. Anyway, it doesn't matter now." She gathered her things and got to her feet. "Goodnight, Aidan." Girls usually give me their ration-book smiles, like they're saving something for someone else, for later, but Catherine was different.

She always smiled like she meant it. I always lied to her.

I stood up, but she was already walking away, heels on the hardwood floor. She stopped, turned. "You're staying?"

"I think so," I said, hoping she'd sit back down.

"Would you tell my friend I've gone?"

"The blond kid?"

She nodded. "The blond kid. Y'know, you should look for a job somewhere else. Maybe you can do better?" She turned and left. It was one of the few times she tried to talk to me. I should have said something else, I thought. Something better.

Isabelle Rossiter came back an hour or so later. Her skirt was hiked another inch up her thighs and she drifted across the room to the Ladies'. The bar manager had come back five minutes before. He watched her like the other men in the room, through the corner of his eye. When she reappeared from the toilet, she looked awkwardly around, and slunk to the side of the bar that her new friend wasn't serving.

I guessed, after whatever they had done out there, he'd told her to beat it.

The barmaid passed her over for other customers, avoiding the age question, and Isabelle seemed to shrink down to almost nothing. After a few minutes of this, she inched slowly round the bar, a pleasant, vacant look on her face. She wiped her nose, took out her phone and half-pretended to read something on it. It was quite cool in the room but she wore a light sheen of sweat, and I guessed that she was high.

The bar manager was laughing with a customer when he saw her coming through the rabble. He made a show of turning away, shouting something about the pipes and going out the back to avoid her. Isabelle looked like a lost child in a supermarket.

The customer who the bar manager had been laughing with turned to her. His face was heart-attack red and swollen with drink. He let his left arm fall from the bar and brush against her thigh. When she looked up at him, he cupped a hand to her ear and said something. She was seventeen years old. He must have been in his late fifties. She frowned, took a step back and shook her head. *No*, she said, with her own ration-book smile. *Thanks.*

She'd live, I thought. I was young as well. I thought sex and money were half of everything. She walked toward the door with slow, gliding steps. The red-faced man turned and lifted up her skirt as she went. She pulled it back down and kept walking, but a cheer went up around the bar.

I stared into my drink again, saw myself caricatured in the liquid. When I got up, I got up slowly, willing her to be gone by the time I got outside. She was standing on the pavement, though, watching her breath in the air.

"Isabelle," I said. She turned with a bright, stage-managed smile. She held it even when her eyes gave away that she couldn't place me for a second. Her hands drifted to her bag. "We met at Zain's . . ."

"The astrologist," she said, brightening, taking a step forward. "What's going on?"

"Just having a drink. I'm actually glad I caught you." Her face straightened. *Oh?* "I ran into Cath and she asked me to tell you she'd gone."

"Oh." She seemed hurt. "Say where?"

"No. Was upset about something, though." She pulled a face to cover a blush. I felt bad for pushing it but I still needed to talk to her. "My friend just left, too, and I feel like having another. If you're up to it, I'm buying . . ." She thought about it for a second and walked past me, back into the bar. She looked like she was doing an impression of someone else.

2

We left the dance floor shaking but still trying to shake it. I'd been buying and Isabelle laughed like a whipcrack, throwing her body forward and then back again, covering her mouth with her hands. A flash of chipped orange nail polish and matching lipstick. Occasionally her eyes drifted over my shoulder, and I knew she wanted someone else to see us together.

There was no problem sitting back at Catherine's deserted corner table. Last orders had rung out and almost everyone was on their feet, dancing or queuing at the bar. Even Cath's abandoned drink was sitting there untouched. It was around that time when lovers start pairing off, and Isabelle leaned back, watching the boys and girls leaving together. Some arm in arm, some stone-faced.

She thought out loud, over the music. "I wonder which ones just met and which ones are real couples?"

"The ones all over each other just met. The ones not speaking are the real couples."

She swirled her drink, tried to sound offhand. "Like Zain and Sarah?"

I looked at her. She'd been shivering since we sat down and tried to cover it. I wondered again what she was on. If it was the same thing I'd tasted at Fairview.

"Izzy, that bottle of wine you gave me the other week. Where did you get it?"

She tried to remember. "I don't know, maybe Neil?"

The barman had put something in her drink. I think she had an idea what I might ask next, so she improvised. Stared right at me while pulling out a cigarette like the smoking ban never was. Her hands were shaking so much I had to help light it. She took a drag and blew smoke in my face.

"You don't like Zain very much, do you?" she said, changing the subject.

"Not particularly."

"Why?"

"He's a user." She frowned. "People," I said. "Not drugs."

"He doesn't use people like you do." I tried to smile but her youth made the opinion sound like mundane fact. Like X-ray results. "You use your disadvantages," she said. "Same as me."

"What are your disadvantages?"

She acted like she hadn't heard me, started moving her head to the rhythm of the music. Screaming laser effects and something about going wild for the night.

"I love this song," she said. I waited. "People don't like me very much. They don't like you very much, either." Her teeth were chattering and she took a deep drag of her cigarette. "It's good in a way. Means we can creep right up on them."

"Who are we creeping up on? Zain Carver?"

She watched the smoke leaving her mouth. "He's something different . . ."

"From what?"

"A loan, a debt, a job."

"So you're just taking a gap year?"

"Why not?"

"You might leave it with nothing."

"*No future*," she said, a perfect Johnny Rotten drawl. We both laughed. "You're right, I should probably go backpacking round a cultural wasteland with people my own age."

I touched my glass to hers. "Suddenly the drug trade sounds more appealing."

"You're OK, y'know? Everyone else is always telling me to go home."

"Like who?"

"Zain, Cathy, Grip. The lot of them."

"Where is home, Izzy?"

"I don't wanna talk about it . . ."

"What even brought you here in the first place?" She looked at me. "You just don't seem like a natural fit."

"Why not?"

"You look like you grew up rich."

"Fuck you," she said. "You look like you grew up poor."

"That's what brought me here."

She smoldered for a second. "For me it was all the anorexic girls I grew up with. All the boys who only wanted to hold my hand and write poems about me . . ."

"I suppose not much rhymes with Isabelle."

"No," she said. "Not much."

"They'll get older, though. Better."

"Is that what people do when they get older?" I didn't say anything. She flicked ash across the table, singed my arm and went on, "You and Zain spoke the other night. Call him a user then?"

"It didn't come up, no."

"What did he want?"

"Advice."

"Oh?"

"He's having the house painted. Wondered if pastel green would go with his dreamy eyes."

"You said he's a user . . ."

"Yeah, let's talk about something else."

"Come on," she said. "Tell me who he's using."

I sat there until she saw something in the way I looked at her.

"Fuck you," she said again, meaning it this time. She stabbed her cigarette out on the table. Her orange lipstick had rubbed off on it. "I make my own decisions." She pulled her scarf tight and I thought of the scar on her neck. I looked away, across the room and saw the bar manager staring, dead-eyed, at me again. I thought of his acquittal. The evidence that had gone missing and the laced wine he'd given to Isabelle. Tonight, he'd have to go through me.

I waved at him.

Isabelle lifted Catherine's abandoned glass of vodka and started to drink. Neither of us blinked until about a third of it was gone.

"Stop," I said, reaching a hand across the table to lower the glass. We were two people in a crowd of a thousand, and we sat in deafening silence for a minute.

"Look at us now," she said finally. "We're like one of those real couples."

It was the bitter end and the lights were turned up, exposing us all. The men and women who'd looked so alive in the cool darkness seemed trampled and beaten somehow. The music, which had seemed to hold up the ceiling, had been gutted from the room, leaving it lifeless and empty. The bar manager was collecting glasses, snaking around tables toward us. He still stared at me from sunken, ashtray eyes. As he drew closer I saw that his face was drawn and hard.

"Closing time," he said, heavily dropping his basket of half-empties onto our table. Isabelle's nose had started bleeding, and she checked it in her compact mirror. "You wait for me," he said to her. She blushed, looked up at him and gave a small nod.

"Thought I'd walk her home myself," I said.

"Why's that?"

"Never know who's around these days."

"He bothering you?" the barman asked Isabelle. She gave me a long, exhausted look. I could see the comedown somewhere in her eyes, but she wasn't acting naturally now. I thought she was scared of him.

"Yeah," she said quietly. "He's bothering me."

The bar manager wiped his nose and let his head loll. Then he grinned. He lifted one side of his drinks basket and threw it violently upward. Everything hit me at once. I was drenched in broken glass, backwash and beer, and saw blood running from somewhere, mixing with the liquid as it drained through my legs. Isabelle shrank back into her chair. There were gasps. Conversations stopping dead around us. A group of men started cheering. The defeated people who had been quietly leaving looked over at us.

"Sorry about that," said the bar manager, still smiling. He took a handkerchief from his shirt pocket and bent to dab at a spot of liquid on my face. His shoulder hit mine, hard, as he did so, his name-badge connecting with my collarbone.

I got my breath and climbed to my feet, my chair fell back behind me. I could feel coarse, broken glass in my face.

"Neil," said the barmaid. She was standing behind the manager, a hand on his arm to calm him down. I swayed forward but he pushed me firmly back. More people had stopped on their way out to watch us argue, some laughing and cheering. There were enough of them staring to make things feel ugly. To make me feel like a drunk.

"Sorry," I said to Isabelle, nearly falling over my chair as I walked to the toilets past ten or more burning pairs of eyes.

"Wait outside," I heard the bar manager say to her.

When I went into the Gents', bleeding, drenched below the waist and stinking of drink, the two men who'd been talking in there exchanged looks and left. I thought of Isabelle, her shrinking voice, and then of Smithson, smiling on the court steps. I caught a glimpse of myself as I passed the mirror, red-faced and shaking.

I went straight to the cubicle I'd started my night in, stood on top of the toilet and tore the light fixture off the ceiling. Two-thirds of the plaster tile surrounding it came down, too, and several bags of drugs plopped onto the floor around me. I ripped them open, one by one, and upended them into the toilet. I flushed until there were just a few pills floating up through the water. I flushed it one last time and left the cubicle.

When the door opened I knew it would be him. I turned slowly. The lights left trails behind them like ghosts. The bar manager walked confidently across the room and shoved me into the wall. My collarbone screamed beneath my skin.

He wrapped a hand round my jaw and squeezed.

"She's mine," he hissed, staring into my eyes. My vision was blurred, and he was so close I could smell the vodka on his breath. He slapped my face once, twice and drew his hand back for a third.

I nodded and he let go. He checked himself in the mirror, swinging his shoulder quickly as he did so. I winced and he laughed a little. Happy with his appearance, he took slow, menacing steps toward the exit. The implication was that he might turn around and kill me any second. I let him cross the room, pull down the handle and push open the door.

"Glen," I said.

He turned at the sound of his real name. "The fuck did you just say?"

The door swung shut.

"Glen."

"Who called me that?" he said, staring at me. "Who fucking called me that?"

"That's your name, isn't it? Glen Smithson?" He took two efficient steps in my direction and ground me back into the wall.

The air left my lungs.

"Name's Neil," he said, holding up his name-badge. "Get it right."

"My mistake," I said. "Thought you were that bloke from the papers—"

Glen Smithson punched me so hard in the chest that I almost passed out. As I slid down the wall I saw that my impact had made the lights in the room start flickering. I was on the floor, crying for a breath. Smithson stood over me, breathing hard through his nose. Then he crouched and said he'd kill me if I didn't get lost.

I believed him.

"Fuck off," he said, kicking me in the direction of the exit. I got to the door and held on to it to help myself up. When I looked back, the flickering light made him look like something supernatural. I slunk out, soaked in sweat now as well as drink.

The huge, unnaturally lit beer hall was empty. Shaking, I picked up the nearest chair and dragged it back to the toilet with me. I opened the door and found Smithson combing his hair in front of the mirror.

"*What?*" he said.

"I think your UV light's on the blink."

He glared at me until the meaning of my words sank in. Slowly, he turned toward the cubicle I'd found the drugs hidden in. He pushed open the door. When he looked comprehendingly up at the destroyed fixture, his mouth fell open.

I wish I'd seen his face when he saw the empty bags. The dust around the toilet. The pills floating up through piss and shit. He knew what Zain Carver did to the arms and legs of people who lost his product.

I let the door swing shut and secured the chair up against the outer handle. As I walked through the post-closing-time quietness of the huge, empty hall, I heard Smithson's shoulder repeatedly slamming into the toilet door behind me. It echoed through the building, regular and deep, like the heartbeat of something we'd been swallowed by. I pushed through a fire exit. Fresh November air froze the beer and sweat against my skin.

Isabelle was standing under a streetlamp. She looked blue. She did a double take when she saw me walking toward her. I smiled. She took it the wrong way, took a step backward and tripped on a pothole in the pavement.

3

W ha' happened?" She was slurring her words. I took her by the
arm and pulled her toward a taxi rank. "What did you do?"

Her shoes scraped along the ground. As we drew near to a taxi she
tried to pull away from me and I let go of her arm. She crumpled to the
floor. I was just glad she wasn't going home with the barman. When
I lifted her up again she weighed nothing at all. She passed out beside
me on the back seat and the driver winked into the rearview mirror.

"Good lad," he said.

After what I'd seen in the bar I'd decided to take her back to her
family, Rossiter's wishes be damned. I went through her bag for some
ID, some home address for her father. We were driving toward his
constituency. I found myself looking closely at Isabelle. Stirring occasionally, she seemed to do the impossible. She looked like the girl in
the photograph again.

Her phone wasn't password-protected and I went to her sent messages. There it was, the only one to my number:

Zain knows.

I remembered her telling me twice that I wouldn't have been let
in unless they knew me. I wondered how far that went. I wondered if
the text was a joke, a warning or even some elaborate manipulation
from Carver himself. Had he found my number? Given it to Isabelle?
Used her phone? I scrolled through her photographs, saw nightlife
stuff with Franchise members. It looked like there was voice mail, too,
but when Isabelle shifted in her sleep I put the phone back in her bag.

My heart sank when I found the money.

I couldn't confirm my suspicion because the driver was glaring
at Isabelle in the rearview, so I waited ten minutes until we hit traffic, until he adjusted the mirror to look up her skirt. Once he started
up again I thumbed through the notes. Hundreds of pounds in tens

and twenties, wrapped in red rubber bands. She'd made the collection when she disappeared with the bar manager.

I stared out the window. Saw neon lights streaming past, promising the world, then Isabelle, asleep, reflected in the glass.

"Could you pull in here?" I said. The driver indicated and turned. "I think we need to go back."

4

We arrived at Fairview after midnight. The street was quiet. I leaned over to pay the driver and saw he had an erection, pressing through greasy jeans. He ran his hand over it as he fumbled through a money bag.

"No change," he said.

I nodded and dragged Isabelle out of the car. "Can you wait a minute?"

He glanced at the girl, passed out on my arm, and winked. "Course I can, mate."

I took my jacket off and draped it over her shoulders. I was still holding her upright when I turned to face the Carver house. The night seemed endless. The nearest streetlight had burned out, but even in near pitch-black I could see that we were being watched.

Two lit cigarettes glowed in the darkness at the end of Carver's path. I'd wanted to send Isabelle up there on her own, so as not to antagonize him, but once we got closer I wasn't so sure. One of the cigarettes was thrown down and stamped underfoot, rendering its owner invisible.

I heard a car engine come to life behind me and turned to see the cab moving slowly away. It pulled up a little farther along the road. In the glow of its sidelights I could see the outline of a girl, sitting slumped on a wall. She looked up and laughed at something the driver said through the window, then she stood and leaned closer to him. After a few more exchanged words, she walked round the cab and got in on the passenger side. The car started up again, turned the corner and took the light with it.

Fuck him.

When I looked back at the house I saw that the remaining cigarette had been stamped out, too, and I couldn't see the person who'd been smoking it. Isabelle was still draped around me. I went up the path fast and banged hard on the door.

The house was quiet that night, in contrast to my first few times there. The only sound was the wind, rocking the trees that lined the path. I felt the adrenaline lapsing in my bloodstream, humanizing me. I felt the pain in my collarbone where the barman had connected, and the light weight of Isabelle on my arm. I leaned against the door and lost time. The sound of the bolt made me stand upright.

The door opened and Sarah Jane stared out at us. Her red hair was wet, and spilt out wildly over her shoulders, making her skin look paler than usual. She must have been showering before bed. I realized I'd been hoping for Catherine. Sarah Jane looked at Isabelle, still passed out, then at me, like I was all the bastards in the world combined.

"What happened?"

"If she's lucky she won't remember."

"She's never been lucky yet. Better bring her in."

She stood aside and I carried Isabelle through, shouldering the door closed behind me. The echo that went through the house was like a memory of life from the party. Stripped of revelers, the place was pretty civilized. There were oil paintings, ornaments, stained-white wooden hall chairs.

"Through here," said Sarah Jane reluctantly. She turned the lock on the nearest door and we walked into a well-ordered, dimly lit study. The room had been off-limits every time I'd been before. I set Isabelle down on a leather sofa. She stirred but didn't wake up.

"Have you got any water?" I said.

Sarah Jane didn't move for a second, then turned on her heel and left the room. Something about her seemed different. She came back carrying water and painkillers.

"Leave the pills. I'm not sure what else she's taken."

Sarah Jane looked dubiously at my beer-soaked clothes.

"She was like this when I found her."

I'd worked out what was different about her now. She wore no makeup and looked disarming for it. Without the backdrop of dark eyeliner to blend in with, her lashes seemed delicate and long. They made a better frame for her green eyes, more affecting and intimate, and she knew it.

I held Isabelle's head and helped her drink a glass of water for the second time in a few weeks. Then I took the money from her purse and nodded at Sarah Jane. We left the room, closing the door quietly behind us.

"Where was she? When you found her, I mean."

"That bar, Rubik's. Near the Locks."

"Good of you to carry her things . . ."

"Especially when they're so heavy," I said, passing over the cash. She held eye contact as she felt through it, then took a breath.

"Why'd you bring it back?"

"Doesn't belong to me."

"What about her?"

"She doesn't belong to me, either."

"More's the pity."

"She's not welcome here?"

"I didn't say that."

"As good as."

"We just have a knack for attracting strays . . ."

I felt like she was talking about me more than Isabelle. "Well anyway, I'll get out of your hair."

She glanced at the cash in her hand then at me. "We haven't been properly introduced . . ."

"Aidan," I said, holding out a hand. She gave it the smallest shake possible. Her skin was cold. I wondered if she'd been smoking a cigarette outside a minute before and, if so, who with.

"I'm Sarah Jane." She said her name like it was a job she hated.

"Does Zain need to know about this, Sarah?"

"What do you think?"

"That you could get her in trouble."

"She's used to that by now." I waited. "Teenage girl. Tearing round at all hours with strange men."

"Strange men?"

"You're not the first, Aidan. Anyway, you've been trying to get in here for weeks. Might help if I tell Zain you saved his collection?"

"Don't go to any trouble on my account."

"I wouldn't do anything on your account, Detective." I looked at her. "Don't worry. I'm the only one who knows." Besides Zain and Grip. Zain had told me that Sarah Jane didn't know about me. He'd either told her in the meantime, or she'd worked it out for herself.

"Did you send me a message from Isabelle's phone?" She smiled, but it was to keep me at a distance rather than draw me closer. "How'd you get my number?"

"I think you should go."

"I think you're right." We heard Isabelle moving in the next room. "Shouldn't she be at home? Her real home, I mean."

"Trouble there, too. Some girls just generate it."

"How sympathetic of you."

"She wouldn't be here if I weren't sympathetic. Now," she said, walking past me to the door, "you said something about leaving?"

"It's probably warmer outside anyway. Thought I saw a familiar face on my way in."

"Oh?"

"Yeah, a Burnsider."

"What?" She stepped away from the door.

"Who do you think's out there, Sarah? Sheldon White?" I wanted to see how she reacted to the name.

"Who's that?" she said. It wasn't convincing. I opened the door and stepped out into the darkness. When I turned around, she'd edged away from me, back into the house.

"He's the man who made Zain's last girlfriend disappear. I'd keep an eye out for him, if I were you." I could hear the wind in the trees again, an ambulance somewhere off in the distance.

"Take her with you," Sarah Jane called after me.

"You just said—"

"She stays in a room round the corner." She bent to a small table, scribbling an address onto a pad. "And she's much too young for you, Detective. I'd keep an eye out for that, if I were you."

"Thanks," I said, accepting the slip of paper. Even in a hurry, Sarah Jane's handwriting was angular, thin and neat. It suited her. I went back into the study for Isabelle. She'd moved and, although her eyes were closed, I wondered if she'd been listening to us.

We got to the bottom of the garden path and I stopped. Looked back at the house. There was a soft glow coming from a window upstairs, probably from the screen of a mobile phone. In spite of what I'd said, I hoped that Carver had seen me deliver his money home.

5

Isabelle was staying in an unmissable, brutalist, concrete box of a building. Before the crash it had been intended as an office block, but they changed tack halfway through and it became flats. Jagged red spray paint above the door said:

FERMEZ LA FUCKING BOUCHE.

Inside there was a huge staircase, softened with a carpet the color of dying grass. Isabelle's arm was wrapped around me, and she was upright, but her feet brushed along the floor. On the way up I heard occasional voices behind doors. The only constant sound was a low buzz from the halogen lamps overhead.

Her flat was a sad little shithole. I flipped on the light: a bare, bright bulb in the center of the ceiling. It was too powerful for the room and left hellish neon sunspots in my eyes, even when I blinked or turned away. The place was a studio apartment, one medium-sized lounge with a sofa bed and bathroom.

I laid Isabelle down on the sofa and cast around awhile, trying to justify my being there. There were clothes on hangers around the lounge's periphery, bright summer dresses that seemed unworn. There was a defeated-looking desk and a curtained window. In the bathroom there were a couple of toiletries and a towel that said *SMILE* in bright yellow letters. It looked sarcastic.

That was it.

I found some vodka, mixed it with tap water and sat down in a corner, where I had a clear view of both Isabelle and the door. The flat was neater than it had any right to be. There was almost nothing to suggest that someone lived there, let alone a seventeen-year-old girl going off the rails for a month. Something echoed through my mind and I realized what the room reminded me of.

Her father's penthouse.

They were different in every way, aside from a studied anonymity. This lack of definition, of any personality at all, made the two rooms nearly unique in my experience. I'd spent a few years crawling through the homes of victims, innocent people with nothing to hide. They were usually cluttered with an accumulation of objects defining their life experience. This didn't remind me of that. It felt like the home of someone who'd done something wrong.

I realized then that so did David Rossiter's.

The vodka had woken me, and I stood to take a closer look around. The only object of any interest was the IKEA desk rammed up against the wall farthest from the door. It had been poorly fixed together in the first place and unloved ever since.

Isabelle was still sleeping.

I didn't find a diary or a notebook, but I did find some pictures. Several bunches of glossy black-and-white photographs, made with a high-spec home printer. They seemed to show the Isabelle Rossiter of another dimension, as though some crucial fork in the road had occurred, sending one on to happiness and damning the other.

I glanced over my shoulder.

The girl in the photographs, given over to friends and fits of laughter, linking arms with boys, seemed a world away from the anorexic slip on the sofa. There was some joy in the pictures that I was glad to see she'd had once.

I wondered where it had gone.

The bottom drawer jingled when I pulled it out. It was filled with broken glass, the remains of a mirror. When I began sifting through the shards, expecting traces of powder, maybe a straw, I was surprised to find crusted blood. Looking through the pieces I realized that more than one shattered mirror had been hidden in here. There were parts from three or four differently shaped pieces of glass.

Isabelle had taken one last look at her pictures, the person she was, and turned away. She hadn't left her life behind by accident. For the first time it dawned on me that she might not be running from rich kid problems.

I thought of the phone again, and crossed the room toward Isabelle, holding my breath. With my eyes on her, I took it from her bag and walked slowly away. I stepped into the bathroom, drew the door shut and dialed into her voice mail.

One new message. Received today.

There was a pause, a breath and then a voice.

That unmistakable Oxbridge accent.

"Isabelle, I wish you'd pick up the phone. I know I'm the last person you want to hear from, but we need to speak. The police have been here, asking about you. Your whereabouts. They mentioned a Zain Carver. Said he was involved in drugs. Isabelle, I can protect you, but please call me." There was a pause. *"You know I love you."*

David Rossiter. Lying to his daughter about her situation, trying to manipulate her into going home. I was surprised to hear his voice. He'd implied that he had no means of contacting her. I hung up and opened the door.

Isabelle was standing, barefoot, by the sofa. Tousled punk-rock hair and blotched eyeliner. Her heels hadn't been particularly high but without them she seemed much smaller. This loss of height, combined with her bare feet, made her look frighteningly young.

Her eyes went to the phone in my hand. "What are you doing?"

"I was just—"

"Going through my things?"

I put the phone down on the floor. "I brought you home, Izzy. I was just looking for something to pass the time." I saw then that her fist was clenched around her room keys, holding the longest one out like a knife.

"Pass it elsewhere, please."

"Of course." I edged round the outside of the room toward the door. "I'm sorry," I said, once I'd got it open.

"I know you're working for him."

I turned but didn't answer. Her scarf had fallen open and I could see the scar across her throat. She'd tried to kill herself once. She'd tried to run away from home after that. She'd tried drugs and a relationship with an older man. And all of it was there in her scarf, hanging open at the neck. It was there in her shrinking voice, the awful room, her cold blue feet with the chipped nail polish. She was seventeen years old and she was trying not to cry.

"Izzy . . ."

"Just go."

"Can we talk about this?" I said. "Tomorrow?" She shifted on her feet and looked at me for a long time, until I became conscious of day-light seeping through the nylon curtains.

"If you don't talk to him first."

"He'll never know I was here."

"I've never had a secret from him in my life." I saw all the breath go out of her, like the first moment before a panic attack. She went on in a small voice: "He pays my boyfriends to tell him what they've done with me. He gets them drunk and records them. Sometimes he plays me the tapes." She took a breath. "He knows everything."

"He'll never know I was here," I said. I wanted her to feel safe, so I walked out and closed the door behind me.

"You can come back," she said quietly.

I wasn't sure whether she meant that moment or the next day, so I stood outside with my hand on the door, listening. I heard her land back down on the sofa, breathing deeply. For a minute she had it under control, but began to breathe faster. She started to laugh and then she started to cry. When I left it sounded like she was laughing and crying at the same time. I wondered if it was the drugs, whatever she was on, or waking up to find a strange man in her room. I didn't want to believe what she'd said about being monitored. She'd sounded paranoid, delusional.

I took a night bus, exhausted, back to my own rented room and lay down on the bed. I couldn't sleep but I had his card in my hand for a couple of hours before I called. He answered the phone on the second ring.

"Waits."

"We need to talk."

"I'll send a car," said Rossiter. Sitting there, waiting for the knock, I couldn't help thinking of the graffiti I'd seen earlier in the bar.

Forget the night ahead.

6

'd arrived home with family on my mind. Absent parents, secrets and lies. I felt inside my pocket for the letter that Sutty had passed on to me. I laid it flat on the table but still couldn't open it. Isabelle Rossiter and I had more in common than I'd realized. I hadn't trusted anyone when I left my family.

The Oaks was a large Victorian complex. Closed down, boarded up and burned out now. The grown-ups were nameless, faceless to me, and I had trouble telling them apart. I was eight years old when we arrived, and my sister was five. I was scared to death. I remember my hot cheeks whenever Annie looked to me for an answer about what was happening, and I couldn't tell her because I didn't know.

The male dormitory was filled with boys like me. Around my age, and all new arrivals. Now I see that the personality types—quiet, sullen, outrageous and violent—were all just different expressions of fear. I suppose mine was somewhere in the middle.

I watched everything and gave away as little as possible about myself.

We hadn't been allowed to take our things with us, and I thought of the facts of my life as a kind of currency. Not valuable, but the last thing I had left to hide on my person. Only to be used in case of emergencies. It's a bad habit I've never quite broken.

Annie and I slept in separate rooms but spent most of the days together. I usually just kept her in my sight. Watched her at play but pretended not to. I was scared of her asking when we were going home. Asking where our mother was. I was scared of her telling me more about her dreams.

We hadn't been there long when they first tried to place us with a family. It was never explained or expressed to us in that way. The thought of a child knowing that they're auditioning for new parents is too hateful for the carers to conscience. We were simply told that we'd be meeting some nice people, that we had to be good.

In truth, most kids understand what's happening and, even at that age, you could see who'd be picked first. They try to keep siblings together but, be realistic, who has a home or heart big enough?

I remember walking down the corridor toward the director's office. I was nervous and snappy with my sister. She couldn't keep her clothes straight, didn't know how important it was. When we reached the office we were taken through by one of the nameless, faceless women. The room smelled of polish, and every surface gleamed varnish-brown. There was an intimidating bookcase on one wall and a desk at the other. In between there was a window, looking out onto the grounds, and a chesterfield beside it. Sitting on the sofa were a young couple. They looked like they were on their way to church.

They stood when we walked in.

The lady smiled so much at Annie that I thought she must know her. Her smile faltered when she saw me. We answered some simple questions. What our names and ages were. What food we liked and what games we enjoyed.

We were asked by the faceless woman to go and play. Annie went to the playbox with a sigh and overturned it. She stepped through the assortment of toys that spilled out, examining them like it was her day job. Her small, concentrating frown said she didn't know or care if she was being watched.

I looked from her to the couple.

Saw them glowing.

Saw she was doing the right thing.

I went over a little too eagerly, then. Started playing with her in earnest, trying to look inseparable. When it was time to say goodbye I all but wrapped myself around my sister. I was excited and on edge for a few days afterward, but the couple never came back.

Absent parents, I thought. Secrets and lies.

7

was awake when the knock came. The rain had been coming down like heels on a cobbled street. I opened the door to Detective Kernick. He stared past me, over my shoulder, into the room. He took it in at a glance and turned round without even looking at me.

I followed him out to his car and made that same journey along Deansgate. It was still morning but Beetham Tower was hidden by a thick rain mist, temporarily repairing the city's skyline. We rode the lift up to the forty-fifth floor but something felt different. Kernick escorted me along the corridor to Rossiter's suite. He used his key card at the door and motioned me forward. He didn't come inside.

Rossiter was sitting in an armchair. He left me standing there for a minute as he read through a sheet of paper on his lap, occasionally rubbing his right temple. When he reached the end of the document he lifted it between forefinger and thumb, checking the other side.

The clouds I'd seen from the ground were wrapped around the building and the room was gloomy, sparsely lit by an occasional lamp on the coffee table. From where I was I could see that the other side of the paper was blank. Rossiter replaced it on his lap and began reading it through for the second time.

"I'll come back later."

"Take a seat," he said, without looking up. I crossed the room and sat. Rossiter straightened his cuff links as though he had to be somewhere else.

"You've been a busy boy."

I ignored him. "I'm afraid things may have escalated."

"The investigation?"

"Your daughter."

"Oh?"

"I explained Carver's business model?"

"All too briefly," he said, sounding bored. "Drugs in pubs and clubs, girls collecting the money."

"I think Isabelle may be collecting for him."

"You think."

"I know."

"You said you only know what you see. Did you see it or didn't you?"

"From a distance."

"Distance," he said, looking up at me for the first time. "Go on."

"There isn't much else. The rest pertains to an ongoing serious crimes investigation that doesn't involve her."

"And let me guess. The position she's in now makes her vulnerable. So vulnerable that she shouldn't be pulled out too suddenly."

"The opposite. She should be dragged out kicking and screaming. Now, today." He didn't say anything. "Whatever your problems with each other, there has to be somewhere else she can go. A friend or relative."

"Is that it?"

"What else is there?"

"I assumed you were saving the best part for last."

"Look, I've seen your daughter, Mr. Rossiter. I thought you'd want to know."

"Come now, Waits. You've done a good deal more than just see her."

I didn't say anything.

There was a brown envelope on the table between us. Rossiter leaned forward and slid it across the glass in my direction. On it was written: *I. R. 30th October.*

"Open it," he said.

I slid the envelope back at him. "Do it yourself."

He exhaled through his nose. It was a theatrical frustration, the kind of rehearsed tic that debaters often pick up. He piled a disarming smile on top of it and tore the envelope.

Inside it were photographs.

He threw them across the table and they slid to a halt at my knee. They were full color but blurred. Most likely from a camera phone. I could see the sheen of sweat on Isabelle's skin.

They showed the two of us, together, at the first house party I'd been to. In the first I was holding her close in a crowded hallway. We were staring into each other's eyes, bodies joined at the hip. The second shot showed me handing Isabelle a bottle. Another showed her drinking. Each subsequent picture showed us closer and closer together, until we were damningly knit.

Our lips almost touched.

Rossiter watched me, eyelids half-mast, gauging my reaction. When he finally spoke he sat back in his chair, as though he wanted to be as far away from me as possible.

"Anything to declare?"

"It's—"

"Not what it looks like? Spare me the shit, Waits." He searched his pockets and lit a cigarette. "So why don't you start again. From the beginning. And this time, don't leave out the juicy bits."

I got up, walked to the door and opened it. Detective Kernick was still standing on the other side. I closed the door in his face. I stood there for a second, then walked back across the room toward Rossiter and sat down.

8

I t was starting to go dark again when I left the penthouse. Between the morning mist and the early evening, it felt like there'd been no daylight at all. Detective Kernick was gone when I left, so I took the lift down alone and stood at the taxi rank on Deansgate. I gave the driver Isabelle's address. A part of me believed the Franchise was better for her than home, but she wasn't safe. There had to be another way.

The city was moonlit by the time I got there, and I wondered if I'd even find her in. The lobby to her building was unlocked and unguarded, and I walked the three flights up to her room without seeing anyone. Same disembodied voices behind closed doors, same buzzing halogen light bulbs.

I ran my hand over her door, feeling the grain of the wood, recalling the bitter night before. I realized it was slightly ajar and pushed it open.

I was hit by the stale smell of sex.

Isabelle was naked on the carpet, staring up at the doorway. Her eyes were open and there was a needle in her arm. Her white-blond hair looked dull somehow.

She was very quiet, still and dead.

The whole left side of her body had turned a light shade of blue. In some places I could see the network of veins, intermingling, creating the effect. The arm with the needle in it was a darker shade, almost black around the injection site. I turned, kicked the door as hard as I could and then went to her.

"Izzy . . ."

My hand hovered over her forehead for a second before I could touch it. The sweat on her skin was cold. Without thinking I stepped back out into the corridor and drew the door closed. My legs went weak and I slumped against the wall, trying to think.

I rubbed the sweat from her skin into my trousers.

People don't die from overdoses. Bad needles, bad dealers, a lifetime on the streets, but hardly ever from overdoses. I needed to walk back inside and slap her. Call an ambulance and put her in the shower. But I just stood there. Time lapsed and I heard footsteps coming up the stairs.

I panicked, pushed off the wall into Isabelle's door, pretending to call for her, hoping the person would pass. As the steps came closer I even rapped my knuckles against the wood, knocking lightly. There was a shadow in my periphery, the person coming down the corridor toward me. As the shape came closer, I fixed my eyes on the door. The person stopped and I turned.

"Hi," said Catherine, surprised to see me. "She in?"

"No answer," I said.

She mock-rolled her eyes. "Come on, Izzy, rise and shine." She banged twice on the door and gave me a small matter-of-fact smile when it opened slightly. I didn't stop her when she walked by me, into the flat. The sharp breath she took made it real. I followed her inside and closed the door behind us.

9

Catherine raised both hands to her mouth. She was so unconscious of me that I felt like a voyeur, like I was watching some private grief.

I crouched beside Isabelle and felt pointlessly for a pulse. The tips of my fingers were clammy, tingling with pins and needles, and I could barely feel anything through them. I replaced her wrist on the floor, lowering it gently as if I might still wake her. Isabelle was staring at me with what would be the last look on her face. It wasn't the blissful daze you associate with heroin.

It was horror.

Her jaw was tensed, clamped shut, and the muscles in her face spasmed. When I ran a hand down over her eyelids I thought I felt a moment's resistance, as though there was something still left of her. We didn't move for a minute but Catherine cleared her throat like she was about to say something. Instead, she smoothed down her clothes and walked calmly into the bathroom, eyes raised away from the body. She closed the door behind her and started to retch.

I stood and let my eyes wander down Isabelle's naked frame. I didn't feel anything looking at her skin, the blue left-hand side of her body, but my eyes glazed over the old scar on her neck. She'd tried so hard to keep it covered up in life. Her ribs jutted out sharply, like the bars on a cage. Her nudity, her beauty, her youth, all combined to make some point that I felt like I was missing. Some final, wicked criticism against life.

No future.

Her left arm was such a dark shade of blue that I couldn't see if there were other injection marks on it. There were none on her right, though. Her knees were together, leaning to one side. I thought I could see some kind of rash on her legs . . .

The toilet flushed and Catherine opened the door. Light mascara tears had run down her face and she walked out wiping her mouth with a towel. She was shaky on her feet, and leaned on the wall to steady herself. I thought she was in shock. She stopped when she saw me beside Isabelle.

"What were you doing here?" she said. Her eyes were fixed on the doorway that led back out into the hall. Hopelessly, I thought. I could see her mind working, wondering if I'd killed her friend, wondering if she could get to the door faster than I could get to her.

"I brought her home last night. She asked me to come back today."

Catherine nodded, not really believing me. "I have to go," she said, starting to walk.

I blocked her way.

"What were you doing here?"

"We were working tonight," she said. "Collecting."

"When did you speak to her last?"

"Last night in Rubik's." She tried to keep the accusation out of her voice. "When I asked you to tell her I'd gone."

"What was the argument you were having with the bar manager?" She looked up in surprise. "I was watching you; you said 'no more.' No more what?"

"Who are you?"

"No more what?"

"No more drink, I expect. We'd had more than enough."

"Catherine."

She shrugged. "He was trying it on with her."

"Had that happened before?"

"I don't know. Neil likes 'em young but it's a fine line. Zain'd kill him if he found out."

I thought of the barman. Of flushing the drugs, probably forcing him underground.

"Tell me where she got the stuff."

"I don't know, Zain doesn't let us use . . ."

"He's a saint, that guy. Where did she get it?"

"I don't know."

I started to take my phone from my pocket.

"Not the police," she said. "We can deal with this ourselves."

"Girls like Isabelle Rossiter don't just disappear."

"But she *has*, she's already run away from home."

I started to dial.

Catherine put her hand on my arm. "We could call anonymously, once we're away from here . . ."

"They'd find us. Believe me." I held on to her with one arm while the phone was answered. I told the operator that we'd found a teenage girl, dead, overdosed, and gave him the address. Fog Lane. When he asked additional questions I hung up. I knew that whatever I'd wanted to hold back from Parrs, from Rossiter, would have to come out now.

Catherine looked like she was going to be sick again. I went to the fridge, searching for the vodka I'd found the night before. The bottle was still there. I took three burning mouthfuls and handed it to her.

"Have a drink."

"I can't," she said.

"It'll help."

"*I can't.*"

I lowered my head to look her in the eyes.

"Not now . . ."

"What?"

She looked at me from very far away. "I'm pregnant," she said quietly.

I felt a vein throbbing in my head. A sharp pain went through my collarbone and a dull one went through my fading black eye. I stayed very still, clenching my fists and waiting for it to pass.

"What?"

"I said—"

"You're sure?"

She looked at me. Rummaged in her bag and produced a pregnancy test. I took it from her. Held it up to the light. It was positive.

I handed it back without saying anything.

"That first night at Fairview . . ."

Neither of us spoke for a moment.

"What are you gonna do?"

"Not what are *we* gonna do?" she said. "Have it in prison, I suppose."

I heard sirens down on the street. I thought of the questions they might ask her and the answers she might give them. A flash of hate went through me, at myself, at Catherine in that moment. I wished I'd never met any of them at all. She pulled away from me, walked around Isabelle's body and sat down on the sofa.

"No," I said, lifting her by the arm. "You have to go."

"What?"

"I'll leave you out of it, but you have to go."

"They're here."

I dragged her out of the room with me, along the corridor and toward the stairs. I looked down the three flights and saw two police officers on their way up. We went back up the corridor, past Isabelle's flat, toward a fire escape.

I hit the bar.

The door opened onto a black back staircase. The fire alarm went off. A piercing, high-pitched sound. Catherine walked in and looked back at me. In the darkness of the doorway I couldn't see her features. She was just the shape of a person.

She hesitated. "The bathroom, there's something in the bathroom—"

"Get to Carver," I said. "Tell him to make sure Fairview's clean. The police'll be searching." She squeezed my hand and disappeared down the stairs. I closed the door and strode back up the corridor. People had started to appear from their rooms, startled by the alarm. I went toward Isabelle's.

I was standing outside, breathless, when the officers reached the top of the stairs. I moved smoothly back into the room, hoping I had a minute before they found me.

I only looked at Isabelle to step over her. Shaking, I threw myself round the flat. Wiped my prints off the bottle.

I thought of the phone.

The message she'd sent me:

Zain knows.

I went through her bag but it wasn't there. I couldn't see it anywhere. Cautiously, I went on, into the bathroom. The alarm was so loud in there that it felt like it was going off inside my head.

I started when I saw the mirror. It was fractured in the center where someone had struck the glass. There had been a message written across it in thick red lipstick before the blows.

NO ONE CAN EVER KNOW

I couldn't move. It hadn't been there the night before. Now Isabelle was dead. Her phone was missing. Someone had written a threat across her mirror. I didn't hear the police come in. When they found me I was still staring at that message. I could see myself reflected in a kaleidoscope of shattered glass, those words written across my face.

There was a uniformed officer at the door. He said something but I couldn't make out the words over the alarm. I tried to read his lips but it frustrated me and I turned away.

NO ONE CAN EVER KNOW

I shouted. I wanted to be louder than the alarm, and I threw all of my weight at the mirror, hoping to smash the glass off the wall entirely. Make a scene and give Catherine time to get away. The officer came at me and I threw a wild fist at him. He got his hands around my wrists. The alarm was screaming in my ears. I struggled until his partner came in.

She looked me in the eyes and spoke slowly. At first I thought I knew her, but I just recognized the expression on her face.

Something like sympathy.

I stopped resisting and relaxed back into the male officer's arms. The policewoman calmly raised her truncheon. She was still speaking slowly, as though explaining some harmless procedure. Then she brought the truncheon down, very precisely, onto my forehead. It snapped against my skull. My body went slack and a warm wave of relief went through me.

Then the second blow came and everything went black.

10

White noise. The glitch and crackle of a police radio.
   Aidan.

Someone was saying my name but I didn't want to own up to it. I felt my body being moved and wondered if this was what Isabelle had gone through. If she'd still been aware when we found her, and then slowly tuned in to a different frequency.

Static.

It cut through my head, eventually becoming the beautiful bubble and squeak of a radio searching for a station. I woke up in the off-white hysteria of the Royal Infirmary.

My head was killing me.

Superintendent Parrs was standing over the bed, gray-faced, red-eyed and staring at the wall. His eyes moved down to mine when he saw that I was awake, then he said something over his shoulder and looked away again. The male police officer who'd restrained me was standing in the far corner of the room, hugging his body. Tissue protruded from both nostrils and I realized I must have caught him on the nose. He had a pained look on his face, like he could only keep his hands from reaching out to kill me by exerting superhuman inner strength.

His eyes were fixed on mine.

When Parrs spoke, the police officer leaned forward off the wall. He turned and pushed through a swing door, still hugging himself. He didn't come back.

At length, a young Asian doctor appeared. He strode into the room with the ease of someone who was doing what he loved and had his whole life ahead of him. He had a bright temperament and an even brighter smile. His teeth looked as though they'd been artificially whitened.

"Think you could turn those things down?" I said. He shone a torch aggressively into my face, then gave me the middle finger and asked how many I could see.

"Just the one."

"He's fine," said the doctor, turning on his heel and pushing through the swing doors.

Parrs scowled down at me. "Anything you want to tell me, son?"

I shook my head and winced. "She was like that when I got there. Did you find anything?"

"My office. First thing tomorrow."

I nodded. It hurt.

He looked down at me pityingly and left.

I lay there alone for a while, listening to the strange rhythms of the building, imagining the lives attached to passing voices, feeling unreal. Catherine was pregnant. It compromised me on every level, my disgrace come true. I was too stunned to know what to think, what to do. I thought about how frightened she must be. I'd almost shoved her down a staircase as soon as I heard the news. I felt another pulse of self-loathing work its way through me. Then I rolled out of bed, put my feet on the floor and got my things together.

11

Detective Kernick and his dishwater-blond partner, DS Conway, were waiting for me when I left. Kernick gave me a hard look and almost said something. In the end he just shook his head and walked me outside to his car.

My head was spinning. I felt numb. Stupid and confused. I'd left her, alive in that room, after a Saturday night. Between then and 5 p.m. on Sunday she'd had sex. Someone had left a message on her mirror and then smashed it. Her phone had gone missing. She'd used Eight. She'd died.

We drove out to an ugly business park somewhere and checked into a cheap hotel. I was never left alone for a minute. Kernick put it gently: "Wouldn't want you taking the easy way out, now would we?"

We slept with the light on. I should say I was so damaged and sad about it all that I lay awake that night. The truth is I was exhausted, starving and hollowed out by the stabbing pain in my head. I dreamed of traffic. When I sat up, awake, my jaw hurt. I had been grinding my teeth so hard that I'd woken Kernick. He was sitting at the edge of his bed, staring at me, frowning slightly. He looked away when I sat up.

"Coffee?" he said.

Over breakfast I read the morning paper. Monday, 16 November. Isabelle got the entire front page of the red-top rag that Kernick had brought up to the room.

ISABELLE ROSSITER DEAD AT 17
Squatting with notorious Northern drug lord
"Dangerous, destructive sex life"
History of mental illness

Inset was a picture of David Rossiter, undoubtedly from the files, but caught in a moment where he was frowning, looking concerned. The caption beneath it said: *MP and daughter had been living "sad, separate lives."*

The story continued on page four, mentioning six times that David Rossiter was Secretary of State for Justice. The rest of it was just padded-out facts of the Rossiters' lives. That the mother was born a millionaire, that the father was a world-player, that Isabelle had been a bright, beautiful child.

The quotes, attributed to a source close to the Rossiters, told a different story. They hinted that there was madness and unhappiness within the family. The tone implied that, even with all that money, they still weren't satisfied. When I looked up from the paper, Kernick was watching me closely. I got up and got ready. Took a shower. I stood motionless under the burning water until one of them banged on the door.

12

We parked a few streets over from the station and walked the rest of the way. When we arrived I saw why. Dozens of hacks and photographers, shouting questions, taking pictures of anyone who went by. From a distance I heard the same repeated words:

"*Sex?*"

"*Drugs?*"

"*Suicide?*"

We made our way to the south entrance. I'd never felt scared walking in there before. Inside the station, every person we passed had their ear pressed to a phone. Even so, others rang endlessly in the background. Uniformed officers were bursting out of every door, and there was a frenzy of people coming and going in all directions. I was escorted into the lift, to the fourth floor. Superintendent Parrs's office. No one was worried about blowing my cover now. His frazzled secretary dispatched three callers in the time it took us to pass her desk. Detective Kernick took me right up to the door and knocked.

"Come in," said a voice from the other side.

Kernick opened it. "Waits," he said.

Parrs was sitting behind his desk with his back to the window. He looked more gaunt than usual, his jawline like a downward-facing arrow. There were two telephones in front of him, and lights blinked from both. There was someone holding on every line.

"Thanks," he said as I came in.

Kernick closed the door, staying outside.

Opposite Parrs sat David Rossiter. His face was puffed up from lack of sleep and his suit was crumpled. The top button of his shirt was undone. It seemed unnatural to see him without a tie.

When I walked in he got to his feet and paced to the far corner of the room, leaning into the wall with his back to us. Even in grief there was an otherness about him. He hunched his shoulders, shied away from his full height. Diminished himself. I knew by now that this political theatricality was hardwired into him, that he wasn't necessarily playing to the crowd.

There was a man I didn't recognize in a third chair. He had the formal, relaxed look of an excellent lawyer. He was in his early thirties, older than me, but seeming younger somehow. There was no darkness around his eyes, no lines on his face at all, and his hair was perfect. He looked like he'd been in bed by nine o'clock every night of his life. I felt cheap and exhausted just standing in the same room as him.

Parrs turned his red eyes on me. "Sit down," he said. I did. Neither Rossiter nor the other man looked in my direction. "Tell me what happened."

"She was dead when I got there."

"You let yourself in?"

"I knocked and saw the door was open."

The third man in the room exhaled loudly.

"Detective Constable Waits, this is Christopher Tully," said Parrs. "Mr. Rossiter's lawyer."

"Mr. Rossiter's friend," said Tully. "And lawyer."

I nodded at him, but he just stared straight ahead. Each of us kept our voices low, out of some respect for Rossiter, standing grieving against the wall.

"Let's start at the beginning," said Parrs. "Why were you there in the first place?"

"As you know, Mr. Rossiter asked me to keep an eye on his daughter." Rossiter turned from the wall but didn't speak. "I'd seen her the night before. She was drunk, so I took her home." I knew how it sounded. The room was suddenly quiet. The way things get when something unspoken and ugly hangs in the air. I went on quickly to fill the silence. "As I was leaving, she asked me to come back the next night. The night I found her."

"Why did she want you to come back?" said Parrs.

"She wanted to talk to me about something."

"What?"

I could feel Rossiter's eyes burning into me. The silence swelling back into the room, drowning us all.

"I don't know."

"Don't lie to me, boy," said Parrs.

I just looked at him.

"Fine," he said. "Let's talk about what we do know." He had notes to hand but spoke from memory. "Isabelle Rossiter was found dead in her rented room on Fog Lane yesterday. Your call," he nodded at me, "came at seventeen hundred and twenty hours. A syringe containing what is thought to be an opiate was recovered from the scene. Tests are ongoing, but this is thought to be the cause of death. There was evidence of recent sexual activity." He paused. "Now, what did she want to talk to you about?"

I didn't say anything.

"Detective," said Tully, turning to me and speaking for the first time. "If you're trying to spare Mr. Rossiter's feelings, then you can stop that this instant. I think I can speak for him when I say that he will accept damage to his pride, his reputation, even his heart, if you can shed some light on what happened to Isabelle."

"I can't."

He frowned. "Superintendent Parrs tells us that pathology and forensics will take time, and we appreciate that. We have the probable cause of death in the syringe. What we don't have is the supplier. What we don't have is her state of mind. What we don't have is the reason. You said she'd been drinking. Did you know she was using drugs?"

"Not Eight."

"Eight?" said Tully, looking around.

"Heroin," said Rossiter darkly. It was the first time he'd spoken since I entered the room.

Tully feigned confusion. "So you didn't think she was using heroin. Just other things?"

I looked at Parrs. His unreadable red eyes.

"She drank, took the odd pill. She was acting out."

"Acting out?" said Tully.

"She was a teenage girl."

"A teenage girl," he said. "And you didn't think to have her removed from the influence of a drug dealer twice her age?"

"I had her halfway home," I said, turning to Rossiter. "I had her halfway to your house the night before she died." He looked at me, unguarded. All the politics and premeditation fell away for a moment. He was just a father.

"What happened?"

"I found money in her bag."

No one spoke for a second and then everyone spoke at once.

"Gentlemen," said Parrs, taking the floor. "What money, Waits?"

"Franchise. She'd been collecting for them."

A sound like a restrained scream came from Rossiter, and he turned to face the wall again.

"I'm sorry," said Tully. "Are we talking about drug money?"

I nodded, not looking at anyone now.

"So, you were approached by the Secretary of State for Justice to extricate his seventeen-year-old daughter from a bad situation. You observed her drinking, doing drugs, collecting drug money—*acting out*, as you put it—and did precisely nothing." He let that sink in. "You've made rather a farce of things, Waits."

"I wasn't there to extricate her."

"That's actually a fair point," he said, feigning enthusiasm. "According to Mr. Rossiter, he asked you not to approach his daughter at all. Is that right? Because from what we're hearing now, it sounds like the two of you grew rather close. Unprofessionally so, in your case."

My eyes went to Rossiter.

I thought of the photographs.

"She approached me—"

"She approached you. And you went along with it."

"It would have looked worse if I'd ignored her."

"No one asked you to ignore her."

"You can't have it both ways. You can't tell me I got it wrong for talking to her *and* got it wrong for not talking her into leaving."

"My point, Waits, is that once you were in contact with her anyway, once you saw her using drugs, once you saw her collecting drug money: why didn't you just get her out of there?" Tully's voice had risen throughout the exchange, but he looked away from me and spoke quietly now. "My point is that she clearly needed your help."

"This isn't getting us anywhere," said Parrs.

Tully looked over at Rossiter, who was still turned away from us. His frame shook slightly. "Perhaps you're right," he said, standing to comfort his friend. As his hand touched Rossiter's shoulder, the MP shuddered, suppressing a sob. It cut through the room like a death rattle, the sound of something powerful and natural becoming extinct.

He shook Tully off him, took a handkerchief from his suit pocket and dried his eyes. He stood still for a moment and then began to compose his appearance. He started by pulling his sleeves straight and then fixing his collar. He rose up to his full height, at least half a foot taller than anyone else in the room, and looked at me with his face set, welded in hate.

"You said something there, Waits. You said Tully couldn't have it both ways." His voice broke. "Well, I was her father, and I can. You *were* wrong to talk to her. And you *were* wrong not to talk her into leaving." He walked toward the door. When he snapped it open the aggressive sounds of the station filled the room again. "Save the world one person at a time?" he said. "Like shit." He walked through the door and closed it behind him.

Tully gave me a hard stare but spoke to Parrs. "Next time we meet, Superintendent, I hope the Detective Constable can express some sensitivity for the grieving." He gathered up his things. "You know, when David came to me for advice about all this, I looked into you, Waits. Told him he should steer clear. Your record's starting to look like the bloody obits." When I didn't reply he looked at me with genuine surprise. "But you don't really care, do you?" he said. "Not really."

I started to speak.

"Don't bother." He walked the long way around me, like I was contagious. "We'll be in touch," he said over his shoulder, and followed Rossiter through the door. The air was heavy with heat, sweat and argument.

Neither Parrs nor I spoke for a minute.

"So," he said finally. "No news was just bad news biding its fucking time." He exhaled, loosened the collar on his shirt and stretched his neck. I was grateful when he opened a drawer, taking two glasses and a decanter of whisky from it. He poured himself one while I stared at the other.

"Eyes off the glass, son," he said. "Today. Tonight, tomorrow, next week. Everyone can smell it on you. Trouble you're in, you don't need any more." He downed his drink. "I certainly don't."

"Sir."

"What were you really doing there?"

"She'd asked me to go back."

"So you fucking said. Why?"

I paused for a moment. Wondered whether I could risk taking Parrs into my confidence. As I saw it then, there was no choice.

"She implied that her father was sexually abusing her." Superintendent Parrs's head went slowly backward. When he looked at me again, he spoke so quietly that I had to read his lips.

"Did she say or do anything that could corroborate that implication?"

"No."

He locked his red eyes on me. "Then I suggest that you never say that out loud again."

"I—"

"Don't even hum it in the fucking shower."

"She was running away from something."

"Herself," said Parrs firmly. He eyed me for a moment then opened a drawer and took out a file. He pushed it across the desk and I opened it. Crime-scene photographs from her room on Fog Lane. They focused mainly on Isabelle's body. "Start from number seven," he said.

I flicked forward. Picture number seven was focused on one of Isabelle's inner thighs. What I'd thought looked like a rash when I found her body. I saw now that it was actually a series of fine lines.

Fine self-harming cuts, to be precise.

I went through the pictures. Each cut had gone deep, carved into the soft flesh of her upper inner thigh. From the precision of the marks, I guessed they had been made at different times, using something very sharp. I thought of the bloody broken mirror I'd seen in a drawer.

"They're tally marks," said Parrs. Looking closer, I saw that he was right. They were engraved into her skin in sets of five. The way a prisoner might count years in a cell. Most of them had healed over in ridged scar tissue.

"What do they mean?"

"That she was sick. We don't know what else."

I counted the lines. Three sets of five and one unfinished set of three. Eighteen in total. The final picture was a close-up of the final cut. This single line looked fresh and had even bled out a little. I'd known Isabelle, liked her even, and I was sure that they meant something.

She'd kept a diary after all.

I pushed the file back across the desk to Parrs and he closed it. As far as he was concerned, it proved his point.

"The girl had a history of mental illness. Self-harm and manic depression. I wouldn't put too much stock in anything she said."

"And that's that?"

"She was another victim of our city's drug culture. Far from *that's that*. But from our perspective, we have to grasp the opportunity here."

I couldn't believe what I was hearing. "What opportunity?"

He smiled. "Daughter of MP dies at the hands of a problem dealer."

"Zain Carver didn't give her the Eight."

"Why not?"

"Because he doesn't want to die in prison."

"Perfect place for him."

"He didn't do this."

"Why are you so sure?"

"He doesn't let his collectors use. Was there CCTV in the building?"

"Never hooked up, as far as we can see." Selfishly, I was relieved. It was too late to explain about Cath. "What about her friends? Who'd she hang around with?"

"*Friends* is putting it strongly. She was a hanger-on, seeing how the other half lived for a while. They all knew that."

"And?"

"And from what I saw, they were pretty protective of her."

"What did you see?"

"Not much."

"Clearly," he said. "I have a thing about all these half-truths, son. I don't fucking like them. Tully's got you sussed for a breached duty of care and an inappropriate relationship. There'd better be nothing moldy in the cupboard."

I thought of the photographs, of being pressed up against Isabelle in a steaming hot hallway. *Our lips almost touched.*

"She was a teenage girl."

"Well remembered."

"Did you find her phone?"

He looked up. "What phone?"

"She had a mobile. It was in her bag the night before, when I took her home."

"You're certain?"

"Absolutely."

"Christ," he said, rubbing his face. "No. No phone. Do you have the number?"

I thought of the message she'd sent me:

Zain knows.

"No," I said. "I never got it." I said it as naturally as I could, but it felt like he was staring straight into my mind.

"I'll look into it."

"I could—"

"No, son."

"I need a few more days to sort this out."

"How could you possibly sort this out?"

"I'm close to these people already . . ."

"Too close," he said. "There'll be a full debrief in a few days' time. Until then, disappear." I had a bad feeling. Parrs's obsession with the Franchise made Isabelle a statistic. Something he could use to make a case for his one-man war, whether Carver was responsible or not.

"You know they won't give you anything."

"Do you not understand what's happening here? Have you not seen what it looks like outside?" He motioned at the door. "This place is the most expensive call center in the country today. If you're very lucky and I can crucify Zain Carver, you might keep your job. But I wouldn't trust you to talk to a brick wall. Without bloody drinking it or driving it up itself. If we can't have Carver, Chief Superintendent Chase will be asking me for the next best thing." I looked at him. "When someone shits the bed, Aidan, it gets hung out to dry."

"Just like that."

"Just like that?" he said, "*Just like that?* Your instructions were to leak intelligence to some scumbags and you went fucking . . ." he searched for the words, "method actor on me."

I didn't say anything.

"You were picked up by Special Branch, literally off the street, spoke to an MP while suffering from the DTs and turned up here with a black eye."

"I didn't have the DTs. Someone hit me when I was leaving Rubik's."

"Oh, come on."

"It's true. Before Rossiter's man picked me up that first time. I woke up facedown on the pavement."

"Shit-faced, no doubt. You used to be better at this, son."

Neither of us spoke for a minute.

"So what do we do next?"

"Who's *we*, Aidan?"

"What?"

"We. Who's *we*?"

"Us," I said, not fully understanding.

He scratched his ear and opened a drawer in his desk. When he took out a small digital recording device, I knew my mistake immediately. I wanted to reach out and stop him, but I just sat there. Parrs cued up a particular track and pressed play. When I heard it, I saw sunspots pass in front of my eyes, I felt the blood beating through my ears. I could hear my heart. It was a recording of my own voice.

"*Police,*" I said, "*Nineteen Fog Lane. Third floor of Grove Place. Flat 36.*" I didn't want to hear anymore. "*We've found a body,*" I said. "*A young girl's overdosed.*"

Parrs stopped the recording and stared into me with his red eyes. "Who's *we*?" he said. I thought of Catherine. The questions they might ask her and the answers she might give them.

She looked at me from very far away. "I'm pregnant."

Parrs still hadn't taken his eyes off me. "This is beyond self-preservation, son. Beyond right and wrong. A young girl's dead and the whole world's watching us. Who was with you in that room?"

I didn't say anything.

"Was it Carver?" he said.

"I was alone."

"If you weren't then, you are now. You're suspended. I want detailed reports on my desk tomorrow morning at the latest. I want to see you here, my office, Monday next week. Not a second before. And if I find out you're lying about anything, son, even what color socks you were wearing that day, it won't just be your job. You'll be finding out how fucking handsome you are in prison. This is your last chance to tell me what's going on."

She looked at me from very far away.

I looked into his shining red eyes.

"There's nothing going on."

13

went through the city with no direction. I'd always been an insomniac and walking aimlessly like that used to help. Every time I looked up, though, I saw that my feet had taken me somewhere familiar.

Muscle memory.

I saw the neon lights of bars where I used to drink, and thought of the people I'd known in them just five years before, when it still seemed like I might do anything.

My mind was recalibrating. Adjusting to Isabelle's death. I wondered what she'd wanted to talk to me about. I thought of the eighteen tally marks cut into her thigh. Too many to be counting the years she'd been alive. I thought about the smashed mirror, the message, the missing phone. I thought about Parrs, already spinning her death in his favor.

But when I thought about Isabelle herself, I changed direction. I walked into roads and oncoming cars. Pushing her to the back of my mind brought Catherine to the fore. The baby. I'd lied to her, lied about her, destroyed evidence and put us both in an impossible situation. I wondered where she was, if she could be feeling any worse than this.

Intermittent rain had been hazing the streets, and puddles glowed beneath the lights like portals to other dimensions. My feet had taken me home. To the rented room that was just a part of my cover.

The hallway light that had been flickering, on its last legs for days, had finally given up. Climbing the stairs in the dark was difficult, but the promise of sleep kept me going. I stopped on the first-floor landing. My door was ajar. I ran my hand over it, felt splintered wood where the lock had been forced.

Quietly, I pushed it open.

The only light came from the street, but I could see that everything had been turned over. In the lounge the sofa had been shredded. The coffee table had been smashed in. The few paperbacks I'd brought with me had been pulled down from the shelves and torn to pieces.

I looked through to the kitchenette.

The drawers had been turned out, the cupboards swept empty. Everything that had been in them—packages, plates, glasses—had been shattered or gutted out onto the floor. I was glad I hadn't been in.

I walked through to the bedroom, half expecting to find someone in there. The mattress had been knifed. Cross-sectioned and tossed. The bathroom was the last place I looked. Even in the dark I could see that someone had smashed the mirror. First they had written across it in bright red lipstick:

NO ONE CAN EVER KNOW

I stood with my back to the wall, wondering who'd left the message on Isabelle's mirror. Wondering why they'd do mine as well. What enemy did I have in common with a dead seventeen-year-old? Zain Carver didn't make sense. Not his goons or girls either. My mind drifted toward David Rossiter and I closed my eyes, feeling everything at once.

There was a cool draft coming from somewhere. I tried to remember if I'd closed the door at the street entrance when I came in. I thought I had.

I knew I had.

When I opened my eyes again they'd adjusted to the dark and I took a step forward. The breeze came stronger, and I could hear street sounds drifting up. I moved out of the bathroom as quickly as I could, through the bedroom, then into the lounge. I was holding my breath when I got to the door. I walked out onto the landing and looked down to the street entrance.

The door was open again.

I could see someone in silhouette, standing at the bottom of the stairs, glaring up at me. The kitchen knife in his left hand caught the light. Neither of us moved for a second, then we both moved at once.

The shape slipped smoothly out of the doorway and I pushed myself down the stairs after it. I landed in a heap at the bottom, threw myself up and out onto the street.

A shadow turned the far corner and I ran into the road after it. A taxi tried to swerve around me, and someone pulled me by the shoulder, back onto the pavement. I hit the ground hard, the wind knocked out of me, and lay on my back, staring up at the night sky.

A shape blocked out the streetlight above. Grip was standing over me. He looked off at the corner I'd seen the person run around, and sniffed. Then he looked down, holding out his good hand for me to take.

"C'mon," he said. He helped me up and led the way, back into my flat. I didn't say anything but I watched him closely. I wondered if he was seeing it for the first time.

14

'd offer you a drink . . ." I said, walking past him, into the destroyed room. I turned on the light and crunched across broken glass to the sofa. Its arm was the only piece of padding that had made it. Grip stood in the doorway. I realized that if he didn't want me to leave, I wasn't leaving.

"Any tips for getting boot marks off the floor?"

"Bit of white spirit'll sort it." He looked round the room. "Y'might just wanna pour it over everything and drop a match, though."

"I might. What are you doing here, Grip?"

"Get a look at the fucker?"

"No," I said. He let out a breath. He moved out of the doorway, stuck his head into the kitchenette and whistled. Then he leaned on a wall, looking at me. He seemed more disjointed than the first time I'd met him, and that was saying something. Then, he'd looked like a reanimated corpse. Now it looked like he'd been built in the dark out of three or four different bodies. His clothes were mismatched. His arms were different sizes. His legs were malnourished, funny even, beneath the overdeveloped upper body on top of them. One side of his face didn't even match the other. He looked ill, exhausted, but unique, I suppose.

"What about you?" I said.

"Huh?"

"Did you get a look at him?"

He sniffed. "Nah."

"What are you doing here, Grip?" I repeated.

"They say anything?"

"What are you doing here, Grip?"

He glared at me and I realized I'd shouted at him.

"Wants to see you," he said.

"It's not a good time."

"Not a good time for anyone, mate."

"Did someone smash your cups, too?"

His face darkened. I remembered who and what he was, and broke eye contact in a way I hoped implied apology.

"Isabelle," he said. Her name sounded strange in his mouth. "What happened?"

"Cath must've told you that by now."

"Let's hear it from you."

"All I know is how we found her. The police think it's an overdose. A bad batch or something."

"Police?"

"Had me in all day."

He grinned. "Makes sense."

"Why's that?"

"Been here awhile," he said. "Saw 'em come in and take their time with the place. Makes sense, I s'pose, if they knew you weren't coming back anytime soon . . ."

I motioned to the room. "Police don't do this."

"When you're on our side of it, they do." He looked away. "Don't forget what side of it you're on now."

"Is that what you're here to remind me of?"

"I'm here because he wants to see you. No games."

"Thanks for earlier," I said. He sniffed again. "I mean it, I'd have gone under that cab. Who's doing all this, Grip?"

"Started round the time you showed up."

It wasn't a serious answer and I waited.

"You know who's doing it," he said.

"Why now, though?"

"It's her anniversary, innit."

"What?"

"Joanna Greenlaw. Went missing November, ten years back."

15

We drove in silence. Grip ran an unexpectedly neat, classic-looking muscle car. A dark-colored Mustang hatchback. Strong, sturdy and compact as its owner. Even goons want to be James Dean. I could see that it took concentration to drive with his bad arm. I thought he was nervous, on edge.

"Did you see the man at my flat, Grip?"

He didn't answer.

We arrived at Fairview, parked and walked up the path. There were raised voices coming from inside. Grip knocked at a certain rhythm and they went quiet. Then he opened the door.

Carver was sitting in the hallway chair. He held his phone but for once wasn't absorbed with it.

Sarah Jane was on the stairs, walking up. She stopped halfway and turned to see who'd come in. There were dark lines beneath her eyes. She gave a joyless little laugh when she saw me, then turned and carried on up.

Carver raised his head.

"The fuck happened?" he said. I heard Sarah Jane slam a door behind her. It felt like a full stop at the end of her relationship with us all.

"I should ask you the same thing," I said.

He closed his eyes. "Cath says you found her."

"Yeah."

"And?"

"And she was naked. Smelt of sex. Had a needle in her arm."

"You took her home the night before." He looked at me. "I saw you fucking leaving."

"She was fine when I left her." It was at least half true.

"Sarah Jane says she asked you to take Izzy back to the flat."

"She shouldn't blame herself."

"She blames you. Why were you there the next day? When Cath turned up?" While Carver questioned me, Grip stood staring into the side of my head. I started to have a bad feeling about why I'd been brought here.

"Izzy asked me to be. She wanted to talk about something."

"Talk about what?"

"I don't know," I said.

"Why would she ask you to meet her the next day and then OD?"

"I'm not sure she did OD. There was something wrong with whatever she took. It made her arm go blue. And that's if she took it willingly."

He swallowed, looked at the floor.

"Blue?" said Grip. "This is on you, then," he jabbed a finger in Carver's direction.

"Not now, mate."

"When then?"

"Just not now, all right?"

"She was a kid. Shouldn't have been here in the first fucking place."

"You'd have sent her back, then, would you?"

Grip walked toward Carver and stopped. "I'd have got rid of the shit she jacked." He glared at his boss for a second and then went down the hall, into the kitchen and slammed the door behind him. The whole house shook.

"Drink?" said Carver, standing up and walking into his study next door. I followed him through. It was the second time I'd been in the room, but my first chance to look around. The main event was his desk. A rich, dark mahogany build, too sturdy to have been made recently. I wondered if it had belonged to his parents, or even people before that.

He poured two tall cognacs, handed the first to me and drained his own in one swallow. He poured himself another and sat in the nearest chair, resuming his slumped position from out in the hall. I sat opposite and waited. I didn't even remember drinking my cognac, but when I looked down my glass was empty.

"You did all right."

"How's that?"

"Got Cath out. She was a mess when she got here."

"How is she now?"

Carver looked up. "Dunno," he said, like it hadn't occurred to him to ask. "But she told me what you said. To get Fairview clean. Cops weren't far behind her and it saved me a headache." I wondered why I'd sent him the warning. At the time, I was still undercover; but it had been more than that. My second life would have ended when Isabelle died. I realized I hadn't wanted it to.

"What did the police say?"

"They had a search warrant, first and foremost. Took some stuff away. Took an informal statement." He shrugged. "Could've been worse."

"Anything tricky?"

"They asked when Izzy first turned up. What she got up to. My relationship with her . . ."

I didn't say anything and he looked at me.

"It was nothing much. She showed up one week with Sarah Jane. Some sob story."

With Sarah Jane? I wondered if Sarah Jane was a friend of a friend, or if she was connected to Isabelle Rossiter's life somehow.

"What was the sob story?"

"Personal shit," he said.

"Well, it looks bad for them not to have an arrest for the papers. If they had anything, they'd have charged you already. Can they link the flat to you?"

"Not easily," he said. "Not on paper."

"And did they talk to anyone else?"

He shook his head. "Sarah Jane's got a good head on her shoulders, but not for this shit. She thought we were the good guys."

"You don't?"

"I don't think there are any. Listen, with all this going on, you might be able to save me some more headaches."

"I might."

"Five for getting Cath out of the shit. Ten as a retainer for whatever's next. Ten for what we talked about before." I had to think for a second before I remembered the original operation. Today should have been the day of the sting. In all the madness I'd forgotten to ask Parrs about it.

"Sounds fair. But I can't say yes until I know what you're into. What did Grip mean about the shit she jacked?"

Carver took another drink. "You know what troubleshooting is?"

"Shooting up," I said. "Test batches."

He nodded. "Summertime, we had a problem. First cut from the brick always goes to someone in-house. We rota it so no one's getting burned or addicted."

"How much?"

"A bag," he said. "Hundred mil, fuck-all. Just means we know what we've got. We can amp up a weak batch or cut down a strong one."

"Troubleshooting."

"Well, Grip didn't always look like Frankenstein. He shot a bag . . ." I waited. He went on quietly, like Grip might have his ear to the door. "He got sick. It knocked him out. Fucked his arm. For a while they thought he'd lose it, but he got away with some nerve damage."

"Lucky guy."

He shot me a look. "He was in a coma for a few days. Came out of it different."

"Different how?"

"Argumentative. Emotional."

"Are you saying—"

Carver shook his head. "Opposite of that. He's lost his stomach for the game. I don't think he'd hurt anyone."

"You flushed the Eight, though."

He didn't say anything.

"Zain—"

"I wanted to know what went wrong. I wanted to know if the cook had fucked up or someone had spiked it."

"Who's the cook?"

"What's it to you?"

"It ended up in a seventeen-year-old girl's arm."

He ignored me. "I put it away until we could work out what happened."

"So?"

He drained his glass again and refilled it. "So when I looked for it today it was gone."

"Gone? Where was it?"

He didn't move for a second. Then he nodded over at his desk. I felt sick. Felt the ground dropping out from under me. I tried to speak.

"I . . ."

"You what?"

". . . I left Isabelle in this room the night before she died," I said. "For five minutes, while I spoke to Sarah Jane. I thought I was bringing her home, I didn't know she was staying round the corner . . ."

"Fuck." He thought for a second. Frowned. "Did they find it?"

"What?"

"The brick," he said. "Did they find it at the flat?"

"No." It dawned on me what he was saying. "In which case, it's still out there. She must have sold it or passed it on." We were both standing now. "We've got to find it. Tonight, now."

"Come on," he said, swiping his keys off the desk.

16

We'd been driving for fifteen minutes. We didn't talk about what might happen if contaminated Eight hit the market. I'd waited in the lounge while Carver had short, aggressive conversations with Grip and Sarah Jane. He came back into the room and flashed me a look.

"That retainer," he said. "We good there?"

I nodded.

"You can start earning it."

We sped into the city. I got the impression he was looking at old haunts. Places where friends, lovers, rivals had pushed Eight in his heyday. He'd been off the streets for so long that the people and places he remembered were gone, swept under the rug of the city's regeneration.

"I can think of one person who'd know about it if there was a dodgy brick doing the rounds."

Carver flashed me a look. "The Bug? You're talking about the Bug?"

"Why not?"

"You must be fucking joking."

I let it go, gave him a minute. "So where are we going?" He didn't seem to hear me. "Zain . . ."

"Black-and-white town," he said.

"The Burnside?"

He grunted and we drove on in silence. I'd hoped that I was wrong about the paint smears at Fairview. As we got farther from the center the streets seemed to get darker, uglier, there were no people on the pavements. No laughing girls or boys chancing their arms. The buildings on the roadside were old betting shops or burned-out, boarded-up pubs. We followed the Irwell out of town, north, toward that ugly industrial estate.

The city had written the Burnside off, and the police stayed away. Most tellingly of all, so did the Franchise. As we drove, I watched carefully. The headlights swept across buildings and roads, and the street signs were meaningless. Torn down, redirected or painted over. Responding police cars would get lost in the maze, finally reaching dead ends where they might be firebombed or worse. I thought I caught odd smatterings of black and white paint but only in the corners of my eyes. It was there and then gone again.

"This fucking place," said Carver.

"Do you know anyone here?"

"Wouldn't want to."

I looked at him.

"One of the girls," he said, eyes on the road. "Addie. She was collecting here. Papers say the industry went abroad and ripped the heart out of estates like these. Truth is, there wasn't much heart in the first place.

"The rule was that Grip always went with them. No one came here on their own. The Siders weren't what they had been, but they were still about. And the junkies'd grab a girl as soon as look at her.

"Anyway, I didn't know it but Ads was using. She thought she could control it, keep it to the clubs, but they always start taking it home. She was skimming money from collections. It was just a conversation waiting to happen and that would have been that. Only I left it too long. One night she was short, came here collecting by herself."

"What was she like?"

"Confident, funny. On brand. Some smiler held her down while another stabbed her through the ear with a syringe. Injected Eight into her brain to see what'd happen."

I looked out the window. "Don't you ever get bored of this?"

He didn't say anything, but I knew the rest. The Carver Franchise pulling out created a gap in the market for low-rent, low-down dealers like the Siders to sell the worst-quality stuff imaginable.

Tar.

It burned people down from the inside out. Sutty said he'd even seen users here potholing. They'd nurture one sustained open vein in their arm and then not let it heal. The skin grew up around the wound like split, puckered lips. At the time I'd thought he was exaggerating, but as we drove I wasn't so sure.

We passed through streets of dismal concrete gray, with flecks of black and white dotted about. It was worn down and burned out now, but the aggressive ugliness of the place could only have been intentional. A part of the design back when it had been an industrial estate. A message to employees that they were here to work and nothing else.

"I'd pull it down," said Carver. "To the last fucking brick."

We pulled up beside a hulking, derelict warehouse. I don't know if Carver knew the building or if he just picked the worst place he could find. Looking closely I saw it was spotted with faded, cracked-up, black and white paint.

Sutty had been right.

Whether the Burnsiders were still operating was up for debate, but their tag seemed disused. That only raised more questions about who was leaving it on Carver's doorstep. He turned off the engine and flexed his fingers over the steering wheel. We got out and started walking. His car looked ridiculous here, like a rare animal transplanted from somewhere exotic into dull, monochrome captivity.

As we walked I heard what sounded like animals, howling in the distance. I stopped for a second, realized that they were people. The warehouse had been built with thin sheet metal. In places there were gaps in the walls where the sheets had either fallen out or been stripped away. Through these gaps we could see the glow of flames from makeshift fireplaces, where users would be sitting around, trying to stay warm. The city seemed colder here. November digging its nails in.

Sitting in the doorway was a toothless, drunken woman and her boyfriend. She was crying, a guttural, painful sound, while the man laughed at her. Carver stepped between them, through the door, and I followed.

The building was beyond huge, and it was difficult to imagine it ever having been filled before it fell into disrepair. A short hallway led us past what would have been a reception area and into the colossal main room of the abandoned warehouse.

It was lit only by the fires burning in three different spots, each illuminating four or five wasted, skeletal people. They were either lying down or staring intently into the flames, but none of them looked at us as we entered. Carver walked toward the nearest group and I followed. He bent to a man, lying passed out by a fire, and rolled him over. A smiler. Scar tissue either side of his mouth. Carver held his arm up to the light, searching for some sign that the missing brick had been here.

"Hey," said the man. The only protest he was capable of. He watched dispassionately as Carver removed a tin-foil package from the man's hand. He opened it, looked inside and threw it back down, disgusted.

He was out of his depth. We both were. He repeated the process at the second fireplace, finding nothing but tar and bad conversation. Carver was already checking the third when we heard some commotion from the doorway. Someone was talking to the toothless woman we'd stepped over on our way in.

"Finally," said Carver. He turned from what he was doing and strode in the direction of the door, eager for confrontation. Three shapes appeared. The man in front was bald and wiry. He was white but, even in the low light, looked so dirty that his skin had been permanently colored. He had golden teeth and tattoos on his face. About ten feet behind him were two younger men. They were bigger than him but it was more fat than muscle. They both had tired, sulky expressions on their faces. They kept their distance while the bald man came closer.

"Zain Carver," he said. "To what do we owe the pleasure?"

"Do I know you?"

The man laughed. He sounded like a punctured accordion. "Nah, mate," he said. "I bet you don't. Think of me as the nightwatchman."

"Once I walk through that door, mate, I'll never think of you again."

"Best make the most of it then, hadn't I? What brings you here?"

"You've been tryna get my attention for weeks," said Carver.

"Have we, now?"

"The black and white paint at Fairview."

"So?"

"So, ten years since Joanna went missing."

The bald man smiled. "Oh, it's a matter of the heart . . ."

"Where I'm least fucking vulnerable. I'm here to ask you a question and then we can all go home."

"You still can go home, then?"

"What's that mean?"

"We hear you're famous now. Michael fuckin' Jackson in Neverland. Police an' press campin' outside. What'd we hear, Billy?"

"Famous," said Billy, the larger of the two boys. "Got his name in the papers."

"Got yer name in the papers," said the bald man.

"Don't believe everything you hear."

"Know what you mean," said the man. Each time he finished a sentence he counted it off on his fingers, like he only had so many left in him and wanted to keep track. "Sheldon'll never believe it when he hears this."

Carver took a step forward, looked at him. "Why's that?"

"You don't call. You don't write . . ." The man licked his lips. "Ever since we gave that girl of yours some earache."

In one movement, Carver took the man by the shoulders and head-butted him. I heard a sharp, wet crack and saw blood explode into the air, hanging there for a second like mist. The man's head went back so quickly I thought he'd broken his neck. By the time I got to Carver he was strangling him.

"Zain," I said. I looked at the Burnsiders who'd been standing behind the bald man. Neither moved. Billy, the older of the two, wasn't even watching. The other one stared at Carver, strangling his boss on the floor. He looked bored. Carver's thumbs were pressing into the man's neck so hard they were turning white.

"Zain," I said. "Stop."

He wrung the man's neck for a few seconds more and then threw him down on the ground. The man let out an anguished scream for breath. His nose was obliterated, his face was covered in blood.

"We're leaving," said Carver, wiping his hands on his trousers. He got to his feet and strode up to the young Siders. Went toe-to-toe with Billy. "You heard about that girl? Isabelle Rossiter?" Billy nodded. "The stuff that did it is still out there . . ."

"Nothing moves here unless it's from us," said Billy.

Carver grunted and walked out, back the way we came. "Tell Sheldon we said hi," he shouted over his shoulder.

I couldn't look at the man on the floor but I could hear him struggling for air, inhaling and exhaling bone fragments as he did. The two Siders drifted slowly out of the warehouse. I dialed 999 for the second time in two days and asked for an ambulance. I gave them the address, rolled the man over and followed Carver.

"That's the only reason we came here? To prove some fucking point?"

"What?"

"I thought we were looking for the Eight."

"We are," he said, wiping blood from his forehead, getting into the car. "Any bright ideas?"

I got in on the passenger side. "Just one. Don't lose your shit again. Don't leave any more broken noses where we've been." He started the car and put his foot down.

"That's what you call supply and demand. Someone asking for something and someone getting it." I watched his hands, gripping the wheel tightly. I checked the time. It was more than an hour since we'd set out and we were leaving the Burnside with nothing.

I tried to focus. "If the Siders are anything to do with the missing Eight, they'd never sell it on their own doorstep."

He thought about it. "They'd sell it on mine." He leaned forward, dialed a number into his mobile.

Grip's voice came through the speakerphone. *"Any joy?"*

"Not at the Burnside," said Carver. "Check all the bars from Rubik's down. If they're setting us up, they'll sell it in the city, not here."

"No one knows anything. Or no one's talking about it. Got ourselves another problem."

"What?"

"Am I on loud?"

Carver took the phone from its cradle and pressed it to his ear. "Gone?" he said. I assumed they were talking about the bar manager from Rubik's. The drugs I'd flushed. I assumed he'd run for his life. I needed to talk to him about his relationship with Isabelle and wondered again how I'd do it.

Carver spoke quietly. "Get around everyone. Get around everywhere. Put out a cash reward. Find it." He hung up and we drove on in silence for a few minutes.

I took a breath. "The Bug." Carver didn't say anything this time and I went on. "Stuff gets cut down and sold on every day. There's a roaring black market for Eight."

He still didn't say anything.

"If someone was trying to move a brick, he'd hear about it."

"He's a fucking psychopath."

"What have we got to lose?"

Carver looked at me. "My temper." He drove on for a minute. "Grip can go with you."

"Mr. Levelheaded? Leave him out of it."

"You wanna talk to the Bug on your own? You must have something I haven't seen, brother."

"Turn left here," I said. "Yeah, we go way back."

He didn't say anything else. I couldn't tell if he was disgusted or impressed.

17

The Bug was an urban legend made flesh. He'd been a heroic user of heroin in his day, perfecting a style known as cannibalization. He was the rag-and-bone man of the scene, picking up the stuff that even hardcore users wouldn't shoot and finding a home for it. He considered using another person's needle a high in its own right, and would mix together the dregs from several syringes, recutting it into one cocktail.

But it wasn't until he got sober some years later that he picked up his nickname. Injecting had always been sexualized for him and, once he stopped, he spent even more time around users. Especially young ones.

They called him the Bug because he would hover around a group of kids, salivating as they shot up. Then, once they were high, he'd lower himself down and kiss, gently, along their arms until he got to the vein they'd shot into. Then he'd suckle at the wound, letting out low, satisfied moans. His primary physical threat was being literally infectious. He bragged about an entire alphabet of hepatitis in his bloodstream.

He became a cult figure in the gay scene, performing a transsexual BDSM act under the name Daddy Longlegs at unlicensed saunas and sex clubs. He made existential, art-house pornography. Wrote cheap but well-selling chapbooks of poetry and sold his own artwork for hundreds of pounds a go.

Among a subculture known as bug chasers he became infamous. These young men saw HIV as a status symbol and pursued it with a suicidal vigor that was both sad and compelling to see. He practiced unprotected sex with people who considered it a gift to be infected by him. The rumors were outrageous, awful and—sometimes—true. He was well-spoken, wore tailored clothes and reveled in these contradictions in his character.

He lived in a converted church off Alexandra Park. Carver pulled up across the road without looking directly at the place.

"If I'm not back in ten minutes . . ."

"Don't bother coming back at all," he said.

18

I got out and crossed the road. It was gone midnight and these ten stress-free seconds, breathing the cold air, made me feel light-headed. I got to the door and pressed the intercom. The building had been renovated and modernized. It was a world away from the Burnside and I was grateful for it.

"*Yesssss,*" buzzed a bored, mechanized voice.

"Waits."

There was silence for a few seconds.

"*Come on in, handsome.*"

The place was decorated in sedate, pastel colors that belied the Bug's wild reputation. The main room was large and spacious, resplendent with solid, load-bearing beams. A teenage boy was sitting at a piano, naked to the waist, playing a sonata. Some of the less bombastic Beethoven, I thought.

On a bed in the center of the room a young couple lay in their pants, kissing, grinding slowly against each other. At first I thought they were both boys, but saw that the girl simply had short hair, an angular, androgynous face and a flat chest. The bed was low, Japanese in style, and had a glaring spotlight above it. Neither of them looked up when I walked in.

A haggard man was sitting on a sofa opposite them, swilling a glass of red wine. He was dressed in an outrageous parody of femininity. He wore a huge pink wig with a tight corset and miniskirt. The look was finished with thick, slick makeup, sparkling tights and red high heels.

"Detective Waits," he said, not looking away from the kissing couple. "Excuse me if I don't rise for the occasion."

"I need to talk to the Bug." I leaned against a wall, felt the cold sweat under my clothes.

"He's out," said the man, "foul little shit that he is. Are you out?"

"I'm afraid not."

"Aidan Waits for no man," he said, looking at me for the first time. "They say it's very liberating . . ."

"I know they do. I'm all for it. I also know he's here, so go get him for me, sweetheart."

The man smiled, did his best to look bashful. "What's in it for me?"

I pushed an expensive-looking vase off its stand. It smashed onto the floor and the piano playing stopped. The teenage couple looked up at me from the bed, still holding on to each other.

"I need to talk to the Bug," I repeated.

"You want the organ grinder," said the man. "Fine, I'll go and get him, but he's so serious lately, I don't know if he'll grind your organ or not." With that he stood up, gave me a wink and walked out of the room, caressing the boy at the piano as he went. The kids on the bed stared at me blankly and we waited a few minutes in silence.

When the man came back, he'd taken off his wig, thrown a shapeless gray jumper over the corset and clawed off some makeup. He had a face like a nun's knee.

He was barefoot now and acknowledged me with a grunt as he sat down.

"Dick," he said to the boy at the piano. "Dom," he said to the boy on the bed. "Give us a minute." They got up sluggishly. The boy on the bed gave his girlfriend's arm a tug or two, but she'd passed out. He shrugged his shoulders and left her there, facedown in the pillow, following his friend into the back.

"No hurry," I said.

"Excuse me for taking my time, but you never come here with good news."

"If it were up to me, I'd never come here at all."

"Funny we see so much of each other, then."

"I need some information."

"What's new?"

"About drugs."

"Bor-ing," said the Bug, getting to his feet.

"Sit down. A pound of Eight got snatched from Zain Carver the other day. I need to know where it is."

He sat forward, fascinated. "Why haven't the police been here?" I didn't say anything. "It's true, isn't it? You really have gone over to the dark side. All the way."

"Have you heard anything?"

"I heard you've been stealing evidence. I heard you've been eating speed for breakfast, dinner and tea. I even heard you rattling on your way up the drive like a pack of Tic Tacs." I didn't say anything. "I also heard that hot mess Isabelle Rossiter got some *bad* Eight inserted inside her," he said with a smile. "Wouldn't have anything to do with that, now, would it?"

"No."

"Pity," he said to himself. "I just love the thought of it . . ."

I waited.

"You're no fun anymore. Remember when we first met?" The Bug had grown up in The Oaks group home, same as me. When I knew him, he was a sensitive soul, ten years old and just realizing he was gay. He'd lent me books and albums, expecting nothing in return. At the time I'd thought he was trying to convince me that there was some life, some hope, outside the place. Now I see that he was probably trying to convince himself.

He smiled. "I'd say something outrageous and you'd come back with a little one-liner. Something funny and cruel. You've stopped doing that now, haven't you? You've run out of funny things to say." He took a sip of his wine. "You're such a disappointment."

"If I'm disappointing you, I must be doing something right."

The Bug threw the wineglass over his shoulder, laughed and clapped his hands.

"That's more like it. You give something, you get something. There's a kid I know," he said, flashing me a candid look, "eighteen years old, officer, I swear. A kid I know got extra lucky this morning. Not only did he see yours truly, but when he went buzzing down to the Burnside afterward he ran into someone trying to shift a pound of Eight. Got it half price."

"Name?"

"Oh, Slimmer or Swimmer or something like that—you know how they are these days. Comes from a very good family, though. Lives on Sycamore Way."

"West Dids?"

The Bug nodded. "Mum and Dad are out this weekend so Daddy Longlegs is going over to entertain the troops." He was referring to himself.

"House number?" The Bug didn't say anything. I stepped toward another vase.

"Thirty-one."

"Stay home tonight. I'm doing you a favor."

"I'd rather not owe you one."

I nodded at the girl, passed out on the bed.

"Get her a cab and we'll call it even."

19

I t was after 1 a.m. when we arrived. Sycamore Way was lined with huge, ageless trees. When I was young, the other kids at school made pilgrimages there in couples, carving their names inside love hearts into the bark.

I only knew it by reputation.

November had already stripped the leaves away when we arrived and, in the winter gloom, the trees looked like enormous skeletal hands, reaching to the sky.

The road was broad and commanding, giving an impression of wealth and success without going to any great lengths. The homes on each side were restored Victorian mansions.

Carver had stared off into the street for a minute when I told him where we were going. I think he knew then that he was nearing the end. It was one thing for spiked Eight to wash up at the Burnside, another thing entirely for it to arrive in the pristine upper-class greenery of Sycamore Way. He drove in silence until we pulled up outside a grand property.

"Thirty-one," he said.

We couldn't see a number on the gate but had both counted down from the bottom. The house itself was at the end of a private lane. Although it was hidden behind an embankment of trees, we could make out the roof from the road.

"Yeah," I said. "You should probably wait here."

He looked at me.

We both got out of the car and walked toward the property. An impressive automatic black-and-gold gate stood at the end of the drive. Having been left ajar, either by malfunction or by human error, it off-set the perfect symmetry of the place.

We passed through it, up the driveway. There were cars parked alongside the lawn, all of them incongruous against the backdrop of the mansion. They were small hatchbacks, probably first cars belonging to teenagers. A dull, insistent beat was coming from a sound system inside.

Carver nodded up at the house.

Illuminated in a window was a young girl. She was standing in a kitchen, at a sink. As we drew closer, her face split into a perfect white smile. We both stopped before realizing that she couldn't see us. She was smiling at her own reflection in the window. She wore a tight, brilliant-white vest over tanned skin. With her dusty blond hair, from inside that house, she conveyed an air of health and well-being.

Carver walked up the path to the door. The monotonous beat from the sound system was louder inside. Thick and heavy.

The door led into a large hallway. There was a table littered with junk mail and bills and, beside it, a coat stand covered with distressed-denim jackets. I followed Carver to the right, heading for the kitchen, where we'd seen the girl.

He stopped.

Dominated the doorway so I couldn't see past. The beat of the music grew louder as I moved around him.

The girl was standing in a large puddle of blood. I forced my eyes up to her face. She was still smiling at her reflection as though we weren't in the room. It looked like she'd been carrying a tray of glasses and dropped them. She'd been walking up and down on the shards for some time, oblivious to the pain. Her feet were cut to pieces and had bled out all over the white tiles.

The girl turned our way, crunching more glass beneath her bare feet, repeating the perfect white smile we'd seen through the window. Showing us the arm she'd injected into. It hung, limp at her side, blue veins standing out like motorways on a map.

I pushed past Carver, walked over the glass and held her upright. She looked me in the eyes and nodded slightly, still smiling, like she had no control over it. I picked her up, carried her to a sofa at the far side of the kitchen and set her down.

Turning to look at Carver, I saw he was following the sound of the beat to a closed door. The music had seemed sharper since we arrived in the kitchen, but when he opened the door it cut loudly through the air.

He walked inside and didn't come back out. I looked at the girl and her eyes locked onto mine. She was still smiling but it had started to twist into something else.

"It's OK," I said, out of breath. There was a reading lamp positioned next to the sofa, lighting her up more than I would have liked. Close up, I could see that her left-hand side was turning a pale almost pastel shade of blue. Her feet glistened with blood and shards of embedded broken glass.

I crossed the room toward the beat of the music. The door that Carver had gone through. I shouted his name but he didn't answer. The beat felt louder, more aggressive, and I was hit by the smell of sick. The room was a lunatic asylum of pain and shining, sweating, naked limbs. I counted five girls and three boys. All teenagers. Some were facedown in their own sick, some had contorted blue faces. Some slept serenely.

They'd all injected.

Carver was standing in the middle of them. He had his back to me, his head hung low. He straightened to his full height and went forward. I thought he was looking more closely at one of the girls, twitching on the floor. Instead, he walked past her to the sound system. He examined it for a second and then switched it off.

The lack of music exposed the low moans coming from the kids. I didn't know what to do. He turned, took his phone from his pocket and started to dial.

"Who are you calling?"

He didn't answer.

"Put that down," I said, walking toward him. He reached out, grabbed my collar and held me at arm's length by the scruff of the neck. He didn't look at me while he waited for the phone to be answered.

"Police," he said. "Ambulance and police."

20

C arver killed the connection on his phone and walked out. I heard gurgles and low moans from the dosed kids. Some were curled in the fetal position. One was lying on his back, drawing his knees up like Isabelle had. Soon they all started doing it, faces turning blue.

The girl closest to me was throwing up blood. I rolled her over so she wouldn't choke on it and walked back into the kitchen. I pulled the door closed behind me. I pulled and pulled until I heard the click of the handle.

I'd been holding my breath and steadied myself against the wall, absorbing the rush of air into my lungs. I walked to the window, tried to look outside. All I could make out was my own thin reflection. I realized that the girl we'd seen through the window must have been looking at herself, wondering if her face was changing color like the others. I could hear her fitting on the sofa.

Then I saw lights.

Headlights and flashing blues, bleeding into one another, illuminating the room. I heard car doors closing. Voices. Booted men and women, crashing in on the quiet.

I was lighter than air when I left. I went out a back door, into the pitch-black night, through the garden. I walked carefully at first, then through trees, bushes, ponds, paying no attention to where the path was. I climbed over a fence, went across another lawn and came out on the next road. First stumbling, then walking, then running.

III

CLOSER

1

The daylight was awful. It floodlit the insane, the terminally ill, turned loose again for the day, laughing and crying and pissing their pants through the streets. It was like the lights going up at last orders, turning the women from beautiful to plain, exposing the men for what they all are at their worst. Ugly, identical.

It was Monday morning, almost a week since Sycamore Way. A week since I'd last taken speed. I'd heard bar-talk about Franchise doormen getting kicked in. About Carver cabs being turned over. Collections taken by force. No one was talking too loudly, though, and I hadn't heard who'd been held up or hurt. I thought about Catherine.

Driving through the city I saw a jarring addition to its color scheme. Uniformed police presence had been ramped up, with reflective Day-Glo jackets blaring out from every corner. They were ostensibly there to stop-and-search, to engage with the herd and give them whatever the agreed story was. Their role was mainly cosmetic. Lipstick on a pit bull.

Dressing for my interview with Parrs, I'd pulled on a suit I thought I could still fill. It hung loosely, a hand-me-down from someone I used to know. I'd walked quickly past the police officers standing on the street and found myself at headquarters a few minutes early.

It was uncharacteristically quiet. I could hear the air conditioning overhead. The last time I'd been around was after finding Isabelle Rossiter, when it seemed that the building might come apart at the seams with activity. On this Monday morning it was a ghost town. Every free body was standing outside, reassuring the public.

I showed my card and signed in.

My signature flowed out automatically, but it looked like a stranger's handwriting. I stared down at it for a second until the officer at reception politely cleared his throat. I accepted a visitor pass and moved on. My mind was elsewhere, already running through what I had to tell Superintendent Parrs. I took a lift up to the fourth floor, hoping not to see anyone I knew. I was almost at his door when my phone rang.

"*Waits*," said the man on the other end. "We need to talk."

"I'm about to go into Parrs—"

"I know that," he said. "Meet me in the stairwell." I didn't say anything. "You'll thank me." I hung up, carried on going and then hesitated. I stopped and checked the time. Then I turned, walked back the way I'd come and pushed through a fire door. The staircase was lined from top to bottom with exposed pipes. They kept the air perpetually heavy and warm. The lighting was variable, too, with long stretches of bulbs having burned out at different points without ever being replaced.

I saw a shape, a man, walking down from the fifth floor toward me. He stopped with three steps between us.

"Aidan," said Detective Kernick.

"Sweetheart."

He stepped into the light. For the first time I noticed that the charcoal color of his hair was spotted with lighter grays and whites. I wondered if it was a recent development. He looked about five years older.

"I'm glad I caught you," he said.

"You sound it."

"Mr. Fucking Insight. Your debrief with Parrs. You'll have a lot to talk about . . ."

"So if you don't mind . . ."

"Course," he said, standing to one side. Out of the light he was just a shape again. "That's the great thing about you, Waits. Always so keen to walk into the shit."

"What am I walking into?"

He craned his head forward, back into the light. Glared at me. "You really haven't got any friends here, have you?"

"What am I walking into?"

He took two steps down, leaned into my ear. "*They know*," he hissed. I took a step back. He was entirely lit up now. "The drugs," he said. "The drinking, the screwing. Who the fuck did you think you were?" I tried to move past him, but he stopped me with a hand on my chest. "Just a second, son." I could feel the sweat on his palm, bleeding through my shirt. We were both standing in the light now and he looked me dead in the eyes.

"Were you fucking her?"

"Who?" I said, giving away more than I would have liked.

The flicker of a smile. "Isabelle."

"No, I wasn't."

He looked at me for a second. "Those pictures," he said. "The ones of you and Izzy, cozying up at the Carver place. They're off the table."

"What about Rossiter?"

"He's the one who asked me to source them in the first place. To check up on you. He knows what it means for his job and mine if they come to light. Thought you should hear it before speaking to the Super." He peeled his hand off my chest. "One less thing for you to talk about."

"Who took those pictures?"

He smiled. "Fuck yourself."

I walked away from him.

"He doesn't need to know," Kernick said to my back.

I stopped in the doorway. "Doesn't need to know you illegally carried out your own investigation?"

"You little—"

"Don't dress self-preservation up as charity, Kernick. It's a bad look."

"Some self-preservation might save your life, son," he said, coming after me. I let the door close in his face.

By the time I got to Parrs's office I felt sick. I took a breath, walked into the small waiting room. Standing there, then, in that brand-new building, in that old suit, I felt like the wrong man. Like I should never have gone back. Something in the way his secretary looked up at me made me think:

Fucking run.

2

Superintendent Parrs stood as I walked into his office.

"Waits," he said, directing me to a chair. I sat opposite and, after some arrangement of the papers at his desk, he resumed his seat. He looked like he hadn't slept since Isabelle died. I could only imagine what Sycamore Way had done to him. The deaths had been national news. His red eyes stared straight through me and his Scottish accent, always hard and low, was a brick wall.

"This is an informal conversation. It serves mainly as a handover and debrief for your work with the Franchise. It's my hope that—"

"Did we get him?" I said.

"As you know—"

"Did we get him?" I repeated.

"No." Parrs blinked. "As you know, the sting was set for Monday, November sixteenth . . ."

"The day after we found Isabelle Rossiter."

"The drive was wiped. Our man was definitely in there. Unfortunately, due to the increased workload that day, room 6.21A was reassigned without my authorization."

It felt like a joke. "I don't understand. We were keeping the room empty . . ."

"Personnel overflow working the Rossiter girl's death was assigned to 6.21A. Thirty-five people went in and out. Twenty-three of them long-serving enough to be our man. No," he said. "We didn't get him."

I couldn't speak.

"Believe me, I know how you feel." I wanted to get up and walk out, I just couldn't put enough thought together. "Let's talk about you, son. Your future."

"I was under the impression I didn't have one."

"That's up to you, to some extent."

I reached into my jacket pocket, handing him a sealed envelope.

"In that case, I should be clear from the start." I wasn't interested in sitting through more threats. I wanted to take the gun out of his hand.

He held up the letter. "What's this?"

"You received my reports?"

"I did. They were very clear."

"I'd like them to serve as the basis of my handover."

Parrs looked at the envelope, which he was still holding in the space between us. "This your fucking suicide note?"

"My resignation."

He put the envelope down. "What makes you think you're in any position to resign?"

"If there are charges for removing drugs from evidence, then I'll face them."

He swept the letter to one side so it lined up perfectly with the corner of his desk.

"Bold choice. Corruption. Theft. Intent to supply. Five-year sentence? Three, four years inside? Be difficult to qualify for good behavior, though, the amount of glass you'll be shitting."

"Fine," I said, standing to leave, thinking I still might run.

"Sit down," he said. "What's this really about?"

I sat. "Joanna Greenlaw's disappearance. Zain Carver. The Franchise. Contaminated drugs. Fine." I looked at him. "But I won't cover up Isabelle Rossiter's death. It's one compromise too many, even for me."

"What do you plan on doing? Aside from some hard time?"

"I'd leave," I said. In my head it sounded sensible, like something he might want to hear. Out loud it sounded like a childish dream. "I'd go as far away as possible."

"You don't want to see this through to the end?"

"I don't want to know how it ends."

His eyes narrowed. In interrogations, Parrs would ask simple, direct questions and then wait. Even after the interviewee had answered them. It made people uncomfortable, forced them to break the silence and keep on talking.

I didn't say anything.

"I'd make sure it fucking followed you, son. Wherever you went."

"What can I do?" I said. "What do you want me to do?"

Parrs glared at me. "You asked me before about Joanna Greenlaw. I sent you to the *Evening News* appeal. You got the facts but didn't quite get the truth."

"What's the truth?"

"There's an awful lot of it outside the facts, if you look and listen. Joanna Greenlaw agreed to testify against Carver and the Burnsiders ten years ago, that's a fact. A friend of hers was killed in the Burnside, that's a fact. What the papers won't tell you is the truth. That it was me who turned her. The papers won't tell you I worked with that girl every day for months. Painstaking stuff. We changed our pattern of communication every three days. Orchestrated a rotating cast of operatives. Made sure no other officer knew the scope and scale of the operation. So when I say I know how you feel . . ."

"Why all that?"

"Carver had enough near-misses under his belt to convince me there were leaks, even then. That's the truth but not a fact."

"You must have someone in mind for the leaks."

"A rogue's gallery, son."

"What really happened to Joanna Greenlaw?"

"Your guess is as good as mine. Black and white paint found at the scene. No sign of her."

"Did you look?"

"To my shame, no. My Chief Super said she'd just got stage fright. Done a runner before she said or did anything too damning to her old boss. I was reassigned and told in no uncertain terms to leave it alone. I'd wasted enough time already. Once the dust settled, I tried to follow it up, but her last-known associates were Zain Carver and Sheldon White. Neither of them talkative. The trail, if she left one at all, was cold by then." He paused. Went on quietly, "I suppose I hoped she had run. Then with each year that she didn't turn up, saw it was less and less likely . . ."

"Grip—Danny Gripe—thinks Sheldon White's making noise for the anniversary. Ten years since she went missing . . ."

Parrs thought about it. "Psychological warfare seems a little advanced for the Burnsiders. It's convenient that White just got out, but that's all it is. He's not the type to own a calendar, much less use one."

"Who else could it be?" He didn't move. "You don't think Joanna Greenlaw's still alive?"

He ignored that. "What I'm saying is, sometimes you have to play the long game. You could still see this right." I didn't say anything and he went on, "Fine. You have about a month of unused leave. I was going to suggest you take it anyway, but I suppose, given the circumstances, I'd agree to you taking it to see out your notice."

"And the charges?"

"We'll see about the charges. But only after a satisfactory debrief."

"My reports—"

"Are, as I said, very clear. Very factual. I think it might be helpful for us to step outside those facts into your reactions and impressions. You only ever see the worst in people, son." He flashed me his shark's smile. "Only fair I reap the benefit, eh?"

"Sir."

Parrs picked up a sheet of paper from his desk. I saw it was a part of my written report. Although he didn't look down or refer to the paper, it was clear he had fully assimilated its contents. In meetings he often wrote detailed notes and then discreetly binned them afterward. His memory was excellent and I assumed he took the notes to assure others that he was taking them and their work seriously. I assumed he held my report without looking at it now for the same reason.

"When you took Isabelle back to Carver's place in a cab, you went through her bag. Why?"

"From what I'd seen at Rubik's—that she was at least drinking and probably using—I'd decided to take her home. Her real home," I said. "I only vaguely knew where the Rossiter family lived. I thought I'd find something with their address on it."

"Take me through what you did find."

"Money. Lots of it. I realized she'd made the Franchise collection while out of my sight line. I thought she'd be in more danger if she didn't take the cash back to Carver."

"What else was in the bag?"

"Cosmetics, a purse, a mobile. She still had that mobile when I got her home. Whoever took it from her flat must have been the last person to see her alive."

"Don't get excited. We found the phone."

I tried not to react. I thought about the text Isabelle had sent me. The text that I'd seen sitting in her sent items folder.

Zain knows.

I braced myself. I had already told Parrs that I never got her number. This would prove me a liar.

He went on. "Her father had the number and we were able to trace it. When we saw that its last signal came from inside her flat, we took the place apart. The phone was found hidden. Taped to the bottom of a drawer on her desk."

That didn't sound right. I wanted to ask what was on it. Why it was hidden. If they'd found the message she sent to me. I knew how it might look to an outsider: *Zain knows about us.*

Parrs left an excruciating silence.

I thought of the photographs.

Finally, he said, "What was the reaction when you got her back to Fairview?"

"Subdued."

"You didn't speak to Carver?"

"Sarah Jane answered the door."

"This redhead of his?"

I nodded. "She was more interested in the cash than Isabelle. I think I saw Carver in a window when I was leaving. To be honest, I wondered if the whole thing was a setup."

"How so?"

"He likes to play games with people and he was trying to work out if he could trust me. He's had me followed. He wouldn't be above having the barman spike Isabelle to see what I'd do once I found the money. He was certainly more trusting of me afterward."

"You say he likes to play games. Why?"

"Part of the fun. He considers himself a strategist. Whatever it looks like he's doing, he's probably working on the opposite."

"He's a big guy. Sometimes men like that only respect their own kind. What's he make of you?"

"More than I thought he would."

"Go on."

"I think he enjoyed me racking out some home truths. Seemed to enjoy me talking out of turn. He always knew how and when to put me back in my place, though. I think he likes to talk and probably doesn't get much chance to with the goon squad. The one thing he said that really rang true was that he doesn't go around hitting people. He doesn't have to."

"Tell me about this Grip character."

"Little less conversation, a little more action."

"Dangerous?"

"He'd pick a fight with the floor if it looked up at him funny. He spat in my face the first time we met."

"You can have that effect on people."

I smiled. "No, he's the type. I've seen Carver have to talk him down once or twice."

"Interesting," said Parrs. "Bonkers enough to have spiked the Eight? Or sold on stuff that he knew was bad?" I hadn't told Parrs that Grip had, in fact, been the first victim of the bad batch.

"Emotional was the word Carver used. Says Grip's lost his appetite for the game rather than gained it. My impression is, he's like the rest of them. Scared of something else."

"Tell me more about the house."

"Transient population. Especially when there's a party on. I stayed there my second night, no problem. Kids kipping on floors every other room."

"What kinds of kids?"

"White middle-class ones. College age up. Most in their mid-twenties. Creatives, I think they call themselves."

"And there are two exits?"

I looked at him. "You're raiding." He didn't move.

"The night of the next party."

"Those parties camouflage the Franchise with a couple of hundred drunk kids."

"Noted."

"They'll get hurt."

"It's a nebulous concept to you, Waits, but I'm following the orders I'm given. I happen to think, given the circumstances, they're the right ones. Carver's been given too long a leash for too long a time. When you're a dealer and kids start dying from toxic batches, you get your door kicked in. Simple as that."

"Why not just go round now with a warrant?"

"We did. He was waiting for us. Fucker'd had his whole house deep-cleaned from top to bottom." My warning. "Now, the exits."

"Two, from what I saw. Front and back. The back's a double-glazed doorway leading out into the garden. Since there'll be a crush when you kick the front door in, it might be worth letting people filter out that back way and having men on the garden gate down the path."

"Something to keep in mind."

"Is there anything else?"

"You've heard about the cabs being turned over?"

"Just pub talk. Cabs plural?"

"Aye, looks like we're in for a regime change whether Carver's arrested or not. One cab on Friday night and one on Saturday. Both unreported but called in by witnesses. Each car was hit by a large goods vehicle before it could reach Fairview. Then someone got out of said vehicle and forcibly took the cash from whichever girl had collected it."

"Who was in the cabs? Are they OK?"

Parrs looked at me. "Cuts and bruises, far as we know." I hoped it wasn't Catherine. I felt like less than shit for lying low the past week.

"Franchise collections. They're not gonna like it . . ."

"They'd have been paltry in the first place. There was a long article from one of the Sycamore Way mothers in the *Guardian*. As a brand name, Eight's finished."

"It's about sending a message."

"A nail in the coffin, aye. Anyway," said Parrs, sensing my renewed interest and cutting it short, "that'll be all."

I stood to leave, feeling light on my feet. Parrs didn't stand to see me out, just offered a nod in my direction. A part of me wanted to turn around and tell him everything, but I had the door open when he called after me.

"Sorry, Waits."

I turned.

That shark smile again.

"There was one other thing."

I walked back into the office, let the door close behind me, went completely blank.

"Isabelle's phone," he said.

Zain knows.

"I was wondering if you could take a look at it for me?"

Zain knows.

I nodded. I could hear the pulse in my ears. Parrs opened a drawer at his desk. He sighed, closed it and opened another. He rummaged in that one but closed it as well.

He knows.

I couldn't believe that the man who'd memorized my reports had forgotten which drawer he'd left some evidence in. He was raising the tension. Finally, he took out a large-screened, hot-pink mobile phone, wrapped in a clear plastic bag.

"This the one?"

It wasn't. I had never seen it before.

"Yes, sir."

He didn't say anything.

"At least, I think it is."

"Hm," he said, eyes not moving from mine. "Odd thing is, it doesn't seem to have been switched on since Isabelle ran away from home. Doesn't seem like the kind of thing she'd keep in her handbag."

"It was there," I said.

"Thanks," said Parrs, smiling.

3

racked my brain for Parrs's angle on the phone. He knew it wasn't the one I'd seen, or at least suspected it. I walked a zigzag through the city, making sure I hadn't been followed. I found a pay phone. Scrolled through the messages in my mobile for the single one I had received from Isabelle. From the phone that the police hadn't found. The phone that had gone missing from her flat when she died.

I looked over my shoulder, dropped a coin into the slot and dialed. It rang two and a half times and was suddenly cut off. Sent to voice mail.

Someone had it.

I thought of the voice mail I'd heard on that phone. The night before Isabelle died.

That unmistakable Oxbridge accent.

"Isabelle, I wish you'd pick up the phone. I know I'm the last person you want to hear from . . ."

Superintendent Parrs had found Isabelle's old phone because her father had given him the number. If David Rossiter also had the number to her second phone, the one she had only bought since running away, how had he got it? Why hadn't he handed that over as well? And who had taken it from her room?

When I started walking it was still early. I tried to disappear into the streets again, just another vagrant that your eyes scan past as you cross a road. Weak, white-gray light thawed the city, the traffic flowing again like blood in its veins.

I wanted to be swept along with it and forget myself. To see my reflection warp and alter in the bottles behind a bar. I saw the same afternoon tug in other people, too. Invisible lassos around their waists, pulling them into street-side pubs.

It was early evening when I arrived at Rubik's. I stood outside for a long time, working up the nerve to go in. Something here was different, and I knew it was probably me.

4

I ordered a drink and sat in a corner, in the booth that Catherine liked. I wanted to talk to her, and it was the only place we had in common where Zain Carver wouldn't be. I imagined he'd been doing the same thing I had since Sycamore Way. Lying low, getting his story straight. I'd stopped into Rubik's most days since, but no one had surfaced yet.

The tone of the place had shifted, though. Behavior was being tolerated, even encouraged, that wouldn't have been before. I had seen open drug use, simulated sex on the dance floors and men glassing each other. They were climbing up the walls. I didn't know if they were going through withdrawal or just using stuff they weren't used to.

I didn't want to know.

It was early evening and I was into my second drink when Catherine walked through the door. I wondered if she'd come here hoping to see me, but the slight inclination of her head when she glanced over said that she hadn't.

She gave a small smile, a small wave. I waited while she ordered, running through what I wanted to say, watching it fall flat in my mind's eye. Zain had told me that his girls didn't know I was a police officer, but Sarah Jane had worked it out somehow. I hoped Cath hadn't yet. I knew I should tell her myself. She looked subdued in comparison with her usual Rubik's getup. A leather jacket, black pencil skirt and brogues. Her brown hair, usually spilling out over her shoulders, was tied up on top of her head, with two red sticks stabbed through to hold it in place.

Until then she'd always been an idea in my head. A spark of life and a possible future. In the wake of Isabelle's death, in the wake of Sycamore Way, it scared me to think of her as a person. Vulnerable as the rest of us. As if to emphasize this, as she crossed the room toward me a man walked into her, hard, almost knocking her down.

"Hey," I shouted after him, walking to Catherine. I'd never seen him before but he had the same filthy look as the man Carver had head-butted at the Burnside. A Sider. His clothes were out of time, and he was older than most people in the room. Into his fifties, I thought.

"You OK?"

"Yeah, fine."

"Who was that?"

"I don't know," she said, looking after him. The man had crossed the room toward the exit, slamming the door as he went.

"Wait here."

"Aidan, please." She took my hand. "Can't we just sit down?" We walked back to the corner booth. Catherine saw me looking at her half-spilt drink.

"Sprite," she said. I nodded but didn't know what to say, didn't know how to acknowledge it. She saw that, too, and went on quickly. "It doesn't mean I'm—"

"I know."

"I just don't know what I'm doing yet . . ."

"How are you?"

"Good," she said, looking up and then down again. "Bad. Happy. Depressed."

"Four of the seven dwarfs."

"You really scared me that day at Isabelle's place."

"I know. I'm sorry. You scared me, too."

"I got that impression." She mock-punched me in the chest. "Never knocked up a stranger before?" Her arm was half across the table now and our little fingers brushed against each other.

"Actually, no."

"Worth it if you're getting too much sleep at night."

"With your help I'm cutting it out entirely."

She shifted in her seat. "Do you need help, Aidan?"

"How do you mean?"

"Are you in trouble?"

"What makes you say that?"

"Everyone else I know is." She smiled. "Including me. You just appeared out of nowhere one day with a black eye. I don't know anything about you . . ."

"What do you want to know?"

"Am I just something that gets you closer to Zain Carver?"

"I don't care if I never see him again."

She looked surprised. "And what about me?"

"I hope this isn't the last time we talk. We didn't have a conventional start. We probably wouldn't have a conventional relationship. I'd like to try it, though, if you would."

"Don't you want to know anything about me?"

"I'll take it as it comes."

She looked even more surprised. "And tell me what you think about all this, really?" She was talking about the pregnancy.

"I think that, whatever you decide, I'm with you. It's where I want to be."

She moved her little finger over mine, squeezed it lightly. "Actually never heard that one before."

"I wanted to get in touch sooner. I didn't have your number, though. I couldn't go to Zain's after Sycamore Way, and—"

"Sycamore Way," she said. Those words held so much power now that the room seemed to darken with them. Seven of the teenagers had died. "What happened?"

"I don't know. I left Isabelle alone in Zain's study. I think she stole the dirty brick. Then there was a whole day between me leaving her in the flat and finding her dead. I think she sold most of the stuff on and kept a sliver for herself. She used it. Those rich kids from West Dids used it."

"Zain said you were there when he found them?" I nodded. "Were they the same as Isabelle? As bad?"

"I think they all went peacefully," I said. There seemed little point in telling her the truth. She seemed relieved. "Has Zain said anything?"

She looked up. "Like what?"

"Like what went wrong with that brick? Why people died?"

She shook her head. "The stuff's imported. Zain just cuts it. Everything else from that batch was fine."

"He's sure?"

"Tested it all after Sycamore Way."

"So whatever the brick was cut with is the problem?"

She nodded.

"And Zain said the cut was normal?"

"Like he meant it. Like he really meant it."

"Then someone spiked it." She frowned. "You saw what it did to Isabelle. That couldn't have been an accident."

"But why?"

"Zain must have more enemies than he can count. Think about who benefits from him going down." I thought about it myself. Superintendent Parrs had his zeal. David Rossiter had his secrets. Sheldon White had his grudge. Even Grip couldn't be counted out.

"Is that what'll happen? He'll go down?"

"I don't know. They'd have him in already if they could."

"I don't really want to be around when it happens . . ."

I squeezed her finger. "Where would you go?"

"London? Sometimes it's sad, being around all these things that are just . . ." she hesitated, "just ending." I realized then I was probably the last person she hoped to run into that day, that she had already decided about the baby.

"You sound like you're saying goodbye."

"Just don't get to know me." She looked away. "It'll be easier if you don't get to know me." There was always an edge of performance with Catherine, but when I think of her, when I think of the real her, I think of that night. Her hair up, that jacket, that skirt, that conflict. I felt the second drink working on me. Putting the beat back into the music, the shine back on every surface. I didn't know what she was thinking. I didn't know what she was trying to say. I never really got to know her.

5

I was sitting with my back to the main entrance, but saw Cath's eyes widen. Before I could turn, a man sat heavily beside her. The same man who had shoved her, over at the bar.

He smelled of motor oil.

The sight of him sitting by any girl, much less her, was offensive, nearly comical. He gave me the broad, ugly parody of a smile and put an arm round Catherine like she was nothing, working one finger beneath an exposed bra strap.

She hadn't been looking in his direction when her eyes widened, and I knew there was someone else standing behind me. I thought I even knew who it was. Her eyes were on mine now, with the same cornered expression I'd seen a week ago in Isabelle's room. The first man, still wrapped around her, cleared his throat:

"Why don't ya take a seat, Neil?"

I turned to see the barman I had run out of the place ten days earlier. Still running. Still using his fake name. I gripped my glass tightly. I wanted to break it in his fucking face.

He was wired. His barrel chest still heaved out in front of him but the designer stubble had grown all out of shape. Thick black bags hung beneath his eyes. He sat down beside me, sliding sideways, pushing me into the wall. It was an aggressive movement but I thought he'd just misjudged the space. He looked worn out, capsized by too many cocaine nights in a row.

I saw sparkling drops of moisture in my glass, smelled alcohol in the air, half-heard conversations around the table. Rubik's had got busy without me noticing. The room went on as normal, not knowing or caring about us. It was getting late and people were already deep into their evening drinks. I wondered how often I'd been drunk, oblivious, while something ugly happened in the same room.

"Should probably introduce meself," said the man with his arm round Catherine's shoulder. He wore his scowl like a mask. The kind that becomes permanent when you live a hard life. Here, now, he was at his most reasonable, but he couldn't quite pull off the expression. It gave his face a look of concentration that made him seem simpler than he probably was.

"Name's Sheldon White," he said, holding out his free hand for someone to shake. Neither Catherine nor I did. Glen, Neil, the ex-barman, sat beside me ripping up a beer mat.

"Good to meet you," I said. "Can you find him a gram of something? He's stressing me out."

Sheldon tried another smile. He must have seen one once, from a distance. "Y'already know Neil."

The barman came to attention at the sound of his fake name. "Yeah," he said, answering for me. He kept making quick, cokehead movements, his eyes following a fly the rest of us couldn't see.

"Now, I know you kids've got some history, but we're putting that to bed now." I didn't say anything. Catherine didn't say anything. "What's your poison, lad?"

I nodded at the fidgeting barman. "Whatever he's having."

Sheldon stopped smiling.

"Jameson's and soda," I said.

"Double?"

"At least."

"Think I'll join ya. And for the lady?" When Catherine didn't reply, he flicked her bra strap.

"Red," she said, looking at the wall. Sheldon heaved himself up. He was a big man, older than Zain Carver and going to ruin.

"Don't go anywhere," he said.

The room was bustling with people, and all I could see around the table were bodies jammed together. Sheldon pushed through them toward the bar. Once he'd disappeared I got to my feet, nodded at Catherine.

She didn't move.

The barman, still fidgeting, still blocking my way, didn't get up either. Instead, he showed me the hand that had been under the table.

The knife.

Through the crowd I saw blank, bored faces turned in our direction. I thought I recognized the two goons that Carver and I had seen at the Burnside. Others, similar in size and leers, were all around us. I sat back down, tried not to think about it.

I looked at Glen, Neil, whatever. "Was it you I saw outside my flat?"

He didn't answer directly but the pressure of the knife against my stomach said it all.

"You don't need that," said Catherine.

"Truth serum, innit. You should've stayed away from him."

Her eyes moved onto mine for a second. "Why?"

"Tell her why, Aid."

"I don't know what you're talking about."

"Doesn't know which lie he's been caught in. Let's start with what happened to Izzy."

"She was dosed with bad Eight."

"By who?"

"By herself or someone else."

"You took her home that night, dint ya? Where were you when all this happened?"

"My flat. Where were you?" He pressed the knife into me. I thought it had gone through my shirt.

"That's not how this works."

"I found her the next day. I called the police. Why would I have gone back if I killed her?" As I explained myself, I tried to think: the barman's emotional state meant he probably had nothing to do with Isabelle's death. He sounded as confused as I was.

"You might've stayed the night. Or just gone back to clean up."

"He was with me," said Catherine. "We found her together, I swear. I swear on my life." I thought her hand went to her stomach. "And I think it's a fair question to ask where you were, Neil." I could feel the knife pressing into the skin of my stomach.

"Fair question." He laughed. "Was with Mel."

"Mel?"

He nodded across the room at the Australian barmaid. "Aid flushed a few grand of coke. Left me to hang for it." He spat out the words. "Knew I couldn't stay at mine, so she put me up."

"Why would Aidan—"

"It's true," I said.

"What . . . ?"

169

"I was trying to look out for Isabelle . . ."

"Bull*shit*," said the barman. "Looking out for your fucking self. Your kind always do."

"What do you mean, his kind?" said Catherine.

"Tell her, Aid." I felt the knife slip into my skin.

"I'm a detective," I said. For a second her eyes moved onto mine, then back at the wall again. All the color went from her face and I thought she was going to be sick. The barman watched closely.

"Surprise, surprise, you didn't know. Aid sets me up and takes Izzy home. Next day, she's dead. Then them Sycamore Way kids. Then Zain in the shit for it all. Think about it," he said. "They all separate things or one fucking big one?" Catherine's eyes came onto mine again, lingering longer this time.

"Who's he?" she said, nodding at the empty seat beside her.

"Sheldon White?" said the barman. "Old school Burnsider."

She closed her eyes.

"Not like I had a choice, was it?" he went on. "And I wasn't gonna walk out on this prick." He pressed the knife into me again. This time, I could feel the blood seeping into my shirt. "Told the Siders I could set 'em up in here while Zain gets back on his feet. Played 'em . . ."

His hands had started to shake and he looked down at them. There was no need to interrupt, to say that it was him who had been played. It was all there, exposed, in his own version of events.

I wondered if he'd been fed more than cocaine, though. Scared, stupid and running for his life, the Siders had probably looked like a good bet. Some protection while he worked out what to do next. Then they'd just strung him out on drugs for days and gleaned every detail they could about the Franchise's trade.

I thought, bitterly, about flushing the drugs. I could have had him arrested, but I'd had my revenge instead.

"Gotta do what ya gotta do," he said vaguely. "Zain understands that." We sat in silence until Sheldon reappeared with the drinks. Four glasses in two giant, tattooed hands.

"Don't stop on my account, kids," he said, sliding the glasses onto the table and slumping down beside Catherine. He put one hand back around her shoulder and drank with the other. "Name's Cath, innit?"

She nodded. She seemed suddenly very young.

The man looked at me. "And you are?"

"Aidan," I said.

"Right, right, Aidan Waits. Live off Newton Street."

I glared at the barman. "It's no secret. Are we neighbors?"

"Nah, mate, I wish. I'm farther out than that. Round Burnside way."

"Nice place."

"That's right. You an' Zain paid us a visit the other week."

"Kept hearing such good things."

His forehead creased into an ugly, tectonic frown. "You fuckin' gob like that to him," he said, nodding at the barman. "Gob like that to Carver. Gob like that to this bitch, if you want. But don't gob like that to me. Clear?" I nodded. "Yeah, Burnside's a nice place. Untapped, let's say. Bit like here, tonight."

We waited.

"All these people," he said, looking around us. "All this money, all this gash." He breathed it in. "Just cryin' out for a bit of oblivion. And no one selling it? That's criminal."

"Zain's selling it," said Catherine.

"Used to, darlin'," said Sheldon. "Think we can all agree the golden age is over, though." The barman nodded, like he was thinking deeply about it. I think it was dawning on him what he'd done. "His taste in skirt hasn't changed, though, has it, sweetheart?" Catherine didn't say anything. "You might be his best yet."

"I work for him."

He laughed in my direction. "That's how it starts, though, eh, Aid? That other tart just worked for him, too." Catherine didn't say anything, and he kept on pushing. "What was her name again?"

I didn't know if it was out of fear or loyalty, but Catherine's voice broke. "Her name was Joanna," she said.

"Jo-anna," repeated White. "That's the one. Before your time, though, surely?"

"I never met her," Catherine said quietly.

White looked at me. "Slag's buried in cement, somewhere. Not much of a retirement scheme, eh?"

"Fuck you," said Catherine.

"What's that, sweetheart?"

She turned and said it to his face.

I gripped my glass tighter. I thought he was going to hit her. From the look in her eyes I think she did, too. I saw the massed faces in the crowd, watching us. It felt like the hinge of the entire conversation, the entire night.

"You wanted to talk to us about something," I said. "I'm guessing it wasn't the past."

"Look at that," said Sheldon, smiling. "Aid couldn't give a shit about the he-said, she-said. Straight to business. Good stuff."

"I just want to get on with my night."

"So you fucking shall, mate, so you fucking shall. I wanna borrow you for a bit first."

"What for?"

"Call it peacekeeping."

I waited.

"Can't just rock up here without letting Carver know about it, can I? This is his place, after all. You can put something to him for me. An opportunity. Way Neil tells it, the Franchise runs from Rubik's these days. Stuff comes here, gets sold here, gets farmed out to other places. That's right, innit?" The barman nodded down at the table. "But with Zain's rep in the shitter and Neil here on the lam, everything's stopped."

"And you can get it restarted."

His fingers pressed into Catherine's shoulder.

"I can keep it warm for him, yeah." I shook my head and he went on. "That's not the offer. Want ya to tell him I'm prepared to pay." He smirked. There was thick, shining sweat on his upper lip. "One percent of all profits."

"There's only one way he'll take that."

"Lying down," said Sheldon. "He's fucked six ways from Sunday. Hasn't got a choice."

"He's got his pride, though. I can put it to him that you sell here, but that's humiliation enough. You offer him one percent and his ego won't let him take it. You get a war instead." Sheldon looked bored. "He hasn't got a lot left to lose," I said. "Offer ten and he can call it a business decision. Swallow it with his pride."

He sucked his teeth, pretended to think about it.

"Might have something there, Aid." He scrutinized me. "I'll go five."

"Is that what all this has been about?"

"All what?"

"The black and white paint at Carver's house, for a start."

Sheldon frowned, laughed. "Paint's nothin' to do with me, mate. Nice to know Zain's got some new enemies, though. An' imitation's the highest form of flattery."

I tried to recover. "And why would I be your message boy?"

The barman interrupted us, spoke to White. "You said I could tell Carver—"

"That was before we ran into Aid, though. Now I'm improvising." The barman looked at him, breathing heavily. His plan to explain himself was already in tatters.

White went on: "Y'interrupted me before, Aid. When I was talking about Joanna sod's-law. You said I wasn't here to talk about the past. You were wrong." His hand went to Catherine's breast, gripping it through her top. She closed her eyes. "Cath's gonna wait here with me while you explain it to Carver. Aren't you, Cath?"

She didn't say anything.

He pressed his thumb and forefinger through her top, squeezing her nipple. "Aren't you, Cath?"

"Yes," she said, opening her eyes.

I tried to remember everything. The sparkling drops of moisture on the table, the alcohol in the air, the half-heard conversations. The look on Catherine's face. She was staring off at the wall again now, but her eyes were filling. I wanted her to look at me, to trust me again, but I knew that she couldn't.

"Yer phone," said Sheldon.

I found it in my pocket and handed it to him. He nodded at the barman, who clumsily felt me for another. I saw a red circle of blood on my shirt where the knife had pierced my skin. Satisfied, he nodded back. Sheldon handed me a cheap burner.

"Can only call one number: mine. Carver just needs to say one of two words: *yes* or *no*." He took a drink and smacked his lips. "And if he's got a problem with it. If he doesn't agree to five percent. If I don't hear from him by ten o'clock. Cath goes missing." Small beads of sweat were sprouting about his face. "Y'interrupted me again, Aid. Never think you've got nothing to lose, mate. It'll be like she never fucking lived."

Catherine still wouldn't look at me and ten seconds later I was pushing through the crowd toward the exit. My mind was completely calm. Completely clear. Completely focused on Sheldon White and the barman. Just give me the chance, I thought. Give me the chance and I'll fucking kill them both.

6

Outside the hotbox of Rubik's I felt a blast of cold air. There were people on the street going in every direction, wearing winter coats, walking toward families, homes, beds. Two men followed me out of the club and I began walking away. I took out the phone that Sheldon had given me, dialed 999 and asked for the police.

"There's a girl being held against her will on the ground floor of Rubik's nightclub, off the Locks. Brunette, early twenties. In the company of two, possibly more, IC1 males. One is a Sheldon White, approximately fifty years old, form for ABH and drug offenses. One is Glen Smithson, thirties, form for date rape and drug offenses. Armed and dangerous. Armed and dangerous." When I was sure I'd woken the dispatcher up I ended the call.

I went back into the city, trying to dial Parrs, but the phone couldn't connect.

The taxis passing me were all carrying fares, going in the wrong direction. I waved at them anyway. Carver's house was an hour out of town on foot. Fifteen minutes by car. I looked at Sheldon's phone.

The fucker hadn't set the clock.

Two girls went by and I called after them for the time. They stared at me like I was drunk.

"Running late," I said, breathless.

Neither of them wore watches and one reached warily into her purse for her phone. I took a step back so she wouldn't think I was trying to steal it.

"Quarter to," she said.

"Ten?" She nodded.

I was already walking backward, away from them.

I heard the Christmas market congestion of St. Anne's Square before I saw it. Vibrant lights and festive decorations hung above hundreds of bespoke wooden stalls, makeshift bars and shops. The air was thick with the mingled smells of beer, mulled wine, hot dogs.

There was music. People everywhere I looked. Families with tired, food-stunned kids, workers from the surrounding offices, flirting teens on first dates. I forced myself through the wholesome push and pull of a few thousand people, all going in different directions.

Sheldon was staging a hostile takeover. The barman hadn't been wrong to join up the events of the last few weeks.

Isabelle's death.

Sycamore Way.

Carver held responsible.

"They all separate things or one fucking big one?"

It was hard to imagine the events as anything other than the buildup to this moment. There was more to the city, more to the Franchise, than Rubik's. But it was the flagship. And wired or not, the barman had handed the Burnsiders the keys. Offering Carver 5 percent was the real bitter pill. To him it would sound exactly as it was intended.

Like an insult.

All I could do was tell him the truth, or something close to it. Manipulate him with a mention of his precious bloody Joanna. Play on the same anger I'd seen at the Burnside, the same anger that made him almost kill a man for mentioning one of his girls. I couldn't let Catherine get hurt.

Before I got to the taxi rank, I saw a cab coming my way, *For Hire* sign lit. I ran into the road, through screaming traffic, and waved it down. The driver stopped and I gave him Zain Carver's address.

"Fifty quid if we're there in ten minutes."

7

ucky you could get a car tonight, mate."

"Why's that?"

"Massive fire, up Yarville Street. Something like twenty cabs up in smoke."

"When was this?"

"Last hour." Yarville Street was the headquarters for the Franchise's taxi firm. Another move from Sheldon White. I hoped that Carver hadn't heard about it yet.

"Listen, mate, can I borrow your phone? Tenner up front for one short call." He eyed me in the rearview mirror. "It's an emergency," I said, holding up the cash. He nodded and we made the exchange. I called Superintendent Parrs.

It went straight to voice mail.

"I'm blown," I said. "There's a girl in danger. Cath. Ground floor of Rubik's with Sheldon White against her will." I couldn't think of anything else to say. "Help her." I hung up and handed the phone back to the driver. He avoided eye contact and sped up, keen to get rid of me.

We pulled up about a hundred feet from Fairview. I looked at the clock on the dashboard: 21:56. I pushed all the notes from my wallet through the Perspex hatch and got out, running up the street toward the house. I went up the garden path and collided with the front door.

When no one came I kicked it. Kept kicking it, knocking, shouting, leaning on the bell, until the hallway light came on.

I stepped back, making sure Sarah Jane could see me through the peephole. When the door opened I went forward but was pushed back, hard, by Grip. Sarah Jane was standing behind him, arms wrapped round herself. Her bright red hair made her look pale. Sick and thin.

"I need to see Zain, now."

Grip filled the doorway. "The fuck's goin' on?"

"Siders have got Catherine." He took a step back, glanced over his shoulder at Sarah. "Zain talks to them by ten or she goes missing."

I had the burner in my hand. "There's one number on here. He just needs to call it and say yes."

"Yes to what?" said Grip.

"They know he can't move anything at the moment. They want to sell in Rubik's until the shit blows over."

"They've just torched his cars, he won't do it."

"Aidan—" said Sarah Jane.

"He can say yes now and go back on it later."

Grip stepped forward. "He won't do it."

"*Aidan,*" said Sarah Jane, stepping between us. "He's not here."

For a second the only sound was my breath.

"What time is it?" I said.

Sarah Jane looked at her watch.

"Two minutes past . . ."

"Where is she?" said Grip. But I had already turned and started walking away from the house. The phone was slippery in my hand. All I could think about was Catherine, not looking at me. Not trusting me at the end. I unlocked the keypad and opened the contacts.

One entry.

BOSS.

I walked farther from the house light, farther down the path, feeling invisible. I hovered over the call button.

Everything stopped.

I listened to the wind hissing through the trees for a second, and pressed call. It rang for a long time. More than a minute. Then *Click.*

"Yer late," said Sheldon.

"I got here on time. Carver's out."

"Fine."

"I can get to him in the hour—" The line went dead.

I looked down at the phone and saw that my hands were shaking. I could feel my lungs burning in my chest. I was suddenly sitting on the garden path, staring out at the trees. I thought I could see and hear people in them, wrapped around the branches, watching me.

8

called back, but the phone just rang out. When I dialed again, it went straight to voice mail. I listened to the message, the automated female voice, and waited for the beep. I didn't know what I'd say until I said it:

"He'll agree to one percent, call me back."

I hung up and sat there staring at the phone. I could feel the seconds disappearing for good. I tried not to think about how time was passing for Catherine.

I didn't want to go back to Rubik's in case Sheldon called, in case I needed to find Carver, but I was getting up when I heard the door slam behind me. Without that soft glow emanating from the house, the path was thrown into darkness. I turned and made out two shapes, Sarah Jane and Grip, coming toward me.

"What did you tell them?" said Sarah Jane.

"I said Zain wasn't here. They hung up."

"Call them back."

"Straight to voice mail. Where is he?"

"Out." She hesitated. "Where's Cath?"

"Rubik's, but I doubt they'll be there now."

"Let's see." She took her phone from her jacket pocket and called Catherine. We all waited. "Ringing," she said. I stepped closer and heard the tone cut off abruptly as someone sent the phone to voice mail.

"Rubik's," said Grip, walking past me, down the path.

"I'm coming with you."

"Nah, pal. You can find his fucking lordship and explain this shit. What were you doing with her anyway?"

"Talking."

"All you're fucking good for."

"Who had her?" said Sarah Jane.

"Sheldon White. He said I should mention Joanna Greenlaw's

179

name." No one spoke for a second. I couldn't see either of them clearly, but I thought they exchanged a look. "Who did you see outside my flat, Grip?"

He didn't say anything but I could hear him breathing.

"What's he talking about?" said Sarah Jane.

"Someone trashed my flat. Night of Sycamore Way. He saw who did it."

"I told you. Filth did your flat."

"Who was the man with the knife?" He didn't say anything. "I think it was Glen, or Neil, or whatever name your ex-bar manager goes under. He was with Sheldon tonight. He's been with him for a while. If we'd known earlier, we could have prevented this."

Grip was still just a shape, but when he sighed I saw his shoulders slump. "Find Zain," he said, and disappeared down the path. I looked back at Sarah Jane, the outline of her. I couldn't make out her features in the dark but I could see her red hair in the moonlight. I had the phone in my hand and when it went off we both started. The lit screen said:

BOSS CALLING.

I answered and held the phone in the space between us. Sarah Jane moved closer.

"One percent," said Sheldon, laughing.

"Fine."

"Got till ten thirty."

"Let me talk to her."

The line went dead again.

I looked at Sarah Jane. "What time is it?"

She lit up the screen on her phone.

"Ten past." She took my arm. "Come on, I think I know where he'll be."

9

We got to the bottom of the path, into the mild relief of street-lights. I saw her properly for the first time that night. She wore a fox fur over black jeans. It was the wrong side of November and I wondered if she'd taken my arm because she was cold. After a few feet I noticed she was actually limping. It had only been days since her taxi had been held up. I thought some of her confidence had gone with it. We went as fast as we could, heads down against the cold.

"I'm starting to wonder if we can ever have a crisis without you?" she said.

"Sounds like you had one on Friday night and I was nowhere near it." She didn't say anything for a minute, but sped up a little, tried to cover her limp. We reached the bottom of the road and turned into a complex of ugly newer builds. I thought I knew where we were going. When we passed men on the street I saw their eyes darting to Sarah Jane. She didn't notice or she didn't care.

"The cab was an accident."

"Like fuck it was. What's all this about?"

She didn't say anything.

"You and Zain were arguing on my second night at Fairview. Was it about this? Had it already started then?"

"We weren't arguing."

"You hit him. I didn't think you were the type."

She pulled her arm free. "Don't tell me what fucking type I am."

"Levelheaded. What's changed? Why are you walking with a limp?"

She stopped, looked at me. "We were talking about you, actually. That first night."

"Flattered."

"You shouldn't be."

"There was already a bad atmosphere at the house even then."

She started walking again. "I don't know anything about it."

"After that someone spiked the brick," I said to her back. "A house full of kids died. Isabelle died. Any ideas?"

"We're here," she said.

November was everywhere and it had wrapped the ugly gray building in fog. Like something half-remembered. The pockmarked, pebble-dashed walls looked acne-scarred, and industrial halogen lights burned out from behind anonymous windows. The converted office block where Isabelle Rossiter had died.

10

Sarah Jane led the way. Through the vacant lobby and up the stairs. She was three feet ahead of me, red hair trailing behind. Walking there in her wake, I could smell her perfume. It made me feel nostalgic for something. The way a familiar scent can stop you dead on the street, take you back through things you thought you'd forgotten. I couldn't place the memory, though.

Even then, walking with her, toward something, she gave the impression that she was completely separate from me. Like we'd never met before. She wasn't dismissive and she wasn't arrogant. There was just something that set her apart. I got the feeling that I'd never known her, I never would.

I didn't know what Carver would be doing here. I wondered if he'd bottomed out. Taken a room somewhere in the building to get away from it all. As we went farther up, past the first and second floors, I knew that we were going to Isabelle's old flat.

Sarah Jane turned onto the landing. The farther we went, the worse I felt. There was a broken police ribbon on the floor.

Do Not Cross.

Sarah Jane knocked and turned around. I was standing too close. She was backed up against the door, looking up at me. She put her hand very lightly on my chest. I stepped back and she took a key from her pocket. When she opened the door, I was half-expecting to see Isabelle still lying there.

Instead, warm air drifted out into the hallway, a sharp smell of sweat cutting through it. The room was dark, lit only by a lamp on the desk. Isabelle's studied anonymity had been replaced by chaos. I could see national newspapers, a couple of local rags, too. All turned to pages on Isabelle Rossiter, David Rossiter, Zain Carver and Sycamore Way. In pride of place, in the center of the floor, was the appeal for information about Joanna Greenlaw. Some pages had been circled, underlined.

Zain Carver, the criminal mastermind, was asleep in a swivel chair at the desk. His arms were wrapped around his body, and his legs were drawn up close. He looked like a vampire who'd gone a day without blood. I wanted to shake him awake.

Sarah Jane turned to me. "Wait here."

"We don't have time for—"

"We're fine," she said, stepping inside and closing the door. I couldn't stand still. It felt like my bones were itching under my skin. I heard murmurs, back and forth, between them, punctuated by Sarah Jane's raised voice.

A minute passed.

I glanced at the phone.

Nothing.

I looked down the hall at the other doors on the floor. Thought about the lives ticking away behind them. Another minute. Another.

I was ready to go in there and start shouting when Sarah Jane opened the door again. She closed it softly behind her and spoke quietly.

"He's troubleshooting everything we've got left." Her voice was shaking. "I think he's trying to kill himself . . ." She looked away, opened the door and led me inside. Carver was awake and stared across the room, right through me.

He didn't get up.

"Phone," he slurred. I handed it to him, felt how clammy his hand was. It was strange, seeing him that way. I actually felt disappointed. He brooded over the phone for a second then accessed the address book using his index finger. He blinked when the phone was immediately answered. I heard a voice from the other end. Carver sat there listening.

The voice stopped.

A few seconds went by and I felt Sarah Jane's eyes on mine. We looked at each other, neither daring to interrupt.

"Yes," said Carver.

11

Carver dropped the phone on the floor. Sarah Jane was walking toward him as I walked backward, out of the room. Neither of them looked up as I left. The bright, violent light bulbs on the landing buzzed overhead and I tripped down the stairs, holding on to the bannister. I ran across the lobby and banged through the double doors, back into the street.

The night was a flash of images.

There was no sequence of events and afterward I had no idea what order they came in. I remember it as being in twenty-five different places at once. I was on a main road, waving down cars. I was in a cab, I was back at Rubik's. It was gone midnight. The doors were closed and I was talking to the people outside. Interrupting conversations, asking if they'd seen Cath. I was round the back, checking the fire exits.

I was leaving the Locks, walking toward the city center. The clubs were still going strong. Long, loud queues snaked outside most.

Skin, laughter, perfume.

I had watched Franchise girls collecting in these clubs and I was talking to the people queuing up outside. I was talking to the doormen.

Don't know her, mate.

Don't know him, mate.

Don't think so, mate.

I was in a cab, on my way home. I was going through drawers, throwing things on the floor, looking for something.

I found my warrant card.

Took a handful of speed.

Left.

I was back in the city center. I was going by the queues again, looking for Cath, Sheldon, Grip, the barman.

Looking for anyone.

I was in an alleyway, smoothing down my clothes, getting my

breath back. I was rehearsing a smile. I lost track of which bars I had been by and did a second circuit. I was showing my warrant card to the doormen. I was watching them memorize my name.

They let me in. That roar of bass, voices, laughter. I was trying to remember Cath's favorite place in each. I was in the corners. I was shouting over the music. I was splitting up couples, trying to describe her. I was finding different street-side pubs and clubs as I went. It was around one in the morning and this time people looked at me differently. Their smiles were wary.

I saw them wondering who I was.

I was in the street. I was in a cab. I was outside Carver's, banging on the door. I was in the city. I was watching the queues dwindle down to nothing. I was in the clubs again. A man with an earpiece was talking to me, shouting over the music.

"Help you, mate?"

I was showing him my warrant card.

"I'm looking for a girl." He was nodding at the stools by the bar, where the music was a little quieter. We were sitting down, we were talking.

"Same from earlier?"

"Earlier?"

"One of your lot was in here earlier. After a brunette in a leather jacket with two older men."

"What'd he look like?"

"Didn't see him, mate."

"Who did?"

"Pat. On break."

"Get him for me." I realized I was standing up.

"I'll see if I can find him." He was walking into the crowd and I was looking around. The DJ was ending his set with slow songs, and people everywhere danced, kissed, wrapped themselves up in each other. The air was alcohol and energy drinks. Perfume and sex.

"You OK?" said the barmaid.

"Double vodka and Red Bull, thanks." She seemed confused for a second, and I realized that hadn't been what she was asking. Then she turned and started making the drink. I was washing down some more speed when the doorman came back through the crowd with a colleague.

"Someone was asking about a girl earlier. Tell me what he looked like."

He was confused, said something to his friend.

"What did he look like?" I repeated.

"It was you, mate."

I was standing outside Fairview in the pure, perfect darkness. The street was so still I felt like I was indoors. On a soundstage in some impossibly large building. I was in the street, I was in a cab, I was in the city, I was inside the clubs, outside them.

I was walking toward the Burnside. The cabbie wouldn't go all the way. I was at the warehouse, outside it, inside it. I was talking to the junkies, shaking them awake, talking at them about a pretty girl with brown hair.

12

Weak, gray, English daylight. I had reached Fairview an hour before but decided to wait until 8 a.m. before I started knocking. Sometimes speed has that effect on me. Imparts an odd respectability. I walked around the block a few times. Listened to the morning birdsong.

It had been raining lightly for the last couple of hours and my clothes were damp. I saw two girls walking to work, laughing, holding newspapers over their heads to keep dry. Their eyes scanned past me like I wasn't there.

I went with three medium knocks. I decided I'd wait a minute, then knock again. After another minute, I'd break a window in the back and let myself in. Sarah Jane opened the door almost straight away. Her red hair caught the daylight and made her skin look paler than usual. I saw a blanket and pillow on the stained-white hall chair. I wondered if she'd sat there all night.

"Catherine, Grip," she said. "They never came back."

13

I told Sarah Jane to call the police. Carver had passed out upstairs. Grip's phone had been switched off and no one had heard from him. I told her to report him and Catherine missing.

"I can wait here with you, if you like."

She looked at me with a kind of exhausted hate. "I'd really rather you didn't."

I left her standing there. When I got to the bottom of the path I heard her shout something, but didn't turn around. I was tired of hearing what people thought of me. I took a cab into town, toward Rubik's. Outside, I found a pay phone and called Superintendent Parrs again. By the third ring, I thought something was wrong. I held on until I was diverted to voice mail. Again. I waited a few minutes before calling back. This time the call went straight to voice mail.

"One of the girls is missing," I said.

It was around 10 a.m. when I got back to Rubik's. There were a handful of men already drinking but they kept to themselves and the room was quiet.

The cheerful Australian barmaid greeted me. "You're up early."

"I haven't been to bed yet."

"Long day already?" I nodded. "Well, what can I get you?"

I showed her my warrant card. "I have a few questions."

"Oh." She busied her hands. "Didn't realize you were a policeman."

"Nonpracticing. You worked last night?"

She had begun wiping down the spotless bar.

She hesitated.

"I don't care about the Eight. Cath—Catherine—a friend of mine's missing. She was here around ten. Works for Zain Carver. I'm sure you know her."

She put the rag down. "I know her. Served her last night, but didn't see her again after that. She OK?"

"What about the rest of the night? Anything unusual? Anyone?"

189

"I . . ."

"It's important and it goes no further. I need to find her."

She shrugged. "Cath was on the lemonade. That's unusual."

"Anything else?"

"Neil turned up out of the blue."

"The old bar manager . . ."

She nodded. "He looked awful."

"Did you talk to him?"

"You know Neil?"

"Yeah, he's a prick."

"Right. You don't really talk, just listen."

"Your name's Mel, isn't it?" She nodded. "Did you hear about Isabelle Rossiter?"

"That MP's kid?" Her hand went to her chest. "Awful."

"Neil told me he spent that night with you? This would have been Sunday, the fifteenth."

She blushed, nodded. "He was riled up about something. Stayed on the sofa."

"And he was there all night?"

"From closing time till ten, eleven the next morning." It occurred to her what I was asking. "Wait, he didn't have anything to do with it, did he?"

"Apparently not." I could hear the disappointment in my voice. The barman almost certainly hadn't slept with Isabelle on the night she died. Hadn't taken her phone. "Anything else happen last night? Anything at all?"

"Police came by. They'd had a report of some sort of disturbance. Couldn't see anything, though, so they left. Aside from that, there was just the usual fight outside. Saw an ambulance as we were locking up."

An ambulance.

"Last thing: were there any phones handed in last night? This morning, even?"

"Give us a sec?" She gave me a small complicated smile and disappeared into the back. She was gone for a couple of minutes and I looked at the old men, sitting in contemplation of their drinks. I thought back to the same time the previous day. The morning alarm, shower, shave and coffee. My meeting with Superintendent Parrs.

It felt like a month ago.

The barmaid came back with three phones, one of which was mine. I took it and checked the screen. No messages. No calls.

"Do you have a pen?" She found one and I wrote my number down on a napkin. "If Neil or Catherine come around, if anything happens that you're not comfortable with, please, give me a call. I promise you can do it in confidence."

"Sure," she said quietly.

14

I started calling hospitals. I introduced myself as a police officer and dealt directly with the local central trust. First I asked about DOAs. It had been a quiet night and the only instances were of elderly homeless people, freezing to death.

There were two living, unidentified arrivals that sounded more likely. One, a young woman, had been ambulanced to the Northern General before midnight.

Stab wounds to the abdominal area.

Defense marks on her hands and arms.

My heart dropped. In a separate incident, a man had been taken to the Royal Infirmary. He'd been badly beaten.

Grip and Catherine hadn't been together, and I could well believe they'd ended up in separate hospitals. The Royal Infirmary was closer but I went straight to the Northern General. The girl was stable and resting. In sleep, her hands had moved to cover her heavily stitched, bandaged torso. I wondered why she hadn't given her name to hospital staff, and why there was no one there for her.

She wasn't Catherine, and I left without disturbing her.

The Royal Infirmary is right in the center of the city. It was heaving with people feeling the effects of colds, flus and stomach bugs. There were also the ones who had put themselves there. They'd taken one drink or said one word too many.

I knew the feeling.

It was the same hospital I had been brought to after Isabelle died. I'd say it brought back bad memories, but they had never really gone away. I approached the front desk, showed my warrant card and made inquiries.

"Police?" said the clerk. "You look like you're about to check yourself in." I tried to smile.

I was worried about seeing other officers, particularly any who might recognize me, and declined his offer to be escorted to the injured man's room. When I arrived on the ward and spoke to a nurse, she showed me an empty bed. She was coming to the end of her shift, and talked about the man wearily.

"Wouldn't talk to us, wouldn't talk to your lot and walked out of here on a broken leg this morning. Some people don't bloody help themselves." I described Grip but she shook her head.

"This was a big lad. Looked like he was in the life. Coming down off something. Bags under his eyes, messy beard." Glen Smithson. Neil. The barman. Sheldon White had cut him loose. I'd missed him by an hour. I wanted to scream.

The nurse frowned. "If you don't mind me asking, are you all right, son?" I started to answer and then nodded. I thanked her and left.

15

Sheldon White was as good as his word. It felt like Catherine had never lived. And now he'd had full use out of the barman, he'd been cast aside as well. When I arrived back at my flat there was a car waiting. It was a Ford, dark blue, standing out in the No Parking zone. Before I could get to my door, two men climbed out and stood either side of me.

"Aidan Waits?" said one.

"I'm his cleaner. What's this about?"

The first man smirked. "Need to ask you a few questions, sir. We step inside?"

"Cards," I said. They dug into their pockets. The first man was waspish, tall and thin. He had that zealot stare of a drinker on the dry. In a white suit he'd have looked like an evangelical preacher. He had his card out before I finished asking for it, and I made a point of not looking.

His partner was heavyset with bloodshot eyes and hangdog features. He looked like the kind of man who might make up his own nickname. A robust notebook fell out of his jacket pocket and a wedding confetti of scrunched-up receipts fluttered to the ground. He fumbled with the papers at his feet. After a few seconds of this, at the exact moment he was about to show me his card, I turned abruptly.

"Don't worry about it," I said. I felt the look he gave me in the back of my head. I opened the door leading onto the narrow staircase. "Come in."

"You're not much of a cleaner," said the bigger man, looking round the flat. I had, at great length, straightened the room. Reset the lock on the door, swept up the shattered glass and thrown away the broken things that had littered the floor.

The gutted sofa still stood out, though.

The thin man closed the door behind him and turned to the room. He walked ahead of his partner, past me, stepping over the previous night's turned-out drawers, where I had frenziedly searched for my warrant card. Not mentioning them, their obvious disarray, was his way of telling me he'd acknowledged their significance.

"My name's Detective Sergeant Laskey," said the thin man.

"And I'm Detective Constable Riggs," said the larger.

I took the double meaning of their arrival. To cut my personal ties with the Superintendent, and to show Catherine's lack of importance to the bigger picture. To put me in my place.

"Parrs sent you?"

They exchanged mystified looks.

"About the girl?"

"What girl would that be?" said Laskey, folding his arms. His partner, Riggs, took the fat notebook from his jacket pocket and began idly flicking through it.

"The missing one," I said.

Riggs licked his index finger, found a page and read aloud: "Brunette in her early twenties, wearing a leather jacket and pencil skirt, in the company of two older men." He looked up at me. "That girl?"

Laskey took over. "No problem if your memory's a bit fuzzy, Waits. We've got five or six doormen from the Locks to the city center who were carded by you last night. One of them even remembered you'd been done for stealing drugs." So they hadn't been put in the picture.

"I haven't been done yet."

"Close enough."

"Drink?" I said.

"Bit early for me, thanks. Bloke was wondering why a suspended police officer's running around town at gone midnight looking for a missing girl? Interesting question."

I didn't offer anything to Riggs, but went to the fridge and found a cold beer. It was still before eleven and Laskey made a face. I made sure it foamed slightly when I opened it and took a good long pull, more to annoy him than anything.

I looked up. "You were saying . . ."

"No, *you* were saying. Why a suspended police officer—awaiting a corruption trial, no less—used his warrant card to question people about a missing girl."

"A missing girl," I said. "Did you come here to answer your own questions?"

"Why didn't you report her missing?"

"I did. It's complicated."

"So uncomplicate it for us," said Riggs.

"She was reported missing by her friend this morning. My connection to her's tentative."

"Explain."

"Tentative means something isn't quite certain or confirmed."

He slow-clapped me. "How do you know this girl?"

"Through an old case." I looked at him. "A case is a situation you get assigned to and then try to resolve." He stared back at me for a second, then walked to the other side of the room and leaned against the wall with his fists in his pockets.

I spoke to Laskey. He was so thin it looked as though daylight might pass straight through him. "The person in charge of that case was Superintendent Parrs, so I reported it to him. Last night."

"And what did he say?"

"I haven't heard back. I guess the two of you are what he says."

"We're just here for your warrant card, mate."

I think I actually laughed.

"We can do this the easy way or—"

"Please," I said, crouching to the drawers pulled out on the floor. I sifted through some paperwork until I found what I was looking for. The suspension notice that Parrs had issued as part of my cover and the receipt stapled to it. The receipt covered items I had handed back to the police until such time that I could be trusted with them again. It stated that I had handed back my card, although I hadn't. I walked past Laskey and handed it to his partner. It was the most irritating thing I could think of at the time. He read the receipt then handed it to his colleague. Laskey read it then looked back at me.

"When's the trial?"

"I thought it had started already . . ."

"Y'know, this could be a lot more serious. We could've come down here and kicked your fucking head in. Still might do. Card or not, you've been up to something. This girl, who is she?"

"I don't know her surname."

"Address?"

When I told them they looked at each other.

"That's Zain Carver," said Riggs.

"Yeah," I said, sitting on the gutted sofa.

"And she *has* been officially reported missing?"

"This morning. By a girl living at that address. She'll have reported a man missing as well. He went searching for her last night and didn't come back."

"What's his story?"

"Danny Gripe," I said. "Grip to his friends. Franchise muscle. You're looking for a fourth- or fifth-generation Mustang hatchback. Black with thin red stripes."

"License?"

"She'll have given that, too."

"Do you know anything that might lead us to their whereabouts?"

"Catherine was last seen in Rubik's with Sheldon White."

"Sheldon White?" Laskey recognized the name. "Rubik's is Franchise, though."

"It changed ownership yesterday."

Frowns all round.

"Sounds like you had a long night," said Laskey. "She in trouble?"

"Speak to Parrs," I said.

"What are you doing with Zain Carver, mate? Sheldon White? Is that how you got caught with your hand in the till?"

"Yeah. You've blown this one wide open. I told you, I know her from an old case. I don't have to tell you that the Franchise is falling apart and things are changing fast. If you've got any sense, you'll take this to Parrs and tell him it's connected."

Neither of them said anything for a minute.

"Sure," said Riggs eventually. "That's what we'll do." He gave me a beaming liar's smile and they left the room.

I went to the window and watched them get into their car. Laskey said something that made his partner laugh. I saw his jowls shaking. Once the car pulled away, the street was quiet. The flat was quiet. When I tried to call Superintendent Parrs again, his phone didn't even ring.

16

The next day I read that Zain Carver had been arrested. The newspapers linked him with the death of Isabelle Rossiter. They linked him with Sycamore Way. I tried not to think about who they should have arrested instead. The only silver lining was that it had happened on a weekday, not during one of the parties. Perhaps I'd got through to Parrs after all.

I needed to speak to the barman. He'd been with Catherine before she went missing and been turned loose by Sheldon White since. I went to his last-known address: an ugly, modern tower block that had been built in the city center with some fanfare during the property boom. It had promised affordable penthouse-style suites, but the funding fell through and the project was abandoned for a few years. It was finished with tighter budgets, lower expectations and smaller, cheaper rooms.

I didn't hold out much hope that he'd be there. He had lived alone, about halfway up the building. I carded a bored-looking security guard for access.

The room had the stale smell of a cheap, lonely life. It reminded me of my own. It had been cleared out in a hurry, with plenty of clothes and personal effects left behind. I found some crumpled drinks receipts in the pockets of a discarded pair of trousers. He'd recently been drinking in a club called the Wiggle Room.

As I was leaving, the security guard called over. "Find anything this time?"

"This time?"

"One of your lot's been out already." I could see he was bored out of his mind and more than willing to talk.

"When was this?"

"Let me see," he said, rubbing his chin. "Must be at least a week." An alarm bell was going off in my head. As far as I knew, the barman had never been reported missing. At least, not to the police. I remembered driving with Zain Carver, though, the night of Sycamore Way. He'd told Grip to put the whole Franchise on the search for Glen Smithson. I wondered if that included his man on the force.

"Was this a uniformed officer or plainclothes?"

"Plainclothes," said the man. "Plain bloody rude, if you ask me. Was late when he came. Barked at me to open the door. Was in and out in five minutes."

"Did he give you his name?"

"Not as I can remember."

"What did he look like?"

"Like I say, plain. Taller than you."

"My build?"

"Near enough."

Terrific. "Do you have CCTV here?"

"We do, but . . ." He thought about it. "This was the Monday before last. Will have taped over by now. Why do you ask?"

"There's a bug in the software at dispatch," I lied. "It's been assigning multiple people to the same jobs. Sounds like this other bloke's one step ahead of me, so it'd be good to get one of us reassigned. Not waste the manpower." I hoped a *Daily Mail* scare story would bring him on board.

"Well," he said. "He might have left a number to get him on . . ."

The man searched through the assorted papers at his desk and found what he was looking for: a Post-it note with a mobile number scrawled across it. I copied the number into my phone, thanked the man and left. Out on the street, I saved the number into my mobile as: Franchise Man. I found a phone box and dialed. It rang out.

After putting it off for as long as possible, I made the drive north, out to the Burnside. It was dark when I got there, but I had no trouble finding the warehouse. Nothing inside had changed, but when I was halfway around I heard a banging sound coming from the entrance. I walked back out to see one of the Siders who'd confronted me and Carver repeatedly hitting the roof of my car with a brick. He didn't seem to notice me, just dispassionately carried on making dents in the bodywork. He looked like he was working on an assembly line. I got in, started up and drove away while he was still doing it. That only left one stone unturned.

17

The Greenlaw house was a remote, dilapidated terrace on an abandoned street in old Salford. Ten years before, Joanna Greenlaw had walked out the door and disappeared. The house had stood empty ever since.

Dull sheet metal covered what would have been windows. The small patch of wasteland outside was unrecognizable as a garden. Under the weight of pollution and rain, the weeds had turned black, and rusting beer cans mingled with the grass like they were growing right out of the ground.

Rain had been coming down all day and the bricks, boards and weeds were all soaked through. I thought there was graffiti on the metallic sheets at first, but when I got closer I saw they were just spray-painted warnings to deter trespassers.

I had brought a crowbar to force the door with, but saw that someone had beaten me to it. The heavy lock that had held it shut had been dismantled and replaced with a makeshift wire latch. I looked down the row of houses. The others, as far as the eye could see, all had intact locks. I prized the wire apart and pushed the door open. It stopped unnaturally, mid-arc. The carpet beneath it was swollen with damp.

I shone a torch down a dark, simple hallway. There was a staircase and two doorways leading off to separate rooms. The wallpaper was peeling, and the ceiling was alive with fungi and rot. I pulled the door to behind me and went inside.

Greenlaw hadn't spent much time at the house, but it was difficult to separate her image from the ruin. She had been twenty-six when she went missing, a little older than Cath. I knew I was looking for a feeling more than anything tangible and, even though the place had been empty for a decade, I found it.

Distilled fear.

I shone the torch straight ahead, into what was left of a kitchen. There were windows, but they'd been boarded up, too. The furniture had been removed, there was a gap where an oven would have been once, and space for a fridge. There was a closed door on the left, leading to what I thought was a pantry. I held my breath and quietly crossed the room. The door opened to empty shelves.

I left the kitchen and turned into the other ground-floor room. It was a small lounge, again with the windows boarded up. I could only see what was lit up by the torch, and it gave me the feeling that, to the left and right of the beam, there were people watching me. That they stepped smoothly out of the torch's path when I moved it.

It took me a moment to remember where I had seen the room before.

The *Evening News* piece.

POLICE APPEAL FOR INFORMATION ON GREENLAW DISAPPEARANCE

I could hear myself breathing. The paper had printed a picture of Greenlaw, standing by a fireplace, in this room. I wondered who'd taken it. If it had been Superintendent Parrs. His story about working closely with Greenlaw didn't explain his obsession, his drive to force a reaction out of Zain Carver. I wondered if there had been something between them.

I went back into the hall, up the stairs. I expected them to creak under my weight, but they were so damp that they just flexed. The windows upstairs were covered with the same sheet metal as on the ground floor and there was no light aside from my torch. There was a filthy, broken-down bathroom at the top of the stairs. Along the landing there were two doorways leading into bedrooms not much bigger than prison cells.

One was empty.

In the second I saw a sleeping bag. There were melted-down candles, some paperbacks and food scraps. I kept my eyes on the door every second I was in there.

When I walked down the stairs, back to the front door, I turned and shone the torch around madly, trying to catch out some imagined watcher. I walked outside, down the path and back to my car quickly. I felt like I wasn't alone.

18

Parrs was a wall. Isabelle was dead. Catherine and Grip had disappeared. Even Zain Carver was under arrest. The world was suddenly smaller. Emptier. The days reclined and stretched out endlessly in front of me. I tried to wean myself off the speed, but it didn't work. I quickly went back to one pill a day. I thought that would help me stay off them in the long run. And if one was helping, it only made sense to take two, three, four. After that I lost track again and the days became a blur. My mind raced, made connections that weren't really there.

"*Think about it,*" the barman had said. Joanna Greenlaw. The Franchise. An MP's daughter involved with them. The spiked drugs that killed her. The spiked drugs that were stolen from Carver and made it to Sycamore Way. Sheldon White's bid for Rubik's. Cath's disappearance. Grip's disappearance. Black and white paint somewhere at the edge of it all. "*They all separate things or one fucking big one?*"

I started to sink down into another possible life. It was 6 p.m. The point of no return. Whenever I stayed in Rubik's later than that, I was always the last to leave. The bar was an open secret, and it was easy to get hold of uppers for the mornings and downers for the nights. Sometimes I confused my uppers and my downers, but then sometimes I confused my days and my nights. Everything bled into everything else. I hoped Catherine might walk in again one day, and everything would come back around.

She never did, though.

I was sitting in my usual seat. Clear view of the window, clear view of the bar. Mel, the Australian barmaid, was starting her shift. She walked in with a small bouquet of flowers, and I arrived at the bar at the same time she did. She filled a pint glass with tap water and put the flowers in them.

"Y'shouldn't have, darling," said a man sitting at the bar. He was a regular. The same man who had tried to proposition Isabelle the night before she died. He came here every day. I knew that now because so did I. I'd even heard him talking about Isabelle Rossiter and Sycamore Way. He'd shaken his head with the best of them and said something about the country going to pot.

He nodded at the flowers. "For me?"

The barmaid smiled. "'Fraid not. Just need something to cheer up my room."

"Pretty girl like you," he said. "Shouldn't be buying yer own flowers. Or cheering up yer own room."

"Oh, I don't mind." She acknowledged me with wide eyes. "Yes?"

"Jameson's and soda," I said. "Thanks."

The man gave me a look. "What d'you think, son?"

"I don't know, I try not to."

"This girl's buying her own flowers. Was just sayin', she wants a man in her life." I paid for my drink and went back to my seat. "Miserable sod," he said.

I was halfway through my drink when the barmaid came over, collecting glasses. She smiled. She'd never asked me about Catherine or referred to the morning I came here looking for her. It must have been clear by now that I had nowhere else to be.

As she went round the room I saw the man at the bar, watching her. When she disappeared round a corner, he leaned over the bar and took her flowers. He couldn't quite reach and broke some of them as he did it. Then he smoothed them down, shook the water off the stems and held them low so she wouldn't see them on her way back.

She came back with a full crate of empties and lifted them onto the bar. The man watched as she unloaded the glasses into the dishwasher. Between that and a few customers, it was a few minutes before she noticed her vase had been upended. She looked around, confused, then turned to the people sitting nearby.

The man produced her flowers.

Presented them to her like a lover.

When she didn't take them, he shook the flowers in her face. She reached her hand out, but he didn't let go. Just looked at her, smiling. After a couple of seconds, he relinquished them and she turned away. She filled another pint glass, put the ruined flowers into it. She stayed like that for a moment, her back to the customers.

A couple of them were waiting and when one called her she turned to serve him with a tight smile. Even the man at the bar noticed the change and tried to imply an apology with his posture. The next time he bought a drink, the barmaid served him with a marked minimum of conversation, and he made a show of tipping her.

"Thanks," she said. He downed his pint in one or two swallows, then pushed away from the bar and went to the toilet. He only came back into the main room to get his jacket and leave.

A few minutes later he was walking away from the Locks, in the opposite direction of the city. He weaved slightly on his feet but otherwise seemed stable. Within sight of the tramline, he paused. I thought he might turn round, but I carried on walking toward him. He looked about, squinting into an alleyway on his right. Then he walked down it, already unzipping his fly.

When I turned into the alley, he was about halfway along it, ten feet or so away. It was dark but I could see him leaning on a wall, pissing in the opposite direction. He didn't hear me walking toward him, and I don't think he saw me, either. When I knocked him down, his piss went haywire in the air, all over his trousers. Then I kicked him as hard as I could, again and again and again and again, until my legs, feet and ankles ached.

I went back to Rubik's, drank gin and tonics until I couldn't speak. The last thing I remember is the lime rind floating up through my glass, like a glowing green lunatic grin.

19

I woke up, against all odds, facedown in a bed. My head felt like a Russian doll. Like I had six skulls, each smaller than the last, placed one inside the other. When I moved or thought too deeply, they rattled together, and it was a long time before I could roll over and open my eyes.

When I did I started. There were two men standing over the bed. Laskey and Riggs. The room was dark but what light there was still seemed to pass straight through Laskey's translucent skin. Riggs was plainly hungover. I didn't want to know how I looked to them. They both smiled and Laskey threw a shirt at me.

"Rise and shine, handsome."

My voice was gone. "You can't just walk in here."

"Door was wide open, mate." It was believable. I didn't remember getting home. "We'll just wait in the lounge, eh?" They went through. Slowly, I got up, got dressed and followed them. They were walking round the flat, examining anything that was out in the open, picking at the gutted sofa. They turned to me and smiled, but neither spoke.

"Cath," I said. They heard the shake in my voice. More fear than hangover. "You've found something . . ."

"There's nothing to find," said Laskey. "We should do you for wasting police time."

"What do you mean?"

"You last saw her in Rubik's," he said. "That right?"

"Yeah."

"In the company of one Sheldon White?"

"Yeah . . ."

"Well, she left with him, of her own free will."

"What?"

He stifled a yawn. "She was seen."

"By who? What does Parrs say?"

Riggs cut in. "*We're* what he says."

205

"You were wound up enough to risk jail time, though," said the thin man. "Why?"

"She's connected with Zain Carver."

"Tell us about him."

"I don't know much."

"Not what we hear."

"Catherine," I said. "Please, tell me."

"What makes you think we're here about her?"

I didn't say anything.

"Where were you on Friday afternoon?" They were standing either side of me. Laskey moved so the light from the window would shine into my eyes.

"What day is it?"

They both laughed and Riggs shook his head. "What fucking *day* is it?"

"We should all get ourselves suspended," said Laskey. He looked at me. "It's Sunday, mate. November twenty-ninth. Where were you on Friday afternoon?"

"Rubik's. Yesterday, too."

"Ah," said Laskey to his partner. "Can't be him, then."

"Y'win some, y'lose some," said Riggs. "Sorry to have wasted your time." They both turned and started walking toward the door.

"S'pose someone could confirm that?" said Laskey, over his shoulder.

"Bar staff. Half a dozen drunks . . ."

"Thing is," he said, turning around, "one of those drunks was having a quiet pint in Rubik's on Friday."

"So?"

Riggs went on: "So he left after six and some bastard kicked his head in."

Laskey smiled. "Just going for his tram."

"Like I said, I was in Rubik's."

"Was only down the road. You were seen leaving soon after him."

"It's open-and-shut, then."

"What it is," said Riggs, stepping toward me, "is circumstantial."

"But sometimes we believe in circumstantial," said Laskey. "There are worse things than the law, Waits."

I just looked at him. "Such as?" He didn't answer. "Get back to me when you can prove something. Otherwise, you know where the door is. Apparently it's open." I turned and walked back into the bedroom. I sat down, feeling sick. After a couple of minutes I heard footsteps, heading out. The change rattling in their pockets.

"We'll leave this as we found it," shouted Riggs, kicking the door for effect. I went to the window and watched them get into their car again. I walked to the front door, closed it and locked it. Then I went back to bed and tried to forget everything.

It didn't work.

Joanna Greenlaw. Isabelle Rossiter. Catherine, Sarah Jane. I'd pushed them to the back of my mind but they wouldn't stay there. I saw them laughing, frowning, dying. I got up, went to the bathroom and found a bag of speed. I flushed it down the toilet, then went through to the gutted sofa and sat down. I forced myself to think.

IV

STILL

1

I set my alarm for 7 a.m. but was already awake, watching the time pass, when it went off. Monday. The last day of November. I got up, shaved, showered and dressed. I found a black suit and ironed a white shirt. I found a slim black tie, put it on and looked in the mirror for the first time in days.

If only I could iron that face.

Weeks of long nights and bad living had darkened it, and my eyes were smaller, sharper. I shined my shoes, took a breath and walked outside. It was just above freezing, the kind of weather that makes you think the planet's trying to shake us off.

There was a car parked on the other side of the road. That BMW, all gleaming black paint and chrome. I walked in the opposite direction. The car started. I heard gravel crunching beneath tires as it pulled alongside me, matching my pace.

I stopped.

The driver pulled up to the curb, left the engine running. The window buzzed down and Detective Kernick leaned one arm out through the frame. He was dressed, like me, in a smart black suit. I don't know if it was the shock of morning light or the stress he'd been through lately, but his gray hair looked a shade lighter.

"Don't do it, son," he said. I could see his breath in the air.

"Do what?"

"Don't go out there this morning."

I didn't say anything.

"Look, I'm sure you've the best intentions. I'm sure it's hard. But I have to think about the Rossiters today. They don't want you there. Hard enough for them as it is . . ." I carried on walking. He started the car again and drove alongside me for a minute. "You look awful." He sighed. "Don't let it ruin your life."

I didn't turn, but heard the window go up again. He drove ahead to the end of the road and indicated. I waited until he'd turned the corner, then went on.

I'd read about Isabelle's funeral a few days before, in a newspaper that had been left lying around Rubik's. Although it was set to be a private ceremony, held in Gorton Monastery, mourners would be allowed on the grounds to watch the procession and lay tributes. It might be interesting to see who turned up, but it wasn't my intention to go there. The funeral just presented an opportunity.

I walked at a pace, running things through my mind. I needed to know who'd taken Isabelle's phone from her flat. Her father had provided police with the number to her old phone, the one found taped to the bottom of a drawer, but I'd heard him leave a message on her new one. If he knew about the new phone, why hadn't he mentioned it? Why hadn't he passed that number on to the police as well? And how had he got the number in the first place? Most of all, I needed to know if he'd taken the phone from her room after she died. I needed to know why it had gone missing, what was on it.

I arrived at Beetham Tower before 9 a.m. There was a group of disheveled men in tuxedos, just walking in from a night on the town. The funeral was due to start in half an hour, so I was sure that both Rossiter and Kernick would be on their way to the monastery. I crossed the road to a bank of pay phones, found a clean one and dialed 999.

"Police," I said. "I'd like to report a break-in."

2

walked into the lobby of the tower and approached the front desk. I
was pleased to see the same young woman who'd been on duty for
my previous visits, when I had been in the company of Detective Kernick. She gave me a perfect white smile.

"Good morning, sir. How can I help?"

"Morning," I said, handing over my warrant card. "Detective Constable Waits, I'm not sure we've met before?"

"Oh," she said. "Might I have seen you with Mr.—" she corrected
herself with a smile, "Detective Kernick?"

"You might have, I'm on Mr. Rossiter's security detail."

She read my card before returning it.

"Such a shame about his girl . . ."

"Sadly the press haven't been so sensitive. I'm sure you know the
funeral's this morning?"

She nodded. "I believe Mr. Rossiter's at the family home this
week . . ."

"He is. I actually just came from there. Our only concern is that
some members of the press might find their way here. Harass guests,
staff, neighbors for quotes. I've been asked to post myself in the lobby
and politely move any lurkers along."

"Of course," she said. "Do you mind if I refer you to building security?"

"That was going to be my next question. I don't think I've met
Mr. . . ."

"Reed," she said.

"If you could give him a call, that'd be great."

I moved away from the desk so that she could explain the situation. The man who appeared a few minutes later had the look of an
ex-police officer. A bulky, no-nonsense gait and searching, observant
eyes. From ten or so people standing around the lobby, he identified
me immediately as the person he was looking for.

"Mr. Reed," I said, as though Detective Kernick had told me all about him. "Detective Constable Waits." We shook hands. "Do you have a minute?"

"Course," he said, nodding us toward two chairs on the right of the lobby. "I believe you're on Mr. Rossiter's security detail?"

I handed him my warrant card. "Seconded to it while the death of his daughter's investigated."

"Hm," he said, looking at my card. "Bloody shame."

"Your colleague told you why I was here . . . ?"

"Press," he said. "Bloody parasites sometimes."

"You were on the force yourself, weren't you?"

He drew himself up. "Ten years."

"Seen your share of ghouls, then . . ."

"To be honest, son, there's more of 'em hanging round here than most crime scenes."

"The price of success," I said, motioning to the grandeur of the lobby. "We were hoping for a little compassion today, but when we saw the state of the church, thought it might make sense to post someone here."

"So they sent the work-experience boy?"

I smiled. "A day off from doing the tea run. If it's OK with you, I'll just sit here with a magazine, keeping an eye on the door, probably just until after the funeral."

He returned my warrant card. "Makes sense to me, son. I've got some bits on, but if you have any trouble, get the desk to give us a call."

We stood and shook hands. "Thanks again, Mr. Reed." He went over to the desk, briefly explained the outcome of our conversation to the receptionist, and gave me a nod. Then he walked back to the lift and carried on with his day. I sat down, opened a complimentary magazine and watched the door.

3

When I had called the police a few minutes earlier, I reported suspicious noises and activity coming from a neighbor's flat on the forty-fifth floor of Beetham Tower. I knew that mentioning Rossiter's name might mean the police would arrive too quickly, so I just said that my neighbor was away and I knew that his flat was supposed to be empty.

Less than an hour after I sat down to my magazine, two uniformed officers walked into the lobby. They wore high-visibility jackets and carried their hats under their arms. I saw the receptionist look over at me as they approached her, but decided to wait in my seat. They lowered their voices, hinting toward a sensitive matter. When the receptionist walked around the front desk and motioned the men to follow her, I stood and walked toward them.

"What seems to be the problem?"

The first officer addressed me. "You are . . . ?"

"Waits."

"Detective Waits is on Mr. Rossiter's security detail," the receptionist said.

I showed them my warrant card. "Is there a problem, Constables . . . ?"

"Turner and Barnes. We've received a report of suspicious activity in a suite on the forty-fifth floor. Apparently that's where Mr. Rossiter lives?"

"That's right. There shouldn't be anyone in there today, though."

"Might be worth us having a quick look."

"I'm . . . not sure that would be appropriate."

Barnes cut in. "If someone's reported a disturbance, sir, we have to look into it."

"I appreciate that, but I'm certain there's no one in the apartment today."

"Have you been in the apartment today, sir?"

"No. No, I haven't."

"Do you have access to the suite?"

"No," I said. Then, to the receptionist, "Perhaps you could call up? Save our blushes . . ."

"Of course," she said. She walked back to the front desk and dialed a number, then asked to be put through to Mr. Rossiter's suite. We waited for a minute as the phone rang. "Sounds like there's no one home."

The officer looked at her. "Can you get us access to the apartment?"

"I believe Mr. Rossiter *is* on the key card system."

"Hang on," I said. "I can't just let anyone up there." The officers looked at me in disbelief. "One moment," I said. I pulled out my mobile and dialed a nonexistent number.

"Kernick," I said. "I'll wait." I allowed an uncomfortable amount of time to pass while the three of them stared at me. "Sir," I said finally. "There's been a report of a disturbance in Mr. Rossiter's suite at Beetham Tower and—" I pretended to be interrupted. "Of course, sir." I lowered my voice. "Yes, sir. Thank you, sir." I hung up and then spoke to the receptionist. "If we could get the key, please?"

"I'll see what I can do," she said, turning back to her desk.

"Sorry about that," I said to the constables. "I'm sure you can appreciate the heightened sensitivity today."

"Course," they said in unison, both avoiding my eyes.

4

insisted that one of them handle the key card. None of us spoke as the lift approached the forty-fifth floor. I don't remember the Muzak, but I'm sure it was still there. When the doors opened, I walked ahead along the corridor and directly to Rossiter's suite. To leave no doubt that I went there often.

When I looked back, they were walking slowly toward me, memorizing the decor and remarking on the layout. The officer with the key card, Turner, stepped forward, inserted it and pulled the handle.

"After you," he said.

"I'll follow up with the neighbor while you look around."

"Whatever you think." He opened the door and walked through it. I stepped aside for his partner and watched them both crane their necks. As the door closed, I heard one of them whistle. I went down the hall and stood by the neighbor's entrance for a minute. When I heard Rossiter's door opening again, I began walking back toward it.

"All good?"

"Yeah," said Turner. "Nice to know the honorable gent's a man of the people, eh?"

"All good?" I repeated.

"Sir. No sign of a disturbance."

"Neighbor's a shut-in," I said. "The only disturbance is in her head. Wants to make a statement about her cleaner stealing plates. She's just getting changed."

The officers exchanged a smile. "Shall we . . . ?"

"I'll take it from here. Thanks."

They walked past me, down the corridor, and pressed the button for the lift. I watched them, waited until the doors were open before I said, "Constables."

They both turned to look at me.

"The key?" Turner stepped out of the lift while his colleague held the door. "Thanks," I said, taking it and walking back down the hall-way.

I heard the lift doors close.

I walked directly to Rossiter's.

Opened it. Entered.

Checked the time: 9:57.

I closed the door, closed my eyes and leaned back against the frame for a second, breathing deeply. I wondered if Isabelle would have been buried by then. I had to be in the lift, on my way down to the lobby by 10:30.

Any later would be suicide.

I pushed myself forward. Looked: I was in the large, anonymous lounge where I had met Rossiter before. Huge floor-to-ceiling panes of glass showed the city below.

I compartmentalized, grid-searched.

I was looking for Isabelle's second phone and I went efficiently about the room. The inaccessibility, the remoteness of the suite, made it the perfect place for Rossiter to keep secrets. This would be my only chance to find them. I moved quickly, aided by the anonymity of the place. In all of that space, there was just so little to look through. I examined the cognac that Rossiter had given me almost a month before. Hennessy.

Zain Carver's brand.

I found nothing else in the lounge and moved through to one of the largest kitchens I had ever seen. It looked unused. There was nothing but a carton of skim milk in the fridge.

I walked back into the lounge and through to a spacious stairwell. It led up to the bedrooms, but first I looked into the study at its base. Although the study afforded the best view in the suite, the desk was turned markedly away from the window.

The sign of a room where work was done.

There was a closed laptop on the desk but no books, notebooks or files. There was nothing in the bottom two drawers. I pulled out the top one and saw it. The brown paper envelope that Rossiter had slid across his coffee table toward me, two weeks before. I lifted it out of the drawer, poured out the pictures and went through them.

Full color but blurred. The pictures were taken at odd angles, clearly from a camera phone. I could see the sheen of sweat on Isabelle's skin. The two of us together at the first house party I had been to.

I thought about taking the pictures. I wondered if that was why I'd really gone in the first place. To destroy evidence against myself and save my own skin. A pulse of self-loathing went through me. I put them back in the envelope, the envelope back in the drawer and left the room.

I got to the stairs and stopped.

Went back into the study and opened the drawer again. I didn't pick up the envelope this time. Just looked at the writing.

I. R. 30th October.

I moved up the stairs, into a dark corridor. There were two large master bedrooms, each bigger than my entire flat. One was plainly Rossiter's and there were some simple things in the adjoining en-suite bathroom, a toothbrush and shaving kit. There were two smaller guest rooms farther down the corridor. The first carried the same vacant anonymity as the rest of the flat.

The second one was different.

Time jumped from 10:25 to 10:30 in what felt like seconds.

The wallpaper was bright pink. The small, single bed had pink sheets and pillows. On it were an array of dolls and stuffed toys. Care Bears and Barbies. Isabelle had been seventeen years old when she ran away. From memory, her older sister was somewhere in her twenties. So whose room was this?

I went to the walk-in wardrobe and opened it:

Several identical little black dresses.

A couple of pairs of blue denim dungarees.

I closed the wardrobe and went to the chest of drawers. Found colorful, childish underwear. Cutesy writing and Disney characters on them. All in what I'd guess would be Isabelle's sizes, but not her style. Not even close.

10:34. I thought for a moment. About the phone hidden in Isabelle's flat. I wondered if it were a regular trick of hers. I pulled the drawers out fully. There was a slip of paper taped to the back of the bottom one. I checked the time.

10:36.

I peeled the Sellotape off the paper and gently pulled it away from the wooden surface. It was a note. It was 10:38 and I was pushing the drawers back. I moved down the stairs and through the lounge. I could still go back for the photographs, I thought.

A piercing, loud telecom sound cut through the room. I froze to the spot. It went off again and I realized it was the doorbell. I held my breath and made my way slowly forward.

I opened the door to Mr. Reed, building security. He was red-faced and breathing hard. "Y'should've bloody called me, son. What's going on?"

"I'm sorry, Mr. Reed. I knew it was nothing so thought I'd save you a job."

"You're not saving my bloody job when there are two cun—" he stuttered. "Cun—" He concentrated. "Constables in the building I don't know about." He'd run out of air halfway through the sentence.

"You're more than welcome to take a look around yourself, but I'm sure it's a false alarm."

He eyed me. "Do I know you from somewhere?"

"I don't think so," I said, off guard. "I've just had a call that the funeral's concluded so I'll be heading back to the family home now, anyway." I walked down the corridor, feeling his eyes burn into the back of my head. I came to the lift and pressed the call button seven times.

Waited.

I watched the lift's excruciatingly slow progress on the small digital screen beside it. I didn't turn around. As it reached the forty-third floor I had a sudden sense that there would be someone in it. Kernick, Rossiter, the two constables.

I waited.

The doors opened.

The lift was empty.

I walked in and pressed for the lobby.

"'Scuse me, son," said Mr. Reed, half-running toward me. "Excuse me." Hating myself, I put my arm forward and held open the door. He got to the lift, breathing hard and sweating. "The key?" he said.

"Of course." I fumbled in my pocket and handed it over. He stepped back and I let the doors close. By the thirty-fifth floor I realized I'd been holding my breath and tried to breathe. Look normal. I was fingering the note I'd found when the lift reached the lobby. The doors opened. I walked out and went straight to the main entrance, exiting onto Deansgate. I could feel the paper burning a hole in my pocket.

I saw police cars on the street. I saw men I thought I recognized.

I didn't look at the note until I'd walked five hundred feet and turned down a narrow, dingy alleyway. I glanced over my shoulder then leaned back against the wall.

Breathed.

I took the slip from my pocket and opened it up, hands shaking. It was written in stark red ink.

NO ONE CAN EVER KNOW.

5

I was eight years old when I made my own bid for freedom, when I started lying for my own benefit. I manipulated everyone else in the room, and it was one of the last times I ever saw my sister.

Annie had stopped sensing or seeing a shadow over her bed at night. Now the shadow was a man who could reach out and stroke her hair. She thought she'd imagined him to life. I remember her, scared, urgently whispering to me the next day: *"If I dream something, can it come true?"*

It's difficult to articulate the powerlessness of a child in care. Everything, from your daily routine, to the building you sleep in, is changeable at a moment's notice. The only things that felt permanent were our names, which fit as uncomfortably as the damp-smelling, hand-me-down clothes we wore, and felt less like identities than scars for life. Vicious parting shots from people who didn't want us. As Annie and I became unmoored from our old lives, drifted further from safety, I saw that our welfare was just an illusion.

An unspoken lie that we were expected to live inside.

The last time we met with a couple I was stubborn, standoffish. When they asked me questions, I shrugged, sighed, muttered my responses. I stood apart from my sister and wouldn't look at her. I could feel her eyes on me. Her big, thinking head turned in my direction. She thought I was angry with her, and tugged one of her knee socks back to its rightful place to appease me. When we were told to go and play, I followed her to the toy box. She peered over the edge at whatever was inside.

As she was about to tip it over, I pushed her. She landed on her bottom and looked up at me, wide-eyed. Then she looked down and cried quietly into her hand, the way our mother taught us to. I threw a toy at her head and shouted a dirty word I'd heard one of the older boys use. I turned my back on her and played on my own. I squeezed a plastic figure in my hand so hard that it broke. The man who'd been sitting on the sofa walked over to Annie.

"Hey, it's OK," he said, picking her up.

Proceedings started that day, and her new parents had no guilt at separating her from her bullying older brother. She fades from my memory soon after that. For years after she left The Oaks I saw her everywhere. On streets, on passing buses, in bars. I did a double take at any girl who might be the same age, and I still see her everywhere. She's Joanna Greenlaw and Isabelle Rossiter. She's Catherine and Sarah Jane. Training to become a detective, it was always in the back of my mind to look her up, to find her and explain myself. I never got further than working out she was still in the area.

Unfortunately, she'd found me.

I felt inside my pocket for the letter that Sutty had passed on, the letter that had arrived at the station after my suspension. It was from my sister. Opening it, I found I still couldn't take in the contents. I felt the hot tears of shame welling in my eyes. I scanned to the bottom of the page. Anne, as she signed her name, had seen my picture in the papers.

Disgraced Detective Aidan Waits.

She'd known it was me immediately.

"You're my family, I can help you," she'd written but, refolding the letter, I knew I wouldn't reply.

Leaving the alley, looking both ways, I had scattered black thoughts. Of girls I'd grown up with, self-harming. Sometimes they'd run away and be dragged back, humiliated, days, weeks, months later. Sometimes we'd never hear from them again.

The dismal gray morning had turned into a dismal gray day. The pavements were blocks of ice under my feet, and I could feel the cold through the soles of my shoes. I thought about the past, the sunspots. The terrifying blackouts of my youth. I thought about never seeing my sister again. I thought about Isabelle. First scared, then alone, then dead.

6

knew her service would probably be over. I drove toward the monastery more by accident than design. It was only three or four miles out of the city and, with Isabelle on my mind, seemed too short a distance to pass up. I kept thinking of the note I'd found in Rossiter's penthouse, the messages I'd seen, smashed into the mirrors. I kept asking myself:

No one can ever know *what*?

The small, low-cost houses that surrounded it had probably seemed incongruous when they were first built. It's the monastery that's out of place today, though. An obsolete show of power and wealth from a God that the world decided, all at once, didn't exist. It had recently been refurbished at a cost of millions, but the money had come from heritage funds rather than the Church. The building's main use was as a conference center, and the service had been humanist.

When I drove past, there were still a few people standing around. Some girls about her age talked in a group. They wore smart black dresses, stark red lipstick, perfect shaded veils. I wondered what kind of friends they'd been. What kind of people they'd grow into. I wondered if they'd hung on there to attract the attention of some photographers, still taking pictures of the grounds. Then I saw one of the girls comfort a crying friend and wondered what my fucking problem was.

There were a couple of uniformed officers moving the photographers along. As I pulled away, I saw an old hack I recognized, those bloodhound features, sitting in his car, calling in his copy. I saw him idly try to place me as I went by.

Yesterday's news.

Although it hadn't been reported in the press, I had a good idea of where the burial itself would be. Gorton Cemetery was just a few minutes away. When I arrived, there was still a hearse parked up alongside the black saloon cars that family and friends had been driven in. I parked a little farther down the road and walked away from this, the

224

nearest entrance. Felt the white-hot anger burning a hole in me. A photographer was trying to long-lens the mourners.

There were two funerals taking place. It was the perfect day for it, and I joined the back of the smaller one. There were only five or so people standing around, but I kept my head down, kicked my heels, and no one noticed me.

About a hundred feet away I could see that Isabelle had already been buried. Some people were standing in groups, talking or hugging. Some were alone. Most were already walking back down the path to the black saloon cars. The official who had led the service was working the crowd, shaking hands and offering her condolences.

I thought of Isabelle, passed out with her head in her hands. Of her toying with the scarf at her neck. Of her nudging me, laughing like a whip crack. I thought of the look on her face, her wide-open eyes when I had found her dead. I thought of the veins in her arms, that unnatural, dark color beneath white skin. The blue half of her body, injected with pain. The smell of sex, the tally marks cut into her inner thigh. With effort, I remembered the pictures I'd found in her desk. A seventeen-year-old girl, laughing with her friends.

Of the few people standing around the grave, the first I recognized was Detective Kernick. I'd expected to see him at the gate, wearing sunglasses and an earpiece, and was surprised that he seemed to be attending the service as a family friend. He was standing with a dark-haired woman and a young girl. His family, I thought. I knew he'd worked with the Rossiters for years but hadn't realized they were this close. His girl was around Isabelle's age, obviously upset, and I wondered if they'd been friends.

When Kernick put his arm around her, I felt a stab of guilt. I remembered him in the stairwell at the station, staring right through me, trying to see if I had taken advantage of Isabelle. He'd acted more like her father than Rossiter had. He'd visited me earlier, insisted I stay away, because he didn't want to work today. He turned the girl from the grave and nodded at the dark-haired woman. His wife? They began walking toward the gates.

My eyes went to a solitary young woman at the graveside. She wore a dark-gray coat and a small black hat, standing with her arms wrapped round herself, radiating grief. A couple walking away gave her a covert look, then began talking about her like she was famous. She didn't look up. She didn't seem to notice anything going on around her. She had the same pixie features as Isabelle, and her hair was a similar blond color—albeit a shade darker.

The older sister, the runaway found.

She let out a long sigh and stepped back from the grave. Just as she was about to make her way down the path, David Rossiter appeared. Her father. For a moment I didn't recognize him. He'd messed up his hair by running his hands through it, and his face seemed bloated, haggard and tired.

He'd been crying.

He and the girl looked at each other. They were only a few feet apart, but it seemed farther. His mouth opened to say something but the words didn't come. The girl's expression darkened. She gave a small shake of her head and walked past him, down the path. Rossiter didn't turn to watch her go and when his knees buckled I thought he was going to fall down. He drew himself up, messily wiped his face with his forearm and looked about the people still in the cemetery.

The only other person of note was a tall, attractive woman in her mid-forties. The streaks of gray in her hair just made the blond stand out more, and the veil did nothing to diminish her striking appearance. I recognized her from the reports of Isabelle's death as Alexa Rossiter, Isabelle's mother. She wore her grief with an upright, almost iconic kind of elegance. Her face was set, with very little emotion allowed through it, just the squint in her eyes hinting at what must have been behind them.

She and her husband glared at each other.

His face, his mouth and eyes, were open in some kind of communication, some kind of apology. Mrs. Rossiter's expression didn't change. She returned his look until he couldn't take it anymore. He turned and walked down the path. After he'd gone far enough away, she followed.

The service I was standing with had come to an end, and people began shaking hands and dispersing. I walked down the path, keeping a distance from anyone who might recognize me.

Mrs. Rossiter strode past her husband, got into the back of a car and closed the door. She spoke to the driver and he indicated to pull out into the road. Rossiter looked round, lost. Kernick appeared, offering his arm. Rossiter allowed himself to be led to another car.

I remembered meeting David Rossiter for the first time. Remembered his wedding ring, cold to the touch because he'd only just put it on. Remembered him telling me about his depressed daughter. Her suicide attempt. That he'd called the ambulance. That he'd kept it out of the news. That he'd gone to the papers himself and begged them.

I remembered him telling me about his basket-case wife. I thought of the way she'd looked at him. The way she'd strode past him. The way she'd left, head high, the picture of self-assurance, without him.

He'd been lying to me.

7

On my way back into the city I stopped in a pub to warm myself up. A TV over the bar was showing the news on mute, a report of Isabelle's funeral. The scrolling text at the bottom of the screen reminded viewers that she'd been sexually active from a young age, that she'd overdosed.

A zooming camera showed a small group of people standing around the grave. I ate some peanuts, drank a couple of slow beers and left.

I parked a few streets from my flat and walked the rest of the way. It was dark and the buildings hung over my head like black thoughts. I kept my eyes low. The pavement was frosted with ice and I thought of the city freezing entirely. Everything and everyone in stasis for a few months while the evil dissipated, while the people got their breath back.

My shoes crunched the light ice. I was almost surprised when I turned onto my street without having thought about where I was walking.

I looked up.

Stopped.

On the other side of the road, parked right outside my flat. A fourth- or fifth-generation Mustang hatchback. Black body with thin red stripes of detail. The engine was running and I could see the exhaust fumes under the streetlights. Grip's car.

Grip.

I stepped into a doorway and looked about the street for him. There were a few silhouettes, a few people walking in or out of town, but none with his uncomfortable, laboring gait. I looked at my building. The street entrance. The door was closed and the hallway was dark. I looked up at my flat. The window above the street. The light was off but I couldn't remember how I'd left it.

"Can I help you?"

I started. It was a voice from the intercom in the doorway, which I must have leaned on. I glanced around, up at the building I was standing beside. A young woman was in the window a few floors up, wondering why I was hiding in her building's doorway. I gave her a small wave of apology and walked out onto the street.

I went slowly toward the car, walking on the other side of the road. I could still go straight past. As I got closer I heard the low rumble of the engine. Coming alongside it, I gave the car the most casual of sideways glances. Then I stopped and looked again. There was no one in the driver's seat. I checked both ways before I crossed over.

More for Grip than for traffic.

When I looked through the window, I saw there was no one in the car. The keys were in the ignition and I knew something was wrong. The car was the way Grip defined himself. Even ducking into my flat for a few minutes, he'd have taken the keys.

He'd have locked it.

I took a breath, opened the driver's-side door. I had been expecting a little warmth but the interior was cold, no better than street temperature. I saw that the heaters were turned right down. No one had been sitting here waiting.

I looked about the street again.

Reached in and turned the key. The low rumble of the engine cut out. I took the keys and closed the door. Walked to the rear and stopped.

Looked round again.

It was dark and there was no one within fifty feet of me.

I turned the key and narrowly opened the boot. The interior lit up when I did, and I saw inside for a moment before closing it.

I tried to breathe out the smell.

My hands were shaking and I spread them flat on the car. It was the only thing holding me upright.

I heard street sounds again and turned my head. There was a group of people, drunk, singing, coming down the pavement toward me. Couples, arm in arm.

Silhouettes in doorways.

The girl I had seen a few minutes earlier.

She was still standing in her window. She was still looking down at me. Talking to someone on the phone. I walked round the car, got in at the driver's side and turned the ignition. I started it up and pulled out into the road.

8

The Mustang's engine had been designed to give off a certain sound, even within the speed limit. It growled, low, insistent, a voice in my head. As I drove, I thought I heard tapping, rattling sounds coming from the car boot.

I knew that was impossible.

It was after five when I arrived at Fairview. I parked on a parallel street, got out of the car and stood for a moment, breathing the cold air. I walked to the house, up the path, and knocked on the door.

I heard footsteps inside.

They stopped abruptly as someone looked through the peephole. Sarah Jane opened the door. She consciously softened her expression when she did. It was the first time I'd ever noticed her doing that, and I wondered if she was lonely. Isabelle dead. Zain arrested. Grip missing. Catherine, too. She gave me a small, nervous smile and I thought how young she must be.

"Hi," she said.

"Hi," I said. We looked at each other for a second too long and then both spoke at once.

"Would you like to come in—"

"I've found Grip," I said. She peered over my shoulder for him. "Not here."

"Is he OK?"

"He's still in one piece. I can take you to him." She had an ear for cruelty, and I saw her wondering why I'd phrased it that way. Why I'd turned up here unannounced, and why I was trying to take her away.

"No," she said, but it was more like a reaction to bad news than an answer. I could see the blood draining from her face.

She stepped back.

Started to close the door.

I got my foot in the way and pushed it open. I walked in and slammed it behind me.

"I know, Sarah."

She didn't move but her eyes lost focus on me. She stood there stunned, as if I'd slapped her in the face. I moved past her, found the fur I'd seen her wearing before and started to put it over her shoulders. Her arms moved into the sleeves automatically. I gave her a little push forward, toward the door, and she went.

She didn't open it. Just stood there with both hands on the wood, like she was checking for fire on the other side. When she turned to look at me there were tears in her eyes.

"What do you know?" she said.

"Most of it."

"Oh."

I leaned past her and opened the latch. I led her by the arm and closed the door behind us. By the time we got to the bottom of the path she was leaning against me to stay upright. When we got to Grip's car, she put her hand to her mouth. Tried to pull away. I took her to the passenger side and put her in. I walked round the car, climbed inside and started it up.

9

I knew we had to go somewhere quiet and remote, and I drove toward, through, past the city limits. Sarah Jane fidgeted with her seat belt.

We went by dozens of half-finished, half-forgotten building sites and I slowed down by one or two of them. When I did, she looked out her window, sometimes with a hand on the glass, wondering if it was where Grip had ended up. Wondering what would happen to her now.

Once we'd left the city, once there were fewer streetlights on the roads, I caught her looking at me. Car headlights swept past us as we went and I saw her eyes lit up in my periphery.

I kept my face blank and kept on going. The Barnes Hospital was a survivor from the 1800s. An enormous gothic redbrick building, it had a couple of wings and a turreted clock tower that hadn't told the time since the late nineties, when millions of pounds were cut from the local health trust's budget. The hospital was closed down and immediately listed as a place of historical and architectural interest. In spite of that, the real estate company who bought it let the building slide into ruin.

Sarah Jane and I pulled off the motorway, into the drive. There was a red sign at the entrance which used the word "opportunity" three times, urging interested parties to call an 0800 number. A chain-link fence had been put up around the hospital's perimeter, but someone had removed the bollards blocking the driveway. I took us in closer. When the headlights lit up the huge, abandoned building, its stone steps and wrought iron railings, I saw Sarah Jane's hand drift to the passenger-side door handle.

I stopped the car, killed the engine and waited.

There were no lights in the grounds and, without the growl of the engine, all we could hear were the sounds of the motorway. After a minute or so I became aware of the sound of Sarah Jane's breathing, too.

"They buried Isabelle today," she said, staring straight ahead, trying to sound conversational. Trying, too late, to put some common ground between us.

"I know, I was there," I said. She didn't say anything but turned in my direction. "Would you have gone if you could, Sarah?"

"Of course I would."

"What kept you away, I wonder?"

"Why are you doing this?"

I didn't say anything.

"Where is he? Where's Grip?"

"Grip's here, don't worry about that."

"Then take me to him," she said, putting a hand on my arm. She was so cold I felt it through my sleeve.

"I need to ask you some questions first. What happens next depends on how you do with them."

She took her hand away. "You know why I couldn't go. She died because of us."

"Us?"

She turned, stared straight ahead again. "Because of me."

"That's not why you couldn't go, though, is it?" She didn't say anything. "The question I keep asking myself is, how did David Rossiter know so much about Isabelle, even after she'd run away from home?"

Sarah Jane straightened. When she spoke again there was something of the old hardness in her voice. "She was seventeen years old. I looked out for her."

"You got her killed a second ago, now you were looking out for her." She didn't say anything. "Well, which is it?"

She mumbled something.

"Say again."

"I was looking out for her, and I'm not apologizing for it."

"I don't want an apology. I want an explanation. You still haven't answered my question."

"What question?"

"How did David Rossiter know so much about Isabelle's life after she ran away from home?"

"Because I told him," she said.

Neither of us spoke for a minute. The car was warm. Beads of condensation massed together on the windows.

"You reported back to him about Isabelle. About me."

She didn't say anything.

"You took photos of us together. Gave them to him."

She didn't say anything.

"You gave him her new number."

"So?"

"You told him where she was staying. When she was there."

"So?" she said again, but this time it was barely audible.

"So why do you think she ran away from home?"

"Little rich girl problems."

"Try again."

"Big rich girl problems."

"Again."

"Oh, you know everything, Aidan. Why don't you tell me?"

"Because your boyfriend was fucking her."

"What?"

"I didn't believe it myself at first, either." She didn't say anything. "When we found her, she was naked. She'd recently had sex."

"What does that have to do with—"

"Your boyfriend? There were self-harming cuts on her inner thigh. Tally marks. One for every time they'd been together. There was even a fresh cut there, for that last time."

"Zain was with me when Isabelle died."

"Who said anything about Zain?"

She didn't move.

"I was talking about your other boyfriend. I assume there are just the two of them?"

Sarah Jane opened the passenger-side door and took a step out. The interior light flicked on automatically, surprising her, and she froze for a second. I hadn't realized that she'd been crying, and her makeup had run with it. A blast of cool air blew her hair about her face. Stark red on pale skin. Smudged eyeliner.

"I don't know what you're talking about," she said. She stepped out of the car and slammed the door. The interior light flicked off. I opened my door and it came on again. I left it ajar so I could see. Sarah Jane was walking, fast, back toward the motorway. I went after her, took her arm and dragged her back to the car.

"I don't know what you're talking about," she said again, but there was less force in it this time. I didn't say anything. I was tired of banging my head against the wall. I led her to the driver's side and took the key from the ignition. We were in darkness again.

The motorway around us.

The sound of her breathing.

Her freezing-cold fingers on my arm.

We walked to the car boot and I fumbled with the key. She started to panic, to pull away from me, and I held her by the scruff of the neck. I pointed her at the car. Opened the boot. The light flicked on, lit us up with it.

Sarah Jane screwed her eyes shut. "Please, don't—"

"Look," I said.

She took a breath, looked and then leaned on me to stay upright. Grip's wide eyes stared back at us. They seemed bigger than usual, swelling right out of his skull. He had been forced inside too small a space and they'd broken his legs, bent both knees the wrong way, to do it. The rictus of pain on his face suggested he'd been alive when it happened. His wrists were bound in front of his body with cable ties.

There were deep cuts in the skin where he'd tried to struggle free.

His arms had been in front of his body so they had easy access. So he could see what was being done to him.

There was a syringe in his left arm and the injection site had turned black.

The left side of his body had darkened. The same nightmare shade of blue I'd seen on Isabelle. The same I'd seen at Sycamore Way.

I watched Sarah Jane's eyes filling with pity, as she traced the torture on her friend from head to toe. When she looked at his face she went limp against me and started to cry. He'd vomited heavily before he died. He'd been forced to drink a large quantity of paint. The sick down his chest, crusted inside and outside his mouth, was black and white.

10

I held Sarah Jane's arm and walked her to the passenger side. I opened the door, lowered her in and walked round the car. When I got in she spoke in a steady voice.

"What happened to him?"

"He went after Cath."

She pulled the fur around her. "Is she . . . ?"

"I found the car at my flat. No sign of her." I thought of what Sheldon had said in Rubik's: *It'll be like she never fucking lived.*

"Why at your flat?"

"A warning, a guarantee he'd be found. Look," I said, leaning toward the dash. "You need to answer some questions."

"Don't turn the light on. Ask me whatever, but don't turn the light on." I knew there was a good chance that we'd never speak again outside this car and, for whatever reason, had wanted to see her. I sat back and we talked in the dark.

"How long have you been sleeping with David Rossiter?"

"A year, give or take. How did you know?"

"He knew more than he should have, but that could have been from anywhere. It was the pictures of Isabelle and me, really. They were too suggestive to have been taken by someone who didn't understand sex. Caught the moment too well to have been taken by a man."

"So I was too good?"

"No, not quite. When I brought Isabelle back to Zain's that night, you asked me to take her to the flat round the corner. You wrote down her address. I saw the same handwriting on the envelope Rossiter had the pictures in." She snorted. "Carver and Rossiter both drank the same brand of cognac as well. I wondered if that came from you."

She nodded. "I'm sorry for getting you in trouble."

"Who with?"

"David, Zain, the police." She shrugged. "You're in trouble with everyone."

"I don't work for the police anymore."

She looked at me again but didn't say anything.

"How did you and Rossiter meet?"

"It doesn't have anything to do with—"

"If I have to ask again I'll put you in the boot with Grip and walk home."

I was afraid that I meant it.

"How else would a girl like me meet a man like him?" I felt a stab of jealousy. I tried to keep it out of my voice but didn't quite manage.

"Where was this?"

Sarah Jane caught the tone and began responding faster, happy in the knowledge that at least each answer hurt me on some level.

"The Cloud," she said.

A bar on the twenty-third floor of Beetham Tower. A view of the city and cocktails at Prohibition-era prices. There's a four-meter overhang with a glass floor so you can see all the way down. There are usually traveling businessmen. Occasionally there are young women keeping them company. For most people, The Cloud felt like going up in the world.

For David Rossiter, it was twenty-two floors beneath him. I wanted to tell Sarah Jane it was beneath her, too, but I'd heard the tone in my voice as well as she had. I didn't want to start acting on it.

"You were working."

"Whoring? I don't think of it as work, really."

"He paid you, though?"

"Nothing to trouble the expenses scandal."

"Yes or no."

She paused. "Sometimes."

"Tell me about him."

"I can even tell you his safe word, if you like?" I didn't say anything. "Mine's 'harder' . . ."

"Let's start at The Cloud."

"I was only there for a drink. You get so tired of drinking in basements around here. Especially the dives Zain sells in. Sometimes a view can take your mind off things.

"I'd have been wearing something nice. Black for the way I felt, or red for the way I wanted to. I used to go there when I was young. Made more in an hour than my mum did in a month."

"You're still young," I said. "Rossiter approached you?"

"With David it would've been more mutual than that—I fucking love money. I don't remember exactly, though. I'm sure we'd have locked eyes and bought each other a drink."

"Where did you go?"

"All the way to the top."

"His penthouse? He wasn't afraid his wife might come home and find you?"

"Says she's never set foot in the place."

"And you believe him?"

"It's true, I think. Crippling vertigo and more money than sense. She bought the highest flat in England to try and get over it."

"How's that?"

"She was gonna stay in the Hilton for forty-five days straight. Go up a floor every night until she got to the top. She had a panic attack on the fifteenth and never went back."

"So David started using it for himself?"

"He said things weren't working at home. They were only married on paper, really." I thought of him putting his ring back on every time Sarah Jane left. She heard herself, and went on quietly. "I know they all say that."

"Isabelle didn't suffer from vertigo, though."

"No."

"And you met her at the penthouse?"

"She went there every so often, when she knew David was out. We started running into each other."

"Sounds awkward."

"A little, at first. He'd left for work one morning and I was waiting for the lift when she came up in it. She was cutting school. Had a boy with her. She looked scared to death."

"And she knew?"

"More or less. She started to work out our routine. David likes . . ." She paused, corrected herself. "David liked to leave the suite first. I'd go ten, twenty minutes later. More often than not I'd see her get out of the lift. You don't pass many people on the forty-fifth floor of Beetham Tower."

"Did you tell Rossiter?"

She didn't say anything.

"Sarah—"

"No. No, but I think he knew. Some days they only missed each other by minutes. I thought they must be passing each other in the lobby . . ."

"How did you and Isabelle end up talking to each other?"

"David and I spent a night together. Usually I felt at home there, but I couldn't get comfortable. When he left in the morning I was right behind him.

"The lift came up but Isabelle wasn't in it. It wasn't right. I wondered if that was why I'd felt weird. If there was something wrong. I waited a few minutes, but she never showed.

"I had this horrible feeling that she'd been hiding in the penthouse all night. Watching us. Listening. I went back and knocked on the door. Sure enough, she opened it."

"Then what?"

"Said she'd just wanted to know for sure. No hard feelings. I bought her a drink. I felt sorry for her. Got the impression her parents didn't pay that much attention. One always thought she was with the other."

"Is that how she was gone so long before they realized?"

"That they didn't know?" She paused. "I guess."

"Did she ever say anything to you about her father?"

"Not really . . ."

"Anything off? Anything at all?"

"I'd have remembered."

"What about him? Did he say anything about her?"

"Like what?"

"Like anything."

"Those clichés about men paying whores just to listen aren't really true, you know."

"Stop calling yourself that, I get it. How did you end up taking Isabelle to Zain's?"

"I didn't. I wouldn't have. She started following me round."

"And you of all people couldn't give her the cold shoulder? You've got two of them."

"Her sister had left. She had no one else . . ."

"She flattered you."

"I suppose. No one had thought of me like that before. She got in the same way you did. I saw her round the bars, putting it about for a few weeks, then one night she showed up at Zain's."

"And he took to her?"

"I told you, he has a habit of attracting strays."

"What were you and Zain arguing about the second night I went there?"

"You, at first—like I said. Told him it was stupid to let you in."

"How did you know who I was?"

"David told me a policeman might be snooping around. He only told you about Izzy so it wouldn't look weird that he hadn't reported her missing, but . . ."

I waited.

". . . I don't know, sometimes it seemed like he didn't want her back."

If Rossiter had heard about an investigation that might locate his daughter, a daughter he hadn't even reported missing, it might make sense to bring me in unofficially. Then he could impede any contact between us. Keep tabs on Isabelle and keep his secrets safe. If worst came to worst, he could use the pictures he'd got of us to keep me in line.

"What about Zain? He knew who I was before I introduced my-self."

"If he sees a face twice, he wants to know who it is. A few of us had seen you hanging round the bars."

"But who ID'd me?"

She swallowed. "He pays someone on the police force. They ID'd you . . ."

"From a picture or in person?"

She didn't say anything.

"Sarah, this is important."

"In person. Before you came to Fairview that first night."

"Someone hit me that night. I woke up on the street outside Rubik's." In the darkness I saw Sarah Jane shift position to look at me. "Did you have anything to do with it?"

She nodded.

"Go on."

"Zain just called him his friend. Said his friend was gonna wait for you in Rubik's. ID you and call it in. I knew you were something to do with Isabelle. Something to do with David. I told Zain he should have you scared off." She stopped abruptly and started to cry. Not for me but for herself, or whoever she'd been before. "When I saw you at the door with a black eye, looking at me like that . . ."

"How did I look at you?"

She wiped her nose. "Like I was something good."

"I need the name of Zain's friend on the force . . ."

She shook her head.

"Man or woman?"

"I don't know. It's one of the only things he's precious about."

"You said I was the first thing you argued about. What was the second?"

"Isabelle."

"You wanted her out?"

"I forced her out. She was staying in the house at first. I made Zain move her to that other place."

"Why?"

"I was scared she'd let slip. About her dad and me."

"Does Zain own the flat she went to?"

She nodded. "It's not true, is it? David and Isabelle?"

I thought for a second. "When I got close to Isabelle, she saw through me pretty quickly. She asked if I was working for him, started having a panic attack."

"But what does that mean?"

"She said he was obsessed with her. He interviewed her boyfriends, got them drunk and found out things about her sex life. He played the tapes to her sometimes." As I spoke, she started to breathe deeply. "I need to ask you a few more questions."

She nodded.

"Your sex life with David Rossiter. Was there anything unusual about it?" Even in the dark I could feel her eyes on me. "I need to know." I could hear her concentrating on her breathing. A minute or so went by as she steadied herself to talk.

"Role play," she said.

"Age stuff?"

She nodded. "Uniforms. Voices. I didn't know . . ."

"There's a room in the suite. Done up like a young girl's."

"We usually went there. He likes me to call him Daddy." She turned away. "Did he kill Isabelle?"

"Did you tell him I'd taken her home that night?"

"Yes," she said quietly.

"Then he knew where she was and in what state. I saw him the next day and he confronted me about the pictures. He was afraid we were getting close."

"So why wouldn't he kill you? I mean—"

"I'm only one of a dozen people she could have told. Anyway, he's had me sidelined from the investigation. Had his man remind me of the pictures." Sarah Jane was completely slumped against the passenger-side door now. "There's one other thing. When I found Isabelle, there was a message written on her bathroom mirror. *No one can ever know.*" I was hoping Sarah Jane might recognize the phrase, but she just said:

"OK . . ."

"After my last conversation with the police, with my boss, I got home to find my flat wrecked. Everything had been broken or cut. Someone had written the same thing on my mirror and then smashed it."

"Right . . ."

"And when I was in Rossiter's suite, when I searched the room where you two slept together, I found this." I reached into my pocket and handed her the note. She looked down at it for a second then found her phone in her pocket. She lit up the screen and held it like a torch over the paper.

No one can ever know.

"Do you recognize the handwriting?"

She put her phone away and shook her head.

"Do you know Rossiter's handwriting?"

"I think so."

"Do you have any of it anywhere? A letter? A signature?"

"He was careful."

"How do you usually arrange things?"

"I've got a phone specifically for him. He has one specifically for me. Texts. No calls."

"When was the last time you spoke?"

"The night before Isabelle died. You . . ."

"Go on."

"You smelt of drink. She'd passed out. I was worried about her."

"Do you have it with you?" She fumbled in her pocket, held the phone out like she was glad to be rid of it. "Hold on to it for a minute," I said. "I need you to do something for me." I believed Sarah Jane but I needed to be sure. After I dictated the message and she sent it, we drove back to Fairview in silence.

11

Need to see you urgently. Sx.

12

Things felt different between Sarah Jane and me. In some way we were strangers again. Sarah Jane fidgeted compulsively for the entire journey. Picked, plucked and scratched at her body, like she was slowly disassembling herself.

It was late when we got back to Fairview and I gave her the choice. Face the police or leave, I didn't care which. She decided to leave. I told her she could stay the night, pack her things the next morning. I locked us inside, asked her to hand over her phones and unplugged the landline.

"Just for the night," I said. She shrugged and went to bed. I brushed my teeth, thinking of Isabelle blacked out on the bathroom floor. When I spat out the toothpaste there was blood in it.

I woke up in the night to a creak on the hardwood floor. All I could see was her silhouette against the dim glow from outside. When she took a step forward, I saw that she was holding a bedsheet around her body with one hand and something sharp, metallic in the other. She took another step and a thin strip of light crossed her face. She stood there for a minute, not knowing if I was awake or asleep, and I watched the conflict in her eyes. Finally, she turned and crept quietly out of the room.

We were both up early the next morning and Sarah Jane packed a bag. Rossiter had replied in the night, in the same clipped style of message we'd sent to him.

Grafton St. 11.

When I asked Sarah Jane about it, she said he was referring to a multistory car park in town. When they wanted to take a drive, go farther afield, they'd meet there, away from prying eyes. She glanced at the message and shrugged. "No kiss."

I took her case outside and down the path. She was standing there, wrapped in her fur, as close to vulnerable as it was possible for her to look. A light wind had caught her hair, sending red strands in a hundred different directions at once, and I watched her for a moment before she turned and saw me. She nodded at Grip's car. Neither of us had referred to his body still being in the boot.

"What'll happen to him?"

"Once you're away I'll report it. He'll get buried."

"He'd want to be cremated," she said. Then quietly: "He didn't like his body." She walked toward the car and put a gloved hand on the boot. "And what about those fucking animals? The Burnsiders? Sheldon White?"

"Try not to think about it."

"I hate . . ." Her voice broke. "I hate thinking I won't see him again." She looked back at the house. "I won't see any of them again, will I? It's like you're killing me as well." I didn't move and she gave me a sad smile. "I know it's not like that really." I nodded. We loaded up and drove into the city.

13

We got to the car park a little after ten, drove inside and up to the third floor. Sarah Jane told me this was their place. It was less than half-full and I reversed into a space with a clear view of the entrance ramp. She smoothed down her fur and spoke quietly.

"What will I say to him?"

"It doesn't matter, I just want to see it with my own eyes. Tell him you're upset about Isabelle. You wanted to see him."

"I am upset about Isabelle," she said. "What if he wants to go somewhere?"

"Say no."

"I'm quite scared."

"If he touches you, I'll kill him."

She looked at me, surprised.

It was before half past when I saw a familiar black BMW coming up the entrance ramp. The headlights were on full beam and strafed the walls before the car turned right, toward the opposite side of the floor. We both sat low in our seats and Sarah Jane breathed a little faster.

My phone started to vibrate.

An incoming call from an unknown number. I canceled it and spoke to Sarah Jane:

"Stand out in the middle of the floor where he can see you. Don't go over to him. He'll come to you." She gave a small nod and got out of the car.

She walked toward the center of the floor and pretended to look around for Rossiter. She wore her fur, a knee-length skirt and heeled black boots. I couldn't see the car but saw him flash up his lights. She squinted, raised a gloved hand to her eyes and turned her head in that direction. It was the kind of vacant expression that men can't help but fill with meaning.

I heard a car door slam. I saw her take a cool step backward as someone walked toward her. A man in a long, dark coat. There was a gray suit beneath it.

Sarah Jane frowned, really confused now, and listened to him talk. He handed her a plain gift bag and walked back to his car. I saw the lights flash again as he turned the ignition. Sarah Jane stepped out of the way, unconsciously looking in my direction as the BMW drove by her. It went past me toward the exit ramp and down, out of the third floor. There had only been one person in the car.

Detective Kernick.

I opened the door and walked toward Sarah Jane.

"What did he say?"

She seemed stunned. "David sends his apologies. Says it's over."

I looked at the bag. "May I?"

She handed it over. There were crisp wads of cash inside. I moved them around, searching for a letter, for something to compare with the note I'd found in Rossiter's penthouse. There was nothing. I looked up and saw Sarah Jane watching me riffle through the cash. I handed back the bag.

"Let me give you a ride to the station."

14

We were sitting in traffic, waiting to make a turn into the northern quarter. She'd been quiet on the drive, idly fingering through the bag on her lap.

"You look like you've got something to say."

"When Zain gets out, will you tell him? About David and me?"

"It's the only way I can be sure you won't come back."

"Oh." She nodded. She turned to stare out her window, and I wondered which one of them she'd be missing. "Would it be so awful if I came back?" She looked at me. "If I never left, even?"

"Think about Isabelle, Catherine, Grip, even Zain. Something's going on, and if you stay . . . yes, it might be awful." She turned, stared out her window again.

"What about you?" she said, quietly.

A bored little boy sitting in the back of a car in front held his fingers up as a gun. I put my hands up but he shot me dead.

I parked round the corner from Piccadilly station, somewhere I was sure there were no cameras. I couldn't drive Grip's car anymore, but I didn't want either of us to be seen leaving it. The police had the details and they'd find it soon enough.

Piccadilly has fourteen platforms, perfect for picking a random destination and disappearing without a trace. Inside, Sarah Jane spent some time scanning the departures board. My phone had started vibrating in my pocket again, but when I looked at the screen it was another unknown number. I ignored it. After a few minutes, Sarah Jane nodded, more to herself than to me, and started walking. I followed her to platform five and set her case down. She held on to the bag that Kernick had given her.

"So this is it," she said, looking at the station over my shoulder.

"What will you do?"

"Who knows?" She paused. There were tears in her eyes. "I am so sorry, you know."

I nodded. "Me, too." There were a lot of people coming and going, and we walked toward the train. She got on and I put her case in beside her. A man on the platform signaled that they were ready to go. I think we both felt something at that point.

"If you didn't tell Zain about David and me, I could stay, or I could come back . . ."

"In a couple of weeks there'll be nothing left to come back to."

"How do you mean?" The doors started beeping and I stepped backward, allowing them to close. The train didn't depart immediately and as I walked away I got the feeling that Sarah Jane was watching me go. When I turned, hoping to see her in the window, she wasn't there.

It was before twelve when I left. I bought a strong coffee, crossed the bridge outside and walked through a gleaming complex of hotels out onto Auburn Street. I passed the Gardens and skirted China Town.

The overcast, static sky buzzed on overhead.

It was the first day of December and I had just put my last friend, such as she was, on a train out of town. I felt my phone vibrate again. This time it was a message but still from a number I didn't recognize.

He's here! Mel.

I had to think for a few seconds before I remembered that Mel was the Australian barmaid from Rubik's. I crossed the road through lunchtime traffic and ran toward the Locks.

15

Rubik's was quiet but there were a dozen people standing around the main bar. I pushed through them, looking for Mel. There was no one serving.

"Where's the barmaid?"

"Been gone awhile," said a man holding an empty pint glass. I took out my phone and called the number I'd received the text from. I heard it ringing behind the bar and walked around to find it.

"Mine's a shandy, mate."

"Get lost," I said. "Police, I mean it."

The men exchanged looks and dispersed. Mel's phone was lit up on the floor and I stopped the call. There was a door at the side of the bar leading into the back. It didn't move when I tried it.

I knocked.

"Mel, are you in there? It's Aidan." There was some movement.

"Is anyone with you?"

"I'm alone." I heard the lock turn and stepped back from the door. She opened it partway and stared out over my shoulder. "There's no one here, it's OK."

"He had a knife . . ."

"I think you're on a break. Come on," I said, leading her out from behind the bar. We went to my usual seat. It had a good view of the room and a good view of the street outside. Over a drink she told me that Neil, Glen, the ex-barman, had come in on crutches around an hour before. He looked and smelled awful, and she thought he must be sleeping rough. That made sense. He had a broken leg and was hiding from the Burnsiders as well as the Franchise now.

"You did the right thing, calling me."

She shrank a little. "He told me to do it."

"What?"

"The police have been here looking for you as well."

"When?"

"Did you beat up one of our regulars?"

I didn't say anything.

"They say you got fired. You stole drugs from evidence—"

"When were they looking for me?"

"Twice. They came for a statement after the assault, and then earlier today."

"About the assault?"

"They said it was in connection with a murder." Her voice trembled. I turned to the window. Wondered if they could have found Grip's car already.

"What did you tell them?"

"That I hadn't seen you. Is it true?"

"What? No. Thank you."

"You've always been nice to me but I won't lie again."

I looked around the room. "It's OK. I'll talk to them, I'm close to getting things straight. Why did Neil tell you to call me?"

"Wanted me to give you this." She pulled a dirty folded envelope from her pocket and pushed it across the table.

"Did he say anything else?"

"Just walked behind the bar like he owned the place. Opened the till and emptied it into a bag. I tried to stop him and he pushed me down. There's a floor safe behind every bar so I locked myself in with it. He kicked a bit and someone asked what was going on. Then it went quiet." She took a shaky mouthful of her drink and nodded at the envelope. "What is it?"

It had been folded down the middle, looked grimy and smelled of sweat. I guessed it had been in his pocket for a few days. There was nothing written on the front of the envelope and it had never been sealed. I opened it and pulled out a familiar newspaper clipping.

It was the appeal for information about the disappearance of Joanna Greenlaw. Someone had laboriously blacked out the words in the article with a marker pen, like redacted information on an old MoD file. With a blue biro they had circled her picture. The biro lines had been scrawled so many times around her that they left shining blue grooves in the paper. I turned it over, searching for something else, a message, but there was nothing. I wondered what it meant. Why the barman would have it. Why he'd give it to me of all people.

"What is it?" said Mel.

I turned to the window. "You said you were getting a new job?"

"Start at Fifth Avenue on Friday."

I looked around the room. "Good. You shouldn't come back here."

I reexamined the clipping, trying to work out what it was telling me. I recognized Joanna's picture. The vacant expression that seemed somehow familiar.

When I looked up again the barmaid was gone.

Had Joanna run away so she wouldn't have to testify against Carver and White? Or was she closer than that? The circling of the picture implied whatever I was supposed to see was in there, but there was no shadow cast over her. No reflection of a killer in her eyes.

Just a girl in a room in a photograph.

I glanced round the room. Over my shoulder. I looked at the text. Some letters had survived the blue marker pen. The remaining ones spelled:

TAKEABATH

I glanced round the room again. Over my shoulder. Out the window. I saw Laskey and Riggs getting out of their car. I crumpled the clipping into my pocket and went down a flight of stairs, banged open a fire exit and left.

16

It was around twilight when I pulled onto Thursfield Street. My head-lights caught the metallic sheets that covered the windows of the houses. Reflected back at me. I cut them and sat in the dark for a second, letting my eyes adjust. Even on a row of run-down, abandoned derelicts, the Greenlaw house felt significant.

I looked over my shoulder. Thought I saw shadows moving in my periphery. I went up the path with a torch and a crowbar.

I clicked on the torch.

The simple wire that had held the door shut was gone. When I shone the light down at my feet, I saw the wire, cut, on the floor.

The door was already ajar when I pushed it, and it wouldn't open much farther. The damp carpet had swollen up from the floor too much. I edged inside and shone the torch down the hallway. Every-thing looked the same. I wanted to be sure that I was alone so went straight along into the kitchen.

Same boarded windows.

Same gutted room.

Same spaces where white goods would have been. I checked that the pantry was still empty, then went back along the hallway into the front room. It was the same way I'd left it. A sad, plain space, about four meters by three, wrapped in gloom. The carpet had been stripped away some time ago, leaving a mismatched, warped wooden floor. The windows were boarded up and no light from the street got in.

I left the front room and climbed the stairs, feeling them flex under my weight. I went past the bathroom and looked into the bedroom. It was empty, exactly as I'd left it. The second room, where I had seen a sleeping bag and food scraps before, was also empty.

It had been swept clean.

I went back to the bathroom. It was so cold I could see the breath in front of my face. I took the newspaper clipping from my pocket and shone the light down at it.

TAKEABATH

I set the torch down so it lit up the bathtub, then took the crowbar and knelt beside it. I tried to jam it in the corner of the side panel. It was well sealed, and so caked in years of grime that I couldn't find the edge. After a couple of minutes of this I swung back and hit it. Then again. I made a dent, a hole. Then another.

Eventually, I was able to get the crowbar inside. I pulled backward and broke the board. I stopped. Thought I'd heard something over my shoulder. I waited a second then swung again.

I made another dent, then a hole. I pulled backward. Broke away more board. Swung again. Finally, a big enough hole appeared. There was a dull, rotten smell. I listened to my breathing. Absorbed waves of paranoia. I dropped the crowbar, picked up the torch and shone it inside.

Contorted into too small a space, between the side panel and the bathtub, was the body of a young woman. Ruined by death and time and damp. I pushed myself backward, tried to breathe. I went out onto the landing and retched.

Joanna Greenlaw had never left the house.

I thought about Zain Carver, Sheldon White. She had betrayed one. Agreed to testify against both. The black and white paint tied things back to Sheldon, but it was circumstantial. And I thought about Superintendent Parrs. His zeal. His close relationship with Greenlaw. I was sure that at least one of them had known where she was for the last ten years.

I heard the front door go. Kicked in. There were footsteps and torches, first one in the doorway, then two, blinding me.

Raised voices and swearing.

A shape came at me. Hit me in the stomach with a torch. I was turned around and shoved into a wall. Teeth on brickwork. My hands were cuffed behind me. The room was filled with panting breaths.

"Turn around," shouted a familiar voice.

"FUCKING TURN AROUND," screamed another.

I turned. All I could see was the blinding white from the torch. It hit me in the face, glass smashed, and I was dragged out of the room.

I could feel blood, brick and loose teeth in my mouth. They shoved me across the landing to the top of the stairs.

"My hands," I said. They were still cuffed behind me.

Then one of the men pushed me down the staircase. I rolled and landed in a painful heap at the bottom.

17

A s you know, I'm Detective Sergeant Laskey," said the thinner of the two officers who'd twice visited my flat. I thought we were in an interview room in the basement of police headquarters. An unventilated black box with no windows and no air.

I didn't know what time it was, what day it was. My hands were cuffed in front of me now, and I was sitting at a desk with a tape recorder and some files on it.

I was fucked.

Detective Sergeant Laskey was standing against the far wall with his shirtsleeves rolled up, hands in pockets, jingling change. Pale. Thin. Tendons standing out from his neck like wires. He kept clenching and unclenching his jaw as though he was chewing on something.

Gray, artificial light bled into the room through a plastic fitting in the ceiling. When I looked up to stretch my neck I saw trapped dust inside it, the vague outlines of dead insects.

"You remember Detective Constable Riggs," said Laskey.

I nodded at his partner.

The larger man had pulled his chair away from the desk and sat with his back to the door. To the average interviewee, this might signify that no one was walking out of the room. To me, it signified that no one would be walking in. Riggs's face was so red with drink that he looked sunburned, the capillaries in his nose and cheeks at absolutely full capacity. He winked at me and a dull pain went through the back of my head.

I remembered him.

I thought the heat and body odor in the room were probably coming from Riggs, but they might have been coming from me. It smelled like stress. Fear. I tried to run a hand through my hair but it was matted with blood.

"You forgot to read me my rights," I said.

Laskey unclenched his jaw. Smiled. "We're just talking, Aid. Don't need to hear your rights for some conversation, do you?"

Riggs cleared his throat. "How long had you been screwing Isabelle Rossiter before she died?" His drinker's blush made him look ashamed of himself, but he smiled at me as he said it.

"Don't think he remembers," said Laskey, unclenching his jaw. "Let's go back a bit further. How'd you meet her in the first place?"

I didn't say anything.

Riggs sighed. It smelled like alcohol and cigarettes. "Come on, Waits, whatever's going on, it's game over. Kids dropping dead. Women crammed under bathtubs. You're not the man we want and every minute with you's one we could spend after the fucker responsible. So help yourself."

It felt wrong.

I'd just found the body of a woman who'd been missing for a decade and they wanted to talk about Isabelle Rossiter. I was confused. Handcuffed, but not under arrest. There was something else going on.

"I met Isabelle Rossiter at Zain Carver's house," I said.

"Seems a funny place for a vodka heiress."

I shrugged. It hurt.

"How'd she get there?" said Laskey.

"Invite only, what we hear," said Riggs.

"I don't know, she'd been there awhile when I arrived."

"Awhile?"

"Months."

"More than one month, less than two," said Laskey. "According to her dad."

Riggs leaned forward, elbows on knees. "In which case, she ran away around the same time you were caught stealing drugs from evidence . . ." Confirmation that they didn't know I'd been undercover.

"No comment."

"Wonder if those two things are connected? We know she liked her drugs . . ."

"I didn't meet her until after I was suspended."

"You *were* stealing drugs, though?"

"No comment."

"Do you have a drug problem?"

"When I can't get enough of them."

"So you were stealing them for yourself?"

"No fucking comment."

"See, her dad reckons she was using something before she ran away. Someone got her hooked, then she went to the source." Her dad. He'd never said she was an addict before. Either he was lying to them or they were lying to me.

"That's one explanation."

"So give us another," said Riggs.

"She was running *from* something."

"From something like what?"

The only sound was the buzz of the light bulb.

"Fair enough," said Laskey, pushing himself away from the wall. "You're an addict but you get suspended. Your supply runs dry. Is it you or Isabelle who first decides to approach Zain Carver for drugs?"

"Laughable," I said. "I just told you, I didn't know her until after I went to Fairview."

A thin smile. "My mistake."

"Which of them did you meet first?" said Riggs. "Zain Carver or Isabelle Rossiter?"

"Isabelle. She was at his house the first time I went."

"What were you doing there?"

"Scoring."

He raised his eyebrows.

"Pills," I said. "Not girls."

"And Isabelle Rossiter was scoring, too?"

"She was sober."

"So you go out scoring—"

"Pills," said Laskey, interrupting his partner. "Not girls."

"Right. You go out scoring pills, not girls, and end up with a bit of both. Nice work, son."

"We just talked."

"I'm sure you fucking did."

"Sounds like Isabelle Rossiter did a lot of talking," said Laskey. "We think it might be why she ran away."

"*From* something," said Riggs, sitting up. "See, she'd fucking talk to anyone, that girl. She'd already talked to every boy in her school. Some of the girls as well, from what we hear. She'd pick up homeless blokes off the street and just talk to them all night. Sometimes she got a hotel room and talked to two or three of them at the same time."

I looked at him.

I realized I was standing up.

I looked away and sat back down.

Riggs chortled. "Anytime, son. Anytime."

"Go on, Waits," said Laskey, sharing a smile with his partner. "You were talking with her . . ."

"We passed each other in the hallway. Said all of ten words."

"Sometimes that's all it takes."

"All what takes?"

He shrugged. "Answer one of my questions and I'll answer one of yours." I didn't say anything. "I'll give you an easy one. How long had you been screwing Isabelle Rossiter before she died?"

"I never touched her."

Laskey stared at me for a few seconds, then leaned forward. He flipped open the first file and slid it across the desk.

"What's this, then?"

I didn't look down.

I knew what it would be. I felt light-headed. Those migraine sunspots in my eyes. Riggs heaved himself out of his chair and walked behind me. He leaned over my shoulder and squinted at the top picture. Full color. Blurred. The sheen of sweat on Isabelle's skin.

"Looks like you're touching her there, mate . . ."

"Care to rephrase your last statement?" said Laskey.

"We're in a crowded corridor. Talking."

Riggs leaned closer, leafed through the pictures and spread them across the table. The booze was so heavy on his breath that I could guess his brand.

"Like I said. Talk to fucking anyone, that girl."

Sarah Jane had done a good job when she took the pictures. They were framed to include as little of our surroundings as possible. Each one showed Isabelle and me slightly closer together. Riggs leaned hard on my shoulder.

"This the first night you met?"

I nodded.

"Don't waste your time, do ya?"

"Where did you get these?"

I didn't want to ask him and sound rattled, but I was.

"Sent in anonymous," said Laskey. "Someone out there wants you burned to the ground, Waits. Who might that be?" I was already thinking about it. Rossiter or Sarah Jane could have sent them the pictures. I knew Rossiter was most likely. I thought about not destroying them when I'd had the chance.

"How many times did you meet Isabelle Rossiter?" said Laskey. Riggs was still pressing down hard on my shoulder. Their focus on Isabelle Rossiter, the pictures, started to give me a bad feeling, worse than the pain in my head.

"I don't remember."

"Then think about it."

I thought. "Two or three times at Fairview. Once at Rubik's. I took her home from there one night. What's this about?"

"Tell us about the Rubik's night," said Riggs, lifting himself off my shoulder, walking round the table. The light glaring off his polyester trousers hurt my eyes.

"I ran into her late, around last orders. She was drunk and I wanted to make sure she got home safe."

"Safe from what?"

"The bar manager was a creep."

"Oh yeah?" said Laskey. "What's his name?"

"Never caught it," I lied. Laskey gave me an odd look.

"You took her back to her flat?" he said.

"Yeah."

"Cab driver says you went to Fairview first."

I tried not to react. "That's true."

"Picking up Eight?"

"No."

"What then?"

"Isabelle was drunk—"

"Passed out in the cab, apparently," said Laskey. "Driver says he was concerned for her safety."

Fucker. "She was fine. I took her to Fairview because I didn't know she stayed in the flat round the corner. We weren't that close."

Laskey gave me a *yeah-yeah* look. "So you get her back to the flat, then what?"

"I left and she asked me to come back the next day."

"Why?"

"Something she wanted to tell me."

"What?"

"I don't know."

"You didn't ask?"

"The next time I saw her she was dead."

"Is that right?" said Riggs.

Laskey sat down opposite me, clenching and unclenching his skinny jaw. "We wondered if she'd just told you something you didn't want to hear?"

"Like what?"

"Like she wanted to go back to her family?"

"Her decision. I'd have told her it was a good one."

"Funny, that. When you and her got in the cab from Rubik's, you started out heading in that direction . . ."

Riggs carried on. "Only, once she passed out, you had the cabbie pull over and turn round."

When I'd found the cash in Isabelle's handbag.

"My word against a cab driver's?"

"The journey was saved in his satnav," said Laskey. "So what changed your mind?"

It was clear I was giving away more than I was getting back. "No comment," I said.

They exchanged a look.

Laskey went on, "Maybe she told you she didn't want to see you anymore?"

"No comment."

"Maybe she told you she'd been talking to this barman you can't remember the name of?" Laskey gave me that look again. *What do you know?* I wondered why he was so interested in the barman.

"You know how she liked to talk to people," said Riggs.

"No comment."

"No comment," said Laskey to Riggs. "S'pose no one can ever know . . ."

I looked at him.

"Oh, that got a reaction."

"Got a reaction at the scene, as well," said Riggs. "Gave a constable a broken nose."

"Why did you lose it when you saw the message on the mirror, Waits? *No one can ever know* what?"

"No comment."

"How come it was written on the bathroom mirror at your place?"

"You trashed my flat?"

"*Searched* your flat: the door was open when we got there. Someone had written *No one can ever know* on the bathroom mirror and smashed it. I think it was you."

"No comment."

"And how come when we grabbed you today, there was a note on your person with the same thing written on it?"

"No comment."

"Not in your handwriting," said Riggs. "Yours slants like a fucking psychopath's. Maybe the note was from Isabelle?"

"She sends you a note saying no one can ever know. She ends up dead. You see it written on a bathroom mirror and assault a police officer."

"No comment."

"You write it on your own mirror and destroy the place."

"You're miles off . . ."

"Who was in the room with you when you found Isabelle's body?"

"No one."

"'*We've* found a body,' you said. I've heard the tape."

"I misspoke."

"*No one can ever know*, what?" said Riggs.

I looked at him. "You tell me."

"Answer one of my questions and I'll answer one of yours."

"Do we have to keep on doing this?"

"How long had you been screwing Isabelle Rossiter before she died?"

"It never happened."

Riggs raised his eyebrows at Laskey. Laskey gave me another thin smile and slid the second file across the desk toward me.

"Open it."

It was a postmortem report. I knew it immediately. The name at the top was Isabelle Rossiter. I was familiar with the layout and assimilated the information quickly. Felt the pulse, beating through my head. The blood, singing through my veins. I could hear my heart.

I looked at the report again.

There had been heroin in Isabelle's bloodstream when she died. That was expected. She had also been a few weeks pregnant. That stopped me. I didn't move but I was sinking into the ground. Laskey put one hand roughly on my shoulder. I felt his bony fingers, kneading my skin. With the other hand he pushed an evidence bag across the table.

The picture of Isabelle that her father had given me; it had been in my pocket.

A pale, pretty girl with dull blond hair and intelligent blue eyes. In the picture, she was staring above where the camera would have been. At the person holding it. It looked intimate. Laskey smiled about an inch away from my face and squeezed my shoulder again.

"You never touched her, mate. You've got nothing to worry about."

18

We repeated the same conversation several times, the heat in the room rising, until they decided to go out and eat. I'd lost all track of time and my head was a mess of lies and omissions.

They came back into the room smelling of fresh air, fried food and cigarettes. Freedom. I couldn't pay attention or say anything back at first. I could hear my pulse. Ambient noise from the rooms above and around us. The box we were in felt dense with heat and there was no movement in the air. I thought I had a concussion.

Laskey and Riggs were sweating. I was sweating. The walls were sweating. I could see Laskey, looking at me, lips moving, and tried to concentrate.

"Let's talk about the Franchise," he said.

"Can I get a glass of water or something?"

"In a minute, let's talk about the Franchise a bit first."

My words slurred. "What do you wanna know?"

"Tell us how you got involved in the first place." I had my doubts about both of them, and decided to play along with the public record of my disgrace. I improvised.

"It was after I was suspended. I was just looking for somewhere to score . . ."

"But you're an ex-cop. How'd you get yourself invited to Fairview?"

"I met a girl at Rubik's. Catherine."

"This the same girl who dropped off the face of the earth a few weeks later?" I nodded. It felt like an aneurism. "You said you knew her from an old case . . ."

"I did. I ran into her again at Rubik's."

Laskey and Riggs exchanged a look.

"Go on," said Laskey. "You meet this Cath, again."

"I told her what I was after, she told me how to get it."

"And on your first night at Fairview, the only person you spoke to was Isabelle Rossiter?"

"Yes."

"And that's when these pictures were taken?"

"Yeah, listen, can I get that glass of water?"

"In a minute," said Laskey. "Were you using the night you took Isabelle home from Rubik's?"

"No."

"Were you drinking?"

Yes. "No."

"Saturday, November fourteenth. You were seen in an altercation with this barman you can't remember the name of."

"Never *got* the name of," I said. Laskey. The barman again. That same look on his face. *What do you know?* I had a flash that I might not be the only one in the room with secrets.

"Well, we've got a room full of witnesses who say you were drunk. You'd spilt beer all over yourself. Isabelle Rossiter was found dead the next day . . ."

I didn't say anything.

Riggs flicked my head.

"You're drunk. You get in a fight with him and leave with Isabelle. You set out for her mum and dad's place, probably at her request, but once she passes out you get the cabbie to turn around and head to Fairview."

"No."

"Where you know you can score," said Riggs.

"No."

"Once you do that, you go back to the flat," said Laskey.

"Only there's an argument."

I shook my head. Gripped the table to stay upright.

"She wakes up somewhere she doesn't wanna be."

"With you."

"Starts off just drunk talk, but she's used to her own way."

"These rich bitches."

"You're just tryna calm her down."

"Keep her quiet, but it's all coming out now."

"And she plays her last card."

"Ace in the hole." Riggs smirked. "She's pregnant." Neither of them said anything for a minute, then Riggs went on, leaning right into my face, "She hasn't shut her legs in six months, fuck knows whose it is."

"*No one can ever know,*" said Laskey. "Isn't that what all this is about? No man could be himself in that situation."

"Let's get it cleared up now, mate. How long had you been screwing her before she died?"

"I thought we were talking about the Franchise?" I said. I was looking at the table, but I could feel them both staring down at me. I could hear myself breathing. See the sweat dropping off my face.

"Fine by me," said Laskey. "Seems to have fallen apart recently. Why?"

"Sheldon White came out of prison and things started to happen. Black and white paint turning up in places it shouldn't have. Then the spiked Eight, Isabelle's death, Sycamore Way, Carver's collections being turned over."

"Them cabs that were held up?" said Laskey.

"Yeah."

"And the fire at Yarville Street?"

I nodded.

"Were you at Sycamore Way?" said Riggs.

Yes. I hesitated. "No."

"Bloke matching your description," said Laskey. "Maybe you've got a double?"

"God's not cruel enough to put that face on two different fuckers," said Riggs. I didn't say anything. He flicked my face.

Laskey stood.

They were both standing, facing me now.

"It all comes to a head when you meet your friend Cath at Rubik's again . . ."

"White was there. He threatened her." My voice sounded like someone else's. Tired. Pleading. "Said unless I got a message to Carver, she'd end up like Joanna Greenlaw."

"What message?"

"That Rubik's was a Burnsider place from then on."

"Is that when he told you where Greenlaw was?"

I shook my head and regretted it. The room spun.

"He just used her name as a threat."

"And we met you the next day," said Riggs. "Looked like you'd been using . . ." I didn't say anything. He flicked my face again. "Looked like you'd been going from club to club and getting fucked up."

"No."

"Using your warrant card to jump the queues."

"No."

"Then inventing this story of a drug rivalry and missing girl when we called you out on it."

"No." I thought. "Someone else reported Cath and Grip missing . . ."

"Sarah Jane Locke. Another woman in your life who's dropped off the face of the earth. One missing girl's a mistake, Waits. Two's just careless."

"I called hospitals the next day, looking for Cath. Check."

"We have."

"And?"

"And it's true, you called some hospitals."

"So—"

"So you were impersonating a police officer, congratulations."

None of us spoke for a moment, then Riggs leaned on the table, staring right at me.

"You said you never touched Isabelle Rossiter. *Lie.* Said you wanted her to go home to her parents. *Lie.* Said you were alone when you found her body. *Lie.*" I could feel the heat beating off him. "You said you knew this Catherine through an old case. *Lie.* Said she was last seen with Sheldon White. *Lie.* Said you'd handed in your warrant card . . ." He fumbled in his pocket and slapped an evidence bag down on the table. It was my card. It had been in my pocket. "*Lie.*"

"I told you. Talk to Parrs."

"We have. He doesn't remember the girl. Barely remembers you. He thinks you're a fucking fantasist."

Everything stopped.

I sat back in my chair. My chest felt tight and it was all I could do to breathe.

"Look, I'll tell you anything, but I need some water."

Laskey and Riggs looked at each other. They were both breathing hard, shirts patching with sweat. Laskey nodded at his partner.

269

Riggs gave me a nasty smile. "Don't go anywhere," he said, turning, kicking the chair from in front of the door and opening it. He walked out and turned the lock on the other side. There was a gasp of ventilated air from the corridor. It stung my eyes.

Laskey resumed his position at the far side of the room. Hands in pockets, jingling loose change. Now he stared right at me. With some difficulty, because of the cuffs, I ran a hand over my face and looked at the palm. Soaked with sweat. I ran it through my hair. It had been matted with blood where Riggs had hit me in the Greenlaw house, but the sweat had loosened it and I felt the bump.

I thought about Laskey. His line of questioning. His interest in the barman. The look on his face that said: *What do you know?* I thought that if he had a secret then the barman must be his weak spot. I tried to think.

Laskey just stared at me.

Jingling his change.

I touched the spot on my skull where I had been hit. I thought of the night I met David Rossiter. The night I met Catherine. The night I first went to Fairview, and the night I met Isabelle. Someone had hit me when I was leaving Rubik's.

"*Zain's friend,*" Sarah Jane said.

I woke up, facedown on the street. The young couple crossed over to avoid me, and I heard the jingle of small change in someone's pocket.

I looked up at Laskey. "You hit me over the back of the head outside Rubik's." His expression didn't change. "You suppressed evidence against Glen Smithson, the Franchise barman, in that date-rape case."

He jingled his change again and smiled.

19

askey's expression didn't change until we heard someone at the door. Riggs came in with three bottles of water, and I breathed in a blast of fresh air. The door closed and I was left with the edge of sweat coming from Riggs.

Laskey ripped the lid off his water and drained it in one, crushing the plastic bottle as he did so. Riggs did the same, spilling some on his shirtfront as he glugged it back. The water just blended in with the sweat.

My mouth was dry. I could still feel the brickwork from the Greenlaw house on my teeth. I looked at my bottle. The seal had been broken. An old trick, a cheap one, to make me think twice about drinking it. I just left it there.

I felt like my life depended on getting out of that room.

"Riggs, can I ask you something?"

He did a double take, glanced at Laskey and then sat down opposite me. He rubbed his nose on his forearm and nodded. "Course you can, Aid."

"Where were you on October thirtieth?"

"Dunno, mate. Where were you?"

"At a bar. Rubik's. It was a Friday, by the way. I drink too much and so do you. It's why you write everything down. Your notebook's in your jacket pocket, so you can check."

He looked over his shoulder at Laskey.

His partner was standing, stock-still, against the wall. Riggs didn't catch the game, but didn't want to give that away, so he turned to me, shrugged and reached for his jacket. He dug into his pockets and found my wallet, my phone, and dropped them on the table. Then he held up his notebook.

Before he could open it, I interrupted. "Prediction: if you were on duty with him around six p.m.," I nodded at Laskey, "then he either made an excuse and left, or plain disappeared on you." Riggs hesitated and I knew I'd jogged a memory. He leafed back through the pages and shrugged again.

"Yeah, so? How many times did you screw Isabelle Rossiter before she died?"

"Where were you on Monday, November sixteenth?"

"What is this?"

Laskey clenched and unclenched his jaw. "Tell him," he said, steadily. He was staring right at me. That same look on his face. "We've got time."

Riggs leafed forward in his book and found the day.

"Prediction," I said. "He moved heaven and earth to get assigned to the Isabelle Rossiter investigation after her death."

"So?" Riggs frowned. "Explain."

"Friday, October thirtieth. Zain Carver asked his man on the force to rough me up. Detective Laskey makes an excuse and leaves you at around six p.m. I was assaulted at seven." Riggs shifted in his chair. "Monday, November sixteenth. Said man made sure that room 6.21A here was reassigned so he could go in and out without being noticed. A hard drive which he believed to be evidence against him was wiped."

Riggs shrugged. "Meaningless."

I looked at Laskey. "I was sent undercover to flush him out. You need to get Superintendent Parrs. Now."

Riggs smiled. "Parrs thinks you're full of shit—"

"Did you hear that directly from him? Or did Laskey tell you?"

He didn't move. Laskey didn't move.

"What about that first day you came up to my flat?"

"What about it?"

"Franchise doormen wouldn't speak to the police in their wildest dreams. If some mad bastard was using his warrant card to get into Franchise clubs, they'd report it to their boss. Zain Carver. He'd get his man on the force to look into it."

"You're in space—"

"There's one more: Glen Smithson."

"Should I know him?"

"He's that Franchise barman that Laskey keeps derailing this interview to talk about. Was charged with date rape a few years ago, but the evidence went missing."

"So?"

"So a couple of weeks ago he went missing, too. It was never reported to the police, though."

"And what's that gotta do with Jim?"

"When I went looking for Smithson, the guard in his building said I was the second cop who'd been there. The first burst in on the night of Sycamore Way, stuck his head in the room and left. The same night I heard Zain Carver put every man in the Franchise onto the hunt."

"And you're saying it was Jim?" Riggs mulled it over. "Prove it."

"The first man left his mobile number with the guard, in case Smithson turned up. I saved it onto my phone." Laskey stepped forward, but Riggs swiped my phone off the desk.

"Saved as?"

"Franchise Man."

Riggs walked round the table so he was standing to my right. He and Laskey were either side of me, facing each other. He frowned and scrolled through the address book. He looked up and hit call.

Laskey's phone went off, a shrill factory-setting ringtone. Calmly, he took it from his jacket pocket and canceled the call. His face twisted into a smile. He spoke to his partner but he was staring at me. "Why don't you go and wake up the Super," he said quietly.

Riggs was confused.

I spoke to him. "If you leave me alone with Laskey, he'll say there was an accident. That I tried to run . . ."

Riggs looked at me. "Have you completely lost it?"

"Go and get Parrs," said Laskey again, eyes not moving from mine.

". . . And you can't get a junior officer in here cuz you never officially booked me in. It'd take some explaining."

"Go and get Parrs," said Laskey.

"Yeah," said Riggs, thinking he was joining in on the joke.

"GO AND FUCKING GET HIM!" screamed Laskey, the veins pulled tight in his neck. Riggs gaped at his partner. "That's an order."

He put the phone down and backed away from the desk. He fumbled with the door and walked out, letting it close behind him. Laskey looked at me as we listened to the footsteps going down the corridor.

First walking, then running.

Laskey jingled his change one last time then took his hands out of his pockets. Took a step closer.

I stood up. "That's a secure place," I said, improvising. "CCTV, time stamps . . ."

"Dunno what you're talking about."

"The guard ID'd your picture," I lied.

"Shh," he said, taking another step. I could see his mind working. Making it up as he went along. He picked up my phone and threw it down on the floor. Then he stamped on it, ground it under his heel. He ripped the lanyard off his neck and threw it on the table.

I looked down.

His clearance card. Then he stepped back and leaned on the bright green Panic button. An alarm went off but I didn't move. He shrugged, picked up the tape deck and hit himself, hard, in the face with one corner.

He leaned back against the far wall and looked at me, blood spotting from his nose into his teeth, down his chin, onto his shirt. I decided in less than a second. Picked up my wallet, the clearance card. I opened the door and went down the hall. Through two sets of doors, banking left into a fire escape.

The ground-floor exit led out into the captivity of the station car park. I hit the doors so it would look like I'd gone that way and went on up to the first floor. I tried to breathe. When I heard a sound behind me I started to run. Followed the exposed piping round to the south side of the building. I went down a floor and banged through the fire doors, out onto Central Park, thinking:

Fuck. Fuck. Fuck.

CONTROL

1

I was in the cab before I knew where I was going.

"Know the Wiggle Room?" I said to the driver. He grimaced. The Wiggle Room is a ramshackle, semilegal nightclub off Sackville Street. A five-minute walk could take you to the gay quarter: color, vibrancy and life. The Wiggle Room was the other side of that coin. In the daytime it was difficult to spot, the entrance caked in crusted, overlapping show posters for BDSM and Trans-Queer cabaret. I hoped it went some way to explaining my appearance to the cab driver. I was still handcuffed, scared of what I might look like.

Bawdy street-laughter from the queue blended with old show standards escaping from inside. I paid the cabbie and climbed out of the car.

Two enormous drag queens wearing bright feather boas were working the door. They were balanced on brick-thick high heels made from sparkling, see-through plastic. The plastic was filled with water and each shoe contained several live goldfish. The shock to the senses was intentionally comic and absurd. Your mind took in the queue, the leather, the makeup at a glance, but then it stopped.

Was that a host from ITV news? Someone singing the Lady Di version of "Candle in the Wind?"

The queue itself was diverse.

Some were drifters from the gay quarter, wanting to see it for themselves. Some were outright BDSM enthusiasts, swelling out of PVC corsets. Some were curious, blank-faced men, turned away from the street, hoping not to be noticed. The first night of every month was a guaranteed sell-out because of the residency of their biggest draw.

Daddy Longlegs.

The Bug's stage name was more than just an alter ego for him. He put on an entirely different personality with the makeup. Demanded they be treated as two separate entities. They agreed on nothing and the Bug was generally the more reasonable of the two. It was technically December second, but only the early hours of it, and the show still went on.

I joined the line behind a shivering middle-aged man in stilettos and a miniskirt. We moved fast, a few of the blank-faced men suddenly remembering appointments, disappearing off into the street.

I caught my reflection in the door. Dried sweat and matted blood sent my hair out in wild directions. The handcuffs made me fit right in, though. I handed a fiver to one of the 300-pound he–she's and was waved inside without a second glance. I felt dizzy, light-headed. Electric. I went through the door, where a shrunken, evil-looking old man in pinstripes stamped my hand. A lightning bolt.

I'd found receipts for the club in Glen Smithson, the barman's flat. I needed to talk to him, badly. Aside from his connection with Laskey, he had given me the letter that led to Joanna Greenlaw's body. It raised more questions than it answered.

I needed an explanation.

I went through to a poorly lit hallway on a thin, squelching-wet carpet. The cloakroom was down here, along the hall, and there was another diverse queue. I walked through some hostile looks, up a flight of stairs to the main room. The city treated them like outsiders and this was where they came afterward. At best I was a tourist. At worst I was trouble. I pushed through double doors at the top of the stairs.

The smell of stale booze and bleach burned my eyes. The room was a mass of people, moving in crazy light. Two or three hundred, crammed into enough space for half that, going backward, forward, with the music.

The heat was a wall.

I could feel drops of condensation falling from the ceiling. The gender balance was hard to speak on. Men, women and everyone in between. Kissing couples and threesomes in every conceivable combination. Although about a third of the room wore theatrical, *Rocky Horror* getup, most were in their street clothes. This was their real life.

Everyone was screaming, sweating, swaying forward, toward the stage. There was an illustrated backdrop:

Daddy Longlegs and the Delicious Little Titbits.

I went right, through the crowd, toward the bar. A pretty, young post-op was serving and I ordered three large bourbons. Two neat and one with ice. I drank the neats at the bar, taking a look of gentle reproach from the girl. She touched my hand and said *"Easy, tiger,"* over the music. I nodded, turned toward the stage with my remaining drink.

Daddy Longlegs wailed into the mic, gyrating against the stand. Three large black drag queens, The Titbits, accompanied him, acting as his backing singers. Longlegs wore elbow-length black leather gloves and a burlesque outfit modified to look like a Nazi SS uniform. By the time I'd fought my way to the front, he was on his closing number, bending over to the crowd, miming a sex act with a dildo the size of a fire hose.

He was singing a lounge version of "Moon River."

When the song ended the crowd went insane and glitter bombs exploded onstage. Longlegs and his backing band were doused in pink, sparkling confetti. Someone threw a bouquet of black flowers wrapped in barbed wire and Longlegs picked them up, pressed them to his chest. He bent to take a bow, sweeping a half-empty bottle of champagne off the floor as he did so. He threw back his head, took in a mouthful then showered the front row with it. He bowed again, holding hands with the backing singers, and left the stage. The crowd started to disperse almost immediately. They would already be moving on to the next place.

I followed a rotten hallway, backstage, down a flight of stairs to the dressing room. There was a star on the door:

Daddy written in the center.

I could hear a conversation going on. It stopped abruptly when I knocked. There were footsteps and then the door opened a crack.

"Yeah?" said one of the Titbits. He was dressed casually, in street clothes, and dominated the doorway.

"Can I talk to him?"

"Daddy's taking his face off," he said, low and smooth. "No calls right now."

"Tell him it's Waits."

He frowned. "The kind you lift?"

"No," said a voice from inside the room. "The kind that drag you down. Come on in, Aidan."

The man stepped back from the doorway, revealing a neat dressing room where Daddy Longlegs sat with his back to me. He was in front of an old-style showbiz vanity mirror, lined with light bulbs. He went on removing his makeup and didn't turn around.

"You after an autograph or just some lipstick on your collar?"

I held up my hands.

Rattled the cuffs.

"Thought if anyone could get me out of these, it's you." I saw him frown into the mirror, then he turned around. He actually looked surprised. "I need a favor," I said.

"Lewis," Longlegs monotoned, not taking his eyes off me. "Could you give us a minute?"

2

I gave him my story. What I understood of it.

He'd taken the makeup off but still wore his costume. He was sitting cross-legged on a chair opposite me, twirling the handcuffs round his index finger. He'd had a key for them in his handbag.

I stopped talking, but he carried on playing with the cuffs, twirling them until they caught his attention. He shook his head sadly.

"Hiatts . . ." he squinted at them ". . . 2103s. Where's the *craft*?"

"Have you been listening to me?"

He gave me a hateful look. I couldn't tell if he was playacting or really meant it. "Why should I help you, Aidan?"

"I can get you money."

"I can get me money. Why should I help you?"

"I thought that was your friend there at Sycamore Way?"

"My buddy," he said with a smile. It faded and he went on. "They wouldn't let me see him, before he . . ."

"I'm sorry."

"Meaningless, coming from you. *Sorry*'s been your default setting since you were a kid. You should let someone at you with a screwdriver. Open you up and have a play."

"Another time."

"You still haven't told me why I, of all people, should help you."

"There's nowhere else I can go," I said. I meant it. "I don't believe all this shit about you, this act. You looked out for me once." He didn't say anything. "You could call the police now and turn me in. It'd be one way to end all this."

"What's the other?"

"There are drug dealers involved. Police. Politicians." I closed my eyes. "If you help me, we could ruin a lot of lives." When I looked at him, he was staring at me, absolutely expressionless. Then a flicker at the corner of his mouth.

Then another.

Then he burst out laughing, hysterical and delighted. He leaned forward, touched my knee and gave me an affectionate smile. He shook his head, cocked it to one side and leaned back in his chair.

"You always know the right thing to say."

3

The Bug drove. He'd changed out of his Daddy Longlegs outfit and into street clothes. I sat low in the passenger seat. We went through backstreets and alleyways, toward the lock-up where I'd left my old life. Where I'd left the five grand that Carver had given me. I tried to tell myself that going to the Bug was smart. An unpredictable, off-radar move. The truth is that without him I don't know where I would have gone. There were as few friends in my old life as my new one.

I didn't know what the scale of the search for me was, or if it had even kicked in yet. Laskey had needed me out of that building badly, while he hid or spun or obfuscated what was going on. I'd been dragged to headquarters after hours. Never officially booked in. Legally, I'd been free to leave whenever I wanted.

The assault made things different, but how Laskey might explain that, and to who, was anyone's guess. I thought he'd try to keep it between himself and Riggs until he could eliminate all traces of his ties with Carver, or until Riggs finally cracked.

I hoped that gave me a day.

"Are we there yet?" said the Bug.

"Left here."

He'd borrowed the car, a dark, puttering compact, from Lewis, one of the Titbits. The Bug's own car was a white Cadillac we decided might not blend in. The most noticeable difference between this and his other persona was the mess of twitches and tics that seemed to itch his whole body. He smoked, almost literally, constantly because:

"Daddy hates it."

When he had changed out of the leathers and into a smart-casual, crumpled black suit, he'd become immediately bad-tempered about the prospect of helping me. I'd reminded him about the money. Past a certain point, all these compromises seemed of equal value. I wondered what the next one would be.

"Tell me about Neil, the barman," I said, going through the motions.

The Bug drove on. "Tell you about who? The what?"

"Neil. He was the bar manager at Rubik's until recently."

"I wouldn't drink in there if Zain Carver's blood were on tap."

"Neil's been drinking in the Wiggle Room."

"Even Franchise employees can possess good taste, Aidan."

"Believe me, he doesn't."

"I can categorically say I've never met a Franchise employee by the name of Neil."

"Used to go by the name Glen . . ."

"Well then, that's another story," he said, amused, happy to spill the beans. "Oh, Glen and me go way back. We have a few things in common." I thought of the barman's acquittal and it must have shown in my face. "Oh, not that, you filthy-minded man-child. He cut bricks from the Franchise for me."

"Hang on"—I actually laughed—"you were stealing from Zain Carver?"

"Good, eh?"

"It's something. How'd it work?"

"Everything went through Glen, or Neil, or whatever. Once the Eight was delivered to Rubik's, he'd shave some off and pass it to me at a healthy discount."

I thought of Glen. Neil. The barman.

His calculating eyes. He was at the center of so many things. Laskey had sabotaged a court case against him. He'd been in some sort of relationship with Isabelle Rossiter. Possibly supplied her with drugs. He'd been the fulcrum of Carver's Franchise operation. He'd betrayed them for the Burnsiders, and been betrayed himself in turn. He'd known where Joanna Greenlaw's body was hidden. And now it turned out he'd been playing everyone, selling on Eight shavings to the Bug.

I thought again of flushing his drugs in Rubik's.

Sending him underground.

I thought of him standing outside my flat, gleaming knife in hand. The same one he'd pressed into my stomach the night that Cath went missing. Why had he come back? Where had he got the idea that Joanna Greenlaw was hidden under the bath? And why had he passed that idea on to me?

"When was the last time you saw him?"

"Now you mention it, he might have been to the Wiggle Room . . ."

"Did you talk?"

"We communicated. Things weren't going well."

"Did he want money?"

"He didn't want money so much as what it could buy . . ."

"Eight?" I looked at the Bug. He drove on, twitching, smoking, impassive. He nodded. "What did you tell him?"

"Well, he was my source for Eight. I told him he'd got things arse about face. Now," he said, "in my personal life, that's how I like it. But business is different."

"You say things weren't going well. Why?"

"He was nervous. Always looking over his shoulder. Now, in my personal life, I like a boy looking over his shoulder. But business is different."

"How'd he look?"

The Bug smirked. "Like he had a bad taste in his mouth. Now, in my personal life—"

"OK . . ."

"Luggage under his eyes and beard all messy. I thought the only reason he'd want more Eight was for the spirit in the sky."

"And when was this?"

"He came to Wiggle the week after Sycamore Way."

That made sense, matched up with the receipts I'd found in his flat.

"Have you seen him since?"

"Only the once . . ."

"At the Wiggle Room?"

The Bug shifted in his seat. "No, he called me."

"Did you go to him?"

He nodded. "He was at the Royal Infirmary. Needed someone to come and get him."

The night Cath went missing. His broken leg.

"Where did you take him?"

"I'll show you."

"Now."

"When you . . ." he mumbled something.

"When I what?"

He threw back his head. "SHOW ME THE MONEY!" He took his hands off the wheel, let out a whooping scream and put his foot down. The car veered to the left and I reached across to steady us. The Bug let me steer for a second, then cleared his throat and took over. "Sorry about that, old boy."

When we arrived at the lock-up, I told him to wait outside. It was a dark, damp space with a few stacked boxes. I had already started moving them aside when I noticed he'd come with me, that he was standing by the door, watching.

"This is where you put your stuff?" he said.

"Yeah."

He frowned, looked almost sorry for me. "Where's the rest of it?" I ignored him and found the satchel where I'd hidden Zain Carver's money. I handed it over and the Bug thumbed through the notes. Pacified, he slung the bag over his shoulder and nodded.

"Where did you take the barman?"

"It was quite the tour," he said. "Come on, I'll show you."

We drove back into the city. It was past 3 a.m. and there was barely any traffic on the road. I was confused when we arrived at the Royal Infirmary, but realized we were retracing his journey with the barman.

"I got here to find him hobbling out on a broken leg with two black eyes."

"Did he say what'd happened?"

"Said he'd run afoul of the Burnsiders. Sheldon White in particular."

"He was with a girl who went missing that night—Cath. Did he say anything about her?"

"No, nothing about a Cath." I felt my heart physically sink. "Had some choice words on the subject of you, though."

"Like?"

"Said you'd killed Isabelle Rossiter."

We drove on for a minute. "Did he say anything else?"

"Is it true?"

"No," I said. Just hearing someone say it made me want to take a shower.

"That's what I told him," said the Bug. "No, didn't say much else. He was exhausted. In a lot of pain. Not making much sense."

"Where did you go?"

The Bug twitched. "I'll show you." From the direction we drove in, and from the evidence I'd found in the spare room, I thought we were probably heading to the Greenlaw house. The Bug pulled into the curb and turned the lights off.

Police cars up ahead.

A white forensics tent pitched around the front door.

"He picked up his things from here. Insisted I go inside with him because he was scared of something. All he had was a holdall. We got it and drove back to my place. I put him up for the night."

"Then what?"

The Bug stifled a yawn. "In the morning the news said Zain Carver had been arrested. It gave him an idea."

"Of what?"

"Somewhere to stay."

"Fairview?"

The Bug shook his head. "Some other flat that Carver owns. He used to put his girls up in it. Glen said that, with the Franchise broken up, Carver in prison, his girls missing or dead, it might be a good spot for him to recuperate."

"Is this on Fog Lane?"

"You know it?"

The building where Isabelle Rossiter had died.

"Yeah, I know it. He still there?"

"Well," the Bug snorted, "if he isn't, he won't have got far on that leg."

He started up again and we drove. I could see the building before we got anywhere near it. That brutalist, pockmarked concrete block. When we turned onto the street, the Bug pulled over and killed the lights.

Police cars there, too.

I wondered. Were they here by chance, doing street patrols in light of all the drug activity in the area, or had something happened with the barman? I needed to speak to him but I couldn't argue with the Bug when he started up the car, turned around and drove away.

"Not tonight," he said.

We went back to his house, the converted church beside Alexandra Park, and he put me up in a spare room. My ears were still ringing from every hit I'd taken in the last twenty-four hours, head still spinning from what I had and hadn't learned.

I slept like the dead.

4

We got up early the next morning. Sleep seemed to have relieved the Bug of some twitches and tics, and I felt better for it, too. I'd showered the dried sweat and matted blood out of my hair, and the marks on my wrists from the handcuffs had faded. Looking at myself in the mirror, I wondered for a second if it had really happened.

We drove back out to Fog Lane. I didn't know what to expect that morning, and I was relieved not to see the police. It was early, though, before nine, and didn't mean they weren't around somewhere.

"Wait here," I said, getting out of the car. The Bug sighed and gave a theatrical bow. I crossed the road to that gray, pebble-dashed building and entered beneath the graffiti sign:

FERMEZ LA FUCKING BOUCHE.

Three flights of voices behind doors. Dim, buzzing light bulbs. I crossed the landing. Stopped. Listened. Dreaded it. If the barman was inside, he wasn't making a sound. I wondered if he was dead as well. I stood with my hand on the door, wondering whether to knock, then thought of Isabelle the night before she died.

I stepped back and kicked the door at the lock. The wood was cheap and light, it broke apart easily. I went inside, closed it behind me.

The room was dim. Dull winter sun bleeding through the curtains. I flipped on a light—that bare bright bulb in the center of the ceiling—and confirmed what I thought I'd seen.

Glen Smithson. Neil. The barman.

Passed out on the sofa. His beard had grown out, taking over most of his face and all of his neck. His eyebrows nearly met in the middle. His right leg was encased in an almost satirically off-white cast, the exact color of mold. The room was a wreck, and I recognized some of the chaos from when I'd found Zain Carver in a similar state.

Newspapers, food wrappers, notebooks.

The barman didn't move when I went toward him, and I saw the small wooden box that Carver must have left. There was a needle beside him, but the Eight must have been clean. He didn't look like Isabelle or the Sycamore Way kids, and I was relieved.

I nudged him to no response. I slapped him and he murmured slightly. Finally, I heaved him up and into the bathroom. I dropped him in the shower, so his upper body would be hit by water, and turned it on.

Ice cold.

He sat up when it hit him, taking a deep, sharp breath like he was coming back from the dead. I let the water run a few more seconds, then turned it off. His quick, calculating eyes flashed about the bathroom, then up at me, scared, confused.

"The fuck?"

"I need to ask you some questions."

"Where am I?"

"You're in Zain Carver's flat on Fog Lane." The name spooked him and he tried to sit up, sliding back down wet tiles. "He's not here. He's under arrest. You'd passed out so I put you in the shower." He tried to look around me. "I came alone."

"You can leave, same fucking way."

"I can't leave until you've answered some questions."

"Got shit to say."

I crouched down so I wasn't standing over him. "You've got shit in your veins, Glen. Shit for friends and shit to say. They're all things you can change."

"You? You're gonna come here, dishin' out motivational speeches? You ruined my fuckin' life." He was already crying and started to shiver. "They broke my leg . . ."

"I'm sorry," I said, standing up. Looking at him then, I meant it.

I let him cry a minute while I went next door and found a towel. "Here." He squinted at the towel for a second like it was a trick, then he took it and began drying himself. While he did, I looked at his cast. A new color, somewhere between yellow, brown and gray. It smelled awful. He saw me watching and began toweling it down, embarrassed.

"You should get that seen to."

"Can't show my face outside, though, can I?"

"Why not?"

"White'll kill me."

"If he wanted you dead he'd have done it already."

He looked up at me.

"You're not important enough." I sat down on the bathroom floor. "Don't be offended. I'm not important enough, either. We're the only ones left, Glen. Isabelle's dead. Carver's in prison. Sarah Jane's left town and Cath's missing."

" 'Bout Grip?"

"He's dead. White killed him, the same night he broke your leg. So, if he'd wanted to do you as well . . ." What color there had been in Glen's face drained from it. But he nodded, finally.

"How . . ." He frowned. "How long's it been? Since we saw each other?"

"A few weeks."

"You look older," he said, like I was trying to trick him.

I nodded. I felt it. "I've got a suggestion. Answer some questions, off the record, and help me clear this up. That'll be your part in it over. After that, we'll get you something to eat. Get you to a hospital. They'll take care of that leg and get you straight again, if that's what you want."

He screwed his eyes shut. An unexpected show of kindness can be more effective than threats or shouting. It can make a person come apart after too long holding the same pose. He cried again, holding the towel over his face, then looked up at me, scared.

"Did you kill Isabelle?"

"No. And I know you were with Mel that night." I got up and held out a hand to help him. "So let's talk about who did."

5

I sat him back on the sofa in the messy studio room.

I began by asking about his relationship with Isabelle Rossiter. He told me they'd met for the first time in Rubik's, a few months ago. That tallied with what Sarah Jane had said about Isabelle doing the rounds for a while before running away from home. Glen had seen that Isabelle was underage from the off and hadn't wanted to serve her in the bar. He'd been careful not to turn her away, though.

"Looked like she had nowhere else to go." He sniffed, wiped at his face to cover some emotion. I assumed he knew the feeling.

"Were you sleeping together?" He looked away. "No judgment, Glen. I just need to know."

"Why? Why do you need to know?"

"She was being, or had been, sexually abused. If she slept with you, you might know something—even if you think you don't."

"Know something like what?"

I shrugged. "What she liked, what she didn't, what her experience was . . ."

"This a frame-up?"

"No."

"Yer not pinning that on me."

"I'm not pinning anything on anyone. It was a member of her family. I just thought there was a chance you might know something, if you were close."

"Member of her family?" He slumped down on the sofa, ran a hand over his face. "Jesus. Listen, I liked her. Much for her gob as her looks. We kissed once, but nothing else. She . . ."

"She what?"

"She started losing her breath. Crying."

"Like a panic attack?"

He spoke distractedly. "I s'pose . . ."

"Did she tell you what it was about?"

"Dint ask. Worried it was me. What member of her family?" I didn't say anything. "Her dad?"

"Did she ever talk about him?"

"Nah," he said, thinking about something else. "I once asked her why she'd run off, though."

"And?"

"She said she hadn't really."

"How do you mean?"

"She said: 'He knows where I am, right enough.'"

I asked about his deal with the Bug and he confirmed what I'd been told. He was selling stuff on the side. He'd thought I was trying to get Isabelle drunk the night before she died. The night he'd thrown a drinks crate in my face and I flushed his drugs.

After that, he'd run.

First to Mel's, then to the Siders, and finally to the Bug after Sheldon White broke his leg.

"Tell me about that night," I said. "What happened after I left Rubik's?"

"White took me in. Was sound with me at first. Then he started pressin' for details on the Franchise. How it worked. Went in there knowing I'd have to give some things away, but it didn't stop. Just got more and more intense. They kept me awake for a few days, out at the Burnside. Made me drink the whole time. Do lines." He went quiet for a minute, then swallowed. "I told 'em everything.

"That last day, they put me in a van. Drove a bit. Scary stuff. I started wonderin' how useful I'd be with nothing left to say. Was actually relieved to pull up at Rubik's. White wanted me to show him about. See things firsthand. We had a scout, then I saw you, sat in Cath's usual booth. I pulled Sheldon aside, told him about you. What I knew." He looked at me. "I fucking hated you, Waits. He buys us a drink and we sit on the other side of the room, watching you from behind. He says we'll give you a scare. I never thought he'd end up hurting Cath . . ."

"What happened to her? Once I'd left?"

"I was drunk. High. Don't remember it too well." He went on quietly. "They argued, though." I thought of her hand going protectively to her stomach when she swore on her life for me.

"Did he hurt her, Glen?"

I could see him concentrating, trying to remember. "They were talking about Joanna Greenlaw. Zain's ex from back in the day."

"What about her?"

He shook his head. "I don't know. Just remember the name being thrown about. In the end, she agreed to leave with him, I think. Go somewhere. I was really spinning by this point and walked out with 'em. White turns to me an' says: "Bye then, Glen.""

"I was respectful. Fuckin' respectful. But I said, didn't he owe me anything? For all the help I'd given him?" Glen touched his broken leg. "Well, this is what I got."

Sheldon White had beaten Glen in the street, then broken his leg by stomping, repeatedly, on the knee.

"Had his hand round my throat and I started to go light-headed, but then Cath ..." He was shaking, scared at the memory. "Is there someone outside?" he said, trying to look past me.

I glanced over my shoulder. "There's no one outside, I promise."

"I can hear someone."

"There's no one there. Go on."

"Well, Cath calmed him down. Got her hand on his arm, started rubbing it. Talking into his ear. She gave him the come-on and he got off me." *The come-on.*

"Where did she go?"

"With him. Right off."

"They must have said where."

"They didn't."

"What direction did they go in?"

"Didn't see ..."

Useless. It felt like he'd told me nothing. I tried to think. "Greenlaw," I said. "How did you work out where she was?"

"Eh?"

"Joanna Greenlaw, Zain's ex. You gave Mel from Rubik's a note about her ..."

"That was Cath."

"What?"

"When White got off me, she pressed this letter in my hand, said to get it to you. I was gonna keep it. But I didn't know what it meant. When I heard Cath had never turned up, I felt bad. Wondered if it might help." He looked up at me, hopeful, keen to have done something, anything, right. "Did it help . . . ?"

"In a way," I said. "Do you know where they might have gone, Glen?"

"Burnside somewhere. Was always in the van when they moved us. You think she's . . . ?"

"Is there anywhere else she might have gone?"

"Like where?"

"Like anywhere. Anything she mentioned? Friends? Family?"

"Not to me."

"What about other Carver places?"

"Wha?"

"He owns this place, Fairview . . . There must be more."

"None I know about."

I stared at him.

There was a cough from behind the door. Glen tried to get up, but put the weight on his bad leg and sat down again in pain. The Bug walked into the room. The twitches and tics were gone. He spoke to the barman in a low, steady voice.

"Now that's not what you told me, Glen."

Glen looked at me, panicking. "You said you were alone."

"What's he talking about, Glen?"

The barman had started to cry. The Bug stepped forward, cradled his head.

"Shhh, come on now, you need to let that go. Tell Aidan what you told me."

Smithson sniffed. Wiped his face. "Cath gave me a key an' all . . ."

"A key to what?" He didn't answer. "A key to what?"

"Some flat in London," said the Bug. "One of Carver's. A safe house, I believe, for when it hits the fan. She gave him an address, too. Told him to pass it on to you."

"Why didn't you tell me?"

"I . . ."

"He wanted to see if there was anything there he could sell first," said the Bug.

I couldn't even be angry with him. It was a direction. It was hope.

"The key and the address," I said. "Now."

We helped Smithson up, down the stairs and out to the car. None of us spoke on the way to the Royal Infirmary. The Bug took the car as close to the entrance as he could get it and turned to Glen. "You'll be all right from here."

Glen nodded, seeming to take some comfort in that assessment.

"I hope you find her," he said, before he got out and limped away. The Bug sat back in his seat and sighed. Then he took the address from his jacket pocket and held it up to the light.

"Who is this Catherine, then?" he said. When I didn't answer he put the note back in his pocket, smiled to himself and started the car. "It was funny, listening to you talk in there. Anyone'd think you cared about the girl . . ."

6

The Bug merged onto the M56 without saying anything else. Took it to the M6 and kept on going. Stoke. Birmingham. Milton Keynes. A hundred places with no names at all. He stayed a steady five to ten miles an hour above the speed limit and I was grateful. Tired but expectant. Willing the car forward through gray skies, gray streets and gray people. It was a four-hour drive, and neither of us spoke for the first one. I realized I'd been grateful for the madness. Without it, memories swelled, bruised and blossomed, until I thought I must be wearing them on my face like black eyes. I turned and looked out the window.

Gray Britain.

I couldn't help but wonder what we'd find at Carver's London flat. On one level, I hoped it wouldn't be Catherine. Like a coward, I let myself imagine her, happy, on the other side of the world somewhere. I thought of Grip, tortured, scared, murdered. Like a coward, I hoped I'd never see Catherine again.

"There something between you and this girl, then?" said the Bug. I saw a sign for a service station.

TIREDNESS CAN KILL.

"Can we pull in here?"

"Hm," said the Bug. "You're the boss." He indicated for the turn. I needed to make a call to Superintendent Parrs. A mobile would be stupid. A phone in the city would have placed me too easily. A service station on a motorway seemed like a more infuriating place to be traced to.

It was still early. After ten on a Thursday morning. The Bug rummaged on the back seat for a neon-pink wig and headed toward the canteen.

He shrugged. "I'll go put a scare into the straights." I watched him go, then went to the bank of pay phones at the station's entrance and dialed. It only rang once.

Click. "Parrs speaking."

"It's me."

"Waits," he said. "Where are you?"

"Laskey's our man."

He took a breath. "You need to come in, now."

"I can't do that."

"You've been playing both sides, son. They say they found you at the Greenlaw house last night. You assaulted Laskey. You ran."

"That's not what happened."

"It's what her fucking ladyship Chief Superintendent Chase thinks happened." His voice dropped. "You're lucky you even caught me. I'm clearing my desk."

I held the phone away from my ear, thought about hanging up.

"Riggs can back me up if you apply some pressure," I said finally. "Laskey had him believing they were under orders from you. I assume that's a lie. An easy one to catch him in."

Parrs didn't say anything.

"They had me in headquarters at gone midnight yesterday. All but kicked my head in."

"Central Park? There'll be a record."

"They didn't book me in but if Laskey hasn't got to the tapes yet they'll make for interesting viewing."

"Assuming I believe you, what did he want?"

"I think he wanted to see how much I know. How much of it he can spin."

"What do you know?"

"Glen Smithson," I said. "Checked himself into the Royal Infirmary this morning with a broken leg. Find him."

"Why do I know that name?"

"A rape trial against him collapsed a few years ago due to missing evidence: Laskey's doing."

"Why?"

"Smithson was a bar manager for the Franchise at the time. He's recently fallen afoul of them. Recently fallen afoul of everyone. He'll probably give you the lot, if you can keep him safe."

Parrs didn't say anything.

"You need to ground Laskey now. He'll be cleaning up his mess while we speak."

Parrs waited. Five seconds or so for me to twist in. "No, son. I need to go home and you need to turn yourself in."

I steadied myself. Looked around.

"What was your relationship with Joanna Greenlaw?"

He spoke quietly. "Excuse me?"

"I just found her body under a bath. Answer the fucking question."

Steady. "Not what you think."

"Tell me what I think."

"I think you've had a long night."

"You took the picture of her that ended up in the appeal."

"What makes you say that?"

"She's standing in the safe house, so it was you or another cop. She looks like she's with someone she trusts, though. She's about to laugh or frown."

"Aidan Waits, telling *me* about people."

I waited.

"Yes, I took it."

"Were you sleeping with her?"

"*Sleeping with her?* Jesus Christ, son. Don't be so fucking squeamish."

"Did you kill her?"

"No."

"Did you leak information that allowed the Franchise or the Siders to find her?" I could hear him breathing into the phone. "She'd agreed to testify against Carver. She'd been working against Sheldon White for years. She had secrets with you . . ."

"I was keeping her safe," he said, a rare edge of emotion in his voice.

"How did you miss her, crushed under a bath?"

"How did you find her?"

"We're not talking about me."

"No, son, we never are."

"Did you have anything to do with Joanna Greenlaw's disappearance?" My voice sounded strained, insane.

"No."

"Find the surveillance from Central Park. Interview Glen Smithson."

"We're not done here, Waits. Tell me where you are."

"I can't trust you."

"Then who can you trust?"

The Bug was walking out of the service station, carrying his pink wig in one hand and a carrier bag in the other. A family of four stopped and watched him go by, the youngest child hiding behind his mother. The Bug got halfway past them, then turned and shouted:

"Boo!"

They all jumped and he carried on to the car, laughing to himself.

"I've got to go," I said, and hung up the phone.

7

West Kensington. We arrived around two in the afternoon. It was like driving into another world. The buildings were sand-blasted, brilliant white, and the people were slim, tanned. Happy. The address took us off North End Road to a gated Victorian mansion block named Fitzgerald Avenue. The Bug pulled up and squinted down at the address. There was a six-foot gate operated by an intercom system. Between it and the ornate building there was a well-tended garden, and a driveway about the size of a tennis court.

I examined the keys that Smithson had given me. The fob on the chain.

"Coming?"

The Bug twitched. "I'm all for ruining lives, Aidan, but I draw the line at my own."

"Keep the car running." I got out, crossed the road and held the fob to the touchpad on the gate. The lock shot open. I crossed the courtyard to the building's entrance. The larger key opened the front door. Into a quiet, neat hallway.

I went up the stairs, onto the first-floor hallway and came to 1C. The address that Smithson had given me. I took a breath and unlocked the door. It opened to silence and stillness. I stepped inside, looked about me. I was standing in a small corridor, leading through to a good-sized lounge. I went straight on into the two bedrooms. There was no one there. It seemed like no one had been there for some time. I went back through to the lounge, to the one thing out of place, there, on the coffee table.

It was a mobile phone.

It was Isabelle Rossiter's mobile phone.

I picked it up, stunned, and then stopped.

There was a note beneath it. Clear, looped handwriting.

I'm sorry, it said.

For a second I couldn't move. Then I walked out, closing the door quietly behind me.

The Bug started up smoothly and pulled out into the road. He weaved from block to block for a few minutes before parking up in an anonymous row of family cars and turning off the engine.

"What was it?" he said.

I took out the phone, hardly believing it myself.

"So?"

"Belonged to Isabelle Rossiter. It went missing from her flat the night she died."

If the Bug'd had eyebrows, they might have shot up.

Shaking, I examined the phone. Switched it on. It immediately began to vibrate with accumulated backlogged missed calls, texts, voice mails. I tried to ignore them. Accessed the messages. Sent items. I went straight to the message she'd sent me at gone midnight, one of the first times we ever spoke.

Zain knows.

I deleted it.

Returned to the sent messages folder. I worked from the oldest through to the newest. The early ones were mundane. Where and whens.

I reached the texts from the night she died. There'd been a rally, back and forth, after I left her flat. They made certain things very clear. I scrolled through them, reading and rereading. Sinking. I backed out of the messages.

To the pictures folder. I had seen files there before. Throwaway, night-out stuff. Every shot of Glen, Catherine, Sarah Jane, Zain and Grip had been methodically erased. There was just one video file left. It had been recorded after I left her flat. Sunday, November fifteenth.

The day she died.

I opened it. A tab at the bottom of the screen showed it was twenty-three minutes long. A blurry moving image of Isabelle's flat appeared.

Then, so did she.

She was breathing quickly. She placed the phone down on a surface. The sofa, I thought. Then she adjusted it so the camera watched the other half of the room.

The desk.

There was the sound of the bolt. Isabelle unlocking the door. Then she crossed the room to the desk, still wearing her going-out clothes from the night before. She was shivering. Cold or scared or both.

Then she waited for someone.

We were two minutes in. There were three bleeps and the screen went blank. The battery had died. I could hear the Bug, breathing heavily next to me.

"Now what?" When I didn't say anything, he went on: "You need a charger for that, you need—"

"We can get one on the way."

"Why? Where are we going?"

"Back," I said.

8

North.

Milton Keynes. Birmingham. Stoke. We hit traffic on our way back into the city. People were getting off work, sluggish and beaten by four days of the week. Then the slow-drip, water-torture commute to and from it all. Personally, I was grateful to sit and wait for a change. For the first time in a long time, I gathered my thoughts.

Looked around, watched the world, saw things and forgot myself.

It had been dark for a couple of hours. When our headlights penetrated the gloomy interiors of surrounding cars, all kinds of characters were lit up like staged vignettes. Some looked back at us, blank-eyed, wondering what kind of couple the Bug and I were. Some stared vacantly straight ahead. I felt something lurch inside me when we started up again. A part of me could have sat in that traffic forever. The end, I thought. It's only the end.

Once inside the city, we made our first stop. I bought a phone charger, looked up an address and got back in the car.

The second stop was more difficult. The Bug made a face when I gave him the directions. We drove out there, that undisturbed suburban tension. There was only one car in the driveway.

"Whatever happens, don't come inside," I said to the Bug. "I mean it this time." He nodded, not sure what was happening.

I went up the path, calm, cold, and rang the bell. There was nothing but the wide-open silent night around me. The girl opened the door. She was very pretty. Very young. She reminded me of Isabelle, and I had to force myself not to ask about her. The girl tilted her head when I didn't say anything. The start of a smile. She didn't feel any way about me. She was just nervous. I asked if I could speak to her mother.

"What about?"

"I'm afraid I have some bad news." She took a step back, hesitated, and called her mother.

"Come in," she said. I stepped inside and closed the door behind me.

It was almost an hour later when I went back down the path. Heavy. Low. The lump in my throat felt like a tumor.

I got in the car and closed the door.

"Everything OK?" said the Bug, looking me over.

"Beetham Tower," I said. He nodded and started up.

I put a hand to my chest, felt my heart beating, then the bulk of Isabelle's phone in my jacket pocket. I pressed, searching, until I found it. The smooth, firm outline of the wedding ring.

9

Detective Alan Kernick began his career as a police officer. He'd bounced around divisions. Serious Crime. Murder. Vice. Before landing protection detail in what was then called Special Branch but is now commonly referred to as Counter Terrorism Command. The role sits somewhere between the security services and police work. Although its officers aren't part of the CID, they're entitled to use the prefix "Detective," and many of them do.

I had no doubt he was an above-average operator, an intelligent man and a tough customer. Through the role, he had come into contact with a string of high-profile VIPs, MPs, their families and friends.

Among them, David Rossiter.

Unfortunately for him, I needed to exploit that connection. I needed to get back into David Rossiter's penthouse on the forty-fifth floor.

Detective Kernick walked briskly toward the BMW. All gleaming black paint and chrome. The same car that had picked me up off the street a month before and transported me to Beetham.

Out of the frying pan.

He stood beside the car, clicked the automatic unlock button on his key and opened the door. He sat down with a satisfied sigh. I waited a moment, reached both hands over his head, drew the cord tight around his neck:

Pulled.

He jumped. Struggled for a second and then started to panic, banging his hands on the dashboard.

"Stop," I said, relaxing the cord a little. He put both hands to his neck, trying to get his fingers beneath the noose. "Stop," I said again. "Hands on the wheel." He moved them immediately. Held them up to appease me. "On the wheel."

He grabbed it, gripped it tightly with both hands.

I relaxed slightly. Let him breathe.

Panting. "Wha-what do you want?"

"I need to see David Rossiter."

"*Waits?*" He thought about it while he got his breath back. "Fuck you."

I sat back, pulled the cord tight and counted to five.

He struggled again, hands straight to his neck, then waving in the air as a signal to me. *Stop.*

I relaxed it again. "You get five seconds added every time."

"Fuck y—" I sat back, pulled the cord tight and counted to ten. He made a desperate, hoarse shouting noise from the back of his throat, using up a lot of air. Afterward, he slumped noticeably. When I relaxed the cord he went into a weak, dry coughing fit. I gave him a minute to get his breath back.

"I need to see David Rossiter," I said.

"I can't just—"

"Deep breath, Alan." I sat back, pulled the cord tight. About five seconds in he started panting, gulping. Trying to say:

OK, OK, OK.

I counted to fifteen. When I relaxed the cord again, he went slack with it. Took a couple of strong, deep breaths, in then out, in then out. Then he started to retch and I smelled sick. I relaxed the cord a little so he could dribble it down his front.

"I need to see David Rossiter," I said. Then quietly, "The next time's twenty seconds, Alan."

He waited a couple of minutes before he said anything.

Playing for time while he got his breath back. Thinking of what he could do. In reality, there was nothing. Even if he could somehow get free, he was in such a weakened state that I could easily overpower him. He cleared his throat. He was finding it difficult to speak.

"OK," he said finally. "OK, OK . . ." He took another minute to breathe. "Whatever's going on, we can talk about—"

I sat back, pulled the cord tight and counted to twenty.

He banged hysterically on the dashboard, the window, then planted both hands on the steering wheel, sounding the horn.

It was a good sign.

He must have known immediately it was his only chance of raising the alarm, and in the dark subterranean car park it was deafeningly loud. If he was doing it now, he was at the end of his rope.

Well that made two of us.

I pulled back as hard as I could, almost garroting him with the cord. He took both hands off the wheel, let out a bloodcurdling sound, somewhere between a gurgle and a scream.

Afterward, he went slack. I finished counting and relaxed again. He went into another coughing fit but kept rocking, minimally, when it stopped. He was crying.

"I need to see David Rossiter," I said.

He didn't say anything now. Just nodded his head slightly as he continued to cry. His hands were shaking and the car smelled of piss, sick and fear. It felt appropriate.

10

We avoided walking through the lobby, taking a grimy car park stairwell up four flights to a different lift entrance. I had taken Kernick's key card. He was still struggling to breathe and walked heavily. There were tears in his eyes.

"Have your fuckin' job for this," he croaked.

"What job would that be?" He didn't answer. "Look, you can come up or not, but I promise you'll be interested in what I've got to say."

"What's it about?"

"Isabelle."

"They've just buried her, for Christ's sake."

"Zain Carver," I said.

Kernick frowned.

"I'm in trouble. I'm going away. I think I can put it all on him and give everyone some closure. But I need to see Rossiter first. I need to know that I'm walking from it."

He glared at me. "You could've just asked."

"You would have said no. If there's still a problem between us in an hour's time, you can do what you want. I know I'm through." I used his key card to call the lift and we waited for it in silence. When it arrived there was no one inside. We got in. Pressed for the forty-fifth floor. Kernick leaned on the handrail, never taking his eyes off me.

His pupils had almost entirely absorbed his irises and it made him look black-eyed and hyperaware. I didn't look directly at him but watched his reflection in the mirrors and reflective steel that surrounded us. We went endlessly up.

"You first," I said when we reached the forty-fifth floor. Kernick walked out of the lift, started down the hall. When he passed the last door before Rossiter's, he banged on it, trying to raise the alarm.

I pushed his face into the wall.

His nose started bleeding.

He looked around wildly, tears in his eyes. Then I slapped him, turned him, shoved him forward to his boss's penthouse. He drew himself up and I took a step back.

"Don't," I said. "The day I've had, I'll overdo it."

He wiped his nose and slumped down again. I went forward, put the key in Rossiter's door and opened it. Kernick went ahead of me. David Rossiter was sitting in a chair with just the reading lamp on the coffee table for light. With the near-panoramic view and the glow of the city from outside, it made me feel like we were standing on thin air.

"Forget somethi—" he said, before he saw that I was standing beside Kernick.

"Pour us all a drink, David. We need to talk."

"What's the meaning of this?"

"Pour us all a drink, David," I repeated. "We need to talk." Rossiter's eyes went briefly to Kernick, absorbing his disarray.

"Quite," he said, standing, moving to the bar and fixing us three strong ones. Using the opportunity to regain control of the room, the situation, he strode confidently toward us, handing both Kernick and me our drinks. Then he went back to his chair, the lamp illuminating his face, making him the focal point of the darkened room. "Won't you take a seat?" he said, with the practiced semblance of a man unfazed.

"You heard him." I pushed Kernick forward. He sat down with his back to me, facing his boss. The MP looked closely at his friend for the first time, then up at me.

"Have you lost your mind?"

I nodded. "I've found out a few things about your daughter as well."

"A few weeks too late," he said, stone-cold. He tried not to let his interest show. "Come on, then. Out with it."

Kernick cleared his throat, also eager to regain some lost ground. "Waits says Carver's responsible. Says he can prove it."

Rossiter's eyes flicked up to me. "Is this true?"

"No."

Kernick half-turned. "You said—"

I didn't take my eyes off Rossiter. "I know what I said. Now I'm saying something else."

Rossiter stared at me until the bitter twist of a smile leaked out from his ego and onto his face. He couldn't help himself. He gave a small sardonic chuckle. Spoke to Kernick.

"Don't you see, Alan. The father did it. That's what you're driving at, isn't it, Waits?"

"You tell me, Mr. Rossiter."

"I'll tell you two things, Aidan. And I know you have a problem with listening, so pay attention. The first is that I had nothing to do with my daughter's death. The second is a piece of advice."

I waited.

"Get yourself out of my sight. Out of this room. Out of this building." His voice had steadily risen and he went on, pure venom. "Get yourself out of this town. Then fuck off this island and don't come back. You're finished."

"No," I said.

"Who do you think are? Beating people up, strong-arming your way into my home. Accusing me . . . *You*. Accusing *me* of harming my daughter?" He stood up. "Get out. Now. I will not ask again."

"There aren't any cameras here, Mr. Rossiter. I can do without the theatrics."

"I assure you—"

"Sit a minute, listen to what I have to say and we can all walk out of here. If you want to fight about it, fine. It doesn't matter to me if none of us leave." He looked at me as if in a new light. He frowned, strode to the bar and made himself another drink. The cognac that Sarah Jane had bought him. He held it up in a toast to me and sat down.

"When Isabelle ran away, you didn't report it for a month. Why?"

"I'm not sure you'd understand."

"Try me."

"As I said before, a delicate situation. My wife's an unwell woman. An unstable one. Isabelle had been gone for some time before it was noticed."

"Your wife seemed fine when I saw her."

"When you . . . ?"

"I was at Isabelle's funeral. Only one of you looked unstable to me."

"Be that as it may."

"Kernick," I said to the detective's back. "It's your job to safeguard your boss. By extension, his family. Where were you during this month?"

"Like he said, Alexa didn't twig until Isabelle had been gone for a while."

"So it was nothing to do with Sarah Jane?"

Rossiter's expression hardened. His eyes drifted subtly to Kernick, still sitting with his back to me. It looked like they were trying to get their stories straight via telekinesis. A few seconds passed, then they both spoke at once.

"It doesn't—"

"I don't think—"

"Let's start from the beginning. The night we all met . . ."

Kernick stretched his neck and sat up. "The night I found you pissed, passed out on the street?"

"When I got into your car, there was a vanilla scent. Some designer perfume. It didn't really fit with you or your partner."

He didn't say anything.

"Later, I met the girl that scent belonged to. I couldn't place it at first. She was Zain Carver's girlfriend." I looked at Rossiter. "For some reason, I didn't see the two of you together."

"Perfume," he said. "Pathetic."

"Then, when I came up here for the first time and you shook my hand, your skin was warm. Your wedding ring was cold to the touch. You'd just put it back on."

"I don't have time for this."

"Listen." He indulged me and I went on. "When I went to Fairview for the first time, it was on your instruction. But you went through unofficial channels, so it couldn't be traced back. I wonder why?"

He didn't move.

"Once I was there, you had compromising pictures taken of me." He still didn't move. "Y'know, I actually thought you might be looking out for your daughter . . ."

"What are you suggesting?"

"That you were looking out for yourself. You knew you couldn't leave it any longer before reporting her missing. Might not play well with the press, if it came out. But you were afraid of what the police might find. So you sent me. The pictures were leverage in case Isabelle and I got too close. In case she told me the wrong thing. Kernick, you put it best before my debrief with Parrs. *He doesn't need to know*, you said. At the time, I thought you were worried about procedure. Illegally carrying out a shadow investigation. In fact, you weren't sure what I might know. What I might tell him."

"I was trying to do you a favor, son," said Kernick.

"What was it you didn't want her to say?"

Neither of them spoke.

"That David Rossiter, MP, was in a relationship with an escort? That he had some wild role-play fantasies? That his Special Branch detail was acting as her taxi service?"

Neither of them spoke.

"You got Sarah Jane to take pictures of me. Used them as blackmail. Best of all," I looked at Rossiter, "you paid her off."

He took a drink then cleared his throat. "I did no such thing."

"You sent your man to do it. Either way, it was under a surveillance camera in a multistory car park. I was there, David, so let's not dance around it."

Rossiter glared at me.

"You were having an affair with Sarah Jane."

He lowered his head. Moved the glass in his hand and listened to the ice cubes colliding.

"You paid her for sex."

He looked up at me.

"You knew that she and Isabelle had met each other." I took a step forward. "You waited a month before reporting your own daughter missing because she was connected to the escort you were sleeping with, and you were afraid what might come out."

Rossiter grimaced, stared vacantly ahead. Finally, he nodded.

"Let's talk about some of the consequences of that decision," I said. He shifted in his seat, but didn't argue. "Because you didn't report Isabelle missing, because you insisted she wasn't to be brought back against her will, she ended up in a relationship with Glen Smithson."

"Should I know him?"

"A dealer with the Franchise. Kicked off his career selling Rohypnol in nightclubs." Rossiter swallowed hard. He stood, fixed himself another drink and sat back down. I waited. "Did you know Sarah Jane was living with Zain Carver when you started the affair?" Rossiter's eyes flicked to Kernick, so I spoke to the back of his head. "Well?"

He twisted himself round. "I'd followed her, yeah. She partied with a criminal. Big deal."

"You were risking her life," I said to Rossiter. "As well as your own. As well as your daughter's."

"Now come on . . ."

"What do you think a man like Carver does when his girl's sleeping with someone else?" I saw that Isabelle had been his weak spot. Sarah Jane was someone he could brush over, and he regained his confidence.

"Give the bitch a good hiding, I'd have thought."

"And then some. Have you ever heard of Joanna Greenlaw?"

He strained. "The appeal recently? That missing woman . . ."

"The woman whose body I found crushed under a bathtub two days ago. Carver's ex. She made the mistake of leaving him." That visibly shook him. He seemed to appreciate for the first time who his daughter had been left with.

"Well, Sarah Jane's a big girl, she makes her own decisions."

"Isabelle told me the same thing about herself."

"They're hardly comparable."

"Why not?"

"Isabelle had a life. A future. Sarah Jane was . . ."

"Nothing?"

"I didn't say that."

I looked at him.

"Oh, fine—she's a perfectly nice girl and I'm a monster, blah, blah." There were tears in his eyes. "I don't believe in people being equal. It's a philosophy one only ever hears from the weak. Where's all this going?"

"Did you know that your daughter self-harmed?" He nodded grudgingly. "Neat, straight lines, cut into her inner thigh."

He bristled at the idea that I'd seen them. It was the first fatherly reaction out of him that night. "Tally marks," he said. "They began a couple of years ago. After she hit puberty. Her doctor thought they were something to do with particularly difficult cycles."

"I think each cut represented a time she was sexually assaulted. Eighteen or nineteen by the time she died."

"Get out," said Rossiter.

Kernick stood, turned, but didn't say anything. His face was drawn and grim. Lifeless except for the bloody nose.

I looked past him. "I'll only take another minute of your time. The night before she died, I saw Isabelle have a panic attack because she thought I was working for you. She said that you stalked her. Interviewed her boyfriends. Played the tapes back to her as blackmail. Intimidation. Harassment."

He was frowning, sweating, shaking his head. "It's not true . . ."

Kernick stepped forward, pushed me back toward the door. "If that's it, Waits."

"It isn't," I said. Then, to Rossiter, "How did you get her phone number, David?"

He was lost in thought. "What? Sarah Jane gave . . ." He paused, corrected himself. "I made Sarah Jane give it to me."

"Why didn't you give it to the police after Isabelle died?"

"They'd have known," he said. "They'd have found out about Sarah Jane and me."

"You could have saved us both a lot of trouble."

Kernick pushed me again. "We don't need to listen to this."

"I found the phone," I said.

Everything stopped.

There was just the glow of the city, surrounding us, swallowing us all. Kernick stepped back and Rossiter stood. Stared down at me, through me.

"It was driving me mad. I'd seen her with this phone the night before she died. But it was missing from her flat when I found her body."

I produced it from my pocket.

"I was sure the killer had to have taken it. Because there was something incriminating on there. In fact, it was someone else. A member of the Franchise who just didn't want their name coming out in connection with drugs."

"What's on the phone?" said Rossiter.

"I'll show you."

"Don't listen to him," said Kernick. "He's making this shit up as he goes along."

"What's on the phone?" Rossiter repeated.

I glared at Kernick until he stepped out of my way. I crossed the room and stood beside Rossiter. Aware, once again, of the intense physical presence of the man. I held up Isabelle's phone, found the video and pressed play.

I handed it to her father.

A blurry moving image of Isabelle's flat appeared. Then, so did she. She was breathing quickly. She placed the phone down on a surface. The sofa, I thought. Then she adjusted it so the camera was watching the other half of the room. The desk. There was the sound of the bolt. Isabelle unlocking the door. Then she crossed the room to the desk, still wearing her going-out clothes from the night before.

She waited.

After a few minutes there was a sound. She jumped. The door opened and then closed. Isabelle looked away, stared at the wall. There were footsteps and a man came into view. He crossed the room toward her. Put a hand through her hair. Isabelle's body went rigid. Then he kissed her. First caressing her neck, then working his way up to her jaw. He kissed her closed mouth until, finally, she began to kiss him back. I stood beside Rossiter but didn't watch anymore. At a certain point he looked away.

"Jump ahead to thirteen minutes."

Dumbly, Rossiter scrolled forward. Isabelle crossed the room toward the camera. Picked it up and took it to the bathroom. She pointed it at the mirror. The message that the man had smeared onto it with lipstick.

NO ONE CAN EVER KNOW

Then the picture blurred. The phone was dropped as she hit something. There was the sound of broken glass and then her voice, shaking: *"I was fifteen when it happened the first time . . ."*

Rossiter lowered the phone.

Stared at Kernick.

Kernick didn't move.

"*You.*"

Kernick still didn't move.

Rossiter threw himself forward. Kernick reacted instinctively, using Rossiter's momentum against him, sending him into the wall. Rossiter got to his feet again, punch-drunk and weaving.

"Please, don't," said Kernick. Rossiter slapped him, hard. Kernick didn't move.

"Stop," I said.

They both stood, sweating, shaking, unable to look at each other. The phone was on the floor between them. Kernick wiped his eyes then shoved Rossiter, hard, into the wall. In one motion, he picked up the phone, stepped over his boss and went for the door. Rossiter sat, panting, on the floor. Kernick snapped open the door, turned and looked back, complete misery.

Rossiter covered his face and began to cry.

"Where are you going?" I said to Kernick. He looked at me for the first time in minutes, only now remembering I was there.

"It's not the way you make it sound."

"She's quite clear about it in the video, Alan. Where are you going?"

He was breathing heavily, rolling the phone around in his hand. "Home."

"I'm afraid—"

"*What?*" He held up the phone. "*You've got nothing.*"

"Neither have you."

His head went to one side.

"I showed that video to your wife and daughter three hours ago." His legs almost went out from under him. "I'm afraid they don't want to see you at the moment."

"You're . . ." He smiled, shook his head and then laughed. "You're full of shit. More fucking talk from the master."

"Didn't you wonder how I got into your car? Kris gave me the spare set." He shut his eyes and I put my hand into my jacket pocket. "She asked me to give you this."

"What is it?" he said, looking up.

"Here," I said, holding my hand out a little farther.

He shook his head. "Nah."

"Come and see." I could feel him weakening. The adrenaline subsiding. "This way you'll be sure." He stepped out of the doorway and crossed the room. He was watching me carefully. His small, black eyes.

I opened my hand. Showed him his wife's wedding ring. "She couldn't get it off her finger fast enough." He took it, examined it and went limp. "There's a good chance you won't see them again," I said.

"What?"

"You'll die in prison, Alan. You know you will. There are police officers on every exit of the building. If you run, you'll just die sooner."

He stood there, head hanging low. I took the phone from him and went over to Rossiter. Helped him up. He looked at Kernick, then at me.

"His family?" he said. "Was that really necessary?"

"Not really, but people get a lot of ideas until you show up where they live." Rossiter took a step back, actually appalled. "I'll never forget where you live, David."

I went back for Kernick, guided him toward the door. Neither of us looked back. Then I took him by the arm and marched him along the hallway to the lift. When it arrived, he stepped inside without resistance. I pressed for the ground floor and the doors closed. His right hand was clenched in a fist, but when he opened it a minute later I saw he was still holding his wife's wedding ring. He seemed entirely unconscious of me until about halfway down the building. He remembered with a jolt what he was going to. He wiped his face with a forearm, tried a smile.

"Of course . . . I've got money . . ."

I just looked at him. Held the handrail as hard as I could until he turned to face the wall. I could see his reflection in the steel. He closed his eyes so that he wouldn't. When we reached the ground floor, he turned, drew himself up. He stepped into the center of the lift, in front of the door. Ready to run. I just watched him. Gripped the handrail. When the door opened, ten or so police officers were standing outside it. He sank back down.

I took him by the arm, led him to the first officer.

He stepped forward. "Detective Alan Kernick. I'm arresting you for the sexual assault of Isabelle Rossiter. You do not have to say anything, but it may harm your defense if you do not mention when questioned something which you later rely on in court. Anything you do say may be given in evidence." Kernick nodded vaguely.

"Get rid of him," I said.

The officer turned Kernick and marched him out of the lobby. For a minute the made-up, elegant people checking in and out stopped and watched. Once the last police officer had left the room, they all carried on and forgot about it. Superintendent Parrs was standing to one side of the lobby and he drifted slowly into view, like smoke.

I handed him Isabelle's phone. "It's all there."

He considered me for a moment, then looked down at the phone.

"Good work on Laskey," he said, with his shark's smile. "In the end."

Then he nodded and turned to leave.

11

It was a few weeks later when I saw the girl again. Around noon, a weekday, although I can't say which. I'd been walking. Emptying my head. The nights since Beetham Tower had been bad. My dreams were tedious, suffocating.

I lived alone in them, and some people I knew had died. I learned to fall asleep with the radio going. Something deeply informative and earnest droning on in the background. With practice, I started to dream about current affairs instead.

War. Famine. Politics.

Anything but the girls.

The days were their own challenge. At first I just drove in and out of the city at the worst possible times. Sat in traffic and watched. It was never as peaceful as that first time, though. So I went back to walking. That day I'd been thoughtless, made the dozen or so mistakes that can lead a man down Market Street in late December.

I had been giving quite serious thought to going after Sarah Jane. Not all the way. I didn't even know where she'd ended up. I just wondered if I should follow her example.

Fill a case and take a train somewhere for good.

I felt myself drifting irresistibly into the slipstream of the street and tried to turn. Each time I did, I was pushed farther forward by the crowd, the way I didn't want to go, until I just went along with it, life streaming past.

I almost didn't recognize her at first. She was a face in the crowd, and so changed from the girl I'd seen last. She was going the opposite way. Pale, sick and thin.

Transformed.

We barely registered each other as she went by. I just caught the edge of a look. That flash of eyeball white, and she was gone. I turned, looked for her.

Stopped.

She'd done the same, but hundreds of people were driving us farther apart. With effort, I held the same spot for a few seconds and saw her, struggling against the tide to do the same. The roar was all around us, too loud to speak, but her eyes were on mine.

Trying to place me.

A man pushed past and I saw her loose coat sleeve, pinned up. Lydia Hargreaves. The girl I'd seen at Sycamore Way. First checking her reflection in the window. Then walking back and forth over broken glass. Her arm had been amputated, and she was the only survivor now.

Perhaps that's what we had in common.

The shared, stunned looks on our faces, not happy and not sad. She got pushed a little farther into the crowd. I tried to get closer but lost her and, in the end, let myself be swept along. A part of the parade. Her eyes had been wide with the surprise of recognition, but I was glad to have seen her.

The crowd was all momentum, and that's probably why I didn't notice them sooner. Being pushed about anyway, the hand on my shoulder, the one on my arm, didn't register. It was when I reached a clearing and was still being driven forward that I looked up.

Saw Billy on one side.

His friend on the other.

Two of the young Burnsiders. I pulled back but they held me fast, pushed me along toward a waiting street-side van. I tried to break away from them. One took my arm, twisted it hard behind my back. The side door slid open. Someone inside took hold of my right leg.

"No," I said. "No! No!"

They threw the door closed on my leg.

I heard a wet crunch, a scream. I was shoved inside in shock. They climbed in with me and the door thunked shut again.

It was dark. I was sitting on a dirty floor, stinking of motor oil, surrounded by three, no, four people. The shapes and smells of men. Everything felt slowed down. Hyperreal. I couldn't see my leg, but it felt like it was detached below the knee. I was lying in something warm and wet. Smelled the piss, pooling beneath me.

I clenched my jaw, swallowed bile. Panicked. One of the men shifted, climbed into the front of the van.

Started up and drove.

Weaving through streets with sudden turns, sending me sliding painfully side to side. At length, a light flicked on.

"Hello, Aidan."

"Zain . . ."

"You look surprised, brother." I didn't say anything. We made another sudden turn and I steadied myself on the wall. "You've met Billy and Alex . . ."

I nodded. "How long have they been working for you?"

"Not long. Not before we took our little trip to the Burnside that night." He smirked. "On my honor."

"What about Sheldon White?"

"What about him? Picked up by your lot. They are your lot, aren't they, Aidan?"

There was no point lying now. "They were," I said. "When I first came to you."

"You spun me some balls about a sting . . ."

"That was the sting." A wave of misery washed over me. "It was to flush out Laskey."

It had worked.

Parrs had gone straight to Riggs when I called him. Compelled him to work against his partner. When they confronted Laskey, he was packing a bag. There was money he couldn't explain. A passport with his picture and someone else's name on it. Smithson was the nail in his coffin.

He was finished.

"Be interesting to hear what he knows," I said. I tried to steady myself on the floor of the van, to save my leg.

Carver shrugged. "Be interesting to see how long he lives inside." He went on, serious for the first time, "Tell me about Isabelle." Everything was spinning now, white-hot sunspots in my eyes.

"She was being abused," I said. "Her father's Special Branch security detail. When she was younger, she tried to kill herself. When she was older, she ran away. He found her, though. Kept tabs. Got to her when she was alone . . ."

"Was it him, then? Gave her the stuff?"

"I don't know. Maybe he just put her in a bad enough place to use it. I guess she stole the brick to raise some cash, so she could run away farther."

"Why?"

"It was me," I said. I swallowed. Looked down at my twisted, bloody leg for the first time. "I took her home, night before she died, and she confronted me. Thought I was working for Kernick, and I didn't convince her otherwise. She must have sold the brick at the Burnside and kept a taste for herself. When Kernick visited her the next day, it must've felt like one more betrayal. One too many. A fix after all that probably seemed like a good idea." I stopped, thought about it. "She didn't even put her clothes back on." The van drove wherever we were going, and we rocked slightly in the back. I tried to anticipate its movements. To stay upright.

"Why me, though?" said Carver. "Why'd she run to me?"

Sarah Jane. Her affair with Rossiter. I had told her that I was going to pass that information on to Carver in the hope that she wouldn't come back. In the hope that she'd steer clear of him for the rest of her life. But I had no intention of actually putting her in danger. He could work it out for himself or never know.

"It was clever, really. Fairview was the one place that Kernick couldn't get to her. She was safe there, until you moved her to that flat."

"And what about Cath? Sarah?"

"I don't know. White said if I didn't get you to agree to terms on Rubik's by ten o'clock that night, it'd be like Cath never lived. I didn't get to you in time, did I?" I nodded at the two Burnsiders standing either side of me. "They'd know better than I would what happened to Catherine."

Neither of them spoke and Carver translated their vacant stares. "They say she left White of her own free will."

I swallowed. "It'd be nice to think so."

The van went over a bump and an incredible pain went through my leg. I thought about Joanna Greenlaw, crushed into that damp space for ten years before anyone found her.

I tried to keep Carver talking. "You said White was arrested. What for?"

"Grip's murder," said Carver. "Apparently there was black and white paint all over his body when they found him. White's fingerprints and DNA everywhere."

"Convenient."

Carver smiled. "S'pose so, yeah."

"And dumped outside my flat, so the police'd definitely find him . . ."

"Is that so? I don't even know where your flat is."

"How would you even get hold of White's DNA?" I looked at the two former Burnsiders. "Ask a stupid question . . ." Carver didn't move. "Doubly convenient that you'd been taken into custody at the time, so couldn't have done it yourself. Who was your arresting officer, by the way?"

"A Detective Laskey, I think," said Carver. "Yeah, convenient that. You don't think I had something to do with it? My best friend?"

Grip had lost his appetite for the game at the same time that Sheldon White had been released from prison. Carver had used one problem to solve the other, framing White for Grip's murder.

"I know you did," I said.

The van came to a sudden stop and the engine was cut.

I thought I was about to die, so I said what I thought. "Is that what happened to Joanna Greenlaw as well?"

"Don't know anything about it."

The door slid open and the two Burnsiders picked me up. Threw me out onto concrete. A shock of unexplainable pain went through me, what was left of my leg. Carver stepped out, stood over me.

"I'll give you this one for free, though. She saved your life."

"What?" I said. I could feel the sweat spiking out from every pore. "Who did?"

"Cath." Carver nodded back at the van. "The lads say White was all for killing you that night. Apparently, she offered to fuck the lot of them if he didn't."

Billy leered at me over his shoulder.

I tried to get up.

I fell back down and Carver laughed at me.

"See ya round, Aid."

He climbed back into the van. I heard the door slide closed and the engine start up. I didn't dare look until they'd driven away.

The street was familiar.

The one I'd been living on for the last few months. I lay on the pavement and looked up at the sky. It was in motion. At first it went clockwise but it slowed. Stopped. Began spinning the other way, faster and faster. I closed my eyes, lay back and covered my face. I cried until my whole body hurt.

VI

PERMANENT

1

Afterward I went back onto the night shift. They'd never trust me in the daylight again. I spent my time responding to 4 a.m. emergency calls, walking up and down dead escalators and trying not to think. I'd been good at that once. I could hardly believe it, a few months later, when I saw my breath in the air again. Saw November coming back around.

Superintendent Parrs saved his job with the Laskey and Kernick arrests. My name had to be kept out of it, though, and I was reassigned, back on the graveyard shift, back on my very last chance. Shackled to my old partner, Detective Inspector Peter Sutcliffe. He took a sadistic pleasure in my low status. When he showed me the news story, the girl's body that had been found, he actually smiled about it.

Time had moved on. Slowly at first, then all of a sudden. Weeks and months went by and it all seemed less real. I spent most of that time in rehab. The break had been ugly. "Acrimonious," according to the first physio, and my leg would never be the same.

I drank, but not like a madman, not anymore. Carver had unwittingly done me a favor. He had no reason to lie about Catherine saving my life and, somehow, that added value to it. She deserved better than me just throwing it away again. I'd been keeping my head down when the phone rang, almost a year later.

"Yeah," I said, surprised. "I can be there within the hour."

Although he'd made it sound urgent, the Bug was twenty-five minutes late. I saw him through the window, smoking a cigarette down to the filter. He walked into the café in a three-piece suit, looking just like one of the straights—with one crucial difference. The rigid, side-parted wig. It was turquoise.

"My natural color," he said, sitting down, ordering an impossible combination of two extravagant coffees. I laughed and he asked how I'd been.

"Same as ever," I said.

"You wanna watch that."

"I just wish I'd seen it sooner."

"A copper, a father and a rapist walk into a bar. *Evening Alan*, says the barman." The Bug studied the table. "Not that simple, is it?"

"I just can't stop thinking about it." He snorted and I looked at him. "We can't all have two personalities."

He looked back at me, surprised but amused. "Course we can." He slid a slip of paper across the table, winked at me and got up to leave.

"What's this?"

He shrugged. "Five grand seemed like a lot for a drive to London and back. Maybe you should take another?" He walked out again. His painstakingly brewed designer coffee arrived a minute later.

"Thanks," I said to the barista, taking a sip so he wouldn't think it had all been in vain. On the slip of paper was an address: 28B West Square, London. I googled it. It was the first-floor flat in a Georgian town house. The first result told me that it was for sale. Idly, I called the estate agent and booked a viewing for that night. It would mean a long drive, there and back, but I had the time. I might even get lucky and be late for my shift with Sutty.

2

I arrived early, found a spot round the corner, and went to the square on foot. Four blocks of Georgian town houses surrounding about an acre of idyllic leafy park. Children from a nearby school were sitting in a circle, taking a nature class in the middle. I didn't know what I was doing there. I took a slow walk, the long way round, to number 28.

The estate agent was standing outside, unmistakable in a suit, pink everyman tie and gravity-defying quiff. We shook hands and he introduced himself as Marcus. I could see that he was good at his job, even more so when he took in my own appearance at a glance. My black, lived-in suit. The shirt to match. The lines under my eyes that I couldn't quite sleep off. The idea of me buying a flat on this street, in this city, must have looked laughable.

He led me up a short flight of stone steps, telling me about the neighbors, the square's history, the period features. I barely heard him. I was staring at the intercom buzzers for the building: 28B was *Cat G.*

When I hesitated at the door, he put a friendly hand on my shoulder and rang the bell.

"Just to let them know we're here," he said, searching his jacket pocket for the key. He found it and let us in, into a fine, well-lit hallway lined with law books, looking like something straight out of the National Trust.

"It's Marcus from Harvey Street," he called out.

I heard a movement upstairs.

A happy, singsong: *"Be right down."*

And then she was.

Alive. Healthy. Glowing. I looked up. Past strap-sandals, skin, a light cream dress. It was a miracle when my eyes met hers. She stopped on the staircase, took half a step back. As if my being there, my walking through the door, was a physical blow.

Marcus saw this immediately, looked to her and then at his watch. "Not early, are we?"

"No. No, it's fine," she said, eyes on me.

He looked between us. "You two know each other?"

"A long time ago," I said. "It was Catherine Greenlaw, wasn't it?" Her eyes on mine. That same cornered look I'd seen in Isabelle Rossiter's flat. The same one I'd seen in Rubik's.

"That's right," she said.

I'd thought a lot about this moment, but now I didn't know what to say. How to fill it. There was a silence and Marcus took the floor.

"And this is Aidan, erm . . ."

"Waits," she said. "Yes, I remember."

"Oh," said Marcus. "Perhaps you want to give us the tour?"

"I have some jobs on." She was already backing up the stairs. "Shout if you need me."

"Thanks, Cat," said Marcus.

The tour didn't take long. The house was set over four floors, not including the basement, and 28B was on the first. It was a two-bedroom flat. The fixtures, furnishings, tones and colors were minimal. Tasteful. Discreet.

When we stepped into the kitchen, Catherine looked up. She'd been staring absentmindedly out a window. At a small garden set behind the house.

"Perfect for the kiddies," said Marcus, following her gaze.

I looked at Catherine. "Do you have children, Miss . . . ?"

She turned from the window. "Greenlaw," she said again. The same defiance I'd seen her speak to Sheldon White with. Thin winter light strained through the window, perfectly illuminating her features. She looked more like an art student than a drug dealer, and I wondered how I hadn't seen it before. "Call me Cat," she said. "Please."

I waited. She didn't go on.

"Do you have children, Cat?" In the silence, even Marcus's welded-on smile started to slip.

"No," she said finally. She gave us both a perfunctory smile, got up and left the room. Marcus guided me in the opposite direction and carried on the tour. We didn't see her again, and before I knew it we were back at the front door. Marcus called something over his shoulder to her as we left and then we were on the street like it had never happened. He spoke to me and I nodded vaguely along, only thinking about getting rid of him.

"Mr. Waits," he said with a nod. When he shook my hand I walked to the edge of the square and he walked to his car. I heard him start up as I got to the corner. He followed the one-way road around the square, and out the other side.

The street was quiet aside from the voices of children playing. I walked back to the house, up the steps, and reached out to press the intercom. The door opened a crack before I could. Catherine stared out at me.

"Come in," she said.

3

She went through the hallway, up the stairs, and I followed. At first I thought she was playing for time. Running through a version of events she might give me. But in her automatic movements I was reminded of people I'd door-stepped with death notifications. She was in shock.

When we reached the first floor she drifted into the flat. I saw a hard-shell suitcase standing by the door. It hadn't been there before. She led the way into the kitchen, still on autopilot, and said the same thing that the newly bereaved often did:

"Can I get you anything? Tea, coffee . . ."

"I thought you were dead," I said to her back.

She turned. "I wanted you to."

"Why?"

She shrugged. "I wanted to be."

"Well, what happened?"

I could see her trying to formulate a response. Something harmless. "When you left Rubik's—"

"What happened to the baby?" I said.

"Oh." She turned to the kettle. Busied herself with mugs. "There never was a baby." She had that mark of a great actor, putting just enough truth into each role to keep it convincing. Even when she switched persona mid-sentence, one didn't make a lie out of the other. She turned back. Looked at me. "I was scared. The police were coming. All I could think of was getting out of that room. I found the pregnancy test in Isabelle's flat." I closed my eyes. "Was she . . . ?"

I nodded.

"Whose was it?"

"I don't know. Neil says he never got that far with her. Odds are on Alan Kernick." Catherine frowned, unfamiliar with the name. "Her father's security guard."

"The man from the video?"

I nodded again.

She began picking dead leaves from a potted plant. "Is that why she ran away from home?"

"More or less. Where did you find the phone?"

"In her flat, when we found her body, when I went to be sick." She paused. "I remembered that she sometimes kept stuff in the toilet cistern."

"Stuff?"

"Weed, blow—nothing hard. I just wanted to flush it so they wouldn't find drugs with her body."

"What did you find?"

"Money. Lots of money on top, some drugs. Underneath it all, there was a sealed plastic bag with her phone in it. I knew there'd be messages, pictures of me, so I took it. The pregnancy test was in there, too." She stopped. Breathed. "Once I got out, I looked at the phone and found the video. I wanted to tell you, explain it that day we were in Rubik's. Then everything with Sheldon White happened. I had to improvise. Was it any use?"

I ignored her. "Joanna Greenlaw was your mother."

She shook her head. "Not really. She got rid of me when I was a baby. I grew up in care." She looked at me, through me. "You wouldn't understand what that's like, especially for a girl. You get good at acting. Faking things. You live the lies so long that they get twisted into memories. You start believing them."

"I'm sorry," I said.

"The law changed at some point. I was given the right to find her. I hadn't thought much about it until then, but something just broke in me when I read she'd gone missing. I didn't go at Zain for revenge. Something else pulled me there. And he liked me." She laughed. "He thought I was good. I worked well in the Franchise. I think I reminded him of Mum." She paused. "I knew she had to be dead, but it got so important for me to work out where she was. Physically, I mean . . ."

I waited.

She was turned fully away from me now. "My only idea was to fuck him. Betray him. Tell him I was going to the police, just to see what he'd do. Just so I'd know for sure what he did to Mum. I used to dream of his hand round my throat and actually wake up happy. Because at least I'd *know*."

"But you changed your mind?"

"I wish I hadn't. Zain and Grip used to troubleshoot. Take small amounts of their cooks to see how strong they were."

"You got the idea to spike them."

"Amazing what you can find online," she said. "Cyanide pills, strychnine, banned pesticides . . ."

I thought about poor Isabelle. "Is that what went into it?"

"A cocktail, in the end. Anything they'd sell me," she said blankly. Then there was a flicker of life in her eyes. "I regretted it as soon as I saw Grip. And Zain never even touched the stuff. I didn't know he'd kept it. Then Isabelle stole that brick and used from it. Sold it on. All those kids," she said. "All those kids at Sycamore Way . . ."

"You couldn't have known. You left the black and white paint at Fairview?"

"I wanted them to *fucking* remember her."

"How did you find out where Joanna was?"

"Grip told me. Matter-of-factly one day, after he came out of the coma. Zain tracked her down, after she'd agreed to give evidence against him."

"And you left the city after that night at Rubik's?"

She nodded, lowered her eyes. I thought about what Zain had told me. *She saved your life.*

"I looked for you," I said.

"You shouldn't have." She raised her eyes. "I'm sorry, but you shouldn't have. I asked you. I told you not to get to know me. I suppose you didn't, really. Are the police outside, Aidan?"

"Of course not. But you should leave, now, go as far as you can. If I can find you then so can he."

"I . . ." She looked at me. "I don't understand."

"You need to leave. Now. Don't tell me where you're going, either. You can close this deal remotely if the flat's yours."

She tilted her head, didn't move for a moment. Then she took a step closer, searching my eyes for the cruelty. The lie.

"Why can't I tell you?"

"You never know who might ask." A dull pain went through my leg. "Or how they might put the question."

She raised a hand, put it on my skin, the way a blind person might memorize a face. It felt like my whole life might change. She took another step and kissed me lightly on the cheek. I moved so we were eye to eye, but we just stood there, neither one daring to go any further. It was just a moment and then she broke away. Walked past me to the door. I heard it close behind her. For a minute I could still smell her scent. I went to the window and waited. It was dusk, somewhere between day and night.

True to Carver's prediction, Laskey didn't live to see trial. Detective Alan Kernick was convicted of statutory rape, among other things. He went to prison for the rest of his life, which didn't turn out to be very long, either. An autopsy showed that Grip—Danny Gripe—had drowned on black and white paint before the agonizing effects of the spiked Eight could take hold. I wasn't sure if that was a good thing or not. When they cremated him, I was the only person there. Sheldon White was convicted of his murder, and Zain Carver walked the streets again, good as new.

Sarah Jane went back to whoring.

I didn't find out until a year after I'd put her on the train, when Sutty showed me the story. They found her, asphyxiated, crushed inside a suitcase in the dismal industrial town she was born in. That pretty girl I'd known.

I watched Catherine from the window, my hand pressing hard into the glass. There should be a word for it. That phantom limb, reaching out from your chest, toward things you'll never have. She crossed the road with wide, lovely strides, and I always wonder what she went on to. The last shred of sunlight caught her hair when she turned the corner, like the start of one thing and the end of another. The dusk itself. I never saw her again.